AURORA BOREALIS BRIDGE

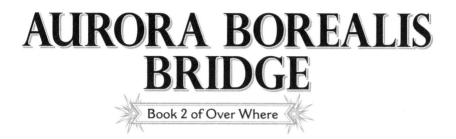

AURORA BOREALIS BRIDGE

Book 2 of Over Where

JANE LINDSKOLD

BAEN

A Baen Books Original

Baen Publishing Enterprises
P.O. Box 1403
Riverdale, NY 10471
www.baen.com

ISBN: 978-1-9821-2602-5

Cover art by Tom Kidd

First printing, April 2022

Distributed by Simon & Schuster
1230 Avenue of the Americas
New York, NY 10020

Library of Congress Cataloging-in-Publication Data

Names: Lindskold, Jane M., author.
Title: Aurora borealis bridge / Jane Lindskold.
Description: Riverdale, NY : Baen Books, [2022] | Series: Over where ; book 2
Identifiers: LCCN 2021059053 | ISBN 9781982126025 (trade paperback) |
ISBN 9781625798602 (ebook)
Subjects: LCGFT: Novels.
Classification: LCC PS3562.I51248 A94 2022 | DDC 813/.54--
dc23/eng/20211203
LC record available at https://lccn.loc.gov/2021059053

Printed in the United States of America

10 9 8 7 6 5 4 3 2 1

❧ ACKNOWLEDGMENTS ❧

Aurora Borealis Bridge is part two of the story that begins in *Library of the Sapphire Wind*, so, for that reason, I have many of the same people to thank—but my thanks are no less heartfelt for all that. First, always and ever, thanks go to my husband, Jim Moore, who encourages me to go after even the wildest ideas, serves as my sounding board, first reader, and best pal.

My gaming group—Cale Mims, Rowan Derrick, Dominique Price, and Melissa Jackson—saw the light in my eyes as I was working on this, and kept wanting to know what had me so excited. I hope, now that they've read the tale, they understand.

My beta readers, especially Paul Dellinger and Sally Gwylan, gave me valuable comments, but thanks as well to Julie Bartel, Maria Boers Morris, and Scot and Jane Noel.

Chuck Gannon's valuable advice applies to this book as well. Thanks, old friend. Sometimes dreams do come true, don't they?

Finally, many thanks to Toni Weisskopf for thoughtful editorial feedback and, most importantly, for her over-the-top enthusiasm for both Over Where books.

AURORA BOREALIS BRIDGE

❧ CHAPTER ONE ❧

"Y'know, I think this would make a great movie," said Peg, pausing where she was sorting through a tray of weirdly varied items she'd gathered from one of the shelves in the wrecked artifacts repository beneath the Library of the Sapphire Wind. "Three fine ladies far beyond the first bloom of youth are drawn through a portal into a shrine in a strange world. Their mission: Help three young people succeed in their quests."

"Inquisitions," corrected Meg dryly, pausing in her review of a battered tome. She laughed. "I remember how we all reacted when the translation spell chose that word. Honestly, though, it is a better choice. All three of our young friends have questions far larger than any simple quest. I'm not sure that the complexity of this tale could be grasped in a movie. I'd prefer a book. I suppose it would need to be a novel, since no one would ever believe this was nonfiction."

From where she was working at the base of a bank of broken lockboxes over to one side of the repository, Teg rocked back on her heels and looked with great affection at her two friends. It was hard to believe that not all that long ago, they had been nothing more to her than a couple of members of the monthly book group to which they all belonged: people she mostly saw there, although occasionally at some open lecture at Taima University.

Meg Blake, silver-haired, very pink and white of complexion, looked every inch the retired librarian she was. Her blue eyes, faded now with age, were quick and alert, rarely missing anything that went on around her, even when you would have sworn she was absorbed

3

in reading or in scribbling notes in her omnipresent journal. Somewhere in her seventies, Meg was the eldest of their trio.

"All right," Peg countered. "How about a miniseries then? My kids prefer them anyhow. My Esmerelda says she likes talking to her friends about what might happen next. You've got to admit, our story has lots of suspense and reversals of expectations. Grunwold and Vereez both didn't tell us the full story behind their inquisitions, and I bet anything the same will prove true of Xerak. Then there was the appearance of sultry Kaj and his crazy mother, Ohent—not to mention what we learned about how our inquisitors' parents had shared a life of crime in their youths."

Teg swallowed a chuckle at the familiar "My . . ." Although only in her sixties, Peg Gallegos had started having kids young, and remained devoted to all of them: four of her own, four step, as well as in-laws, and a growing herd of grandkids. Currently divorced, Peg had been married at least three times. Somehow, repeated disappointment had never quelled Peg's enthusiasm for new experiences.

Peg had even taken aging on as a challenge, remaining physically fit, and deciding that the greying of her dark brown hair was an excuse to incorporate "sun-streaked" highlights. Although she'd spent a lot of her life in California, Peg had moved to Pennsylvania when one of her kids (was it Diego?) had taken a job as a city manager in Taima, a once sleepy community which was in the process of reinventing itself as a combination archetypal college town and retirement destination.

She's in good shape for her age. I'm definitely still fit. Meg's the oldest of us, but she isn't exactly frail or fragile. I wonder if our good health, both mental and physical, was part of our appeal when Hettua Shrine started casting about for mentors that fit the needs of our three inquisitors.

"So, Teg," Peg said, "Movie? Miniseries? Novel?"

Teg considered. "How about graphic novel? Or animated? I know special effects have gotten a whole lot better, but this world is different, really different. Could CGI get it right? I mean, we're used to it by now, but you have to admit, learning that everyone here is therianthropic—mixing animal and human traits—was a real shock. Now I don't think twice about Vereez, say, having the head and tail of a fox, but it did take a while to get used to."

"If animated," Meg cut in, "it would need to be done in one of the more serious styles. Our inquisitors are fascinating young people, but their appearance is more mystic and noble than 'cute.' Disney would positively ruin them, and probably make us three all short, wrinkled, and impossibly adorable, like older versions of those three Fairy Godmothers in *Sleeping Beauty*. That's why I'd prefer a novel. We wouldn't be locked into some art department's idea of what we are."

"Oh, I don't know," Peg said. "I wouldn't mind seeing our adventures live. Me at the wheel of *Slicewind* as we tear through the skies. Teg using her archeologist superpowers to solve the mystery of where the doorway into the Library of the Sapphire Wind had vanished. Meg channeling the *genius loci* of a ruined magical library. The mysterious necropolis..."

As Teg went back to using her "archeologist superpowers" to sweep up potentially interesting debris from the floor of the repository, she swallowed a sigh. Peg might talk about Teg's "archeologist superpowers," but one thing about spending time with three talented "twenty-somethings" (Vereez was actually only nineteen) was that despite Meg and Peg being older than her, there were times Teg definitely felt the weight of her fifty-some years: menopause, aches and pains, and all the rest. Listening to Peg chatter about her expanding family, Teg often wondered if she'd missed out on important aspects of life when she chose to focus on her career, never marrying or having kids.

But I'm in good shape, Teg reminded herself. *And it's sort of nice being in a world where my mixed race heritage isn't the first thing anyone sees about me. Here Meg's not an American woman of Scandinavian descent or Peg a mix of Spanish and Irish, or me just about everything else, topped off with a funky, purple highlighted punk cut. I'm Teg Brown: archeologist, mentor...* Her fingertips drifted to the sun spider amulet that she kept in a pocket, within easy reach of her right hand. *Apprentice user of at least some sort of magic. Hey, I'm cooler even than Indiana Jones. Right?*

Grinning, Teg pushed to her feet and brought her dustpan over to where she'd set up a makeshift screen. Meg reached for another crumbling tome, which she looked at reverently before gently opening the front cover.

A moment later, she screamed. Teg swung around in time to see a needle-toothed, bat-winged creature with enormous eyes take shape from the printed page and surge up toward Meg's face.

Luckily, Meg had been wearing her reading glasses, so her eyes were saved when the creature spat a gob of foaming spittle toward her face. Even so, the librarian's hands and fingers were blistered by an acidic ichor that spattered from beneath the creature's wings. Only Sapphire Wind intervening as a compact storm of electric blue sparks saved more of Meg's body from similar damage.

Meg's scream brought the three inquisitors running.

Thundering down the corridor from where he'd been clearing away chunks of broken masonry came Grunwold, his antlered head bent, his hand reaching for the hilt of the long sword sheathed at his hip. Behind him was fox-headed Vereez, nearly running into him in her haste. The young woman ducked under Grunwold's arm, darted out in front of him, then pulled up short when she saw that at least half a dozen of the bat-winged creatures were now flapping around the room. They were unable to get at Meg, who Sapphire Wind had protected with a tent of blue sparks, but clearly not willing to call it quits.

"What the . . ." Vereez said, moving as if uncertain whether to draw her twin swords or to dive under the book-piled table at which Meg had been working.

Down the stairs from reading room, the text he'd been perusing in one hand, the spear that served as his staff in the other, lion-headed Xerak came barreling in.

The young wizard shouted, "Ilusutinni. Magical creations. Grunwold, get Meg out of the repository. Then get her medical help. Vereez, create a wind to push them back. Teg!"

"I'm here!"

"Close whatever book Meg was messing with before more of the ilusutinni get loose. Don't make skin contact with the book yourself!"

"Right!"

Teg felt in her righthand pocket for the sun spider amulet, already formulating a plan. Grunwold had bodily lifted Meg away, and was carrying her up the stairs. The pages of the book Meg had been reading were fanning back and forth, as if moved by a slight breeze. Several of the pages were beginning to morph into wings, while eyes bulged out from the tightly clustered pages near the book's spine.

Oh, no you don't!

Although Teg knew she still had a lot to learn about the sun spider amulet, the one thing she did feel confident about was using it to shoot what she liked to think of as "Spidey silk." Resisting an urge to close her eyes to help herself concentrate, Teg imagined herself talking to the amulet.

"All right. Let's glue the book's pages closed from a distance. Meg might even forgive me for book vandalizing. Eventually."

The amulet didn't talk back, but Teg felt it awakening, considering, enjoying the challenge she had presented it. Not a single one of the sun spider's many radiating legs moved but, nonetheless, Teg felt something that seemed like motion. She raised her arm palm outward, holding the sun spider amulet cradled in her grasp. The minute faceted gems that represented the sun spider's eyes glittered so brightly that the air sparkled. Teg shouted aloud, although she wasn't at all certain it was necessary:

"Let's do it!"

A line of yellowish-white light burst forth from the amulet's circumference and hit the inner edge of the open tome's front cover, solidifying into a solid silken cord as it did so. Teg moved to one side, pulling as she did, managing to haul the cover over so that it flopped shut. The emerging ilusutinni within hissed protest, then the book began to steam and shake.

Pulling on a work glove as she dashed over, Teg used her gloved hand to stand the battered tome on one end, feeling decidedly creeped out when she realized that several sets of eyes were now glaring at her from the spine. She wrapped the sun spider silk cord, solid and sticky now, around and around, binding the book closed. For a brief moment, she thought the trapped ilusutinni were going to use their caustic spittle to burn their way out, but perhaps the creatures were reluctant to damage their portal or home or whatever the battered book served as. The steaming stopped, the eyes that had continued to glower at her closed, then merged back into the spine, and the book was still.

Teg quickly inspected the rest of Meg's collection of books, assuring herself that none of the damaged volumes were giving forth new monsters. To one side, Vereez was holding her hands out in front of her, muttering soft words filled with *S* sounds. Wind is invisible, but its effects are not, and the small flock of ilusutinni were being buffeted back into a corner of the room.

Xerak was saying. "Good, Vereez. Keep them in that corner. It's all stone so . . ."

He said one of those words the translation spell couldn't or wouldn't translate, and there was a "whoomph" sound, sort of like a gas burner igniting, although much louder, followed by multiple shrill voices shrieking, and a smell that mixed the worst parts of burning hair and boiling vinegar.

"Wow!" Vereez gasped. "That reeks worse than one of Teg's cigarettes. Did you kill them?"

"More like banished," Xerak replied. He sounded utterly exhausted, and half collapsed, sliding against a wall to sit tail-down on the floor. "Do I ever need a drink!"

Teg took off the long sleeved overshirt she was wearing, since the below-ground repository was rather chilly. Here at the Library, the three humans often wore clothing from their own world, since anyone who would see them would already know that they were not any sort of creature anyone had ever seen in this world. She then bundled up the bound tome in the shirt. The book seemed quiescent, but she wasn't taking any chances that it might decide to open its eyes to spy out another time to attack. As she was neatly tying off the sleeves, she heard booted feet on the stone stairs.

Grunwold called down, "I've got Meg settled up here, and Peg's with her, so I'm going for Nefnet."

"Good," Teg called. "I'll come right up. Xerak and Vereez can make sure there are no acid bats lurking elsewhere."

She ran up the stairs to the reading room. Peg was gently sponging off the back of one of Meg's hands, while Meg leaned against the table and tried hard not to wince.

"How are you, Meg?"

Meg's voice quavered a little with shock as she replied, "My skin burns where the spittle got through, but I'd be a lot worse off if Sapphire Wind hadn't intervened."

She looked to where the sparkling blue light was still faintly visible. It brushed against her cheek, after the manner of a cat. At that moment, Grunwold returned, escorting Nefnet, trailed by Kaj, with Ohent, veils jangling, bringing up the rear. Once again, Teg found herself thinking about how much weirdness she'd come to accept as normal.

Nefnet, who immediately started inspecting Meg's acid burns, had the head and tail of an otter. Kaj, who was a couple of years older than Xerak, had the head and tail of an African painted dog, but his mother, Ohent, the last arrival, concealed the head and puffy tail of a snow leopard beneath voluminous gauzy veils, not because she was in the least ashamed of how she looked, but because the veils helped control her sporadic attacks of insanity.

Nefnet reached for her doctor's bag, which Grunwold had carried for her. "I have some ointment here that should help. Sapphire Wind's intervention kept most of the ilusutinni's spittle from hitting you, Meg. Your hands suffered the worst injury, and even that seems to have been more like a misting. Still, I think it would be wise if you stayed here at the Library for a few days, so I could continue to monitor you."

Meg nodded, but her gaze flickered to Vereez, whose inquisition would most likely be their next focus. When Vereez had been only fourteen, she had become pregnant by none other than Kaj. By the time she realized she was pregnant, Kaj had vanished, and he had never known about the child. When Vereez' parents had learned of her condition, they had sent Vereez away, lest the situation cause them social embarrassment. Then, after the baby had been born, they had taken it from her, and from that point on had denied its very existence.

Vereez knew nothing about her child, other than that she was female and her age—about four years old. Nonetheless, Vereez had been determined to find the child, so she could assure herself as to the little girl's well-being. This had grown to an obsession that, in the terms of her culture, made Vereez a "holdback," someone who would be unable to move forward in life until her problem had been solved.

Xerak and Grunwold were holdbacks as well, but Grunwold's problem—finding a cure for his mortally ill father—had recently been solved, at least as much as it could be. Xerak's holdback was that his apprentice master, Uten Kekui, was missing. Devoted as he was to his master, Xerak had seemed willing to put Vereez's search first, although there was no doubt that he was eager to move along to his own mission.

Perhaps knowing that Meg was aware of his fanatical devotion, and that he would fret at any delay, Xerak took care to reassure Meg.

"Don't worry, Meg-toh," he said, using the suffix that indicated affection for an elder who was not a family member. "Sapphire Wind is still working on finding the information we need to continue Vereez's inquisition. We're not going anywhere until then."

"And," Vereez said decisively, coming over and putting a hand on Meg's shoulder, "even then, until Nefnet says you're safe to travel, we're not going anywhere. My inquisition has waited years. It can certainly wait a few more days. Rest and heal. All I ask is that you stay away from dangerous books."

Meg managed to look meek. "I promise. I most sincerely promise." Then she cleared her throat and spoke with her usual calm assertiveness. "The reason Sapphire Wind was close enough to intervene on my behalf when the ilusutinni attacked was that it had come to ask me to tell you that it would like to consult further with us regarding the research it has been doing."

"That sounds reasonable," Xerak said, and everyone else nodded.

"Let's go to the reception hall," Nefnet suggested. "Meg can rest on my bed, and I'll brew her an infusion that will help with the pain."

Even though she had been strung out from their encounter with the land squid, when they had arrived at the Library, Teg had immediately noticed the changes that had been made in the Library's great reception hall. When they had first seen the reception hall, it had been rubble strewn, dusty, and poorly lit. Although the reception hall still showed ample evidence of the catastrophic destruction that had rocked through the entire Library, some effort was being made to make it useable once more.

Over near the reception desk, Nefnet had constructed for herself a sort of house without walls. There was a comfortable chair, a table with a reading light on it, a small bookshelf, a crystal reader, and a scroll rack. Not far away, Nefnet had set up a small kitchen/dining room that had been well stocked with mismatched crockery. Freestanding carved screens flanked a makeshift bed constructed from two more bookshelves with what seemed to be a door on top. The bedding they'd left for Nefnet when they had departed for the necropolis was unrolled on top.

"I do like how you've made yourself at home," Peg said with approval as she helped Meg onto Nefnet's bed, propping her up with pillows so she could sit upright enough to drink the promised infusion. "You haven't been too lonely?"

"A little," Nefnet admitted, filling a tea kettle from a large water bottle, "but Emsehu is here, and he can be an interesting conversationalist. Some of the other guardian creatures have begun to escort me when I venture into the stacks, so I feel as if I have pets. Sapphire Wind will occasionally speak to me through one of the guardians but, unless their interests match the topic, Sapphire Wind finds using them to communicate draining."

At the sound of his name, Emsehu came trotting out from where he had, based upon the dust coating him, been rooting about among the rubble. In this magically rich world which Peg had dubbed Over Where, in addition to many types of plants and animals that resembled nothing on Earth, there was a category of creature officially termed a "unique monstrosity." Emsehu was one of these. He looked something like a crocodile, if a crocodile had the stocky body of a pit bull, as well as the spiked carapace and heavily weighted tail of an ankylosaur.

Emsehu had been born one of the therianthropic denizens of Over Where, but a series of bad decisions had led to him being presented with the choice of death or of having his spirit incarnated in one of the guardian creatures of the Library. He had chosen the latter. Now he lived in the Library, more or less content in his new role. Perhaps, Teg thought, thinking back upon Emsehu's history, he was more content than he had ever been in his original life.

Emsehu greeted them all, then moved to one side where he shook off the worst of the dust in a very doglike manner.

"Since Meg has been injured," he said, "Sapphire Wind has asked me to help it tell you what it has learned about Ba Djed. Having served as the guardian of the Spindle for so long, I admit, I am very interested the matter as well."

"Where should we sit?" Vereez asked. "And can we help with anything?"

"If you'd clear off that long table," Nefnet said, "we can sit there. Just move the bits and pieces to one end. I'll put on enough water that we can all have tea."

"I brought some wine," Xerak said, "and I'll even share."

Grunwold went to where he'd left his pack. "I brought supplies for Nefnet, and before we left *Slicewind* we packed a lunch for everyone. How about we eat while we talk? That way Xerak's wine won't go straight to his head."

Xerak, who was pulling the cork from a wine bottle, gave Grunwold a dirty look, but when he filled his cup, Teg noticed he didn't gulp down the contents as he might have done.

"Wonderful," Nefnet said. "I appreciate the supplies. I'm in no danger of running out of food, but it's nice to feel secure."

"It looks as if you've been doing some sort of craftwork," Peg commented as she moved various items aside.

"I once thought that if I had the time, I'd read all day," Nefnet said, almost apologetically. "I have discovered that I need more to occupy me. Emsehu and I've done some limited exploring of the Library, but, as you just saw, it is still hardly safe. So I've been doing some repairing. Many of the data crystals may be salvageable, although there will probably be blank areas in their content."

Teg moved to look at Nefnet's work. "Nice job. Reminds me of piecing together broken pots from sherds. It's satisfying making something whole again."

Peg added, "You studied healing magic, didn't you, Nefnet? So this is right up your alley, fixing what's broken."

Nefnet looked pleased. "I hadn't thought of it that way, but you're right. The tea water will take a bit of time to heat. Did you bring dishes, or should I get some out?"

"We brought utensils," Grunwold said, "and we can eat off of the wrapping clothes." He cleared his throat. "Uh, has my father . . ."

"Oh! You don't know?" Nefnet said. "I wasn't sure. Yes, your father has been here, in company with your mother. I've given Konnel the first treatment. We will reassess his progress in four months, then refine the treatment."

Grunwold's ears drooped in relief. "That's wonderful. Thank you. If you need anything . . ."

Nefnet motioned toward her makeshift kitchen. "Much of that is their doing. Sefit stripped their ship's galley of the stove and several water containers. She even took out the icebox. The cabinet holds every bit of food they could spare. They offered me more bedding, but I really am comfortable, and I'd already salvaged crockery from what used to be the Library staff's breakroom. Over there"—Nefnet pointed to an area shielded by more screens—"Sefit and her servants made me proper bathing facilities and a very nice toilet. I fear they must have had an uncomfortable voyage home."

She paused, then added, "I didn't expect to, but I liked Konnel very much, and Sefit as well. I can understand why you wanted to save him. Now, can you tell me what happened after all of you left here?"

"How much did my parents tell you about Dad's past?" Grunwold asked. "I need to know, because it ties into our own journey."

"Your father was very frank," Nefnet said. "At my request, he began with how he and his fellow extraction agents had come to raid the Library, and what happened after they fled with one third of Ba Djed of the Weaver. Konnel ended by explaining that one of their number had been given the task of being custodian of the piece of the artifact that they had stolen. He gave no names, for he felt that his associates' secrets were not his to confide, but could that be you, Ohent? I remember a young woman who looked something like you."

Ohent nodded. "Me. Custodian Crazy, Keeper of the tiny bird that serves as Ba Djed's cap."

Nefnet nodded. "I'd like to know why you came here, rather than just sending the Bird, especially if being the custodian has been so taxing. Yet you chose to make this journey rather than simply relinquishing your charge. It can't just that be you don't want to lose your stipend. I would have asked sooner, but you were rather— stressed— after your encounter with the tetzet."

"If Sapphire Wind can wait to give its report," Ohent said, "I will explain. It will help all of us for you to have the background."

As they picnicked on the elaborate repast that Grunwold unpacked, Ohent told how, after they had made their escape, she and her fellow extraction agents had been at a loss for what to do with the portion of Ba Djed they had managed to steal.

"We didn't want to hand just a part over to our client," she explained, "because, well, I guess it was too much like admitting to failure. Better if he simply thought we never had it. Anyhow, Fardowsi had custody of the Bird first."

"Fardowsi's my mother," Xerak added. "Konnel-toh may have felt uneasy about giving names, but I, for one, believe the time for such secrecy is long past."

Ohent nodded and continued, ". . . but Inehem . . ."

"That's *my* mother," Vereez cut in, her voice sharp and bitter.

". . . knew that Fardowsi had grabbed the Bird from the start, and so Inehem probably had at least as much contact with it. When Fardowsi began to have horrible nightmares, Konnel took custody of the Bird. I'll admit, I thought they were all neurotic about the thing because they felt guilty about the damage to the Library." Ohent laughed, a harsh, shrill sound. "Funny, now that I think about it. Anyhow, in time I took my turn and—Bang!—nightmares. But in the end, I accepted the job as its full-time custodian. It meant steady income, and someone had to do it."

"Why didn't you just throw it in the river or something?" Nefnet asked.

"Couldn't," Ohent said, starting to shake so hard that the copper disks sewn into her veils chimed against each other.

Kaj put a protective arm around his mother's shoulders. "She can't. She can't let anyone else harm or dispose of it either. Do you think I didn't consider tossing the blasted thing away?"

"I understand, now," Nefnet said gently. "So the reason you came here, Ohent, was because you couldn't be parted from the Bird."

"That's right," Ohent managed. "I think my only hope for relief is to get Ba Djed put all back together again. Meanwhile, here I am, faithful to the end."

Her tone as she spoke the last was heavy with irony.

"Maybe I can help you deal with the nightmares," Nefnet offered. "I saw what Kaj dosed you with after your arrival here, and that's good as far as it goes, but I may be able to brew up something as effective, and with fewer side effects."

"Why," Ohent asked, eyes narrowing, "would you want to? You agreed to help Konnel because Sapphire Wind made treating him a condition before it would unarchive you. What reason do you have to help me? I was a key member of the team that ruined your life!"

Nefnet wrinkled her nose, showing her teeth in an otter's smile. "But harming anyone wasn't your intent—Konnel made that very clear. Nor was harming anyone the intent of the person who hired your team. I was there, remember? I was one of the scholars who was working out here"—she gestured around the reception area—"when your team attempted to make your escape. Among all of the archived, I am one of maybe four who can bear witness that while your theft may have been intentional, you meant the Library and its inhabitants no harm. And you have paid... Twenty-five years of madness is a high price to pay because one of your colleagues panicked and set off a fireball."

"Very generous of you," Ohent said grudgingly. "I will definitely discuss accepting your offer with my son."

Emsehu, now more or less dust free, had shared the lunch, even to lapping up tea from a shallow bowl Nefnet apparently reserved for the purpose. He had listened without comment to Ohent's version of past events. Doubtless he already had heard Konnel's version, so nothing but Ohent's particular slant would be new to him.

But I wonder how Emsehu feels, Teg thought, *learning that the extraction agents he—well, his prior self—hired to steal Ba Djed for him not only failed, but that they kept part of the artifact that he had wanted the most? Well, Emsehu himself is the first to admit that his near death and transformation into a unique monstrosity changed more than his appearance. Still, although he showed no antagonism to Konnel, Konnel didn't have a bond to one part of Ba Djed. Best not to forget that, at least once upon a time, Emsehu had a horse in this race.*

At this moment, doubtless at a prompt from Sapphire Wind, Emsehu made a sort of grumbly throat-clearing noise. "If everyone is ready now, Sapphire Wind would like to give a report."

Nods and murmurs assured him that everyone was ready, and when next Emsehu spoke, his voice held the whispery notes and slightly stilted cadence they had come to associate with Sapphire Wind's manner of speech.

"Although the presence of two thirds of Ba Djed has been useful, their mere proximity has not been sufficient for me to establish where the third part—the Nest—may be. We have not yet put the pieces together, in part because the Bird usually rests upon the Nest, but I believe that fitting them together would be the next logical step."

"It makes sense to me," Xerak said. "Ohent, will you cooperate?"

Ohent, calmer now, replied, "As long as it isn't overlooked that my price for cooperating is that my granddaughter—Vereez and Kaj's offspring—be located and, if she is any way unhappy with her situation, she be given to me to be cared for."

"As long as you remember," Vereez shot back, "that I don't want to be shut out of my daughter's life all over again, you can be assured, we've not forgotten."

"Then very well," Ohent replied with mocking placidity. "Sapphire Wind, what do you want us to do?"

Emsehu spoke for the *genius loci*. "Xerak, take out the Spindle and set it upright on the table. Ohent will then thread the Bird onto the top."

"A moment," Xerak said.

From one of his belt pouches, he took out a pair of tightly woven gloves and pulled them on. Removing the enshrouding container from another pouch, he placed it before him, then pressed gently down on several of the glyphs carved into its surface. There was a faint click, and the lid popped open. Using tweezers, Xerak removed the Spindle—a highly polished piece of bronze about the same size and dimension as one of the miniature candles used for birthday cakes—and set it on the table. It wobbled, just a little, then seemed to latch hold.

As if the base was magnetized, Teg thought, *although I can't think of what would attract metal and wood.*

Accepting Xerak's mute offer of another pair of gloves, Ohent then opened the enshrouding container that held her part, revealing it for the first time: a minute songbird crafted from bronze, every feather perfect. With meticulous care, she threaded it onto the Spindle.

Unlike Xerak, Ohent did not let go of her piece, resting the pad of her gloved index finger lightly on the top of the Bird's head. Sapphire Wind did not protest, but Teg wondered if it was only paranoia that made her see a flicker of annoyance cross Emsehu's face. Certainly, the expression of concentration that followed was real. The crocodilian brow furrowed, the scaly hide creased around eyes and mouth, as first a spark, then a sparkle, then a swirling that melded these tiny lights into a deep-blue opaque mass took form.

The dark-blue mass spun like clay on a potter's wheel, first formless, then rising to take a rounded shape, then rising and falling as details were sculpted, until the whole approximated the missing portion of Ba Djed that they had glimpsed in that initial vision in the Font of Sight. The only difference was that the missing Nest, which in the vision had appeared to be crafted of some matte-black stone highlighted with bronze, was all sapphire and sparkle.

Various sounds of astonishment only made the overall stillness that had fallen over their normally chattering crew more striking. No one asked Sapphire Wind any questions, since the *genius loci*'s concentration was palpable. Then, without a word, blue opacity once again became sparks, sparks faded, and all that was left was the bronze Bird perched atop the bronze Spindle.

Without waiting for permission or direction, Ohent quickly unthreaded the Bird and dropped it back into its enshrouding container, which she snapped shut. Xerak paused a moment, but followed her example, peeling off his gloves as if to punctuate a sentence.

"What did you learn?" he asked. "I could feel something, but nothing I understood."

He glanced at Ohent, who gave a slight shake of her head. "I'm no wizard. Even though I kept a finger on the Bird, I felt nothing. Oh! Your gloves..."

"Keep them," Xerak said gruffly. "You may need them again. Sapphire Wind, what did you learn?"

"I cannot find the Nest! It is gone. No. Not gone. It is so faint I cannot tell anything but that it exists."

Emsehu ended with a growl that might well have been his own, but might well have been meant to demonstrate Sapphire Wind's desperation.

Vereez cut in. "Do you think it would be possible for you to find the Nest if you had more time, more access to the Bird and the Spindle?"

"I hope so. Maybe. Better than none."

"I have a proposal then," Vereez went on. "We already promised Ohent that we'd make looking for my daughter a priority. Xerak, are you still all right with that?"

"Unless Uten Kekui-va can be found easily, yes, I am."

"Then here's my idea. Ohent, you already have an offer from Nefnet that you could be treated here. How about this? You stay here at the Library with the Bird. We leave the Spindle, too. Xerak has taken care not to become bonded with it, so he shouldn't have any trouble leaving it."

Xerak made a sound, then waved for Vereez to keep talking. She narrowed her eyes at him, then did so.

"If Sapphire Wind can locate either my daughter or Uten Kekui-va, then we go after one or both of them. Meanwhile, Sapphire Wind can continue drawing on the Bird and Spindle to locate the third part. Whenever it has a clear direction for us to go, we keep our part of the bargain and do our best to retrieve the Nest. What do you think? Xerak, you seemed about to object."

Xerak nodded. "A small objection. I like your plan, but I don't think that Ohent should need to deal with two parts of Ba Djed. She's already attuned to the Bird, and it's possible that even if she never does more than touch the enshrouding container holding the Spindle, she could be affected. I suggest we ask Emsehu to be in charge of it. He seems to have functioned as its guardian for many years without being affected, even with it outside of an enshrouding container."

"That's an idea," Peg said caustically, with cheerful disregard for Emsehu's feelings, "and if he gets possessive, well, we already know we can beat him if we must."

Teg frowned. "Look, we haven't talked about this, but Emsehu is or was or whatever, the person who hired the extraction agents in the first place. How do we know he won't go after both the Bird and the Spindle?"

"I won't go after them," Emsehu said. "I am a different person. Then I was the misguided son of Dmen Qeres. Now I am first and foremost, down to my very blood and bones, a guardian creature of the Library of the Sapphire Wind. I have no desire beyond seeing the Library preserved and, if possible, restored. My instincts tell me that while Ba Djed of the Weaver may have provided extra mana for Sapphire Wind to draw upon, the artifact was not in and of itself a part of the Library's collection. It is difficult to explain, but I assure you, I do not want it. I would guard the Spindle and, upon your request, I would return it. It would be as if, in the days of the Library's greatness, you had loaned an item to the collection."

Xerak shut his eyes briefly, then opened them, looking at Emsehu in a fashion that made Teg wonder if Xerak was bringing magic into play or only the sense for the motives of others he must have learned during the year he had wandered in search of Uten Kekui.

Grunwold shrugged. "You two have my backing and *Slicewind*'s sails to carry you wherever your inquisitions take you. And the same goes for finding the last piece of this Ba Djed."

Vereez looked hopefully at Emsehu, her fox's ears melting into almost puppyish pleading. "Don't give up, Sapphire Wind. Help us and be assured, we won't forget what we've promised you—even if we're not successful in our own inquisitions."

From where she had seemed to be drowsing on Nefnet's bed, Meg spoke, "Sapphire Wind seems to be thinking. It is not like us, but I think it will understand that our priorities all lie together. Give it time."

Eventually, Emsehu spoke for Sapphire Wind. "I think that Vereez's plan is the best option. I did not agree to the conditions Ohent set for allowing the Bird to be brought here, but I can understand that your agreement with her on behalf of me is binding upon me as well. Even without the parts of Ba Djed linked, I believe I have the ability to scry for what you seek, Vereez, and for Xerak as well. However, if you will open the enshrouding containers and set them side by side, I would benefit."

"Scry Xerak first," Vereez said, surprising them all. "He'll be a lot more help if he's not brooding over the idea that his master is in some prison or somewhere else horrible. I don't love what my parents did, but I can't believe they would have done anything that would bring actual harm to their granddaughter. After all, she's an asset, and they couldn't be sure they'd ever have another grandling."

Once the Spindle and the Bird had been set out on the table, Sapphire Wind became visible as a sparkling curtain draped over both of them. There was a long wait, while the sparkles glittered. Teg found herself almost mesmerized, feeling as if, if she looked intently enough, she would be able to read the sparks, like words in an almost understood language.

Eventually, Emsehu spoke for Sapphire Wind. "Xerak, I cannot find this Uten Kekui. I am sorry. You say he is a powerful wizard, so he may be able to hide himself from me, especially since I do not have the full artifact to draw upon."

"He's been able to hide from me," Xerak said with soft intensity. "Maybe he's hiding on purpose. What can you find out for Vereez?"

Sapphire Wind replied, "Vereez, give Emsehu your hand. You connect the one you seek with those who have hidden her."

Vereez eagerly grasped Emsehu's armored and heavily clawed hand in her own much more slender, more delicate, clawed appendage. The contrast between Vereez's fox-paw black and Emsehu's crocodilian green reminded Teg once again how many shapes intelligent life took here, and how little shape or color mattered to these people.

Emsehu's smile managed to be warm and reassuring, despite being full of horrifically pointed teeth. "Ah . . . Yes. This helps. Wait. Wait."

This time the blue sparkles connected the pieces of Ba Djed and the linked hands. Teg was reminded of the long sparks cast by a Fourth of July sparkler, and somehow the similarity made her feel hopeful.

The sparks faded and, again, Emsehu spoke for Sapphire Wind.

"You will find the child in the sea-surrounded nation called the Creator's Visage Isles, on the island named Sky Descry. She is called Brunni, which is a common enough name, but you should know her by her resemblance to . . . to her grandfather."

"Which grandfather?" Vereez asked urgently. "My father or Kaj's?"

Emsehu blinked, then shook himself so hard that his tail lashed against the floor. "I'm sorry. I don't know. Sapphire Wind doesn't know. This was less a vision than as if we were tapping a river of knowledge and were shunted out. Still, it shouldn't be that difficult, right? The population of the Creator's Visage Isles is relatively small. The language is different, so Brunni's name would be exotic there. You know what your father looks like and Kaj's?"

There was an uncomfortable silence during which Ohent occupied herself with tucking away the enshrouding container holding the Bird wherever within the folds of her veils she kept it. When it became clear she wasn't going to say anything, Kaj replied stiffly, "I don't know who my father is or even whether I resemble him. My mother will not say."

All eyes turned to Ohent who gave a deep sigh and shrugged deeper into her veils. "So Kaj isn't the only one in the family who has screwed around. I, at least, had more excuse than he does. In the early days of my custodianship, I discovered that a lover sleeping close by would help keep the nightmares away. I had so many I really can't be sure who Kaj's father is. Kaj doesn't believe me, but that's the truth."

"Still," Peg said with forced brightness, "we have the child's name and age, a fifty percent chance of knowing what she will look like, and a location. What could be simpler?"

"Well," Grunwold said, "it would be simpler if the Creator's Visage Isles weren't practically on the other side of the world."

❧CHAPTER TWO❧

The following day, Teg sought an excuse to talk with Nefnet away from as many of the others as possible. An opportunity presented itself when Grunwold—who was eager to follow his parents in their example of generosity—offered to further equip Nefnet if he could do so without rendering *Slicewind* useless.

This led to Sapphire Wind suggesting that Grunwold berth *Slicewind* in what had been the Library's main plaza, not far from the pedestal that held the statue of Dmen Qeres.

"Makes sense," Grunwold agreed. "It will be easier to unload things for Nefnet, and most of us can continue to bunk aboard, without having to hike back to the meadow."

"Two more bathrooms, and an extra kitchen would be useful," Peg agreed.

"Nefnet," Teg said, "why don't you come with me and Grunwold? I'm sure you'd enjoy a chance to see the area from above."

"That would be nice," Nefnet agreed. If she thought it strange that Teg would offer to leave the Library, when there was archeology to be done, she didn't say so. Nor did anyone else.

So, while the others remained to continue preparations for their trip to the Creator's Visage Isles, Teg, Grunwold, and Nefnet hiked back to *Slicewind*.

Overhead soared Heru, Grunwold's xuxu, a creature about the size of a raven, that resembled a miniature pterodactyl (bright green on top, even brighter orange on his underside) as much as he resembled anything else from Teg's home world. *Pet* was probably the wrong word for what Heru was to Grunwold, since Heru was intelligent enough to have learned to speak, but *companion* seemed wrong, too, since Heru was more than a sidekick. For now, Teg had decided to just think of Heru as Heru.

"What a beautiful sky sailer!" Nefnet said, in genuine admiration as they stepped out of the cover of the trees and into the meadow where *Slicewind* was berthed.

Teg could have sworn that *Slicewind's* painted eyes crinkled at the corners, as if the ship smiled at the compliment.

"She's smaller than *Cloud Cleaver*," Grunwold said. "That's the ship my parents would have flown here to see you, only a single master, but I love her lines. She's sleek and maneuverable. One person can handle her in a pinch."

"Especially if that one person is Grunwold," Teg put in. "The rest of us usually need a partner. Belowdecks there are three cabins and a galley. Vereez has the smallest cabin. The three of us mentors share the master suite—which is fine, because we take night watch in shifts— and the boys had the bow cabin, but they turned that over to Ohent and Kaj during our latest voyage."

Once aboard, after Nefnet had been given the tour and she and Grunwold had discussed some of what *Slicewind* could spare, they took the ship aloft.

"Let's sail around a bit," Teg suggested, "so that Nefnet-va can see what the area surrounding the Library looks like now."

Grunwold looked quizzical, but launched the flying ship without comment—something so unusual for him that Teg suspected she was not the only one who wanted relative privacy in which to talk.

Nefnet looked down over the lava fields, at the jagged mountains, marveling at how the lake—from whose waters something with many claw-hooked limbs reached out to snag a passing lizard parrot from the sky—had spread from its once modest dimensions.

"I can see," the healer said, "that we will not need to worry about door-to-door vendors even when the Library is up and running again. We were isolated before, mostly by distance from any large population center, but this . . ."

"The change in the terrain is impressive," Teg agreed, then drew in her breath and launched into what she really wanted to talk about. "Speaking of when the Library was up and running . . . You've been relatively calm about learning that more than twenty years of your life were, if not stolen away—since you're the same age as you were, then—shall we say, suspended? How do you think your associates who remain archived will react when they are released?"

Nefnet shook her head, but her words made clear this was not a refusal to answer, only uncertainty. "I wish I knew. Once I got over my own shock, I've thought about that very matter quite a bit. I've even talked a little about it with Sapphire Wind. You're from another world. What do you know about wizards?"

"In our world, wizards only exist in stories," Teg explained. "However, although I don't know anything about actual wizards—except for those I've met here—I'm old enough to know that people who are accustomed to having power are also accustomed to wielding it. Do you have any idea how many of those who stayed over the holiday were actually wizards, how many support staff?"

"I don't." Nefnet's pleasant otter face looked wistful. "I stayed at the Library because I had nowhere I wanted to go. Even better, I was being offered a chance to work on a new research project. The other two you saw in the vision quite outranked me, and I was honored to be invited to collaborate."

Grunwold spoke from where he was busily rooting through one of the many storage lockers that bordered the upper deck. "When I first learned about the Archived, I thought Sapphire Wind had done us a favor, 'archiving' all those people, so that our parents didn't become mass murderers, even by chance. Now ... I'm still glad, but having the fate of the Archived hanging over us is like being at the end of a game of crack the whip: if you let go, you're going to go flying."

"And quite likely crash into something hard," Teg added. "If your parents' secret had ever gotten out, there would have been no avoiding consequences, but now, with the wronged parties still alive and able to plead their case, it could be very bad."

"Yeah," Grunwold said. "The 'extraction agents'—also known as my dad, Vereez's parents, and Xerak's mom, as well as Ohent—had all those years to find ways to justify to themselves what they'd done. Now—if Sapphire Wind wakes those people back up—our folks are going to have a lot of angry people coming after them."

"*If* waking them is what Sapphire Wind plans ..." Teg said, her voice trailing off so that her words became not quite a question.

"That's my understanding," Nefnet said, "and doubtless unarchiving them is the right thing to do."

"Doubtless?" Grunwold asked, quickly hearing the note of uncertainty in Nefnet's voice.

Nefnet sighed and made a sweeping gesture toward the bubbling lake of molten rock, to the sharp, new upthrust mountains. "That sort of massive disaster doesn't happen every time there's a magical accident. If that was the case, we'd have seared ourselves off the globe long, long ago. What you see down there is what happens when there's a magical accident in a magical library and even then..."

She paused, turned so she could face Grunwold and Teg, then sank to sit on the deck, as if by stopping looking at the burbling chaos of the surrounding landscape she could put it out of her mind.

"There were always stories that the Library of the Sapphire Wind existed as more than a tribute to one rich and powerful wizard's vanity. Rumors were always circulating that there was something powerful hidden there, that the Library had been established because the best place to hide something of power is in the midst of other things of power."

"Like the old fairytale about how the best place to hide a needle isn't in a haystack," Grunwold said, "but in a box of needles."

"Exactly," Nefnet said. "If you find a needle in a haystack, you wonder how it got there. If you feel a strange surge of magical energy in a place that is renowned not only for its collection of magical texts, but also for the artifacts repository... Well, you don't even wonder."

"But you're wondering now," Grunwold said.

"I am. There's something I'm not sure you realize... The name of the Library was always one of its little mysteries. Since the Library was supposed to be a tribute to Dmen Qeres's vast collection of books and artifacts, as well as to his ability to secure donations from others, then why didn't he name it for himself? There's ample precedent. When I was awakened by something that identified itself as the eponymous Sapphire Wind, I had one of those 'ah-ha' moments. And I remembered those rumors... And if—when—Sapphire Wind wakes up the rest of those who were archived, I won't be the only one to remember."

Teg cleared her throat. "I've wondered about the Library's name. What is a 'sapphire wind,' anyhow?"

Grunwold and Nefnet both looked startled, then Nefnet asked, "You don't know? Doesn't the translation spell explain?"

"Not really," Teg said. "It's a terrific spell, but when our language doesn't have a cognate, we get a, to us, meaningless sound that is the word in your language. It does this a lot with plants and animals, though, weirdly, if we nickname whatever it is, like Peg usually does, then the translation spell obliges with giving us 'our' word for spike wolves or whatever."

"Fascinating," Nefnet said. "But for the Library of the Sapphire Wind, it didn't do that?"

"No, it simply gave us our words. Library: a place where books and similar items, usually information storage of one sort or another, are kept. Sapphire: a gem-grade corundum, usually blue, though trace elements may cause the gem to have other colors. However, the gem is usually blue, so much so that the name of the gem is often used to describe a certain rich, vibrant shade of blue. Wind." Teg had to pause and think about that one. "Moving air, I guess. A meteorological phenomenon."

Grunwold nodded. "What does the translation spell do with names? Personal names, I mean?"

"Most of the time, it gives us the sound, not the meaning, if any. Maybe that's because in our culture names are identification tags, sounds, even if they have meaning. One of Peg's stepdaughters is named Sunshine, but no one would ever get confused that, when Peg talks about her, she's actually talking about the light of the sun."

"I had a reason for asking," Grunwold said. "You'd think that since Library of the Sapphire Wind is a name for a place, you would have gotten a sound. Did the name of the city of Rivers Meet come as a sound or translated?"

"Translated," Teg said promptly.

"Interesting," Nefnet said. "I see what you're getting at, Grunwold. As with your culture, Teg, our names are often 'just sounds.' Mine is derived from an old word meaning—let me think—*pretty queen*, if I remember right. But place names are often rooted in something specifically descriptive, like Rivers Meet is a city built where several rivers come together. In an odd way, Sapphire Wind is also a descriptive name."

"Which bring us back to my question," Teg said. "What is a sapphire wind?"

Grunwold took up the explanation. "Each of the four dominant winds are associated with a gem. North is diamond. South is ruby. East is yellow topaz. West is emerald. Sapphire wind is a mystic concept: some call it the wind of the soul, the wind of the spirit. Do I have that right, Nefnet-va? I'm a sailor, not a wizard, although I do have pretentions to poetry."

Nefnet nodded. "That's a good definition. Oh, and I would be pleased to have you all drop the '-va.' I appreciate your recognizing me as a wizard, but I never have taken a wizard's name. I see myself more as a researcher and healer."

"We'll tell the others," Teg said.

Nefnet flashed an otter's smile. "So, Teg, you can see that by naming his library for the sapphire wind, Dmen Qeres was proclaiming it a place associated with the magical arts, because magic is often thought of as the art of using one's sapphire wind to manipulate the surrounding world."

"Wow!" Teg said. "Ask a simple question, get a serious answer. That's amazing. I guess that it is very appropriate that the Library's *genius loci* has the same name, since it's essentially the Library's individual soul."

"That's about it," Nefnet agreed. "When the Library was a going concern, most of us didn't think about whether it had a conscious soul or not, but if Dmen Qeres linked the *genius loci* to a powerful artifact like Ba Djed of the Weaver, he intended the place to have a soul even when it was newly built. More usually, when inanimate items have souls, they acquire them over time."

"Kami," Teg said, then, when the other two looked puzzled, she explained. "That's a word from another language in my world: Japanese. It's often translated as *god*, but it can simply mean the spirit that a place or old tree or landscape feature comes to possess over time. Lots of cultures where we come from have the concept, but these days—maybe because we don't have magic to remind us— animism is considered an old-fashioned, even a primitive, way of seeing the world."

"Not that this isn't fascinating," Grunwold said, "because it honestly is, but we were talking about how those people that Sapphire Wind archived are going to feel when they're put into circulation again. I gather that some of them were immensely powerful."

"Definitely." Nefnet got up and began to pace. "When the Library was active, there were elite librarians who administered the collections, kept them from being abused. Some of those will be among the Archived, but not all. As I've been prowling the stacks, I've seen a tremendous amount of destruction, but I've also seen a wealth of materials that could be salvaged. But for whom? The Library as it was doesn't really exist anymore. Who is Dmen Qeres's heir? Not Emsehu, no matter that he claims that his original body was that of Dmen Qeres's biological son."

"And what about the artifacts repository?" Teg added. "That looks as if it was far less damaged than the open stacks, probably because the lock boxes and shelves wouldn't have burned as easily. Sure, individual storage areas were crushed, but much of what was stored within them should be intact. Who owns what's there?"

"I've been wondering about that, too," Nefnet said. "I'm not a particularly power-hungry person—most who go into healing magics are not. Nonetheless, I've found myself tempted to start doing a bit of salvage work for my own benefit. I'll admit, most of the data crystals I've retrieved and begun to repair are those I would love to have for my own personal collection."

"This doesn't sound good," Grunwold said. "I'd been concentrating on how my dad and his fellow extraction agents would be affected. I hadn't thought about the Library itself. Until now, the Library of the Sapphire Wind hasn't been plundered because it was impossible to get in. Now though . . ."

"Exactly," Teg said. "'Impossible' is its own sort of wall. When I was a child, people talked about heart transplants as if they were one-of-a-kind miracles. Now, while they're not exactly routine, no one is surprised to hear of one being done. As long as 'impossible' guarded the Library of the Sapphire Wind, the treasures hidden in the ruins were relatively safe. Now . . ."

"I hate to keep making the situation seem worse," Nefnet said, "but 'impossible' was not all that kept the Library safe. If I understood the tale you told, Sapphire Wind itself was a major force in keeping the Library isolated. It wanted Ba Djed of the Weaver retrieved. Until it sensed that someone who could help it achieve that goal had arrived, it did its best to keep scavengers and treasure hunters away. Now it has you. In a relatively short time, you've retrieved two of the pieces. What will happen when it has the third?"

Teg and Grunwold stared at each other.

"I hadn't thought about that," Grunwold admitted. "I mean, beyond it unarchiving people and a shit storm landing on my dad, that is. What are you thinking about?"

Teg cut in. "It's that rumor, right? The one that the Library was constructed for reasons beyond those publicly given. Do you think Ba Djed of the Weaver is what's behind those rumors?"

"I wish I knew," Nefnet said, "but I do think that Ba Djed has more significance than Sapphire Wind is making out. Sapphire Wind is acting as if the artifact was simply a power source that it drew upon to keep things working. Maybe that's all it is. Maybe, though, Ba Djed is that and also something else."

"Maybe we should just ask Sapphire Wind," Grunwold suggested.

"How would we know if Sapphire Wind was telling us the truth?" Teg countered. "Have you noticed how Meg seemed to have a sense of Sapphire Wind's motivations, even when she wasn't acting as the translator?"

Grunwold and Nefnet both nodded.

Nefnet said, "So there is a continuing connection between them. I wondered if Sapphire Wind asked Meg's permission to reestablish contact, or if it simply assumed the right, as you said it did when you first arrived at the Library."

"I've wondered the same thing," Teg replied. "It's possible Meg agreed. For all that she can be quiet, she's ferociously curious. I think she'd enjoy having an inside track on information—even if she knew she was taking a risk that Sapphire Wind might possess her permanently."

Nefnet returned to her earlier obsession. "I've wondered what will happen when Sapphire Wind unarchives those who are currently dormant. It might prefer some over others, for example, those who are more ambitious, who can be lured into an agreement with a promise of power. Earlier you mentioned how those with power are accustomed to using it—but I've seen the reverse: sometimes the promise of power lets others use you."

Grunwold said, "Given that Sapphire Wind saved your life, you sure don't sound as if you like it very much."

"I'm not sure it so much saved my life as saved a potential resource," Nefnet countered. "There's a tremendous difference. The Library has always been the Library of the Sapphire Wind. I am beginning to wonder if, to Sapphire Wind, everything there—including those who thought themselves in charge—were merely part of the collection."

In the light of her recent discussion with Nefnet, Teg was less than enthusiastic to learn upon their return that Sapphire Wind had suggested that the group search the repository, both for general items that might be useful and, more specifically, for some device—Teg wasn't quite sure what—that might speed their journey to the Creator's Visage Isles.

Xerak and Vereez were already down in the repository with Meg, who had said that her injured hands hadn't robbed her of the ability to read or do light sorting. Kaj and Peg had stayed with Ohent, who had experienced one of her fits and had needed to be drugged. She now lay on the floor, resting on a pallet they'd made from spare bedding.

Nefnet hurried over to examine the unconscious woman. "Kaj, since you can tell me precisely what you gave her and what dosage, I can separate out the drug's effects from whatever other forces may be acting on her. Maybe we can work out what percentage of these nightmares and fits are magically induced and which may be the result of a guilty conscience."

Kaj nodded. "I know my mother, and I don't think it's guilt. I really don't. I'd love to say that it was, because that would make her seem nicer to you, but I'm going to opt for honesty."

"Still," Nefnet said, "if we can rule any element out for certain, then we can . . ."

The discussion rapidly became dually arcane: magical and medical. Teg, who only understood about one part in three, was additionally distracted by the thought that amateurs—treasure hunters at that—were rooting around in a new part of the repository.

"Let's go help the others," she said to Grunwold and Peg.

Peg lifted her knitting. Her current project was a pair of fingerless gloves made from a coarse yarn, probably intended as work gloves.

"I'm at a complicated part. I'll stay here. Besides, my knee is aching. I don't feel like crawling around on the floor."

Teg grinned. "Aching knees couldn't keep me away. C'mon, Grunwold."

Today the repository looked worse than ever. On their first visit, the devastation had been masked by the dust of ages. Now much of that dust seemed to have shifted onto Xerak and Vereez, who had gained access to more broken safe deposit boxes. Meg, her acid-burned hands gloved, sat behind a jury-rigged table, sorting through various bits of detritus.

Grunwold grinned at his two friends. "You guys look worse than the time we decided to dig a tunnel from our fort down to the river. Find anything useful?"

Vereez threw a small chunk of concrete at him. "Actually, we have. Meg, show him!"

Meg held up a large key. In shape, it resembled the heavy iron keys used to undo old-fashioned locks. However, this key was made from a material that sparkled in the light, mostly a rich green but with hints of yellow and blue.

Teg took the key from Meg and turned it over in her hands, giving it a careful inspection. "This looks as if it was grown, rather than carved or cast."

"I believe it was," Xerak replied. "There's a form of enchantment magic where a significant item is covered in a crystalizing solution. It's a fascinating technique, and the end result is much more durable than it looks. I wouldn't recommend jumping up and down on that with heavy boots on, but it should hold up to routine use."

"And its use is?" Grunwold prompted.

"You'll like it," Xerak said, "since it will be helpful next time you decide to steal one of your parents' sky sailers. Basically, that key should open most nonmagical locks and many magical ones as well. In addition, it provides an alert if the lock is warded or alarmed."

"Can't you do that?" Grunwold asked.

"This will be faster," Xerak replied. "Even better, if we charge the key with mana in advance, using it won't drain me in the same way, so I'll have mana to spare for other spells."

"That *is* terrific," Grunwold agreed. "I remember how, in the vision Sapphire Wind showed us in the Font of Sight, Inehem was pretty much trashed by needing to undo all those magical locks. Now, how can I help you and Vereez here?"

"Help Xerak move some of the heavier stuff, Horn Head," Vereez suggested. "While we work, we'll tell you two what we learned about the Creator's Visage Isles."

"I have antlers, not horns," Grunwold responded with what, for him, was considerable mildness, and started pulling on heavy gloves.

Teg handed Meg the key, then stood, hands on hips, happily surveying the mess. "Where would be a good place for me to start? Can I help any of you?"

Meg spoke in her Sapphire Wind voice. "All along the right side of this corridor were safe deposit boxes in which various routine artifacts were kept. Vereez and Xerak have been clearing the way to strong rooms."

Teg bit thoughtfully into her lower lip. "I'll let you young people do the brute labor. Call me if you find something you're worried you might damage getting out. I've some skill."

"In damaging things?" Grunwold said deadpan, handing her a whisk broom and bucket, then moving to where he could help Xerak move rubble off a fallen beam.

"In *not* damaging them," Teg replied, laughing as she hurried over toward the tantalizing array of safe deposit boxes.

"Take the key," Meg suggested. "Some of those safe deposit boxes may still be locked."

When everyone was settled to a task, Vereez began talking, her words falling over each other in her eagerness to tell everything they had discovered at once.

"The Creator's Visage Isles aren't quite all the way on the other side of the world," she began, "but even using *Slicewind*, we could be months getting there."

Teg started to ask a question, but Meg anticipated her.

"Teg, we're used to flying in jets that can carry us to the other side of the world in less than a day. Even though *Slicewind* can move through the sky, it does rely on the winds. Even if we were able to stock up on stored wind or Xerak could keep the winds in our sails all day and all night . . ."

"Which I can't," Xerak interjected, grunting slightly as he and Grunwold lifted a beam so that Vereez could shove a prop under it.

". . . still *Slicewind* is best thought of as a small plane, not a long-range jet."

"Thanks," Teg said. "Go on, Vereez. Let's skip the getting there for now. What are these Creator's Visage Isles like? Do they have a similar culture to what we've seen in this part of the world? What about the language?"

"They speak a language different from ours," Vereez replied. "Happily, it's a language often associated with poetry and culture, so all of us studied it in school. The translation spell should work for you three mentors."

Xerak drew a quick map on a dusty cabinet top. "If you'll look at this, you'll see why the islands have that mouthful of a name. Look at my sketch from this end. See? Two eyes, two ears, a long nose, and a big mouth."

Teg leaned eagerly forward, immediately noting a few things that Grunwold wouldn't have thought to mention. The "ears" were vaguely pointed and set high, rather than to the sides as with a human. The "nose" was indeed long, more like that of a canine or equine, rather than the dot or triangle often used to represent a human nose.

"So, why is only one of the islands called Sky Descry?" Teg asked. "Shouldn't both eyes be looking up, descrying the sky?"

Xerak said, "I learned a story about how the islands got their name from my master. It goes sort of like this." He cleared his throat self-consciously. "When the Creators had finished their work, they looked down and liked what they saw. In fact, they liked it so much that they came down to live in this new world. However, lest they crowd those who were already there, they sank deep into the sea, leaving only their face exposed. This became the islands."

"Odd," Teg said. "Multiple creators but one face. Anyhow, go on."

Xerak gestured toward his sketch as he went on. "The legend goes on to say that because of the proximity to the Creators, the isles became a magically rich place, known for miracles. Those who lived there were delighted to be so blessed. However, as always seems to be the case, over time the populace asked for larger and more frequent miracles. This went on until, one day, what was asked was so enormous that, when the power latent in the Visage Isles attempted to grant the miracle, it failed spectacularly. Instead of a miracle, a volcano erupted, ruining one of the divine eyes entirely. Now the two islands are known as Blinded Eye Isle and Sky Descry Isle."

Meg sighed contently. "Good story. And little Brunni is apparently on Sky Descry."

"I must admit," Teg said, "that, as interesting as the local history sounds, halfway around the world seems a long way to send a baby just to keep it from being discovered. Do you think that location was intentional on your parents' part, Vereez, or did they just give the child up for adoption and not care what happened after? I hope you don't mind my saying so, but they seemed a bit too controlling for the latter option."

"That's a good point," Vereez admitted, "and one I've wondered about, too. Letting her just vanish doesn't seem like them. What I mean is, they're capable of getting rid of an investment that has gone bad, but I've seen them hold onto ones that have gone soft but have potential to recover. Maybe I'm sentimental, but I'd think their only grandchild to this point, maybe ever, would be a resource they'd want to keep an eye on."

"Do you want to try talking to them again?" Xerak asked.

"Given that the last time I tried to talk to them, they put me under house arrest," Vereez replied, "I think I'd better not. They're weird about the whole subject, completely overboard."

"Listen," Grunwold said, "while it's just us, there's something I want to bring up. Are Kaj and Ohent planning to come with us?"

Xerak shrugged and became intently interested in some broken bricks. Vereez swept some dirt into a bucket, then replied.

"I haven't asked. I'm not sure if we have the right to keep them away if they want to come. And if we do find this transportation device that Sapphire Wind has us looking for, we wouldn't even be crowded together on *Slicewind* for months on end."

"But Ohent is nuts," Grunwold said bluntly. "I actually kinda like her, but trying to see the kid may be hard enough without a woman shrouded in a veil, jagged on stimulants or doped to the gills, trailing along. And Kaj . . ."

He stopped, perhaps seeing some warning in the cant of Vereez's ears that stilled even his usual bluntness.

Teg spoke before the pause could become awkward. "I think that we could argue for leaving them both behind. Kaj may be the child's biological father, however, even when he learned he had a daughter, he didn't seem very interested. If Ohent really is concerned for the child's well-being, then she's not going to want to risk any peculiarity that might keep us from learning more about her. If we can find a delicate way to broach that topic, she might be easily be convinced to stay behind, especially since Nefnet has offered to treat her."

"It has only been a few days," Vereez said hesitantly, "I mean, for Kaj. Ohent never told him what she suspected. Given how proud she is of not lying to him, I think he was shocked. Even more shocked, I mean."

Teg remembered how, after Kaj's recent attempt at seduction, Vereez had admitted that she wasn't quite over him. She'd never get over Kaj if the real person remained intertwined with her accumulated fantasies.

It might actually be better if Vereez had a chance to see the person Kaj is now. I don't think he'd live up to four years of fantasies. Who could?

"You have a point, Vereez," Teg said, promising herself that she'd speak with Grunwold and Xerak privately later. "If Kaj wants to come with us, then we should let him. He deserves a chance to show what sort of man he is."

"Or isn't," Grunwold muttered, but although the tip of one of Vereez's ears flickered, she let the comment pass.

"Now that we've settled that," Xerak said, "shall we make plans for what we'll do when we get there?"

"Point one," Teg said, "I know you've all gotten used to how odd we humans look, but will you have any trouble bringing me and Meg and Peg along? I feel that as your mentors we should be there."

Unspoken was *in case one of you needs to be gotten out of a jam via unconventional routes.*

"That's right," Vereez said. "You were off at *Slicewind* when we discussed that. Taking you three humans shouldn't be a problem. Sky Descry is a pilgrimage location, since it's famous for miracles. Many of those who come there are badly disfigured. Your masks may elicit pity, but they shouldn't attract any unwanted attention."

"Okay. I have another question... Why is there a need for miracles in a world where magic works? I mean, don't you experience miracles on a daily basis?"

Xerak stopped to scrub dust off his nose leather before replying. "Magic and miracles are as different as..." He paused again, struggling for an analogy and failing. "Magic follows rules. Miracles don't. That's an oversimplification, but it's the best I can do."

"So who grants these miracles?" Teg asked. "Gods? Saints?"

"That's a matter of great debate," Xerak said, motioning for Grunwold to help him lift yet another chunk of masonry. "There are two general schools of thought. Gods or their agents certainly are one theory. The other is, well, basically that there are areas where there is a superfluity of magical energy that warps the region in which the miracles occur, so that the rules of what usually can and cannot be done are twisted, even bent. Some factions of the 'gods' school tries to have it both ways, saying that the gods create these areas of high magical energy so that those with strong enough will or faith or need or whatever can change reality to create miracles."

"Sounds dangerous," Teg said.

Meg, now clearly Meg, not Meg/Sapphire Wind, said thoughtfully, "Into which category does Hettua Shrine fall? Is it a place of miracles or of magic?"

Xerak scratched his head, shaking his mane in dismay when he realized how much grit was caught in it. "Before meeting the three of you, I would have said magic—a highly specialized form of divination. However, after what we experienced at the shrine, I may need to rethink that. Summoning three mentors from another world seems miraculous to me."

Teg said, "My question about miracles isn't as off topic as you may think. Vereez, is there a reason your parents would have sent Brunni to a place known for miracles? If we know that, it might help us find her."

"I hadn't really considered that the location might be on purpose," Vereez replied. "I'm not used to thinking about magic and miracles in relation to my parents. To me they've always been hard, practical investment bankers. Remember, until just a short time ago, I thought my mother's magical ability was as limited as my own."

Xerak cut in. "As limited as your parents led you to believe your magic was, Vereez. If you dedicate yourself to serious study, I think you will surprise yourself."

"One thing at a time," Vereez said. "I assure you, I haven't forgotten that my magical abilities might be yet another area where my parents lied to me, but my holdback is still, well ... Holding me back."

Xerak, perhaps all too aware of how his own obsessions continued to hold him back, gave her a sympathetic smile. Grunwold opened his mouth as if to speak, then stopped himself. Teg suspected that he wished to ask Vereez whether what had held her back was her desire to find a child she'd never really known, or a chance to confirm dreams of a love that, after all, might never have existed.

Teg would have liked to feel surprised when the next day, in one of the buried strong rooms, they found a transport artifact that could be used to construct a gateway. Even more convenient was that it was already "programmed" to take them to the main population center on Sky Descry. This town shared the name of the island, probably because it took up most of the land area in one way or another. Teg suspected that Sapphire Wind had known precisely where the transport artifact was all along, and that their few wrong turns and mistakes as they sought it had been to keep them from suspecting just how much they were being steered.

The transport artifact consisted of a number of brightly colored polyhedral shapes ranging from those with four sides, all the way up to twenty. Each was about the size of a golf ball, and were cut from translucent semiprecious stones: amethyst, rose quartz, smoky quartz, quartz crystal, and others. There were multiples of each shape, with the exception of one multicolored piece, roughly the size and shape of a hen's egg, that balanced neatly on its wider end.

When they brought their prize upstairs to their camp in the reception area, Peg—after glancing at Xerak for permission—selected a pink twelve-sided shape and gently rolled it across the table.

"Just like the gaming dice my granddaughter, Anna, got for

Christmas last year. Well, hers were smaller and not gems, but if these had numbers inscribed on them..." She trailed off, inviting Xerak to explain what they could expect from their find.

The young wizard looked up from a booklet with an embossed leather cover that had been in the same box as the polyhedrons.

"The shapes are related to setting destinations: four for the major compass points, then those with more sides for longitude, latitude, and the like."

"The like?" Kaj asked, picking up a twenty-sided shape cut from smoky quartz and examining it closely.

"For example, some polyhedrons can be positioned to indicate elevation," Xerak explained. "Whoever owned this set has already done the calculations for both the Creator's Visage Isles and the Library of the Sapphire Wind, which is going to save us a lot of hassle."

"Any other places?" Teg asked, curious.

"A few," Xerak said. "Rivers Meet is one, which isn't a surprise, since Zisurru University is there. But there are also a few locations I've never heard of."

"When can we leave?" Vereez asked, bouncing lightly on the balls of her feet, as if she was ready to charge off that instant.

"Not for several days yet," Xerak said.

"What!"

"We're lucky that whoever owned this set left instructions," he said, hefting the booklet. "Do you really want me to be standing there with the instructions in one hand and the box with all these pieces in the other, trying to set out a complicated pattern while we're trying to get away with a kidnapped kid?"

"You have a point," Vereez agreed reluctantly. "I'd hoped we could get Brunni away—I mean, if she needs to be gotten away—without raising a fuss or needing to rush."

"Me, too," Xerak said. "Profoundly and wholeheartedly, but we can't count on that. I'm going to memorize these instructions, do a bunch of dry runs on setup, then make a practice jaunt. And, you, my pointy-nosed friend, are going to do the same."

"Me?"

"You. You're the closest thing to another wizard who's going to be part of this venture. You need to know exactly what to do in case something happens to me. Now that I think about it, Teg had better join our training sessions as well. She's shown a real gift for using the sun spider amulet. Time for her to see if she can extend her abilities."

The several days' delay did have advantages. For one, Meg's hands had ample time to heal. For another, after much argument, Ohent was convinced to remain with Nefnet in order to continue her treatment. In the end, Ohent only agreed because, "This way there will be someone to come to the rescue if you get yourselves into deep shit."

Kaj did ask to accompany them and, given that they were going to look for his kid, it was hard to find an excuse to leave him behind. Kaj admitted to no skill with a sword—that was a weapon for soldiers and upper-class idlers—but he was good with a long knife (which he had with him) as well as with a short club, rather like a policeman's baton. Xerak shyly presented Kaj with a nice piece of seasoned hardwood that he had found during his "meditation" visits into the surrounding area, and Kaj wrapped one end with rope to create a slip-free handgrip.

"Those of us who use hand weapons should be certain to keep in practice," Peg said. "I, for one, am of an age where a few days break can be beneficial, but after that I start losing tone quickly."

"I can bring the practice weapons from *Slicewind*," Grunwold said. "Kaj used a club pretty well when we fought the tetzet a few days ago, but I'd like to see how he uses it against edged weapons."

"I'd like to show you," Kaj said, barring his teeth in something that just barely managed to remain a smile. "You might learn a few things."

In addition to weapons practice, Xerak insisted that Teg take time to practice the magical focus exercises he'd been teaching her.

"Don't argue," he said, when she started to do so. "I know archeology is your first passion, but I insist you train your magic. Who knows? Your latent capacity might be one of the reasons Hettua Shrine selected you."

"What about Vereez?" Teg asked.

"I'd like to get her to resume regular meditations," Xerak admitted, "but between her fixation on Kaj and the fact that we're within days of heading off to find Brunni, asking her to put a calm mind in a calm body seems rather too much."

Over the intervening days, Teg also found an opportunity to brief Peg regarding her discussion with Nefnet about the Archived, and whether they would have legal recourse against the former extraction agents.

"Even if the Archived don't have legal recourse," Peg said, "that doesn't end the matter—the nastier sorts might opt for vendettas or character assassination or the like."

Although they both felt bad about it, they decided to share with Meg only their concern about what might happen when the Archived were unarchived and related matters—not Nefnet's suspicions regarding Sapphire Wind's private agenda.

Meg was becoming all too comfortable with the Library's *genius loci*. She didn't seem to mind sharing her vocal cords with it, and when the group conferred, she and Sapphire Wind now switched back and forth without warning, only the shift in the quality of Meg's voice—slightly breathy, with a more measured cadence—announcing that Sapphire Wind was speaking through her.

"It's not that we don't trust *Meg*," Peg reassured Teg in a manner that made it clear she was also reassuring herself. "It's that we aren't sure we can trust Sapphire Wind."

{CHAPTER THREE}

In addition to dry runs with the transport artifact, Xerak arranged to turn the Spindle of Ba Djed over to Emsehu's custody, just in case there were unexpected consequences. However, the transfer went smoothly.

"But I *am* a wizard," Xerak said, "unlike Ohent. And although Inehem didn't admit it to us, I wouldn't be at all surprised if she did some experimenting with the Bird. I certainly would have been tempted to see if I could tap into its mana if I hadn't been repeatedly warned as to how dangerous that could be."

Oddly enough, this was one situation in which Xerak's monomania about finding his master actually served them well. If he had thought fooling around with the piece of Ba Djed would help him find Uten Kekui, he would have been on it, as one of Teg's aunts used to put it, "like white on rice," but since nightmares and hallucinations would weaken him, Xerak resisted, just as he kept his drinking just on the edge of impairing his ability to function.

After several days, Xerak announced he was ready to make a trial run with the transportation artifact.

"We can try Rivers Meet, which we know, or Creator's Visage, which is our destination. There are advantages and disadvantages to either choice. I have no idea where in Rivers Meet this will take us, but if we emerge at Zisurru University, we're likely to be detected, detained, then asked a lot of questions. We might even find ourselves held and the transport artifact taken from us. The same applies to the Creator's Visage Isles, too, of course, depending on where we show up, but it's not likely they'll have the same alarms set to detect unauthorized magical intrusion as a magical university would."

Considerable debate followed, but in the end they decided on heading directly for Sky Descry. As Peg put it, "Since we don't know where we'll end up anyhow, we might as well go where we want to go, rather than risk getting caught where we don't."

After more argument, Xerak and Kaj were selected to make the first test. Grunwold wanted to go but, even he had to agree that if a rescue expedition had to be sent out, they'd need *Slicewind*'s master at her helm.

"Take my watch with you," Peg said, handing her watch to Kaj, "and try to be back within an hour."

"Right," Xerak said. "If for some reason we don't come back, see if Sapphire Wind can divine what happened to us before racing off to the rescue."

Despite her private certainty that if they were doing anything too stupid, Sapphire Wind would find a way to redirect them, Teg found that her hands were sweating as she stood by with Vereez as magical backup.

"I'm an archeologist, not a wizard, Jim," her panicked brain stated in a parody of her favorite character from the original *Star Trek*.

Kneeling on the floor, Xerak rapidly set the various polyhedral shapes in their assigned places in a ring with himself and Kaj at its center. He activated the spell by grasping the multicolored egg, then speaking a few lines of something rhythmic that the translation spell didn't choose to translate. Light surged up around the two young men, making it look as if they stood inside a stained-glass gazebo. The gazebo started spinning, faster and faster, until the colors shifted to white. A few breaths later, with nothing but a faint popping in their ears to signal the change, all that remained was an empty space.

Waiting for Xerak and Kaj to return was incredibly hard. If Meg hadn't kept track of time with an antique pocket watch she'd brought back on her most recent visit home, Teg would have sworn that hours, not a mere thirty-two minutes, passed before a whistling sound warned them that something was happening. The boys looked incredibly pleased with themselves, and Kaj gave a slight bow as he returned Peg's elderly wristwatch to her.

"We were lucky," Kaj said, his entire body telegraphing

excitement. "The spell took us into a deserted building, part of a largish estate. We hiked out far enough to assure ourselves that the location is within walking distance of the town of Sky Descry."

"I can't help but feel it wasn't all luck," Xerak said, giving Meg, or more probably Sapphire Wind, a sidelong look.

"Luck or not," Peg said, "I'll admit to feeling relieved. What would you and Kaj have done if you'd emerged into a room full of people? Apologized and said, 'Sorry? Wrong room?'"

"Something like that," Xerak admitted. "Then while Kaj answered questions and kept people back, I would have been laying out the polyhedrons in the return pattern as fast as I could. It would have been good practice for if we need to make a fast escape, right?"

Now that the time had come, it was Vereez's turn to be the voice of reason. "We'll wait until tomorrow, so you're fully rested, Xerak, and so that the transport device can soak up more mana. You were lucky this time, but I think it's about time we made some of our own luck."

They spent much of the rest of the day making final preparations. The search through the artifact repository had turned up—in addition to the key and the transport artifact—several more magical "flashlights."

These needed—as Peg put it—"to have their batteries charged." This last did seem to support Sapphire Wind's claim that the ambient magical energy of the area had been drained, but still, Teg found herself wondering about how those things that Sapphire Wind wanted to have work—the Font of Sight, and now this transport portal—could be made to function.

Nefnet suggested something else to add to their arsenal. "Let me make you up a powder you can give to young Brunni. In a light dose, either inhaled or imbibed, it will calm her. In a heavier dose, mixed with water or fruit juice and drunk, it will make her sleep."

Vereez looked horrified. "I hate the idea of drugging a child."

"You say this Brunni is only four," Nefnet countered. "All of you will be strangers to her. It is sensible to assume she will panic, and a panicked child is not what you need if you decide she must be removed from her current home. If you're concerned, you can work with me while I do the compounding. You know enough of herb lore that you will be able to see if I do anything nefarious."

Somewhat ashamed, Vereez agreed that this was sensible. She seemed pleased when Kaj also asked to sit in.

"I know quite a bit about preparations meant to soothe or cause sleep," Kaj said, as if feeling he needed to establish why he was interested. "If this one is new to me, I'll have learned something valuable."

The next morning, they assembled in the Library's main reception hall. Since they didn't know how long they'd need to stay, they each carried a light pack.

"Our cover story for when we get to Sky Descry," Vereez said—the fact that she was repeating what they already knew showed how nervous she was—"will be that the three mentors are pilgrims seeking miracles. We four will pose as your escort. That should provide ample explanation for us going about lightly armed."

"We'll keep an eye on *Slicewind* for you," Ohent promised, "and use her to come to the rescue if you don't check in."

Xerak had been giving the instructions a final review, and now he opened the box containing the gemstone polyhedrons. "Hush now, while I get the spell ready. Since the device won't transport more than three at a time, we'll go in shifts. Get in your groups. Grunwold, Heru, Vereez, you're up first."

Teg was in the second group, with Kaj and Meg.

Although standing within a gazebo of shifting light was impressive, even awe inspiring, for Teg the actual transition seemed almost routine, certainly nothing like as startling as when they'd been taken from Pagearean Books to Hettua Shrine. She heard Kaj give a small grunt, and realized that despite having been on the test run, magical transport would be far from routine for him.

In contrast, we three mentors have been making enough trips back and forth between our worlds—not exactly daily, the seven here to one there time difference makes that unnecessary—that's it's beginning to seem a version of normal.

Teg gave Kaj a reassuring pat on the arm as they stepped from the stained-glass gazebo, blinking in the sunlight that poured in through the dirty glass panes of what appeared to have been someone's parlor. The room was furnished with intricately woven wicker furnishings, and had its own door to the outside.

"Remember," said Xerak, who had come through last so he could make sure the transport device continued working without a glitch, "even though this estate isn't in use, we should take care not to be seen."

"We've had the briefing," said Kaj, shifting foot to foot. "Next step, we go into town and find a hotel."

If he meant to impress Vereez with his decisiveness, it didn't work. She sniffed, slipped her swords into their sheaths, and spoke to Heru as if Kaj wasn't there.

"All right, Heru. Your turn to show off. Remember what you're supposed to do?"

In reply the miniature pterodactyl pecked Grunwold on one antler. "Open the door!"

"Don't *do* that," Grunwold grumbled. "My antler isn't a tree limb."

But he opened the door and Heru soared out. Xerak finished gathering up the polyhedrons. He put most of them in their box, which went into his pack, but he reserved those he would need to make a gate back to the Library. Those he put in a bag that he hung at his hip, where he could reach them quickly.

Heru returned before Teg had finished inspecting the room.

"All quiet . . ." he reported happily, playing a cascade of notes on his crest.

"Idiot xuxu," Grunwold said, but Teg noticed he slipped the creature a small treat, which Heru accepted with many happy chortles.

When they stepped outside, the plants in the deserted garden seemed vaguely tropical to Teg, something about broad, thick leaves, lots of vines, and brilliant blossoms. The temperature was comfortable, even though, if this really was on the other side of the world, the season should be closer to autumn than summer.

Then again, Teg thought, *do the seasons here follow the same pattern as ours? I've never quite gotten straight what causes the shifts. Axial tilt? Distance from the sun? I never realized how little I know about why things work until now.*

Xerak and Grunwold led them briskly along, not slowing until they reached a business district where a group of tourists wouldn't seem out of place. The architecture of the city seemed Mediterranean—wide windows, open courtyards, and balconies suggesting a life lived more out of doors than in Rivers Meet, KonSef Landing, and the small town near Hettua Shrine.

Although the Library's maps, stored in scroll cases, these in turn kept in what had reminded Teg of wine racks meant to hold skinny bottles, had survived more or less intact, texts such as travel guides had fared less well. Still, Xerak's wanderings had made him something of an expert at orienting himself in a new location, and he'd expressed little concern about finding them a good inn.

After they'd been turned away from several promising moderate-sized inns, he was less certain. "It seems there's some sort of festival on," Xerak reported. "People are pouring in from the countryside and surrounding islands, so every affordable room is taken."

"Festival?" Peg said. "That sounds like fun!" When Vereez looked daggers at her, Peg gently patted her. "No. I'm not forgetting your inquisition. What better place to ask a bunch of stupid questions than in the middle of a festival? Xerak, can you get us to where we can learn more about what's going on?"

"What about finding a hotel?" he asked.

Peg waved this concern away. "We'll manage. We can always go back to the deserted house and rough it. Remember, I was at Woodstock. We camped in the mud there."

No one else protested Peg's suggestion, so soon they were sweeping down increasingly wide streets toward a magnificent curving plaza backed on three sides by elegant buildings, and on the fourth by view of a harbor full of tall-masted ships at anchor, smaller ships busy as ants as they ferried people to and from shore.

Commandeering Heru, Vereez grabbed Peg, and they split off to see if one of the grander hotels had a line of credit with Vereez's family business. Teg fell in with Xerak, while Meg asserted her authority as the eldest to claim both Grunwold and Kaj as her escort. There was plenty for them to investigate without going so far that they'd lose sight of the others.

From what she could overhear and read on various banners, Teg gathered that the festival was somehow religious in nature, but beyond that she was lost. Apparently, someone was going to be dedicated to the service of the area's patron: the Grantor of Miracles. Who and when and why now was—if Teg correctly understood what she was hearing—something determined by a bunch of factors that not even the locals were in control of.

"Which explains the generally frantic mood," she said to Xerak.

He'd bought them both big cups of what tasted like a port and over-ripe strawberry punch, accented with something light and slightly sour that made the beverage very refreshing. He'd drained his and was looking thoughtfully at his cup.

"You don't really need another so soon," Teg said gently.

"Oh, yeah, I know." Xerak pointed with his index finger claw tip. "Take a look at your cup. Does it have anything written or drawn on it?"

Teg took a swallow, lowering the level enough that she could tilt the cup to one side. The clay was stamped with a stylized pattern accompanied by writing in a script that the translation spell struggled—and failed—to resolve. Xerak looked at her cup, then showed her his, which was incised with the same pattern. Before Teg could ask what was bothering him, he was dragging her along toward one of the many booths set around the plaza.

Teg grabbed the hem of her robe and trotted to keep up. When they stopped, she had to adjust her mask, so it took her a moment to realize that they were standing in front of a souvenir stand.

It always amused Teg that people thought that cheap souvenirs were a bane of modern society. They weren't. The original Olympic games had had souvenirs. So had various temples in a wide variety of places all around the world. Now, in front of her, was a fresh take on an idea that might just be as old as the desire to have a physical item to provide a connection to a place or event.

Of course, these souvenirs weren't plastic. Teg reached out and picked up a little doll. The head was clay, probably molded. It was attached to a floppy cloth body clad in a kimono-like robe, possibly representational, possibly chosen because the straight lines would be easy to quickly sew. The casting was crude, and Teg was trying to figure out exactly what animal was represented when Xerak pulled her away, barely giving her time to put down the doll.

The young wizard looked shaken and, without thinking, Teg handed him her cup. After he downed the rest of the punch, he seemed to get control of himself.

"Did you see that?"

"The souvenir dolls? Sure, but what's bothering you?"

"I thought you could read." Xerak held up the empty cup, traced his claw-tip along the characters. "What does that say?"

"I have no idea. Remember what we discovered at Kuvekt-lial's. The translation spell doesn't work well with all scripts: the more idiosyncratic or stylized, the more difficulty we have in reading them."

"Right. I remember now. Sorry. I wanted you to confirm what I saw without asking a leading question." Instead of explaining, Xerak looked wildly around. "There're Grunwold and Meg. C'mon."

Grunwold, Meg, and Kaj were over by an ornamental fountain, watching the people passing by. The two young men were pointedly ignoring each other in that way that meant they had no attention for anyone but each other. Xerak and Teg had just reached them when Vereez and Peg, Heru spiraling overhead, also came rushing up.

"Did you find a room . . ." Grunwold began, then stopped. "What's wrong with you people?"

Vereez's dark brown eyes were so wild that the whites could be seen all around. She tried to speak, but she was shaking so hard that she couldn't. When Grunwold grabbed her and pressed her close, she didn't protest.

Peg spoke, "When we went into the hotel, I asked about the festival, explaining we'd just arrived and had no idea we would be here at such a busy time. The desk clerk said no one had any idea. This festival came up just a few days ago."

Meg cut in. "Why is Vereez so upset?"

"I'm getting to that," Peg assured her. "I'd suggest we go to our rooms—Vereez did secure us a suite for what is going to be a poisonous price—but she'd refuse. She wants to look for Brunni."

Grunwold had gotten Vereez calmed enough that the younger woman was able to turn to face them. "I'm sorry. I . . . Peg. Go on. Tell them the good news and the bad news."

The last sentence was spoken with a laugh that was on the ragged edge of hysteria. Kaj, who had been standing stiff as a statue, now moved to commandeer one of the many tables scattered around the plaza. Xerak had vanished almost as soon as Vereez and Peg had arrived. He now returned carrying a tray laden with cups of fruit punch and some sort of brightly colored dough-ball snack.

As they moved over to the table, Peg didn't stop talking. "The good news is we have a very firm idea where to find little Brunni. The bad news is that Brunni is apparently crucial to this festival. I don't quite gather what's going on, but she's the one who is going to be dedicated."

"Well," Meg said with typical understatement, "I can see why Vereez was flustered, but why is she so upset? Surely this means that the child is valued, well cared for . . ."

Kaj interrupted her. "Doomed."

Vereez started crying again. Grunwold glowered at Kaj, his expression growing worried when he saw that Xerak was slowly nodding agreement.

"All right," Peg said, pulling out a chair, shoving Vereez into it, then taking the one next to her. "Time for explanations. Kaj, what do you mean 'doomed'? I can't imagine all these people would be celebrating the death of a four-year-old child."

"They aren't," Kaj said. "They're celebrating the rebirth of their local—I'm not sure what to call him. Hero? Guardian? Protector?"

"Something like that," Xerak agreed. "I asked some questions while I was getting the refreshments. Remember how this area is famous for miracles? Well, turns out the story that I learned in school has a second part. After the volcano that became Blinded Eye Isle exploded, a whole administration system evolved to make sure that requests for miracles would be more thoughtfully handled from then on. At the head of this is a personage called the Grantor of Miracles, Grantor for short. Anyhow, the most recent Grantor died a while back."

"Not at the same time as the Library was destroyed," Teg said with a growing sense of dread.

"No, later than that," Xerak reassured her, "something like ten years ago. The residents of the Visage Isles have been praying for signs that a new Grantor has been ordained because, without him, the bigger, flashier miracles don't happen. Don't ask me about how that works. I don't know, and that's not what's important right now."

"So," Peg urged, "what is?"

"Apparently, not long ago, oracles revealed that a child—an immigrant child—was the new vessel of the Grantor."

"Sounds like the Tibetan lama," Teg said, then explained what she meant.

"Except," Kaj put in, "it's not as simple as one person being born as the reincarnation of another. How much do you humans know about reincarnation?"

"We were told enough to know that you all take it for granted," Teg said. "As well as that there are various theories as to how it works and whether the living can have any influence on the outcome."

"Not bad," Kaj said. "You've got the basics. What's going on here, with the new Grantor, could be called an arranged or forced reincarnation. Sometimes when a particular spirit's return is particularly desired, but the person has not reincarnated, a body is provided for the spirit to take over."

"I have a bad feeling about this," Peg muttered.

Kaj ignored her and continued. "This is one way that families keep a particularly powerful or influential person in their midst. Another advantage is that forced reincarnation prevents there being too great a delay. If reincarnation is left to run its own course, then a spirit may take decades, even centuries to return."

Xerak curled a hank of his mane around one index finger. "One thing puzzles me. Kaj, I thought that forced reincarnation worked best if there was a blood tie between the departed spirit and the . . . host. Am I remembering wrong?"

Kaj shook his head. "No. That's what I'd gathered, too. During the years I worked at various necropoli, I've witnessed more than one instance where a family was negotiating which of their members would supply the host body. Usually they want a close relation—a child or grandchild. They also usually want someone a little older than Brunni."

"Why?" Peg asked.

"Several reasons," Kaj said. "One is that a small child is pretty useless, especially if the person being reincarnated is someone who is valued for magical skills. Even if the spirit returns with a full memory, a child's body simply cannot handle the energies involved. From what I saw—and I'm no expert—the preferred host is usually someone a bit older—ten or even twelve."

"Not nineteen or twenty?" Peg asked. "I'm asking because if a blood tie is crucial, then it would seem that you or Vereez would be a better candidate—depending on what side of the family is involved. If any."

Xerak cut in. "Kaj is way too old. Even nineteen, like Vereez is, would be too old to be ideal. By then the personality of the individual is too deeply engraved on the body. The best a returning spirit could expect would be a sort of co-residency."

"Wait!" Teg said. "Kaj said 'doomed.' What happens if this guardian spirit returns and takes up residence in Brunni's body?"

Vereez crushed one of the colorful dough balls between her fingertips, then spoke very carefully. "Either Brunni's spirit would be pushed out completely or she would face a life as a subtenant in her own body. Either way, her existence as herself is over."

"Don't," Grunwold said, turning to the three mentors, his voice unexpectedly rough, "ask if, since we 'believe' in reincarnation, what happens to Brunni's spirit doesn't really matter. Living is important. Most reincarnated people don't remember their past lives, but those lives still shape who you are. Sometimes you meet someone you feel unexpectedly drawn to—or hate. That's probably your past life coming into play. Or you might have a particular knack for some skill you've never tried before. Again, that's your past life."

"Look," Kaj said. "We could discuss the theories for days. Weeks. The thing is, Brunni doesn't have days or weeks. I can't say I feel particularly fatherly toward her. I'm not going to lie. I mean, I didn't even know she existed until a few days ago. But I've always found these arranged reincarnations repulsive. Maybe I've seen one too many kids suddenly realize that their lives don't mean anything except that they're going to provide a healthy body and sound mind for granddad or great-aunt. If Vereez is still determined to find Brunni, learn if the kid has any opinions about her part in this, then I'll help."

Nods around the little group confirmed that no one's mind had changed. Then Meg, who had been quieter even than usual, cleared her throat.

"I suspect that I am not the only one here wondering if this sudden revelation that Brunni is the designated host is purely a coincidence. Somehow, I cannot believe this is so. Somehow someone was alerted to the fact that Vereez was going to attempt to reclaim her daughter, and the timetable was moved up."

"My parents?" Vereez sounded caught between indignation and disbelief.

"Perhaps," Meg said. "Perhaps the situation is something more complicated—perhaps there was some sort of omen or prophetic response to prayer. But, as Kaj said, such suppositions can wait. First, we need to find out if we can do anything for Brunni."

"If Brunni wants anything done," Vereez said, anxiety transmuting into uncertainty. "Who am I to interfere? Maybe she thinks this is wonderful."

"We can't know without talking to her or at least to someone close to her," Grunwold said gruffly. "At least for your sake, we need to find out that much. If you stop here, you'll be held back for the rest of your life. I, for one, am not willing to accept that—and you shouldn't either."

"Good boy," Peg said, her knitting needles flashing in a fashion that reminded Teg of Vereez's twin swords. "So, where do we start? I'm assuming that we can't walk up to whatever hotel or temple or wherever Brunni is staying and say, 'Hi, we have Brunni's biological mother here and...'"

She trailed off as heads shook all around.

"All right, then what do we do?"

"Find where Brunni is staying," Vereez said, tamping down her emotions with visible effort. "Find if she is secluded or in public. Plan from there."

"Good," Xerak said. "I suggest we split up. Each of us will take one of the humans with us. That way, if it seems that having the excuse of a pilgrim who came here seeking a miraculous intervention will get us sympathy, then we'll have one such at hand."

"I want Teg," Vereez said. "I mean, she's my watch partner, and we're used to each other."

"Then I'll take Peg," Xerak said. "If you're okay with escorting Meg, Grunwold?"

Grunwold nodded. Kaj cut in.

"What about me? Don't I get a human?"

Grunwold's expression tightened. "Sure. I'll share Meg with you. No problem."

Unspoken, but perfectly understood, was "And this way I can keep an eye on you, and keep you away from Vereez until she gets her head together."

After a brief discussion of the best places to find information, the three groups split up, agreeing to meet at the hotel in about two hours.

* * *

Almost as soon as Vereez and Teg set off for their assigned destination—a compound associated with the late Grantor of Miracles—Vereez let out a small groan and started sniffling, tears running from her brown eyes to soak her fur, creating mahogany patches against the brighter red.

"I'm not handling this well, am I, Teg?"

"Which bit?" Teg asked, making her voice deliberately light. "Discovering that the child you're searching for may be out of reach? Kaj and Grunwold shedding pheromones and resentment right and left? Your dread that your parents may be nastier people than you'd ever imagined? I don't know. You're not quivering under the bed. A few tears don't seem out of line."

Vereez laughed. "When you put it that way... I think what's really bothering me is I don't know why I'm suddenly all weepy. That really has never been me. Am I trying to get Kaj's attention by reverting to being a little girl? If so, I really don't like myself very much."

"Then don't do it," Teg said. "If you can only win Kaj by being a person you don't like, then you don't want him anyhow. If you win him over that way, you're just going to make yourself miserable. Besides, I don't think that's what you're doing. You put him off pretty easily when he made a move on you back on *Slicewind*."

"Easily? Not really. A lot of me wanted to go..." Vereez stopped herself in midphrase. "I wasn't lying when I told him I dream about how his arms felt. Or other things. He really was..."

"So he was a good lay," Teg said bluntly. "That's fine. If that's all you want, then go for him by all means. Marry him, even. But accept that you won't be the only one he's screwing, that he'll respect you less for wanting him. That's how that sort of man is."

"I... know. Sort of. But not really. I think I could make..."

"Him change?"

"I was going to say 'love me.'"

"He might love you. But that's not going to make him decide to stop being promiscuous. He needs the conquests like Xerak needs his bottle, like I need a smoke. He's addicted to them."

"But you were saying you might quit. Xerak drinks less when he thinks he's on the trail of something important. Can't Kaj change?"

"Maybe. But he has to change himself. I'm thinking about quitting smoking because this trip has brought home to me how what was just a pleasant pastime has become a need. Xerak only stops drinking when he wants to function unmuddled. The rest of the time, Xerak likes that muddle. But our needs are simpler than Kaj's. His are all tied up in his childhood. Remember, he *knew* his mother was basically the only one of the extraction agents who didn't succeed in later life."

"So Kaj needs to prove he's not a failure," Vereez said.

"And every girl he tumbles—I'm thinking 'girl' because he doesn't seem to care that Xerak's making sheep's eyes at him—makes him feel like a success."

"So you figured out that Xerak isn't likely to be competing for my attentions?"

"Wasn't hard, not once Kaj showed up. Before that, I just thought Xerak was . . ."

"Monomaniacal?" Vereez giggled.

"Oh, he's that, but now I'm wondering if there's an added reason for that mania. I wonder if he might have a crush on his master."

"Oh! I hadn't thought of that."

Teg decided to clear up another point. "You do realize that Grunwold has a crush—maybe more than a crush—on you, don't you?"

"He what?"

Vereez's surprise couldn't have been more genuine.

"I shouldn't have said anything, maybe," Teg said, "but before you fling yourself into his arms next time . . . You should remember: for you it might just be accepting brotherly affection, but it's more for him."

"Grunwold? But he's so . . ."

"Grunwold. Let's leave it there. Just think about it, okay? Don't build his hopes up just because you're needy right now." Teg pointed. "Hey, isn't that the building we're looking for?"

The façade that rose up before them reminded Teg of Spanish Colonial Mission–style buildings she'd seen on visits to Arizona. Here, however, the unornamented white-stucco surface was crammed with intricate bas-relief carvings, and what looked like ideographic writing, that was very different from anything she'd seen in Rivers Meet or KonSef Landing. She made a mental note to ask one of the inquisitors—Xerak probably—whether it was writing or merely ornamentation.

"That's it," agreed Vereez, scrubbing away the damp spots on her face, "the Administration for Miracles. The brochure we picked up at the hotel says there's a sort of museum dedicated to past miracles. Why don't we stop at the museum first, learn what we can without asking direct questions?"

A flight of wide, shallow stairs—almost more miniature terraces than mere steps, and again showing a very different architectural style than she'd seen elsewhere—led up to vast double doors that stood open. The stairs were quite crowded but, since every public area in Sky Descry had been crowded, it took Teg a second look to realize that this wasn't the casual lounging of holidaymakers, but a line so long that it not only went all the way to the base of the stairs, but snaked back and forth, so it would not block access to other parts of the structure.

She noticed that many of the people waiting were leaning on crutches or canes. There were even some who wore masks like her own. At Vereez's query, a tiger-headed woman replied with weary patience.

"This is the line for those who want to sign up for an interview."

"With the child, Brunni, who will become the guardian?" Vereez asked with admirable composure.

"Oh, no! Those won't be granted until long after the ceremony. This is to sign up for a triage meeting—to discover if a miracle is even likely."

"But," Teg asked, feeling her mask justified the question, "aren't miracles by definition something that can't be predicted?"

The tiger face showed deep compassion, eyes widening, ears softening. "Oh, isn't that what we all wish! However, apparently some miracles are more likely than others. Later, perhaps, when the new Grantor has grown in power, more powerful miracles will be likely, but..."

They chatted for a little longer about what miracles were most likely to be made possible by the newly embodied Grantor. Other bored people in the line added their conjectures. Opinions differed as to what sort of miracles were most likely. What didn't differ was a strong sense that it was "about time" a new Grantor was appointed. Very few seemed to have any pity for the child who would give up her identity.

"Let's go look at the museum," Teg urged Vereez when she saw that the young woman was reaching the point where she would be likely to say something imprudent. "Maybe we'll learn whether it's worth joining the line."

Vereez came away meekly enough, but when Teg rested a hand on her slim shoulder, she could feel the young woman shaking. This time her emotion was anger, not grief. Teg had to admire the young woman for keeping quiet while other people discussed Brunni as if she was nothing more than an organic vending machine.

After the twisting lines and crowds outside, the museum seemed deserted, although actually quite a few people were viewing the exhibits. The exhibits that drew the most attention were items donated by grateful people to commemorate successful miraculous interventions. Many of these were crutches, false limbs, or masks. Rather than the doubtlessly shabby and worn discarded items, these were beautiful facsimiles, made from the most expensive materials the donor could afford. Those made from inexpensive materials were often the most beautiful, for the maker had lavished workmanship in place of jewels and gilding.

Teg was reminded of the *milagros* that were common in areas indebted to some extent to Spanish culture. The ones she was most familiar with—from the American Southwest—were usually smaller, but the sentiment was the same: a physical representation of the miracle granted or desired.

Rapidly, Teg grew weary of protecting her false tail and mask from being dislodged by the jostling pilgrims, and moved to where she could view the large mural that wrapped around the museum's walls. Changes in artistic style, fading, and such indicated to her trained eye that this had not been painted all at one time, but had been added to over the years.

Or possibly the decades or even the lifetimes of this Grantor.

Curious, Teg sought one of the earliest segments, wanting to get a sense of this folk hero before his legend built and overshadowed the original person. She found what she was looking for in a back room that quite possibly was the original museum, which had been expanded as the legend grew and—more importantly—there was a need for space to display the expensive gifts.

Vereez trailed after her, caught up in her own thoughts, content to let Teg take the lead. She didn't forget her role as bodyguard, though, and this, combined with Teg's apparently reverent posture as she knelt to better examine some of the mural's details, caused other visitors to grant them a little space.

Teg paused to study a section that showed a figure she took to be an early Grantor of Miracles—a surmise based on the figure's attire, which included a robe and an elaborate headdress; the same costume shown in later art—gathered with a group of similarly costumed figures. Did this depict the Grantor and acolytes? The art style was somewhere between hieratic and representational—reminding Teg somewhat of that promulgated in Akhenaten's Egypt, although lacking the emphasis on the grotesque.

If the conventions were similar, then the size of figures was important. What interested Teg was that the Grantor, distinctive in his towering headdress and dark purple robes, was shown here associating with two other figures the same general size as him. That these were equals—peers—was made very clear by the presence of numerous obviously lesser beings: their robes less showy, their headdresses echoes of the Grantor's own, although with different stylistic details.

"Vereez," Teg began, then stopped. She'd come to a panel where the hierarchs were shown standing side by side. Each held something in his or her—secondary sexual characteristics were hidden by the heavy robes, and even the heads were so stylized they could have belonged to any creature with large ears and a long muzzle—right hand. That which the Grantor held seemed to be an icon of some sort, depicting what seemed to be a tree. But that wasn't what had caught her attention. In the palm of the hierarch next to the Grantor was balanced a shape that, even in the old and faded painting, was clearly recognizable.

"Yes, Teg? I'm sorry . . ."

"Vereez. Tell me, do you see anything interesting about this bit of the mural?" Teg asked, being very careful not to ask a leading question. For all she knew, this was a relatively common shape.

But Vereez's indrawn breath confirmed her own supposition. "That's Ba Djed of the Weaver. The artifact from the Library."

"That's what I thought, too. The Grantor is holding something as well . . . Another artifact?"

"So," Vereez said slowly, her ears flattening. "There is a connection between the Library and the Creator's Visage Isles."

Teg pushed herself to her feet. "A connection between the Visage Isles and the Library of the Sapphire Wind. Not necessarily between what's going on with Brunni and the rest of this mess. Look. There's a third figure, same size, also holding something. Is that a wheel?"

"Maybe. I don't really care." Vereez, noticing her flattened ears were attracting attention, forced herself to look more relaxed. Her words showed she was not. "Remember what Meg said about coincidences? I don't believe in them either. The question I need answered is do my parents have anything to do with Brunni being here, about to be sacrificed to some ancient spirit? If so, I'm not certain I'll ever be able to forgive them. Now that we have a connection between the two locations, my parents' deliberately placing Brunni here has just become more likely."

When the groups reunited at the hotel, Teg could tell right off that she and Vereez weren't the only ones with something to report. They had been the last to return and found the others already helping themselves to a fancy smorgasbord laid out in the central room of the suite. As Teg hurried to get out of her cumbersome mask and elaborate robes, she wished she had time to grab a smoke, but she had a feeling the hotel would frown on that even more than did her companions.

Later, she promised herself. To distract herself, she started building a sandwich of which Dagwood Bumstead would have been proud.

Vereez had regained her composure on the way back to the hotel, and now encouraged the others to give their reports first.

"Teg and I learned some things, but we didn't learn much more about Brunni. Did any of you?"

Grunwold and Kaj, momentarily harmonious in some shared emotion, looked at Meg.

"We found where the child is being housed," Meg announced calmly.

"*She* found where," Kaj said with honest admiration. "Me and

Grunwold were worse than useless. Meg's the one who noticed that there was an area where the traffic flow was different."

"The young men are really very unfair to themselves," Meg said. "They were busily asking questions while I sat at a table on the high terrace near the central plaza fountain. From there I watched the crowd much as you might watch waves, just the ebb and flow, not the specifics. Eventually, I caught on that in one area the waves would only go so far before they flowed back."

"She sent us to wander over that way," Grunwold said, "as if we were just tourists, looking at the stands, buying drinks, like that. When we got over there, we realized that unlike all the other areas, where the stalls are spilling back as far as they can find space, at this location they stopped only a block off the plaza."

"The 'short waves,'" Kaj said, "weren't from anything as obvious as barricades, but from the lack of stalls. People would go that way, see nothing interesting, and turn around and come back."

"So, what's there?" asked Peg. "And how come you're so certain the child is there?"

"What's there is a sort of administration block," Meg said. "Why we're certain Brunni is there is Xerak's story."

"I went to the local wizards guildhall," Xerak said. "I was pretty honest—it's always good to be honest around wizards—said that I had come to Sky Descry for reasons of my own, and had been astonished to find myself in the midst of a major festival. The locals were happy enough to talk about it. Even though they tried to act superior, it was pretty clear that most of them were as astonished as anyone. A few of the oldest had been around the last time the Grantor of Miracles was reincarnated, and they said that there had been none of this rush."

Xerak swigged from a goblet of red wine, then went on. "I'll spare you all the 'in my day' stuff and get to what's going to happen here and now. Apparently, the reincarnation must happen in private. No one agreed why, but the most common theory was that the presence of other bodies and minds create 'bumps.'"

"'Bumps?'" Teg asked incredulously.

"Obstructions, then," Xerak said, waving his goblet in a wide, sweeping gesture. "What they want is a clear stream, a funnel. If too many people are around, they're like rocks in the stream. At the worst, they'll divert the channel completely. Even if that didn't happen—and everyone agreed that the Grantor wouldn't be easily diverted—the bumps or diversion could cause a less than complete incarnation. Memories lost. Skills attenuated."

Vereez looked up from the plate of puff pastries she'd been pretending to eat.

"So, this sort of reincarnation isn't automatically successful? From what Kaj said earlier, I thought it was."

Kaj shrugged. "From what I heard it is but, remember, I'm a necropolis groundskeeper, not a genius wizard like Xerak."

Xerak rolled his eyes. "Don't let your hackles go all prickly, Kaj. What you learned is definitely the case—especially if it doesn't matter if all the reincarnating person's skills and memories come back intact all at once. It's enough to have the spirit and enough of an anchor to past lives that the family—or in this case, entire land—can benefit. If a person remembers some of who he or she was before, then the rest can often be recovered."

Teg cut in. "But here and now, they need the Grantor back and in as complete a form as possible. When Vereez and I went by the Administration for Miracles, the lines of petitioners were ridiculously long already—and this is before the news has had time to really spread."

"Or the reincarnation has even succeeded," Xerak agreed. "It's crazy."

"Is it?" Meg asked. "What would you do if someone offered you a miracle that would get your master back?"

Xerak froze, then slowly, deliberately, he finished his wine. "I see your point. And these people are used to having the Grantor of Miracles to rely on, not like where we come from. Fine."

Vereez hopped up and took Xerak's glass as he was reaching for a refill. "Oh no, Tangle Mane. First you tell how you figured out that Brunni is in that building."

Xerak lashed his tail, but he let her take his goblet and set it out of reach. "After I learned all I could, and the stories were starting to repeat themselves, Peg and I decided I'd see if we could figure out where Brunni was. I had a few hints from what people had said, and while I was searching for the place, we met up with Grunwold, Kaj, and Meg and they told us about Meg's eddies and currents."

Grunwold took over. "There was a sort of park between a couple of the buildings—not a place that would attract the tourists—just a wide area with some benches and a few trees in pots. We found a sheltered area and pretended to be having a quiet picnic while Xerak did one of his magic things."

"I'm good at spells for searching," Xerak reminded them. "Kaj was there, so I had one of the parents. Grunwold just happened to have one of Vereez's old socks . . ."

"Handkerchief," Grunwold muttered. "She dropped it."

"So I had something from the mother. I did the spell three times, triangulating. Brunni's in an office building near the park—or was less than an hour ago. Given that the ceremony is going to be soon—maybe even tomorrow—I'd say they plan to leave her there. The building is close to the plaza, but away from the confusion."

"When we came back to the hotel," Vereez said, speaking rapidly, "they were posting a sign in the lobby saying that there was going to be a prayer service channeling luck for a successful reincarnation predawn tomorrow. They're holding it at the Administration for Miracles—which just happens to be way on the other side of the plaza from the building you say Brunni is in."

"Clearing the area as much as possible to help the incarnation along," Xerak said approvingly. "Based on what I know about such rituals, they probably will start the reincarnation after sunrise. Culmination will be planned for when the sun is at zenith."

Eyeing Vereez, he reached for his wine glass. She shoved it toward him.

"Don't get soused, Xerak."

"Just relaxed," he promised, and carefully poured himself precisely half a glass.

Teg strolled over, found that the window did open, and that there was a convenient balcony there. She was fishing out her pipe and paraphernalia, preparing to climb out, when Grunwold grabbed her.

"Mask," he said. "Vereez got us a penthouse, but that doesn't mean you can't be seen."

Teg reluctantly grabbed her lynx face mask, and went out. The balcony was small—probably meant more for potted plants than a grown woman—but it would hold her and she could hear the continuing discussion while she filled her lungs with much-desired smoke.

"What Teg and I learned probably doesn't change anything," Vereez said, "but it's troubling."

She summarized what they'd seen at the museum, with Teg making occasional anthropological comments from her perch.

"Coincidence . . ." Meg said, drawing the word out into four long syllables ending on a hiss. "No. I think not. Sapphire Wind just happens to know of a magical transportation device that will take us here—to an otherwise obscure island nation. The question is did it expect us to learn that there is some sort of relationship between Ba Djed of the Weaver and the Grantor, or did it think we would be so focused on finding Brunni that we wouldn't? Did it know about this impending reincarnation?"

Her questions met with absolute silence, then Peg said, "Honestly, Meg, if anyone knows, that would be you, wouldn't it?"

Meg looked puzzled, then she shook her head. "I will admit, acting as Sapphire Wind's mouthpiece has given me some insights, but I do not know what drives it. All I know is that it is driven—driven to reassemble Ba Djed, perhaps driven to reestablish the Library."

Teg wondered if this was true or if Meg was simply trying to keep them off guard. Even thinking such things made her feel very uncomfortable. Then she remembered what Xerak had said about it not being wise to lie around wizards. Maybe he'd have detected a lie. She'd need to get him alone, and ask his impressions.

"But," Peg said, "the connection between the Library and the Visage Isles is part of the big picture. Right now we need to focus on one very small picture."

"Brunni," Vereez said, her voice hardly above a whisper as she spoke the child's name. "But how can we get to her? And if we do get to her, how do we get her out? It's impossible."

Peg smiled and put her knitting down. "Impossible? We won't know until we try. Meg, do you have paper? Of course, you do. Let's start planning. First of all, let's not forget we have a transport device—and it's portable."

CHAPTER FOUR

The coming of night had done nothing to diminish the crowds. If anything, they were heavier, and a carnival mood dominated the plaza. Music came from multiple sources, the closest of which was a trio of long-faced llamas playing a haunting melody on panpipes. Vendors with trays slung around their necks hawked everything from programs for the upcoming dawn prayer service to sweets to more cheap souvenirs.

I wonder what they'll do with those souvenirs after tomorrow? Teg thought. *Especially if we're successful, and the reincarnation doesn't happen? It'll be worse than the aftermath of a rock concert when the headline band cancels.*

They left the plaza several blocks away from their ultimate destination and then approached the office building from the back. This had been the first part of Peg's master plan.

"Since they haven't made public where Brunni is being housed," she explained, "they won't have obvious guards. That would be the same as shouting 'She's here!' What obvious guards they have will be at the main doors and probably the service entrances, to turn away people who think it's business as usual despite the public holiday. But there should be other ways in, and we have a magic key."

They hadn't just trusted on finding an appropriate door. Vereez and Xerak had gone scouting earlier and had located a loading dock packed with garbage bins that conveniently hid the door from sight from the street. From the lack of activity, if Xerak's divination hadn't assured them otherwise, they would have thought the building was closed and empty.

In case the magic pass key didn't do the job, Xerak prepared his unwarding spell. Then the inquisitors, Kaj, and the three humans made their way down the alley, through the maze of garbage bins, and to the closed door. Since Teg had already shown some affinity for magical items, she had been nominated to use the key, a decision that meant the therianthropes were able to wait with weapons ready to hand.

When the lock clicked over, Teg pulled down on the latch, bracing herself for alarms or flashes of colored light or some such, but all that happened was that the door swung open, and Grunwold and Kaj pushed past her, taking point as had been agreed upon earlier.

These kids can be scarily like their parents at times, Teg thought.

She went next, hand on her machete, followed by Xerak, Peg, Meg, and lastly, Vereez.

The young woman had asked to cover the rear because she said she was so strung out that she didn't trust her judgement. Now, glancing back and seeing Vereez's fox teeth bared in an expression one stage from a snarl, Teg hoped that being positioned at the rear would be enough to hold Vereez in check. As she closed and relocked the door, Teg gave Vereez what she hoped was a reassuring pat on the shoulder, and received a weak "ear melt" smile in return.

Xerak's earlier scrying had not only confirmed that Brunni was in the building, but that she was on an upper floor. As they had hoped, there were both a freight elevator and stairs near the door they'd come in through. After all, who would want the garbage carried out through the public corridors? The door into the stairwell was open, and the stairwell itself dimly lit.

Kaj crouched and, without a word, Meg accepted a piggyback ride. Peg and Teg had sworn they could keep up the pace but, as she hurried up the stairs, Teg felt her archeologically abused knees complain. She wondered if she could get something magical done about the damage here, rather than waiting for knee replacement back home.

She knew such thoughts were her subconscious trying to distract her from a pattering of her heart that had nothing to do with climbing stairs at a fairly rapid pace. On some level, this breaking into a closed office building was more nerve-wracking than making their way through the monster-haunted forests surrounding the

Library of the Sapphire Wind or even that time they'd broken into the warehouse and stolen *Slicewind*. Those events hadn't seemed real. This seemed all too real, so much so that Teg kept glancing around, trying to spot hidden security cameras.

Xerak had said that the magical equivalent did exist, but that they were very expensive and required a great deal of maintenance, so he doubted there would be any here. Even so, Teg couldn't keep herself from feeling certain that somewhere a security guard was watching them on a monitor, and calling for backup.

At each landing, Grunwold and Xerak would peep out, looking and listening for indications that the area was in use. Second floor, third floor, fourth floor: each time the young men withdrew and shook their heads. On the fifth floor they froze, then carefully pulled back, closing the door with infinite care.

"There are people here," Grunwold said.

"It's about the right altitude for where I scried Brunni," Xerak added. "You folks wait here, catch your breath. Teg and I will go and check the next floor, just to be sure."

Teg didn't know whether to be flattered or dismayed that she wasn't viewed as needing to catch her breath. She even wondered if Xerak planned to grab a quick drink and figured she was the least likely to turn him in, but he was in perfect control. She waited with the key in case it would be needed to open this door, but it swung open as the others had. Xerak listened, sniffed the air, then withdrew.

"Quiet. Stale. If I counted right, this is the top floor. The stair will continue to the roof. C'mon. Let's be sure."

They confirmed Xerak's guess, locating a hatch to the roof, then picked their way down to rejoin the others. In their absence, Vereez had insisted on doing a little scouting, pointing out that she was smaller than either Kaj or Grunwold, and far better at moving quietly. In hushed tones, she reported what she had found, her voice level, her previous tension subsumed into purpose.

"The floor is mostly empty. There are people using a series of rooms toward the back. There's a guard stationed where he can see the main elevator and the central staircase. He doesn't look particularly tense, so I'm guessing he's there more to relay messages than to keep anyone away."

"Still," Grunwold said. "We can't have him giving the alert, but if we knock him out or take him captive, then we'll have a problem if someone comes up."

"I agree," Vereez said. "I think the thing to do is distract him for long enough that we can get into those occupied rooms."

"Perhaps a noise from the floor below?" Peg suggested. "He's likely to go down the public stairs and check."

"Unless he calls for help," Kaj offered unhelpfully. "We didn't see any roving patrols, but there might be some."

"You're acting as if anyone would expect someone to try to get in to Brunni," Vereez snapped, quite literally, her fox jaws closing as if she were breaking a chicken's neck.

"Easy," Xerak said, slinging an arm around her shoulders and giving her a quick squeeze. "Kaj's made a reasonable suggestion. Personally, I agree with you; it's worth the risk of alerting a roving patrol. We can't count on a diversion drawing the guard away, but it's worth trying."

Peg chuckled softly. "When his father and I were getting a divorce, my son, Diego, went through what we called his poltergeist phase. He loved designing booby-traps—anything from the classic bucket of water over the door to more elaborate gimmicks. Can we rig something that will make a noise down below, something we can trigger from a distance—maybe by pulling a cord? It would be best if it looks like something that might have fallen on its own, of course, but we can't have everything."

No one loved the idea but, after Xerak explained that he preferred not to use magic, in case there were wards in place that would be alert to active magic (as opposed to the passive magic in the key or flashlights), the last objection was met. Peg—who had learned a great deal about setting up such things when dealing with Diego—went with Vereez and Grunwold, leaving the others to stand an uneasy vigil in the barely lit stairwell.

When the trio returned, Peg was trailing a length of pale yellow yarn, unrolling it from the ball to keep it from drawing tight.

"There's a slipknot at the end," she explained. "We gathered a collection of janitorial supplies—buckets, mops, and such—and heaped them up. One tug and . . ."

"Are you sure the tug will be enough?" Teg asked anxiously.

"It's a miracle the crap hasn't fallen already," Grunwold retorted. "If we're going to try this, let's do it. Vereez . . ."

But the young woman had already moved to the front, easing open the door, sniffing, and then trotting silently ahead. Xerak padded behind her, motioning for Teg to join him. Kaj followed, Meg and Peg came next, leaving Grunwold to pull the yellow yarn.

Teg wondered if the sound of a few buckets falling would be enough to draw the guard, but when the crash came, even expecting it, she nearly jumped out of her skin.

"What the broken-toothed monstrosity . . ." came an unfamiliar voice, followed immediately by the sound of booted feet going down stone stairs.

Grunwold came loping up behind, motioning for everyone to hurry. Vereez rounded the corner first, hands on the hilts of her swords, clearly prepared to attack anyone and anything who might remain. Teg, the crystal-encrusted key firmly clenched in her right hand, ran after, panting slightly, although whether from excitement or lack of breath she couldn't be sure.

Definitely need to cut down on the cigs, she thought.

Voices trailed up the stairwell. Clearly "their" guard hadn't been the only one to hear the crash. As Teg knelt to touch the key to the lock, she caught fragments.

". . . fucking buckets."

". . . guess janitors got hurried out of here before they stowed their junk properly. Here . . ."

The lock clicked. Vereez shoved the door open, then half dove over Teg to get inside. Teg moved in and to one side, hoping she wouldn't be trampled as Xerak and Kaj raced to provide Vereez with backup. Next came Meg, Peg, and lastly Grunwold. He shut the door behind him, remembering not to let it slam, then Teg put the key in place to relock it. When the door had been secured, she turned to inspect their surroundings.

They were in a large rectangular room. The door through which they had entered was in the middle of a long wall. One door opened off the left wall. The middle of the wall on the right had a door in the middle and one near the extreme end. A neat ideogram proclaimed the middle door as a restroom.

Most of the nearer long wall and the two side walls were lined with chairs. At the far end, dominating the other long wall, were three bulky desks. One desk was stacked with paperwork and detritus probably cleared from the other two. The emptied desktops had been adapted to serve as a sort of buffet on which a variety of food and drink had been spread. The offerings looked picked over, as if whoever had been using the buffet had been sampling over many hours.

A waiting room, Teg thought, *converted into a dining area. I bet the secretaries are going to be pissed when they see what's been done to their stuff.*

The room had been empty but, as Teg turned, the door on the left opened and a child and an adult emerged. The child was instantly recognizable from the numerous representations they'd seen that day as Brunni. The other was a woman with a seal's head. She had her hands on the child's shoulders as if she'd been steering her along.

To the bathroom, maybe?

The pair stopped in midstep when they realized that the room they'd clearly expected to be empty held seven strangers. Then Vereez started.

"Aunt Ranpeti! I was told you were dead!"

"Vereez? What are you doing here?"

Vereez was too shocked to manage anything other than the truth. "I've been looking for Brunni. I . . ."

Brunni blinked sleepily. She was a chubby little girl, as adorable as a polar bear cub in one of those Coke advertisements, and nearly as improbable. She stared around the room, absorbed the presence of the assembled adults, and as quickly dismissed them.

Poor kid has probably had so many people staring at her these last couple of weeks that a few more doesn't even register.

"Mama," she said, looking up at the woman Vereez had addressed as "Aunt Ranpeti." "I still hafta go potty."

"Excuse us," Ranpeti said. "Please, will you wait?"

"Try and get us to go," Vereez said. "'Mama.'"

Ranpeti stiffened, then patted Brunni. "Come along. We'll get you to the potty."

The pair returned just as Teg was beginning to wonder if the bathroom had more than one exit. Grunwold caught the closing door and ducked inside, saying "My turn!" Teg didn't doubt that he was checking to see if there was some way Ranpeti might have called for help, as much as because he needed to pee.

Brunni was more awake now, interested in the new arrivals, especially the humans with their elaborate masks. When Ranpeti tried to get her to go back to bed, she protested.

"I wanna drink. And a snack. There are still proggies. Purple ones." She turned a winning smile on all of them. "My favorites."

Ranpeti surrendered. "Very well," she said, staring at Vereez, hardly seeming to notice the rest of them.

Vereez reached for a bunch of proggies, breaking off some that were an impossibly brilliant violet. She handed them to Brunni.

"These were my favorites when I was your age," she said. "Do you like taga juice?"

Brunni shook her head. "Too sour. I like pa-pa with lots of honey."

"Not so close to bed time," Ranpeti said automatically. "You can have zinz tea."

From how Brunni reacted, this was clearly a frequent compromise, and she accepted the drink with fairly good grace. Ranpeti sank into the nearest chair, then pulled Brunni and her snacks into her lap.

"Vereez," she said, speaking the younger woman's name as if she'd never meant to say it again. "You. Here. Now. Especially now. What does it mean?"

Xerak shook his head. "No time for that. We were lucky to get in here. What we need to know is..."

Ranpeti frowned at him. "Are you Senehem? And is that Gruny"—indicating Grunwold, just emerging from the bathroom—"grown and with antlers?"

"Xerafu Akeru is what I'm called now," Xerak said, leaning on his spear staff, "or Xerak, but, yes, I'm me and Grunwold's him. And I think we both remember you, Ranpeti-toh. Glad you're alive when we'd mourned you. What we need to know is..."

Vereez cut him off. "Aunt Ranpeti, is Brunni a volunteer for this upcoming reincarnation? Or do you want to get her out of it?"

Ranpeti gripped the child more tightly. "We were given little choice. Brunni doesn't understand..."

"Yes, I do." Brunni, the fur around her mouth now slightly purple, looked up at her "mother." "There will be a big party. But it will be for the Sleeping One. Not for me. I don't like the Sleeping One. He thinks I'm a new dress."

Ranpeti began to weep. "I hoped. I hoped if I stayed near, maybe I could keep Brunni awake a little even ... after. She can be very strong willed."

Vereez's ears pinned back. "As she should be. How could you let this happen?"

"Don't you yell at my mommy!" Brunni shouted. She didn't look at all cute now, but as if she'd grown into her grandfather's sinuous carnivore heritage. "Don't!"

Vereez jerked back. "I'm sorry, Brunni. Your mommy is my favorite aunt. I'm just ..." Xerak patted her arm, and Vereez refocused. "Aunt Ranpeti, we can get you out of here. Both of you. But you need to understand, before this is over, we're going to have a lot of talking to do."

"We can't leave the building, not even this floor," Ranpeti protested. "The guard at the stairwell will let Brunni and me walk around the top floor, but that's it. When all is said and done, we're captives, no matter how they pretty it up."

Xerak showed his teeth in a fierce grin, an expression that worked all too perfectly on his leonine features.

"We can leave without using the door. Do you have any belongings you need? Brunni's favorite blanket or something? Get them now. Once we trigger the transport magic, I don't think we're going to go unnoticed for long."

Xerak commandeered Vereez and Teg to assist him as he set the crystal polyhedrons at the various points that would define the transportation circle back to the Library. Kaj and Grunwold kept guard at the door. Ranpeti, good manners surfacing despite her obvious confusion, turned to Meg and Peg.

"Please. Feel free to take off your masks. Even the best made masks can be stifling."

Meg laughed. "They can be, but if you have questions now, you'll have even more then. You'll learn why we are wearing these in good time."

Ranpeti did not press. Indeed, she seemed too stunned to do more than watch as those whom she must still think of as children showed how much growing up can happen in four years. She shook herself into alertness.

"Excuse me, then. I will get our belongings."

Gathering up Brunni, she headed toward the room from which they had emerged. From the doorway, it appeared to be someone's office, hastily converted into a bedroom.

"Let me help you pack," Peg said, and bustled after them.

Meg moved to where she could keep watch out a window without being seen.

Almost immediately, apparently bored with packing, Brunni bounded from the bedroom and made a beeline for the glowing polyhedrons.

"I wanna play with the blocks, too!" she announced. "I wan the purple one."

Xerak snarled at her. "Back, brat. You're going to blow the spell."

Brunni, startled as only a much-loved child can be startled when reprimanded by a stranger, balled her fists, closed her eyes, and opened her mouth, obviously about to let loose. Vereez froze, hands on the brilliant orange four-sided polygon she was setting, obviously torn between duty to the spell and a desire to comfort her newly found daughter. Only Xerak's rumbling growl kept her in place.

Grunwold glanced at Kaj. "Call me if you hear anyone coming." Then he loped over and scooped up Brunni. "I'll make you a deal, roly-poly. If you promise not to make a sound louder than a giggle, I'll toss you in the air. I bet you'd like that more than those dumb blocks, wouldn't you?"

Brunni eyed him thoughtfully, then looked sidelong at Xerak, who had returned to his incantations. "Uh-um, yes? Can you trow me? Mama say I'm too chubby to trow."

Grunwold hefted her. "I'm much stronger than Ranpeti-toh. Ready? Remember, nothing louder than a giggle or the deal's off."

He'll be a wonderful father someday, Teg thought, *one of those only children who cherishes a big family even more because he feels he missed out on something.*

Ranpeti and Peg emerged, burdened with luggage, as the last of what Teg now couldn't help but think of as "the blocks" was set in place.

Grunwold handed a still giggling Brunni to Ranpeti, and accepted some of her luggage in exchange.

Xerak straightened, rubbing the damp fur on his forehead with the back of one hand. "We're going to need to get through fast, before anyone senses the portal has been activated. Vereez and I are going to need to stay to maintain the spell. Grunwold, you go first, with Brunni and Ranpeti. Then you three." He indicated the humans. "Last Kaj, Vereez, and me."

Despite damp sweat spots on her own fur and undoubted emotional upheaval, Vereez was managing to appear coolly efficient. "Line up."

Brunni had started to fuss when Grunwold handed her to Ranpeti. Now he looked at her, and spoke seriously. "Listen, Brunni? We're going to play follow the leader. You're on my team, so don't mess it up, hear? We'll lose if you don't follow the rules."

Brunni nodded, alive with instant hero worship of the sort only children that age can experience. "Rules," she repeated, then grabbed Ranpeti's hand and held it tight. "Rules, Mama!"

Ranpeti nodded, and held the little girl more tightly. "Ready, Grunwold?"

Sword in one hand, duffle over his shoulder, Grunwold reached for Ranpeti's hand and led her into the circle. "Ready."

Xerak gripped the multicolored egg, frowned, then said, "Grunwold, as soon as you see the Library, get out of the spell field to clear the way for the next group."

"Got it," Grunwold said, leaning slightly, as if ready to begin a footrace.

Xerak started muttering the untranslatable words. Despite Teg's fears that something would go wrong, that they'd end up trapped, the transport spell activated as before. However, as the colored lights swirled into white, the varied colors appeared to have acquired an additional flat silver sheen.

I wonder if that's because there's some sort of barrier here, Teg thought, but she didn't have time to ask. Meg and Peg, carrying the rest of Ranpeti and Brunni's luggage between them, were hustling forward, Heru perched on Peg's shoulder. In a moment it would be her turn. Already, Xerak was moving to where he could put the blocks back into their container in the second before Kaj, Vereez, and finally himself would make their own transit.

Meg went through, then Peg. As Teg was about to step into the "gazebo" there was banging at the door of the office suite accompanied by muffled shouting. She paused, but Xerak waved her on.

"Go!"

Teg did, feeling again the increasingly familiar sense of passing through a disorienting space that was both within and outside of the normal passage of time. When she saw the white light shading into color, she braced herself, knowing she'd need to move quickly so that there would be room for the last three to follow.

As she jumped clear of the transport circle, the veil of color vanished, revealing that instead of the increasingly familiar rubble-strewn reception hall of the Library of the Sapphire Wind, she had arrived in a large, high-ceilinged space lined with wooden crates and barrels. The narrow windows where the wall met the ceiling showed nothing but darkness, offering no hint of where this room might be located.

In front of Teg, a few steps away from the still-glowing colors of the transport field, were Meg and Peg. A few paces from them stood Grunwold and Ranpeti, who still held Brunni in her arms. As Teg's feet touched down, she acquired two new pieces of information. First, their group hadn't actually been transported into the warehouse, but were instead standing on a springy surface that possessed the shimmer of oil on a wet road. Second, the warehouse held at least six people, most keeping back in the shadows.

The two people poised at the front of the group within the warehouse were Vereez's parents: Inehem and Zarrq.

Teg absorbed all of this in the brief moment that it took for her short sideways jump to bring her feet to rest on the oddly springy surface of the shimmering path. As she landed, time resumed its normal speed.

"Give me the child," Inehem was saying, her voice silky.

In these words, Teg's back brain heard an echo of the line from the movie *Labyrinth*. Her own lips shaped one of the appropriate responses.

"Wait!"

Ranpeti had been moving forward in automatic response to the authority in Inehem's voice, but now she halted, her feet still on the oil slick surface, inches from the stone-flagged warehouse floor.

We're somewhere between places, Teg thought. *Inehem hijacked the transport portal somehow but, if we haven't reached the Library, where we meant to go, we're also not where Inehem intended to bring us. For some reason Inehem doesn't want to come to us—I'm sure of that or she'd have sent one of those people lurking in the shadows to grab Brunni.*

Taking a step back, Ranpeti turned to look at Teg. "Wait?"

"Don't you want to know *why* Inehem wants Brunni?" Teg asked. "I mean, after all this time, it's a little surprising that she and Zarrq would go all grandparenty."

As she was speaking, Teg felt a flicker of motion in the air and suspected Kaj had arrived, but it was Vereez's voice, sharp and clear, that spoke.

"Mother? Father? What are you doing here? How are you here . . . wherever here is?"

"We came for Brunni," Inehem replied easily. "Do you think we would be unaware of what was about to happen to her?"

Vereez pushed to the front. Teg saw a host of emotions in the cant of her slightly drooping fox ears: confusion, hope, relief. Then the group in the shadows moved forward, and Vereez noticed that not only her father was present, but also the butler, Leyenui, and three armed guards, one of whom held two spike-collared dobergoats on leashes. Suspicion pinned those drooping ears back with a snap.

Grunwold, not ungently, shoved Ranpeti and Brunni behind him, so that now he and Vereez stood between Inehem and her quarry. Grunwold drew his sword with a practiced motion, but Vereez, gaze still fixed on the group in the warehouse, held off reaching for her own swords. Breathing hard, Kaj arrived, then Xerak came through, glancing around him with a mixture of calculation and surprise.

At a head jerk from Xerak, Kaj moved to join the front line.

Staying back, Xerak said almost too casually, "Are you the one who diverted the transport spell, Inehem-toh? Let me guess. You had an anchor on Brunni. If something happened to move her from Sky Descry, you would know."

"Such a clever Xerafu Akeru," Inehem said. "Or not so. The only other person I might have put the anchor on was Ranpeti, and why would I care where *she* went as long as she went alone? Brunni, however, is a different matter. Of course, her grandparents would want to keep an eye on her, especially now that their sole child is proving so troublesome."

As soon as Xerak arrived, Teg noticed that their surroundings were subtly altering. The surface underfoot felt the same, but it shone more brilliantly, less a shimmer than a blaze of weird colors that reminded her of the aurora borealis.

I think I get it. Now that Xerak has closed off the connection to the building on Sky Decry, the transport device is trying to finish its job, to take us back to the Library. But whatever Inehem is doing is pulling us toward her.

Meg had also noticed the change. She paused, almost as if listening, then grabbed the luggage from Peg, and began to drop back. Teg glanced to see where Meg was going and saw that, more outline than reality, the reception hall of the Library of the Sapphire Wind was taking shape behind them.

Tug of war, with us standing on the rope, Teg thought. *Is Inehem strong enough to force us out of this between space to where she is— especially with Xerak and our own transportation device pulling the other way?*

Teg felt a flash of relief that Ranpeti had not gone forward. *That would have done it. Her entering the warehouse would have tipped the balance in Inehem's favor. And once Ranpeti and Brunni had joined them, then I bet that Inehem would have closed off the way to her side.*

Teg would have loved a chance to discuss her conclusions, but events were moving too quickly. In response to a motion from Zarrq, the three guards—Tiger-Head, Boar-Head, and Tapir-Head, the last holding the dobergoats' leashes—had moved to the front. Inehem stepped back, sinking to a seat on a crate, her head bending in concentration. Leyenui, demonstrating a familiarity that startled Teg, given how formal the butler had seemed when they had met at the House of Fortune, placed a hand on the nape of Inehem's neck. Had Teg's own hand not been dropping toward the sun spider amulet in her pocket, she might not have corrected her misunderstanding so quickly.

Leyenui isn't showing undue intimacy with "the mistress." He's feeding her mana.

Zarrq drew his twin swords, a motion his daughter echoed.

Peg pulled her own slim sword, shouting, "They're going to charge. Get back! Ranpeti, get Brunni to the Library."

Meg called, "Xerak has nearly unblocked our portal. Ranpeti, hurry!"

Teg froze, uncertain how best to help. *I'm an archeologist not a fighter, Jim,* she thought. Then she switched back to *Labyrinth*: *"Through dangers untold, hardships unnumbered, I have fought my way..."*

Peg's voice, that of a commander of a thousand Cub Scouts, cut through the panic fogging Teg's mind. "Teg! Help Xerak. We'll hold the line."

Teg wasn't sure exactly how she should go about helping Xerak, but she knew that if the young not quite officially a wizard didn't force whatever block Inehem had put on their transport spell, it wouldn't matter what Teg wasn't, or how hard she'd tried to this point. She darted back to Xerak. Mimicking what she'd seen Leyenui doing, she slid her hand beneath Xerak's mane, resting her fingers on his neck where the heavier fur of his lion's head merged into the lighter fuzz on his human torso. Beneath the heave of Xerak's steady deep breathing, she could feel his pulse and, running beside it, something else, something not unlike what she had sensed the first time she used the sun spider amulet.

Remember your lessons. Quiet mind in a quiet body. Feed your mana into that pulse. Pretend that Xerak is nothing more than an amulet. It can't hurt, right?

Teg felt when Xerak began to draw on her mana. The sensation was unsettling, but provided an unexpected benefit. Now she could "see" more clearly what was going on in the invisible magical battle.

Inehem also had a transport device; she wasn't doing this on her own. The device Sapphire Wind had guided them to was the more powerful. However, it was also striving to bridge a much greater distance. The device Inehem was using was less potent and, interestingly, relied on a link to Brunni in order to set one of the directions. However, Inehem's device was only being used to bridge a short distance, probably to a location on Sky Descry.

Probably a warehouse near one of the docks.

Rather than trying to tug them through to her side, Inehem was concentrating on firming up the shimmering liminal space, doubtless in order to send someone to grab Brunni. Xerak, meanwhile, was trying to work loose the hook Inehem had sunk into Brunni, his task made more difficult in that the child was in motion. Teg could tell that Xerak wasn't going to be able to unhook Brunni before . . .

"Incoming!" Peg yelled.

At the same moment, Meg called out, her voice the calm, penetrating one librarians in all eras have used to remind patrons that the library is about to close and books being taken home need to be checked out, "Pull back. Let's take the home field advantage."

Meg then trotted over to Xerak. "Can you come along, dear boy? Sapphire Wind is going to try to hold open the gate on the Library end."

Teg pulled herself out from feeding mana into Xerak to reply for him. "You and I are going to need to drag Xerak. Right now, he's concentrating on keeping Inehem's transport device from trumping ours."

"I'll take his left side," Meg said, bending at the knees, then grabbing Xerak under his left arm.

Teg did the same on Xerak's right, timing her rising to her full height to match Meg's so that they lifted the young man together. As they started hauling him toward the Library, she was aware of Peg and her small army holding the line as Zarrq, flanked by Tiger-Head and Tapir-Head, ventured forward, stepping tentatively as they tested their footing on the aurora borealis pathway.

The clash of metal against metal caused Teg to pick up her pace, even as that little analytic corner of her brain noticed how much more erratic the rhythm of a real battle was than movies and television would lead one to believe. Nor was there any of the shouting of insults or clever comments that movies took such pleasure in. Four against three, and the four were older, stronger, and much more experienced. The only advantage the three defenders had was that the liminal pathway was not wide enough for Zarrq and his guardsmen to all fight at once, so Tapir-Head and the dobergoats had dropped back.

The first cry of pain came just after Teg and Meg had gotten Xerak into the Library, and propped him against a pillar. Teg bolted toward the gate, arriving in time to catch Vereez as Grunwold shoved her through, noticing out of the corner of her eye that Peg, her sword in hand, had moved up to fill the gap in the line of fighters.

Grunwold yelled something inarticulate and furious, then there was another scream, deeper and masculine, but Teg couldn't spare the attention to see who had been injured. She only hoped it wasn't another of their small company.

Grabbing Vereez around the younger woman's waist and stumbling with her back into the Library, Teg saw a long slice had been chopped through the heavy sleeve that was the only thing protecting Vereez's left arm. The cut was deep enough that white bone showed, and blood was gushing out. Teg clamped her hand down in an attempt to staunch the flow, then Nefnet was beside her, and Vereez was fainting, Teg was catching her, arms holding the young woman against her chest, even as she was turning her head to try to figure out what was going on in the chaos where a gate remained open in midair.

Grunwold, Kaj, and Peg were holding the fighting line, backing further into the Library. The transport portal's aperture was shrinking, dimming to dormancy. That was good. Less good was that whatever Inehem and Leyenui were doing was slowing the process. Their enemies were going to make it through before the portal closed, although they were no longer able to keep a line of three, but had to squeeze through one at a time.

Zarrq had come through first, still locked with Grunwold who, although using his sword, had his head bent as if he'd bring his antlers into play if given the chance. When Tiger-Head emerged, Kaj used his club and long knife to good effect, keeping the shorter but more solidly built warrior well occupied defending himself. Boar-Head managed to slip around the edges of the line and paused, both assessing the battlefield and creating an opening through which Tapir-Head, who was bleeding from a defensive wound to his left hand, came through. Apparently, he'd left the dobergoats behind.

Or maybe they were too smart to trust themselves to such an insubstantial bridge, Teg thought.

Boar-Head muttered something, the slight jerk of his tusks as he pointed with his chin making Teg suspect he was saying something like, "I'll help the boss, you help Tiger."

What can I do? What can I do? Teg was thinking frantically, grasping in her pocket for the sun spider amulet. *If they'd move, I could maybe gum up Inehem when she comes through, but . . .*

She was still shaping her barely realized plan when Peg, screaming as might a banshee from the legends of her Irish heritage, ran forward. In one hand, she brandished her sword, with the other she was ripping off her mask, bringing the full horror—for really she did look fearsome—of her naked, hairless, flat human features into view.

The three guards each froze for one precious moment. With a wild strike of her blade, Peg walloped Tapir-Head directly on his already wounded hand. Kaj caught Tiger-Head under the chin with the full force of his club, then, when the guard's head snapped back, did something complicated that swept his legs out from under him. Kaj then turned to face Boar-Head, who was still gaping at the monster that had been hidden by the pronghorn antelope mask.

Yet Peg's diversion would not have been enough to give them a permanent advantage if Ohent—who had apparently been asleep— had not staggered out from behind the screened-off area. Seeing her son in danger, she went mad.

Robes fluttering, veil skimming from her shoulders like a cloak of black mist, Ohent tore across the room as if she were once again the sleek and terrible warrior of decades past. In vivid contrast to Peg, who had not stopped screaming, Ohent was the silent promise of horrible death. Caught between these terrors, the three guards threw down their weapons and flung themselves on the floor, hoping for mercy or at least a less horrid death.

Evenly matched, Zarrq and Grunwold had continued their clash, and might have continued to do so until someone got in a lucky blow, but another unexpected ally entered the field. Emsehu, snapping his long crocodilian jaws, came rushing forth, clearly with every intention of shearing off Zarrq's legs. Only a gout of white light that smelled like peppermint, but apparently burned, from Leyenui, who had emerged half carrying Inehem just as the aperture closed, saved Zarrq from losing a leg beneath the knee.

Inehem fell to one knee, calling out, "We surrender! We surrender!"

Zarrq immediately shifted to defense, and Grunwold stepped back. With a snap that was more threat than promise, Emsehu also broke combat, although he continued to stand beside Grunwold.

Only Ohent, who was racing toward Inehem, didn't pause.

Kaj shouted at Ohent, interposing his own body between Inehem and the approaching fury.

"Mother! I'm all right. We're all all right. Don't make matters worse! Please!"

Ohent heard his voice and slowed, but she was still growling and there was no intelligence in the snow-leopard-blue eyes that peered over her veil. Looking down at the floor, wet with Vereez's blood, she said in a voice that was all the more terrible for its clinical calm:

"Someone is not 'all right.' That's a lot of blood."

Teg said, "Vereez. She's been wounded. Nefnet's doing what she can."

Meg, also now maskless, had brought a pillow to set under Vereez's head. Once she slid it into place, she started to move away to give Nefnet room to work, but Vereez's uninjured arm came up in mute appeal, so Meg stayed holding Vereez's hand.

The whites of Grunwold's eyes showed, making him look like a stag at bay in some Victorian hunting print, but he kept control of himself.

"If you really surrender, then drop your weapons and let us bind your arms. I'm not ready to trust you."

After weapons clattered down, Grunwold started by tying Inehem's hands behind her back, while Kaj took Zarrq. Neither of the extraction agents protested, and Peg trotted over, cheerfully suspicious.

Bending to make a close inspection of Inehem's bonds, she said, "Redo those, Grunwold. Inehem's got small enough hands that—see how she's held them—she'd be able to slip loose. My Diego, the boy who went through the poltergeist phase, also studied how escape artists did their tricks."

Grunwold snorted a dry laugh. "I bet he did." But he also retied the bonds under Peg's inspection, and Teg didn't think it was her imagination that Inehem's ears drooped just a little as he did so.

Kaj stood back so Peg could check Zarrq's bonds, but most of his attention was for Ohent. His mother had straightened her veils and stood watching her former allies, her hand resting on the head of one of the Library's resident dobergoats, several of which were now milling around.

"Kinda late, aren't they?" Kaj said, jerking his head to indicate the arriving creatures.

Xerak sighed from where he now stood, leaning against the pillar for support. "Our fault. We opened the gate. We announced we were bringing strangers. By the time the guardians realized that not all those strangers were welcome, Peg and Ohent had saved the day."

"Makes sense. I guess." Kaj shoved his club into his belt and jerked a thumb at the captives. "What do we do with these people?"

"Bind any wounds, then stow them in a side chamber where they can't hear us confer," Grunwold suggested, his voice gravelly with barely suppressed fury, "and let the guardians do their thing guarding them. After we have a chance to talk, then we'll decide what to do with them."

No one argued. Even Inehem and Zarrq went meekly. Since Emsehu led the motley assortment of guardians, and Zarrq's leg still oozed blood through its bandage, this probably helped make the captives meek. By the time the invaders had been imprisoned, Nefnet was ready to report on Vereez.

"She'll keep the arm," Nefnet said, sinking down on one of the benches, "but it was a close thing. I'm not boasting. If I hadn't been here, Vereez would have lost the arm—and might have died from blood loss and shock. As it is, given that we've already established that some of the herb gardens not only have survived but that what they grow is more potent for not being picked for over two decades, she should make a rapid recovery."

Grunwold looked where Vereez lay unconscious on the floor, still gripping Meg's hand. "Zarrq did that. To his own daughter. He did that. I saw him. I want to kill him."

"Whether or not to kill him," Meg said primly, "is a decision that Vereez should have some say in, I think. Why don't you and Kaj lift her onto one of the cots? This floor is cold. That is if Vereez can be moved. Nefnet?"

"Definitely move her," Nefnet said. "She won't feel anything for a while, but I could use some more herbs. I've exhausted much of what was in the med kits, and since I will be forced to use fresh, I'll need a considerable quantity."

"While I sympathize with Grunwold's desire to kill Zarrq, or at least stomp him," Peg said, "I agree with Meg that Vereez should have some say as to the fate of her parents. So, since we'll want to wait for her to come around, let's go pick some flowers. I'm too wired to sit still. Teg, too tired?"

"Not too," Teg said. "Let me get this mask and these robes off first, and put on jeans and my hiking boots. Xerak, are you mobile enough to come and make sure we choose the right plants? Otherwise, I think we need Nefnet. Vereez is our other herbalist."

"I can manage," Xerak replied, "but I might not be good for much more than sitting in the sun and watching you ladies pick flowers."

"I will stay here," Meg said. "While we wait, I can fill Ranpeti and Brunni in on our shared history. They've really been very polite even after Peg unmasked, but I'm sure they have questions."

Indeed, Ranpeti, Brunni in her arms, stood wide-eyed over to one side, both so shocked that neither had made a sound. Teg didn't think that would last. Brunni was interested by the faces the humans had kept behind their masks, but not unduly disturbed. Maybe Peg's racing to the rescue had made perfectly clear that these new monsters were firmly on her side. Ranpeti was probably too polite to comment.

Ohent seemed as calm as she ever did. "I'll help nursemaiding the wounded. I like this little girl." Her gesture indicated Vereez, but she was looking at Brunni. "And, even if Ranpeti doesn't remember me, we met several times long ago."

Kaj said, "I'll stay here and keep an eye on the prisoners. Other than Emsehu, the Library's guardians aren't always very smart."

Grunwold grinned at him, whatever resentment he'd been nursing over Kaj's past relationship with Vereez dimmed by their recent shared battle. "Good idea. I'll go guard Teg and Peg. I don't trust myself to hold back if Zarrq and Inehem decide to try to escape."

❦ CHAPTER FIVE ❦

When the herb-gathering expedition returned, Brunni had joined Vereez in sleep, and Ranpeti had been briefed. As Ranpeti thanked all three humans for taking their role as mentors so seriously that they'd extended it to helping Brunni and herself as well, Teg found herself surprised how much weirdness Ranpeti had been willing to accept.

But then, accepting that strange creatures from another world have been mentoring your niece and her friends through a series of increasingly peculiar quests is probably easier when the alien creatures are right there and helping to tell the tale.

As Nefnet began preparing to grind the herbs to prepare her various concoctions, she said, "I think it would be a good idea if as many of you as possible can get some rest so you'll be ready to deal with what is to come. Ohent, Emsehu, and I—assisted by the various guardian creatures—will keep watch over the invaders."

"I'm for my bed on *Slicewind*," Teg agreed.

"Vereez is still sound asleep," Nefnet said. "Why not leave her here? I'm not planning on napping."

"If someone will bring a cot over," Meg said, "I will stay here in the Library as well. If there is an emergency, Sapphire Wind may need someone to speak through. That also will leave space in our cabin for Peg and Teg."

Once again, Teg hoped that Meg was merely being efficient, not that Sapphire Wind was somehow controlling her, but this really didn't seem a good time to raise the subject.

Back aboard *Slicewind*, Peg said, "Toss a coin for the bathroom?"

"You go," Teg replied. "I'm too tired to even brush my teeth. Lending Xerak mana seems to have caught up with me."

But she managed to stay awake long enough to brush her teeth and wash her face, before tumbling into the bed beside a softly snoring Peg, and into a dreamless sleep.

The next morning, Teg was awakened by the sound of someone screaming.

Since they'd taken Ohent aboard, this wasn't as unusual an occurrence as it might have been, but these didn't sound like Ohent's mad cackles. As she swung her legs over the side of the bed, and pulled her sleepshirt down where it had bunched around her hips, Teg noticed that Peg was already up and out of the cabin.

Staggering on legs that had stiffened overnight—*Too many flights of stairs in that damned office building*—Teg got to the cabin door, slid it open, and looked out into the lounge that occupied the middle belowdecks portion of *Slicewind*. The multipurpose area usually seemed roomy enough, especially since at least two members of the crew were pretty much always on duty above deck, but today, although the space only held two people, it seemed positively cramped.

Vereez, her injured arm in a sling, was staring with wide-eyed astonishment at Brunni, who had thrown back her head and was working herself up into a good, solid crying fit.

"I want my mama! I want my mama!"

Vereez got down on her knees in front of the little girl and gently grasped her shoulder with her one free hand. "Your mama is in the shower. She'll be out in just a few minutes."

Now that Teg thought about it, she could hear the shower in the bathroom off the lounge running. *Slicewind*'s two bathrooms were both equipped with showers, no tubs, as well as toilets and sinks. This didn't leave much room, which was doubtless why Vereez hadn't just taken Brunni into Ranpeti. Had she done so, Ranpeti wouldn't have had room to get out of the shower.

Unless they closed the toilet seat and Brunni stood on it, and maybe not even then.

Teg sniffed the air. Poffee. The dark purple beverage wasn't precisely coffee, but it was close enough in flavor and, more importantly for someone just barely awake, provided the right buzz. As she moved from the doorway into the stern cabin, angling around the mutually absorbed pair, Brunni caught sight of her and swallowed her howl with an audible gulp.

"I want poffee," Teg said. "I see a pot in the galley."

"It should still be warm," Vereez managed, glancing guardedly at Brunni from the corners of her eyes. "Peg made it before she went over to the Library to help set up breakfast. She said you'd need it."

"And a shower," Teg agreed.

Brunni offered, "I had a shower. I want poffee."

Vereez shook her head. "No poffee. How about juice?"

Brunni drew in a deep breath, obviously preparing for another howl. Teg found herself impressed by how many sharp teeth there were in the little polar-bear mouth.

If those are baby teeth, I don't envy the parents at all.

"Do you always scream when you don't get your way?" Teg asked, making her way to where the poffee waited, and noticing that Peg had left out what had become Teg's favorite of the deep bowls used Over Where, rather than mugs, the one with the glaze that reminded her of the many-hued green of malachite.

Brunni was smart enough to catch a trick question, and trying to find an answer that wouldn't be unsatisfactory made her forget her annoyance.

So she's not a complete spoiled brat, then. That's good.

At that moment, the shower stopped, and Brunni brightened. "Mama!"

Vereez decided to try being in charge. "Let her have a chance to get dry. Can't you be patient even that long?"

Brunni considered. "Poffee?"

"Juice," Vereez replied firmly, "or water."

Teg waved her bowl at them and recrossed the lounge. "I'll take a quick shower and join everyone at the Library."

As she slid the stern cabin door behind her, she heard Brunni say, "Juice."

When Teg came out a short while later—clean and dressed in fresh jeans and a tee shirt ornamented with petroglyphs, beneath which the slogan "My Life Is In Ruins" was written in an elaborate cursive font—she was surprised to find Vereez sitting slumped on one of the bench seats that lined most of the port side of the lounge, staring into a cup of poffee as if she might read oracles in the inky dark surface.

The younger woman looked up at Teg, her expression confused. "Brunni is nothing like what I expected."

"You mean you didn't expect her to be smart? Pretty?" Teg replied flippantly, crossing to the galley and refilling her poffee bowl, then taking a seat on the bench near Vereez. "Opinionated?"

"I thought she'd be ... I don't know. That we'd somehow connect. Instead, she's a stranger. A complete stranger. I wanted a chance to, I don't know, bond? So when Aunt Ranpeti heard that *Slicewind* had showers, and wanted to use them, I offered to come over and show her where everything was. And since the bathroom is too small for more than one person, I offered to watch Brunni while Ranpeti took her own shower after bathing Brunni. I thought it would be fun."

Vereez paused, and Teg made an encouraging noise. After slurping some poffee, Vereez went on.

"I'd bought Brunni—I mean, not Brunni, Brunni, but my daughter who I was looking for—some presents when we were in Rivers Meet. One was a really cute little dress." She indicated where a mass of frilly stuff in blues and greens had been set untidily to one side. "I'd have *loved* it when I was Brunni's age, but when I offered it to her, she just sniffed and wanted her own clothes instead, even though they were decidedly grungy. Then, I don't know what exactly I did wrong, but the next thing I know, she was howling for her mother and then you came out and ..."

Teg was at a loss. She was an only child, and didn't have any children of her own. She hadn't even done the nearly requisite babysitting that had provided pocket money for so many of her classmates, having been required to work—for free—for various family members instead. Happily, Vereez wasn't hoping for instant wisdom, and had continued talking.

"I guess I was stupid, wasn't I? I mean I'm a stranger and ..."

"And," said a soft voice from above, "Brunni really isn't at her best right now."

Ranpeti briskly descended the ladder into the lounge. "Brunni is currently learning how to make something called 'flapjacks' from

Peg, who apparently is mother to at least half of the people in your world. Brunni's distracted for now, and I came over to see how you are. I gather Brunni wasn't particularly well-behaved?"

"She wasn't too bad," Vereez said forcing a laugh. "I wasn't ready for her to have so many opinions, though."

"Part of that is the age," Ranpeti said. "She's at a stage where she has begun to realize there's more than yes or no . . . If you think she's bad now, you should have met her when the automatic answer to just about anything was 'no.' But she's old enough to have favorite things: colors, pieces of clothing, food, games. Maybe I've spoiled her a bit, but since she's my only child, it's not like she's had to learn to compromise like Inehem and I did."

Teg offered, "And lately, Brunni's been under a lot of stress, hasn't she? She had to have been aware that people were after her, had a use for her. She may not have understood why, but she had to have sensed the threat."

Ranpeti nodded. "I think she not only sensed people wanted to take her from me, but maybe even something as to why. I'll tell you more later. For now, my excuse for coming over here is to let you two know that breakfast is ready. After that, we need to decide what to do about Inehem, Zarrq, and their associates."

Vereez rose, her expression thoughtful, and set her poffee bowl in the sink. "Breakfast, at least, sounds good. Peg's made us flapjacks before, and they're great. Thanks for what you said, Aunt Ranpeti. Brunni might have been a bit unreasonable but, now that I think about it, so was I—and she's only four and has a lot more of an excuse."

After everyone had breakfasted, the group gathered around one of the long tables in the reception hall to discuss what to do with their captives.

"They've been quiet," Kaj reported. "The guardians say that Inehem has mostly been asleep. Zarrq has been keeping watch. When I went in to bring them some more water and a little food, the butler guy asked me flat out if we were going to kill them. Or if the Library was."

"What did you say?" Teg asked.

"Nothing." Kaj bared his teeth. "I just smiled."

Xerak, fully restored by a sound night's sleep, said, "Why don't we just send the lot of them back to Rivers Meet? After making them promise to leave Brunni alone, of course."

"If we can trust them to keep a promise," Vereez said darkly. She traced a line, invisible through the bandage, where her father's sword had cut her. "After what they did . . . I'm not sure I'd believe anything they said. Family feeling seems distinctly overrated."

Teg noted that the young woman's gaze strayed to where Brunni, calm and content now, was chirping happily to herself as she used bits of marble as building blocks under the square-pupiled gaze of two of the Library's dobergoats.

Reality has hit, and not one moment too soon. Just as Kaj has not turned out to be the long-lost beloved of Vereez's dreams, what a real, living, breathing child would be to deal with on a day-to-day basis is also coming home. Can't blame Vereez, really, for her illusions. She's an only child, and probably has had very little contact with children who weren't being tended by nannies whose job it was to make sure they behaved well before visitors.

Ohent cackled. "I know how to shape a promise they won't break. Doesn't mean they won't exploit loopholes—if they can find any—but they'll keep to the letter of their word. That I can promise."

Grunwold shifted uneasily. "I could deal with sending Zarrq and Inehem and their people back to Rivers Meet, since the idea of killing them in cold blood makes me feel very weird, but I'm not sure that showing them mercy is going to make them our friends."

"Probably not," Vereez said, her voice deceptively soft, "but that doesn't change that they're here and alive. I'm tired of lies and sick of deception. I'm going to need to deal with my parents sooner or later, and I think sooner is better."

"Then we'll have a proper business conference," Peg said briskly. "I'm sitting in for sure. Between three divorces and a record contract where I nearly made the mistake of signing away the rights to all my future work, I've learned to read fine print."

Meg nodded. "I will also sit in. My late husband and both of my children have worked in industries where negotiations and contracts are important. I learned a great deal from listening to them over the years."

Ranpeti put in, "I will, of course, sit in, as will Vereez."

Teg said, "I want to be where I can overhear, but how about I go where I can sort through the sage's seats?" She indicated an area of the reception hall where in days gone by experts had been available to answer questions. "Probably better we don't have too many sets of eyes glowering at them."

"Sounds wise," Nefnet said. "I will also stay close, but not actually sit in."

"I will," Ohent said firmly, "and Kaj as well."

"I'd better sit in," Xerak sighed. "It will be easier to catch Inehem trying something if I'm close by."

Ranpeti turned to Grunwold. "I have a difficult job for you, Grunwold. I don't want Brunni in a position to overhear our discussions. I firmly believe that small children remember far more, far longer, than adults believe. She's already been through considerable trauma, and is on edge, as her outburst this morning made very clear. Happily, she also seems to have a solid case of hero worship for you. If I can convince Brunni to accept you as a babysitter, would you?"

Again, Teg noticed the mixture of emotions that flickered over Vereez's face, emotions shaped by twitching of ears, curling of whiskers, but no less real.

She's a bit jealous. A bit relieved. And, I think, the relief isn't all for herself. She's learned her parents are poison, and she doesn't want the child exposed to any more of that than she can help.

Perhaps catching Teg's gaze on her, Vereez forced a smile. "I agree with Aunt Ranpeti. Brunni is better out of all of this."

Brunni proved to be amenable to going for a walk with Grunwold-toh and, since Emsehu and several dobergoats were going along, they should be safe.

"If the meeting runs long," Grunwold said as they headed out the door, "I'll take Brunni up in *Slicewind* and let her pretend to steer. I always loved that sort of thing when I was little."

After he'd taken Brunni out, Ohent indicated the seats around the table. "Put Inehem and Zarrq where they can't touch each other. Better, put them where they can't see each other without actually turning their heads. That will give us a better chance of catching them passing nonverbal signals. We used those all the time, back in the day, and I doubt they've given it up."

"Sounds good," Peg said briskly. "Do you think they need to be tied?"

"Let's not," Meg said. "We'll be watching carefully, and Vereez has expressed a desire to settle matters with her parents. This will be more difficult if they are obvious prisoners."

"Should I bring them out then?" Kaj asked, when arrangements as to seating had been settled.

"I'll come with you," Xerak said. "I want to make sure Inehem-lial doesn't try to pull anything subtle and magical."

Teg noticed that the affectionate "toh" had been dropped, although, conditioned to be polite to those in authority, Xerak had substituted the formal "lial."

"You'll escort Zarrq-lial, Kaj," Xerak continued. "Meg, will the Library's guardians keep watch over the other four if we leave them locked in there? I don't trust that Leyenui won't try something."

Meg spoke in her Sapphire Wind voice. "They are intruders. They are servants of our destroyers. We will watch. Should they attempt anything, we are not human enough to show mercy."

Kaj laughed. "Good line. I'll tell them precisely that."

When Inehem and Zarrq were brought out, the group assembled around the long table where, so long ago, three scholars had been disturbed at their work by a cadre of what Sapphire Wind—despite the fact that this incident had led to the Library's destruction—had initially politely referred to as "extraction agents."

But now it's "destroyers," Teg thought as she moved to take one of the sage's seats, where she could watch but not distract. *Sapphire Wind chose to be diplomatic to win our inquisitors over. Worth remembering.*

A drinking bowl of water had been set at every seat, and Peg had supplied herself with a notepad and pen. These little touches gave the encounter something of the feeling of a committee meeting. Perhaps Inehem and Zarrq mistook the lack of bonds and obvious guards for an attempt at appeasement, because they started out on the offensive.

"You do realize that you may have created a major incident with the Creator's Visage Isles," Zarrq said, his small polar-bear eyes cold. "Their elders have chosen Brunni for a great honor, and they will not care to be interfered with."

"Well," Vereez responded, equally coldly, "that saves a question. I did wonder if you'd been trying to save Brunni, even take custody of her for yourselves, since you clearly don't value me anymore."

A motion of her muzzle toward the arm she had nearly lost to her father's blade left no doubt as to what Vereez meant.

Ohent, silky tone mocking, added, "So, Zarrq, Inehem, you would have returned Brunni to the elders on Sky Descry? What would have been in it for you?"

"And how is that any of your business?" Inehem snapped.

"Well, I am as much her grandmother as you are."

The manner in which Ohent responded made Teg absolutely certain that in those long ago days when they'd been part of the same team, there had been rivalry between the two.

Ohent continued, "But I really don't think that what happens to Brunni is your business or my business. I think it's Ranpeti's business, Brunni's business, then, maybe Vereez's business."

"So you have no interest at all in having a biological link to someone who can create miracles?" Inehem sneered.

In the ugly silence that followed, Xerak spoke with quiet pedantry. "The question would be whether you, Inehem"—for the first time he left off even the polite suffix "lial," and the omission was like a shout—"believe you have a hold on Brunni. Based on the link I pried loose from her, the one that enabled you to anchor a transport spell on her, you clearly have done your best to make certain you do. How excited you must have been to learn that she had been chosen as the vessel of the Grantor of Miracles."

Is there a relationship on Vereez's side of the family to the Creator's Visage Isles after all? Teg wondered. *We'd been assuming the relationship came on Kaj's side of the family. Or did Inehem and Zarrq discover which of Ohent's lovers is Kaj's father? I suppose none of this really matters. What matters is what can we do here and now to assure that Brunni has the life she wants, and that Ranpeti does not have her adopted child taken from her.*

Peg cut in. "Xerak, did you free Brunni from whatever hook or hold or line that Inehem put on her?"

"I believe I have," Xerak replied. "I will need to do a more careful check, but I think we can assume that I have done so."

"Good." Peg turned her attention to Vereez's parents, tapping her pencil against the table in a brisk beat. "So, what are you willing to promise if we agree to let you go? Are you willing to agree to leave Brunni and Ranpeti alone? Let's start there."

Zarrq didn't twitch a muscle, but his very stillness showed that he was reassessing the situation. His small dark eyes moved to study the ruined reception hall, as if for the first time he realized just how isolated he and his group were from their usual bases of power.

Vereez used her one good arm to raise the drinking bowl to her mouth, studying her parents over the rim as she delicately lapped her tea. "I don't really want to make enemies of you."

"I'm sure you don't," Inehem replied with a light laugh. "Your life would be a lot less simple without access to the various accounts we've continued to permit you to draw upon, for one. And, when you get over this ridiculous holdback phase, you will miss having not only our fortune, but our connections to benefit you."

Vereez's ears flickered back, but she managed not to snarl. "You misunderstand me, Mother. I don't want to make enemies of you because enmity, hatred, all of that, is just as intimate in its own way as love, friendship, trust. I can't say I'd enjoy being impoverished, but short of killing me, you can't keep me from publicly presenting my side of why we became estranged. You seemingly dismissed this back when I mentioned the possibility when we last visited the House of Fortune but, given how you put me under house arrest immediately after, I think that shaft hit closer to the mark than I realized at the time."

Zarrq spoke with the coldness he must have frequently used in his business. "This Peg asked what we would be willing to promise in order to be set free. Are you threatening us with illegal imprisonment?"

Meg spoke in the voice of Sapphire Wind. "Not illegal. You invaded this territory with hostile intent. As official caretaker of the Library, I may detain you indefinitely. That is legal. It is also legal for me to take action against you as one who caused considerable damage to this facility in the past. What is additionally real, if not legal, is that no one knows that you, your wife, your retainers are here. You may disappear, permanently, perhaps, and even if someday, somehow, you are traced to this location, many have disappeared forever in these environs. Are you willing to risk that?"

Silence again.

Everyone—not just Inehem and Zarrq—is reassessing, Teg thought. *It's too easy to forget that Sapphire Wind is a force to be considered. I don't think Sapphire Wind will kill Vereez's parents outright, just because they had a role in the Library's destruction. After all, it has let Ohent stay here as a guest. But if Inehem and Zarrq push too hard, then Vereez won't need to worry about having her parents' blood on her hands.*

"May we confer?" Inehem asked.

"No," Peg replied promptly, "at least not privately. Talk all you want, but in front of your daughter, your sister, your former business associate."

No one contradicted her, and Inehem gave a theatrical—"Ah, to find oneself in the hands of children and madwomen"—sigh, and turned to Ranpeti.

"You have been very quiet, sister mine. Do you have any questions to ask, threats to offer?"

"Not yet," Ranpeti said. "I want to hear what you are willing to offer for the freedom of yourselves and your retainers."

"Very well," Zarrq said. He turned his attention to Ohent and Kaj. "For you, we can offer a larger stipend. We could even hire Kaj in some lucrative capacity. How large and how lucrative would, of course, depend on whether Brunni is returned to the Creator's Visage Isles, since a percentage of what we hope to gain could certainly be passed on to you."

Ohent looked at Kaj. "Well, Son?"

"I'd as soon as work for bloodsucking ticks," Kaj said.

"So you already love your little daughter so much?" Inehem cooed. "Or perhaps you think this will get you in good with Vereez?"

"No," Kaj snarled, the fur standing up along his hackles. "I've already told these people. Working in the necropolis, seeing what I did there, gave me a real hatred for people who let their children be booted out of their bodies. That goes for people who'd let that happen to a grandchild, too."

Ohent reached over and gave him an approving pat. "I'm also not interested in having my stipend raised on those terms, and if you try to cut it, well . . . We signed an agreement. I'd be very happy to take you to court. I'd likely lose, but you'd lose more."

"The stipend," Zarrq reminded her, "was for taking custody of that Bird."

Ohent smiled. "I still have it, I assure you."

"Don't even make me an offer," Ranpeti said. "I never wanted to give Brunni over to the Grantor's people, but they didn't give me a choice. Vereez and her friends arriving was... Well, odd as it sounds, it was a miracle. I lived in the Isles long enough to know that rejecting a miracle when it is granted is base ingratitude."

Inehem and Zarrq exchanged glances, then Inehem dipped her nose slightly and Zarrq spoke.

"Very well. Brunni being returned to the Isles is off the table for consideration. We think you're foolish, but we will move to the next matter on the agenda. Rather than asking us what we are willing to give for our freedom, what do you want from us?"

"The question of Brunni's custody left up to myself and Vereez," Ranpeti said. "When I adopted Brunni, I also accepted a considerable sum from you, which I have left invested in the House of Fortune. I would prefer you don't tamper with it."

I bet Ranpeti changes banks as soon as she can, Teg thought.

Zarrq looked at Inehem who flattened her ears momentarily, but nodded, then said, "We will agree, but we would like to request that when Brunni reaches her majority she be told her full history, including her relationship to the wealthy and prestigious House of Fortune."

Ranpeti looked at Vereez, who nodded.

"I meant what I said before, Aunt Ranpeti," she said. "I'm tired of lies and deception. Secrets have a way of coming out at the absolutely worst time. I'd even suggest that we tell Brunni sooner than when she reaches her majority, a little bit at a time, starting with that you adopted her, then later why. I can wait for her to learn that I'm her birth mother. She's been through so much now. Upsetting her with things she doesn't understand would be a terrible way of showing how much I love her, wouldn't it?"

Ranpeti gave her niece a gentle hug, carefully avoiding her injured arm. "Thank you. For me, and for Brunni. Now, I think you have the right to require something of Inehem and Zarrq. After all, so far they're getting away with nothing they haven't already given."

Vereez faced each of her parents in turn. "I want you to officially grant me my adult status. So that our mutual social circle will not be tempted to ask questions, I suggest that you settle upon me the sum traditional at this time so I am not suddenly thrust upon charity."

"Fair enough," Zarrq said stiffly.

"I also want to return to the House of Fortune to remove my personal property, and an assurance that I will be permitted to depart thereafter."

Inehem looked at Zarrq, who twitched his left ear, then spoke, "If we grant you these things, can we have the assurance that you and your associates will not reveal the, uh, more colorful elements of our past?"

"I can only speak for myself," Vereez said, "but I certainly have no desire to publicize that the basis of my parents' fortune, possibly even their ability to graduate from college, was based on fraud and theft."

"I'd agree," Xerak said. "After all, my mother's reputation would be hurt as well. I'm sure Grunwold would agree—especially if Vereez's nest egg was a generous one. Our mentors would probably support us."

"As long as the agreement was kept," Peg said, scribbling rapidly on her notepad. "If not, we have very little to lose."

"I won't agree," Ohent said, "because it's my past, too, so I'm not about to promise to give it up. You'd need to get Konnel and Fardowsi to agree as well, so we'll just consider our past misadventures a secret among old associates, especially if my stipend continues on, maybe even with a little bonus so I can pay for the medical care I need."

Kaj gave a brusque nod. "I'll follow my mother's lead on this."

Meg said, "Sapphire Wind also does not agree to conceal misdeeds past and present. However, as long as Inehem and Zarrq agreed to leave the Library alone, and to abide by the rest of the agreements, I believe we can convince Sapphire Wind to settle."

Her voice changed to that used by Sapphire Wind. "By leaving this Library 'alone' it is to be understood that this means directly and indirectly, all associated property and personnel, named and unnamed, and if any action is taken that can be understood to be in violation of this, punitive action will be taken, the least part of which will be the revelation of secrets you wish kept concealed."

This neat little verbal contract, so spontaneously delivered, genuinely started both Inehem and Zarrq.

Peg laughed and started scribbling again. "That's excellent wording. I think we need to use some form of that to cover all of the release agreements."

"I agree," Meg said. "We should make certain that all of our inquisitors and their allies—including Nefnet, Ohent, and Kaj— are protected from attack, direct or indirect. This last should include character assassination, ruining of credit ratings, and similar subtle forms of assault." She gave a quietly ferocious smile. "It's amazing what one can learn from reading crime fiction."

Meg would make a very bad enemy indeed, Teg thought.

Peg finished scribbling, reviewed her notes, and frowned. "This still isn't enough compensation. They attacked us, tried to kidnap Brunni, invaded the Library, and all they're going to need to do is settle on Vereez what they would have settled in a short time anyhow and leave Ranpeti alone? How about a trust fund for Brunni? How about compensation for grief and suffering for the rest of us?"

Vereez's smile was absolutely wicked. "I think Inehem and Zarrq might actually consider that buying the silence of those who otherwise would just be keeping their secret from good will might be value for money. After all, what if we had a difference of opinion and someone decided to get even with me? I mean"—she looked pointedly to where Ohent sat—"even the best of friends have disagreements, even become adversaries. Wouldn't it be nice if they decided to compensate everyone, not just me and Aunt Ranpeti?"

Good move, Peg, Teg thought, *and good follow up, Vereez. We've been spending pretty freely to this point, mostly because of Vereez's credit line. With that gone, we're going to need funds.*

Zarrq's gaze grew, if possible, even colder, but after exchanging looks with his wife, he nodded stiff agreement and named a figure. "Per person, of course."

"Including Ranpeti and Vereez," Meg put in. "As Peg pointed out, they have been too generous in their terms, asking only to keep what is, by right and custom, already their own."

"We agree," Zarrq said. "Now, is a verbal agreement sufficient or will there be written contracts?"

"Written," Peg said, "and that will take a little bit, so you can go back to your room and inform your attendants what will be expected of them."

Inehem frowned. "There is no need that their agreements mention anything about our pasts or what compensations we have agreed upon. In fact, why do they need to sign anything?"

"To make certain they do not speak too freely about the Library for one," Meg said. "Also, consider this. The agreements will protect you from their speaking out about attempted kidnapping and other uncomfortable matters. Even if you already have some protections in place, you can't argue against extra."

Teg called from where she sat. "Xerak, I know Ohent said she's very good at wording contracts, but is there some magical way of enforcing the contracts? Where we come from, there are sayings about pie-crust promises, 'Easily made, easily broken.'"

Xerak gave one of those smiles that turned into a showing of fangs as he turned his attention to Inehem and Zarrq. "Actually, there are such enforcement clauses, from the simple to the horrific. My master taught us one that gives the violator mange."

Inehem shuddered. "I know that one. It's vicious, but I have no problem with that being included, as long as it applies to everyone involved."

"Since we don't plan to break our bargain," Xerak said, "I don't think anyone will complain."

"Then we will return to our room," Inehem said, speaking as grandly as if she were returning to the deluxe suite of a hotel, rather than to what was, essentially, a prison cell, "and brief our retainers."

"I would like an opportunity to read through the contracts before we sign anything," Zarrq added.

"Very reasonable," Vereez agreed. "We will bring you out as soon as we have made sufficient copies. It may take a while, so make yourselves comfortable."

As before, Xerak and Kaj handled escort duty. Ranpeti hurried outside to update Grunwold, and let him and Brunni know they could come back in if they wished. At one end of the table, Ohent, Meg, and Peg muttered to each other as they designed the basic templates for various contracts. Teg came down from the sage's seat, and glanced at Nefnet, who had been listening with interest.

"I can't say I mind being included as a recipient of hush money,"

Nefnet said, "but I'm not sure where I'll be able to spend it if I stay here, and for now, that's what I intend to do."

Vereez spoke from where she was setting out clean paper and writing materials around the table for the scribing session to come. "Don't worry, Nefnet. I certainly don't plan to leave my funds in the care of the House of Fortune. I have a pretty good idea of what banks are reliable. If you'd like, I'd be happy to set you up an account, perhaps in Rivers Meet, since the transport artifact has a setting for there."

"We should check first precisely where it goes," Nefnet agreed, "but if it doesn't take us to someplace where someone arriving would create comment, that would be a good idea. Except for some classes at the university, I don't have a lot of ties in Rivers Meet, so it would be a good place for me to try integrating into current society—when I'm ready."

Xerak noted, "Remember, the transport device can be set for different coordinates. It's a bit of a hassle, but we could set it up for the location of your choice when you're ready. Consider it our fee for your saving Vereez's arm."

"Does anyone else find it interesting," Teg asked, "that both Inehem and Zarrq left open the question of whether or not Vereez was to be disinherited? Do you think that could be a bribe to encourage good behavior or bait toward future reconciliation?"

"I found it interesting," Meg said.

"Me, too," Peg added.

"Me, three," Vereez said, forcing a laugh. "And as for bribe or lure, I can't say. I wonder if they even know?"

Ranpeti smiled sadly. "I've known Inehem all my life, and even I can't say I am privy to how her mind works. Don't push the point and maybe you'll learn someday."

Ohent looked up from where she had been reviewing each copy of the contract, searching one last time for the sort of loopholes she knew her former colleagues would exploit. "I don't think Inehem— or Zarrq for that matter—would use being disinherited as a light threat. You don't remember your paternal grandfather, Vereez, but although he had very little, he used that threat so often it was almost a family joke. That didn't keep it from stinging."

Vereez's ears canted thoughtfully. "I never heard that story. No wonder my mother was so proud of having made her own fortune, no matter that her nest egg wasn't earned through conventional saving, as I was led to believe."

"Families," Peg said softly, "are very complex."

Ohent handed the stack of contracts to Meg, who neatly separated them into which applied to which person.

"I think we're ready for Inehem and Zarrq," Meg said, and Xerak and Kaj went to get them, while Grunwold went to "play with" Brunni over to one side of the reception hall. They weren't taking any chances that Inehem and Zarrq had come up with a final plan to get their hands on the little girl before the contracts were signed.

However, the signing proceeded without incident, including neatly thumbprinting in each person's saliva over the curse Xerak had written out beneath the signature line.

After the signing was concluded, Inehem turned to her daughter and said with false sweetness, "By the way, my dear, I've noticed how you and your associates all trust that this Sapphire Wind is on your side. Based on my own research, I wonder if you are wise to do so. Consider this warning a parting gift."

Inehem would not say more so, with only the ceremony necessary for activating the transportation spell, the captives were sent back to Rivers Meet—this a precaution to keep them from trotting over to have a chat with the acolytes of the Grantor of Miracles as soon as they returned. Inehem had attempted to protest that they'd left their luggage at a hotel in Sky Descry, but Vereez, still steely eyed and unforgiving as only the newly adult can be, simply said, "Get it shipped back. You can afford it."

They set watches in case Inehem and Zarrq attempted to sneak back, but nothing happened. In any case, Xerak seemed fairly certain—and Sapphire Wind agreed—that the Library would be a very difficult place for someone to invade.

"Especially now," Meg stated, "that Sapphire Wind can draw on the power of the two portions of Ba Djed that we have recovered."

They waited until Brunni was napping under the watchful gaze of the pair of dobergoats who seemed to have taken a particular liking to the little girl to ask Ranpeti to relate how she had ended up in possession of the child and residing so very far away from Rivers Meet. Meg and Ohent had heard part of this story, but there hadn't been leisure for the rest to do so.

"If you'll be patient," Ranpeti began, "I'll give you the long version. By necessity, it's going to be painful at times for several of you, perhaps especially for Vereez, but I want you to understand, I'm not being insulting or cruel. This is how it happened. As has been said repeatedly today, I am tired of lies and deceptions."

"Well," Xerak said, "we can't exactly toss Vereez on *Slicewind* until her physician says she's out of danger. A story would help pass the time."

Vereez gave him a grateful smile, knowing how eager he must be to begin the search for his master, and Ranpeti began her tale.

"When Inehem learned that Vereez was pregnant, she came to me for advice. She and Zarrq had already decided that Vereez would not be permitted to keep the child. They felt this would ruin her prospects, whether for marriage or for whatever career she might pursue. They also felt that it would encourage Vereez in her infatuation with a young man who had already—by seducing a child of fourteen—shown himself unsatisfactory."

She paused, as if expecting protest, but when no one spoke, she continued.

"There was some discussion that they might keep the infant themselves, raise it as a daughter or the child of a distant relation, but that sort of lie is hard to maintain, especially since Vereez must needs go into seclusion, and an infant showing up after that would pretty much defeat the purpose of sending her away in the first place. Therefore, the child must be given up for adoption.

"Inehem asked me if I knew of anyone who might be interested in adopting the yet-unborn infant—preferably someone who lived a great distance away or whose work would take them far away. I suggested myself. I am not interested in men, but I was increasingly drawn to the idea of having a child. This arrangement would solve both my problem and theirs—or so I thought. To my surprise, Zarrq and Inehem were initially opposed. If the unborn child resembled our side of the family, all would be well, but auguries seemed to indicate that she would resemble Zarrq's side of the family. While it is not unheard of for sisters to share a man, Zarrq and Inehem have an unusually close relationship, and neither wished it to be in the least diminished in the eyes of a gossipy public.

"I persisted, though. Vereez has always been dear to me. I liked the idea of raising her child as my own. I persisted in my request and—in part, I believe, because several other promising options did not materialize or proved to be in one way or another unsatisfactory—eventually Inehem and Zarrq said I could have the unborn infant, but only if I agreed to certain terms.

"First, I must agree to be officially dead to my family. For this charade to work, I must move far away—to the other side of the world. It may seem unbelievable to you, but I agreed. I have always loved travel, and other than my sister and her family—who I was feeling oddly conflicted about now that I saw how they were dealing with Vereez's pregnancy—I had few close ties. Zarrq suggested Sky Descry, and promised a very ample settlement, more than enough for the unborn child and me to live in great comfort.

"After much thought and prayer, I agreed. My sister and her husband took care of getting me a new identity which would hold up even under magical investigation. When the child was born, she was given to me while still wet from birth. We left on a ship, and Brunni lived her first few months in a first-class cabin, doted upon by all. I gave out that I was a widow, moving to get away from memories of my late husband. My obvious wealth made any eccentricity seem reasonable.

"All went well for the first four years. Then, a few weeks ago, Brunni began to have dreams about someone she called 'the Sleeping Man.' At first those dreams were benign, but then they transformed into nightmares in which the Sleeping Man was looking for Brunni, because she could help him to wake up. Shortly thereafter, I was contacted by representatives of the Creator's Visage Isles and told—not asked, I want you to understand, told—that Brunni was of the lineage of the Grantor of Miracles.

"They explained very kindly—indeed, I think some of them were ashamed—that although normally they would not take a child to serve as vessel for the spirit of the Grantor, circumstances were such that they felt they could not delay."

"Circumstances?" Vereez echoed, her voice vibrating into a shrill growl. "Circumstances?"

Teg reached out and took the hand that was not in a sling. "Vereez. We promised Ranpeti a chance to tell this tale uninterrupted. You can't imagine this is easy for her, can you?"

Vereez bowed her head. "I'm sorry, Aunt Ranpeti. Teg is right."

Ranpeti dipped her nose in gracious acceptance. "You've been hit with so much in such rapid succession. Bear with me. I'm almost done." She sipped from her tea and then went on.

"I didn't want to give Brunni up. I refused, only to be told that I had no choice. The laws of the land gave them the right to claim anyone—adult or child—if that person was connected to the Grantor's spirit. I did gather that they would prefer to wait until the spirit reincarnated naturally, but forces were at work that made this unpleasant decision necessary. Then I was given the only choice they could offer me. I could turn Brunni over and go my way, or I could remain with Brunni and offer her what comfort I could. I made the only choice I felt was even possible. I kept hoping that something would happen, that the Sleeping Man would fail to reincarnate, something, anything."

She managed a weak smile. "I didn't expect help to come in the form of my niece, her childhood friends, and visitors from another world. But I am very, very glad that it did."

"Will the government of the Visage Isles really leave Brunni alone now?" Kaj asked.

His tone was neutral, as if he was simply assessing possible future problems, not as if he pretended any affection for the child. Teg was dismayed to feel Vereez's hand, which she still held, tighten and hear her soft sigh.

"It's possible," Ranpeti said. "But I'm not certain what legal rights they would have now that we have taken Brunni out of their land. If Inehem and Zarrq break their promise to me, I may lose my fortune. I will almost certainly have forfeited my home in the Visage Isles, but as long as Brunni is safe, I can accept that."

Vereez nodded. "We may be impoverished together, but somehow we'll manage. However, we're not yet and may not be. The agreement my parents signed is very binding, and I can't imagine my mother wants to risk mange."

She forced a smile. "We've done our best on that front. What still interests me is that my mother and father sent you right to where—

if what Teg and I saw depicted on the museum's mural is what we think it is—an artifact associated with Ba Djed of the Weaver is kept; where it is, apparently, associated with the miracles that are the greatest claim to prominence for an otherwise obscure land. Is this one of those coincidences we're supposed to overlook?"

Ohent had been sitting unnaturally still during Ranpeti's recital.

"That's too big a coincidence for me to believe," she said flatly. "Inehem may have been guided—perhaps without her even knowing it—to suggest that place through dreams or visions. Remember, she was, even if briefly, custodian of the Bird. As I am witness, close contact with even part of Ba Djed digs deep grooves in a person's psyche."

"Sapphire Wind," Meg said, "says it knows nothing of this other artifact. I believe it."

"So do I," Ohent said. "I can't say why, other than that I have an awareness of Ba Djed, and Sapphire Wind is... How can I explain this? Secondary? It is not associated with Ba Djed itself, only with its care."

Teg was aware that she was not the only one who felt reassured by this. It was hard enough dealing with Sapphire Wind and feeling uncertain as to its motives regarding Meg without wondering if the Library's *genius loci* had an even larger agenda.

Of course, it could be lying to us. It might already be controlling Meg.

Apparently, Peg was having similar thoughts, for she said, "Sapphire Wind, right before she departed, Inehem made some rather nasty comments about you, about how we are being too trusting. While we're on the subject of coincidence, there's something I've been wondering about. It seems too great a coincidence that so many of the children of the extraction agents who were responsible for the Library being nearly destroyed are holdbacks."

Meg's lips started to move, but Peg held up her hand in a wordless request to be permitted to continue. Meg nodded, and Peg went on.

"Let's leave Kaj out of the equation, because Ohent's illness greatly shaped his options. However, we have three others, all of whom come from if not affluent, then prosperous families, each obsessed with a particular problem to the point that, once they became adults, or near adults, they were unable to move on. Why couldn't a cure for

Konnel's illness be found? Once we came to the Library, Nefnet managed quite neatly, and in a fairly short period of time, yet she herself has said she was still learning her craft. Vereez had the resources of her very wealthy family, but she could not find the least trace of what had happened to Brunni. Xerak's master vanished, and Xerak—who has shown himself extremely talented—again couldn't find even the slightest clue to Uten Kekui's whereabouts. Is it a coincidence that until they came here, these puzzles refused to unravel?"

Meg said in her own voice. "A nicely presented case. Sapphire Wind would like to reply."

By now everyone, even those who were only tangentially affected by the situation, were listening with rapt attention. Meg settled herself, took a deep draft of tea, and leaned back. When next her lips moved, the breezy, sighing voice of Sapphire Wind came forth.

"I did not cause the problems. However, after the disaster, I did what I could to force those who had injured me, stolen from me, to return and make right what had been wrong."

"But these children didn't harm you," Peg retorted fiercely, "and Brunni even less."

"The 'children' did not, but their parents did, and their children benefitted from their parents' profit. Understand me, what I did . . . I cannot really explain it now, because I am so much less than I once was . . . but what I did was put into motion forces that would cause those who had broken and stolen Ba Djed, directly or indirectly, to play a role in it being reassembled and returned."

Grunwold attempted to say something, but Sapphire Wind went on speaking as if it did not notice—which it may well have not.

"I have had the odd thought that, even as I was created to protect the artifact, you three inquisitors were created to reassemble it. This may explain why all of you are only children. If so, your parents did pay for their misdeeds, after a fashion."

"Not Kaj?" Xerak asked. "He's an only child, too."

"I think not. His mother, in a sense, took on part of what should have been my job. She is the only one of the thieves to have taken responsibility upon herself."

Ohent looked astonished. "Somehow, knowing that what I did may have spared Kaj, that makes all the hell worthwhile."

Kaj said nothing, but he laid a hand on her shoulder.

"And Brunni?" Ranpeti softly prompted.

"As for Brunni, I think some other force is at work there. You must remember: I do not use Ba Djed, I was created to hide it, to protect it. I did what I did because that is what I was created to do. I cannot say I am sorry that after over twenty-five years I am finally approaching success. What I can say, although you are not likely to believe me, is that I am sorry that the descendants are the ones who must set right a wrong they did not do."

Meg shut her eyes and when she opened them again, she was once again in control of her body. "I think that's it."

Xerak cleared his throat. "Not that this isn't fascinating, and not that we don't have a few other details to work out—like where Brunni and Ranpeti are going to stay—but I feel I have been extraordinarily patient. We now have two pieces of Ba Djed. We have found help for Grunwold's father. Locating Vereez's daughter became a precondition for us gaining access to the second part of the artifact. That's fine. But I'm no closer to finding my master. Can we please move ahead on that matter?"

"Can we try to scry for Uten Kekui using the two pieces we have?" Peg asked. "Maybe that would be enough to give us a lead. I think Sapphire Wind should trust us to keep our word that we will find the final piece after we have found Xerak's master."

Sapphire Wind spoke through Meg. "I would trust and will. Let us make an attempt."

⁜ CHAPTER SIX ⁜

As before, setting up the ritual that would enable Sapphire Wind to use the Font of Sight would take time. As the only one of their number who knew Uten Kekui, Xerak needed to direct the ritual. Meg joined him within the rounded room that held the Font, so that she could speak for Sapphire Wind. Nefnet excused herself to prepare some new medications for when Vereez's wound dressing would need to be changed.

And probably to get a break from too many people, Teg thought sympathetically. *It can't be easy to go from solitude to a whole mess of guests. And a major battle in what one has probably come to think of as one's living room would definitely be upsetting.*

Since Brunni was still solidly asleep, Grunwold excused himself to do some maintenance on *Slicewind.* Peg offered to sit with Vereez while the young woman napped on the cot Meg had used the night before.

"Teg," Xerak said, "I know you're eager to go poking in the rubble, but if you could do so from where I can call on you for magical assistance, that would be good. Normally, I wouldn't ask a raw apprentice, but with Vereez down . . ."

"I understand," Teg assured him. "Don't worry. There's no lack of rubble here to keep me amused."

As Teg finished speaking, she noticed that Peg was motioning for Ohent and Ranpeti to join her and Vereez. Teg drifted to where she could listen while still being on call if Xerak needed her.

"Vereez can't sleep," Peg said when Ohent and Ranpeti arrived.

"I've offered her a sleeping draught, but she wanted to talk with both of you instead. Can you pull over a bench and make yourselves comfortable?"

The other two women did, and Vereez spoke for the first time. She sounded both extremely tired and very determined.

"When we discussed Brunni's fate with my parents, we were all very polite and implied that Aunt Ranpeti would continue to have custody. That's actually all right with me, especially if my aunt will let me get to know Brunni better, so that if anything happens—all deities of every religion ever practiced or imagined forefend—to Aunt Ranpeti, some sort of arrangement can be made so I can be part of taking care of Brunni. But Ohent-lial, your condition for bringing the Bird here was our finding Brunni, and making sure she was well. I can't sleep until I find out how you feel about Aunt Ranpeti remaining Brunni's main parent."

Ohent's smile was just a little sly. "I was wondering if you would ask, or if you would just hope I'd overlook our agreement. Then, too, Kaj has a sire's claim on the girl, and I felt he should be spoken to once he had a chance to get to know her."

Teg glanced around, noticing that Kaj was nowhere to be seen, but Teg felt certain that he would not be able to get up to any mischief. The guardian creatures, which had increased in visibility even in the short time they'd been away at the Visage Isles, would make sure that, if Kaj's grave robber impulses came to the fore, nothing was taken.

"And?" Peg cajoled. "Have you spoken to your son, Ohent?"

Ohent laughed. "I have and he was horrified, not only at the idea of having to become a father, rather than merely a sire, but that I would even consider taking Brunni from Ranpeti-lial. He's a bit of a mama's boy, my Kaj, and he respects a mother's rights."

Ranpeti, whose posture had been a reminder that, cute and cuddly as they might seem, otters were predators, relaxed so fast she nearly collapsed against the back of the bench.

"And you, Ohent-lial? Do you want Brunni? I assure you here and now, I won't give her up without a fight."

"Call me Ohent-toh," the other woman said, "and I will call you Ranpeti-toh. I agree with what Vereez said to Inehem. Brunni will need to know about her past. What better beginning than that she knows at least one of her grandmothers is friends to her mother? If Nefnet and Sapphire Wind agree, I was considering staying here at the Library, so Nefnet could help me research what course of treatment would be best for the damage done to me by my custodianship. Perhaps you can stay here as well. What better place to use as a refuge from the acolytes of the Grantor of Miracles—half a world away, and magically guarded as well?"

"I like the idea," Ranpeti agreed. "As I said, I suspect my home in the Isles is lost to me. However, thanks to recent negotiations, my fortune is not lost."

Vereez cut in. She still looked tired, but Teg thought this looked like the healthy exhaustion of one who would soon be sound asleep.

"We can make plans before we leave. We're going to need to shift our funds to other banks in any case. While we're doing that, we can shop so those of you who remain behind will not be restricted to camping."

Peg smiled. "There's lots of room here in the Library itself. Surely there must have been proper restrooms and such. You all could be very comfortable if we cleared them out and made repairs."

Teg noticed that Vereez's eyes had now drifted shut, that the hand Peg still held was no longer gripping so tightly. If she wasn't asleep now, she would be soon.

Not long after, Kaj returned from wherever he had been exploring, and joined Xerak and Meg near the Font. Teg noticed that as he made his way into the Font chamber, Kaj's canine nose twitched, as if he smelled something interesting. Nor did he lose interest when a scrying was attempted, failed, and attempted again, nor when that second attempt also failed, and a third begun.

It was a good thing Kaj was there, because he was able to catch Xerak when the lion-headed wizard collapsed. Teg thought it said something about Xerak's level of despair that he didn't seem to appreciate that he was being held in those muscular arms. Instead, Xerak abstractedly nodded his thanks, then let Kaj half carry him out into the reception hall, where he carefully arranged himself on one of the benches, his spear staff braced in both hands so he could lean his head against it.

"I guess," Xerak said, the low rumble of his words deadly flat with despair, "I shouldn't be surprised. Every other attempt to scry my master's location has met with failure. Why should this be any different?"

"I will stomp on your tufted tail if you start whining," Grunwold said, coming into the hall on the heels of Ranpeti, who had hurried to get him. "We're not done yet. Don't forget the words Teg spoke back in Hettua Shrine. They promised we'd find answers to our questions if we came to the Library of the Sapphire Wind. Looks as if we'll need to have an intact Ba Djed of the Weaver before we have sufficient wind in our sails to drive us to wherever Uten Kekui-va is."

He raised his antlered head so his nose was pointed in the general direction of the ceiling. "Hey, Sapphire Wind, are you as fried as our wizard boy here, or can you do whatever it is you do to pinpoint the location of the missing bit?"

"With two pieces close, I should be better able to find the third," Sapphire Wind replied through Meg. "Far better than when I had only one and its desire for completion was split between two points."

Ohent had come to reclaim her portion of Ba Djed. Now she halted, the enshrouding container that held the minute bronze bird nestled in the palm of her clawed hand.

"You'll still need this? Or are you going to wait until Xerak has recovered?"

"I can try now," Sapphire Wind replied. "This seeking will draw upon my abilities, as well as the Bird and Spindle's energies, so Xerak's weariness is not a detriment. As with our other scrying, I was planning to use the Font of Sight to reveal what I find. Although my abstract knowledge is great, I have not travelled, and what images there are may mean little to me, less if they need to be interpreted through Meg's perception, since she knows only slightly more of this world than I do."

"How long do you need to set up?" Xerak asked, after taking a deep pull from his wine flask.

"Not long," Sapphire Wind said. "I was created to draw upon and protect Ba Djed."

Vereez and Brunni had both awakened during the commotion following Xerak's collapse, so their entire company, including Nefnet, trooped to the room that held the Font.

"This Font is fascinating," Peg told Ranpeti, "and extremely useful, but the room is also almost completely round. You might want to carry Brunni over to a seat so she doesn't slip."

The seats in question were mounted into the walls of the room, after the style of theater in the round. A large chalice-shaped sculpture rose from a floor that, like the walls and ceilings, was covered in minute white tiles.

Teg had been in the chamber several times before, but once she was in her seat she looked around, certain something was different. After a moment, she had it: the tiles, white before, now glowed with a soft, nacreous sheen that revealed almost undetectable hints of pastel pink, blue, and yellow.

"Sapphire Wind, you've been housekeeping!"

Meg's voice sounded pleased. "The abau are very useful for dusting and polishing. Now that I have more control, I sent a flock in."

Teg, remembering a less domestic encounter with the yellowish-grey creatures Peg had dubbed "flying pancakes," felt an involuntary shudder run up her spine.

"I'm glad to see they're so useful."

Once everyone was comfortably seated, Sapphire Wind dimmed the lights.

At first, Teg wasn't sure whether she really felt the energies building or if she had been convinced that she should be able to do so. However, when she saw Xerak's mane rising as if charged with static electricity, she decided it wasn't her imagination. Interestingly, the reaction to whatever Sapphire Wind was channeling into the Font seemed to vary from person to person, with Xerak and Ohent the most affected, then Teg, Meg, Nefnet, Brunni, and Vereez. Grunwold showed little reaction. Kaj was the real surprise. The longer bits of the red and black fur along his neck nearly crackled as much as did Xerak's mane.

Teg put this interesting tidbit aside for later contemplation, for an image was forming in the air directly over the Font. At first, she thought that the room they were looking at might be the repository within the Library of the Sapphire Wind, perhaps a vision from the past, before the corridors had been littered with rubble. But that couldn't be. Those were industrial metal shelves filled with cardboard boxes and plastic cases. The labels were about evenly split between handwritten and typed, but the language in which they were written was English—not magically translated characters that somehow made sense—but all-too-familiar English.

"I don't..."

"What the..."

"What sort of place is..."

The muttering was incisively cut by Meg's voice. "I believe that's Jaxine Museum's overflow library facility and repository at Taima University. Teg? Do you agree?"

Teg got up from her seat and walked down to where she could lean into the image the Font had created in order to take a closer look at the labels. "That does look like the correct nomenclature: JMTU for the facility and university; the next digits indicate where the contents were acquired; then classification; finally, date. What the heck is going on here?"

When Peg spoke, her voice was thoughtful. "As soon as we figured out that maybe, just maybe, the three of us being summoned wasn't a mistake caused by impulsive inquisitors, I've wondered: Why us? Why did Hettua Shrine grab onto three people from our world to help provide the solution to our inquisitors' problems? If I understand what more usually happens, help rarely comes from another world."

Nods encouraged her to continue.

"I'd like to think we've been useful to our inquisitors, but I'm not sure we've been more helpful than three people with roughly equivalent skills from Over Where would be. The one thing we have to offer that no one from this world could is the connection to our world. If the last part of Ba Djed of the Weaver is in our world, then that's the unique element we can provide."

"You have a point," Teg said excitedly. "There are certainly people at Taima University who have a closer connection with that repository, but we have something else to offer that would be hard to find—we're more or less disposable."

"Disposable?" Xerak repeated, sounding horrified. "What do you mean?"

"I mean," Teg admitted ruthlessly, "that we could—essentially—vanish for weeks and no one would notice or even care. Peg's family is extensive, but her children are grown and have their own children and activities. Meg..."

"I am not precisely intimate with either Charles or Judy," Meg interrupted primly. "I am certain that they are just as happy to have me off on an extensive holiday."

"And I'm a loner," Teg concluded. "No spouse. No children. Currently on sabbatical, so no job to miss me either. Felicity, my cat sitter, might get annoyed if I landed her with Thought and Memory for too long, but that's it. And since the cats have taken to wandering over here from time to time, I don't even need to worry about them getting lonely."

"We haven't been gone that long," Peg reminded her. "The seven days here, one back home time difference has helped a lot. But Teg is right. We're at a time in our lives and in the lives of our families where we're back-burnered."

"So," Grunwold said, his tone of voice cocky, but something in the tilt of his ears showing he was trying to avoid seeming to pity them, "we've figured out why we got stuck with the three of you. Great. Can you go to this repository and fetch the Nest of Ba Djed or is the repository at this Jaxine Museum as full of monsters as the one here at the Library of the Sapphire Wind?"

Teg frowned. "No monsters, different challenges. The good news is that I actually have researcher privileges at Jaxine Museum. Depending on how that box is classified, I might even be able to check it out and get a look at the contents."

Ears perked and a few muted cheers were heard. Teg held up her hand.

"That's the *good* news. There's another side. First, researcher privileges don't mean that I can expect to take the box home with me. Unless I'm very lucky, I'm going to need to inspect the contents there."

"And even then," Xerak said, nodding slowly in understanding, "you couldn't just take something out of the box and drop it in your pocket. Difficulties, yes, but not insurmountable. Teg, if we managed to get you something that looked like the Nest of Ba Djed, could you manage to switch it for the real artifact?"

"I'd be willing to try," Teg said promptly, "but we'd need to be careful that the materials matched. Sapphire Wind, do you know what the missing part is made from? We've only seen visual images."

A long pause, then Sapphire Wind said, "I believe it is polished jet. We should have some jet here, but it would need to be carved into the proper shape."

Ohent laughed. "I volunteer Kaj to make the duplicate. He's very talented at copying items in stone or wood."

I bet he is, Teg thought. *I wonder if Xerak's mother bought some faked grave goods for her antique store over the years, or if Ohent and Kaj saved those for the tourists.*

Kaj said, "Sure, I think I can do it, especially if Sapphire Wind will show me close-up images of the Nest, so that I can make sketches and take measurements."

"This can be done," Meg said. "Sapphire Wind will also tell Emsehu where to find a supply of jet for you. Using the guardians to retrieve it should be safer."

"From what I've seen of this place," Kaj said with a dry laugh, "I completely agree."

"Sounds like a plan," Teg said. "The time difference between here and home is going to be in our advantage for this, because Kaj will have plenty of time to make his carving. Even if I go and spend an hour there, that's seven hours here. Sapphire Wind, can you zoom in on the box I need to get access to?"

There wasn't a verbal reply but, a few moments later, the image began to shift, homing in first on one shelf, then on one box. Teg leaned forward and jotted down the reference numbers.

"Peg, you've been keeping track of the calendar. What day of the week is it?"

Peg pulled a small notebook from a pocket on the outside of her knitting bag. "It's a Monday."

Teg nodded briskly. "Great! That means we have all week, and probably at least part of Saturday, too, to get an available appointment. Here's what I'll do. I'll go back to my house and call the repository. If I'm lucky, I'll get an answer right away. If so, I'll come back and let you know how soon I can see that box. Meantime, we take advantage of the time lag to get started on making a duplicate of the part we'll be switching—the Bird's Nest."

Ranpeti spoke into the brief silence that followed. "So, in addition to being able to speak our language, you mentors can go back and forth between our world and your own at will? How is that managed?

I understood that of you only Teg-lial seems to have a magical gift, and even she is an apprentice."

Meg smiled, obviously enjoying Ranpeti's enthusiasm. "The translation spell is courtesy of Hettua Shrine. It permits us to understand the languages of this world, and read them as well. It has some difficulties if our language doesn't have a word for something in this world, but we manage. I'm even making a dictionary, just in case someday the spell fails to work."

"As for how we go between worlds . . ." Peg set her knitting needles aside and raised her right arm, pulling her sleeve back from the wrist to show a bracelet made from what looked like twisted wires of copper, gold, silver, and bronze, all highly polished. A single grey stone bead, sparkling with minute etchings, was strung over the wire.

"One of the first things we did after we decided we'd stay to serve as mentors," Peg continued, "was arrange a means for us to get home again. Hawtoor, the shrine keeper of Hettua Shrine, directed our making these. They let each one of us get back to a single location on our world. We each chose our own homes."

"That's wonderful!" Ranpeti exclaimed. "Can you use them at any time or from any place?"

"Within limits," Meg said. "We're still testing just what those are. Hawtoor said that we should think of them as a ferry boat, rather than a door, and that just as a ferry cannot be placed anywhere in a river, so these bracelets will work better in some places than in others. It helps if we're in an isolated location, as well as one that isn't very magically active."

"But how does it know where to bring you back?" Ranpeti asked. "I mean here, in our world, not in your own world."

"It helps to have another of the bracelets present to act as an anchor," Meg said. "I believe that, in a pinch, we could use one of our three inquisitors, since each contributed to the making. See the different color wires?" She extended her own wrist. "The copper began as Vereez's fur, the bronze as Grunwold's, the gold as Xerak's, and the silver from hair from each of us three humans—which is doubtless why there is more of it. The bead came from the stone of Hettua Shrine, so I suspect in an emergency we could return there."

"Do the bracelets work if you're in motion?" Ranpeti asked, clearly fascinated. "For example, when you're sailing on *Slicewind*?"

"So far," Peg replied cheerfully. "When we're in transit has been when we've usually gone back home, to send messages to the kids, or pick up something we need. Hawtoor did warn us that we'd need to learn what did and didn't work as we went along. I don't think he had a lot of examples to go on."

"I don't think," Teg said, laughing as she remembered the pedantic shrine keeper, "he had any, but he was a willing old bird."

Literally, in some senses, she thought, *since his nonhuman elements were taken from some sort of owl.*

"That's wonderful," Ranpeti said with a contented sigh. "When Vereez was telling me about how her parents, uh, grounded, her, she escaped by being taken through your world."

"That's right," Teg said. "We didn't want to take any chances that we'd reappear back in the House of Fortune, so Vereez and I walked over to Meg's apartment, and she opened her door for us."

"That's wonderful," Ranpeti repeated. "I'd love to see another world."

"Me, too," Grunwold said, almost bashfully for him. "If I hadn't been so worried when we were rescuing Vereez, I would have asked to go over into Meg's apartment at least."

"I'd also like to see your world," Xerak admitted. "An added benefit might be to strengthen the bracelets' ability to link our worlds."

Peg chuckled and picked up her knitting again. "A very scholarly excuse for playing tourist. What do you think, Teg? Could you take the boys and Ranpeti with you when you go to make our appointment to go to the repository? I'd take them, but every time I go back to my house to make a call or send e-mail, I worry I'll find someone 'housesitting' for me."

"Sure," Teg said. "I'll check first to make sure Felicity isn't there feeding the cats, then pop back. However, given the risks, I think it would be better if we didn't go anywhere but my house. We managed, just barely, to disguise Vereez by wrapping her up, but this jaunt has to be during the day, and I can't figure out how we'd hide Grunwold's antlers."

No one disagreed, but Ranpeti withdrew from going along at the last minute. "I don't want to not be here for Brunni."

Vereez moved as if she was about to volunteer to babysit so her aunt could go, then said carefully, "She's certain to miss Grunwold. Maybe you and I could play a game with her or take her for a walk."

Good girl, Teg thought. *You're growing up in leaps and bounds, and I couldn't be more proud.*

Within the hour, Teg was ready to head back to her house.

"Remember," she said, "I'll be taking a few minutes to make sure my house is empty, and with the seven-to-one time difference, I'll be gone at least ten minutes on this end."

"Right," Grunwold replied.

"We'll be waiting," Xerak reassured her.

And they were. When Teg came back for them, they followed her through eagerly enough, and looked around with interest when they stepped out of the closet in her bedroom. Teg's two cats, Thought and Memory, who had been sleeping on her bed, started to bolt underneath, then stopped when they recognized her. They didn't seem at all surprised to see Xerak and Grunwold, either.

Which says something, probably, Teg thought, *but I'll be damned if I can figure out what.*

"So," she said, "this is probably the first time I've ever brought anyone straight to my bedroom, but that's where you are. Bed. Dressers. Cats. If you go over to the window, you can see out, get a sense of our architecture and plants and all. This time of day, there should be a certain amount of traffic. Look around inside the house all you want, but stay clear of any window where you might be seen from outside. Meanwhile, I want to switch on my computer and see what I can learn about that box before I call to make a reservation."

"Computer?" Xerak said. "You three all talk about these things as if they're communication devices, but the translation spell seems to insist that they are for calculation or computation."

"They originated that way," Teg said, trotting down the stairs to her office, "but over time they've become multipurpose devices, and communication is one of the purposes."

"Fascinating," Xerak said, sounding so much like Mr. Spock that Teg had to swallow a giggle. She didn't want to waste time explaining the reference.

As she worked, she could hear the boys poking about. As with when she'd taken Vereez on their short jaunt, what was interesting was not what she expected to surprise them—they accepted electric lights as a peculiar form of magic, and Vereez had told them about cars—but what she hadn't anticipated. The ice machine on the refrigerator gave Grunwold quite a start, but that was nothing to when Xerak accidentally turned on the garbage disposal when randomly flipping switches.

They both came in and looked over her shoulder as she worked at her computer, so full of questions that she was pressed to concentrate.

"Okay," she said at last. "Now I need to make a phone call. Why don't you two go watch traffic for a few minutes."

"Peg says 'Go play in traffic,'" Grunwold replied. "Now that I see what your traffic looks like, I have a better idea how annoyed she is when says that."

"Translation can only go so far," Teg agreed. "Now, shoo, both of you."

She lucked out, and was able to catch the person who did scheduling just before he left for a meeting. She scribbled down the necessary information, then went to get the boys.

"Okay, fellows. Let's scoot."

Once they were back at the Library, after Grunwold and Xerak had babbled a bit about their adventure, which had definitely delighted them, limited as it had been, Teg gave her report.

"I have an appointment for tomorrow there," she said, stroking Memory, who had insisted on coming back Over Where with her. "Which is a week here. Anyone interested in what that box contains—and where it's originally from?"

Peg and Meg both nodded.

Xerak spoke for the rest when he said, "It might be interesting, but I'm not certain your explanation would mean anything to us."

Teg grinned. She was feeling curiously elated. The discovery that there was a connection between their world and Over Where had set her brain fizzing with possibilities. She knew that most of her guesses were probably wrong, but conjecture was as much a part of an anthropologist's tool kit as were a trowel and tape measure.

"The box was donated to Jaxine Museum just a few years ago. It contains some interesting, if not very valuable, Egyptian artifacts that were offered to the museum by the widow of an alumnus."

"Egyptian?" Meg's eyebrows arched in surprise. "Isn't that rather outside of your area of expertise? How did you explain wanting to look at it?"

"I lucked out," Teg replied. "There are some arrowheads in there. Nice ones. I made the excuse that I'm considering a popular article on different approaches to tipping arrows, and that I wanted to include as large a selection as possible."

She felt herself grinning again. "Turns out that Jaxine Museum is thrilled I want to look at what—frankly, from the curators' point of view—is just a lot of junk without provenience. If I reference the contents, especially if I include a photo or two, they'll let the widow know and maybe the alumni association will find itself getting a nice check. People are funny that way."

She turned to Peg. "Speaking of photographs, I seem to recall you're pretty good with a camera."

"My stepdaughter, Samantha, was very into photography," Peg admitted. "I went to so many classes, I learned as much as she did. And then when digital cameras became affordable, well, grandchildren are my favorite subject."

"Great! Then I nominate you as my assistant. We'll set you up with a light box and all the paraphernalia. If there are two of us moving things around, taking pictures, and all the rest, it should make it easier for us to switch the real artifact for the fake. Speaking of which, how's that going?"

"Emsehu brought me a fairly good supply of jet," Kaj said, "most of which looks as if it was used in small statues that were broken when the Library collapsed. There are several pieces large enough to provide me with ample material to carve a replica Nest."

"That's great," Teg said. "Take your time. You have a week."

Meg said, "Speaking of which, since you and Peg will be going back, I have a prescription I need to refill, and I wouldn't mind some more moisturizer and toothpaste. Can I give you my credit card and a short shopping list? I'll go over to my apartment tonight and call in the prescription."

"That should be fine," Teg said. "The pharmacy you use is right on our way."

Over the next several days, work on the substitute Bird's Nest progressed quite well. Teg had thought it odd that Kaj had brought his carving tools with him, but that was until he started working. Once he did, he sat absorbed for hours on end, carefully shaving minute bits off the chunk of jet, checking his work repeatedly against the drawings he had made. Clearly, carving was a passion with him. As he worked, he even lost his sullen, bad-boy affect.

Teg almost liked him.

Although Xerak was restless, the Library contained plenty of books to distract him. He also insisted that Teg take time away from searching the rubble to practice various aspects of using her magical gift. These included meditation to make her more aware of her core, training to use the sun spider amulet more efficiently, and learning how to create an internal reservoir of mana.

"We can't have you fainting every time there's a crisis," Xerak commented wryly.

Now that Brunni had been found, and Kaj was too occupied in his stone carving to pay attention to anything else, Vereez was more agreeable to resuming her own training. She'd had lessons in how to meditate and focus, as well as in how to store energy, but she admitted she was out of practice.

"I basically relied on my affinities," she said, "for that extra sense they can give you, rather than doing actual spellcasting."

"Given your sense for weather," Xerak said, "I'm guessing that at least one of your affinities is for Air. Do you remember what you were told when you were tested?"

Vereez drooped her ears, obviously embarrassed. "I'm sorry. My parents repeated so many times that I really didn't have anything more than a touch of talent, just enough to make me a danger to myself and others, that I just shrugged it off. That 'danger to myself and others' was why they were arranging for me to have any training at all, and the repeated warnings didn't make me at all eager to experiment."

Xerak shook his head so hard that his mane swept side to side. "Another of those convenient lies you were told. I feel sure of that. Well, affinities are overrated, which is why I haven't been worrying about where Teg's might lie. Still . . . Are your swords here or aboard *Slicewind*?"

"Here," Vereez replied. "Nefnet said I could do nonimpact sword drills in my PT, so I didn't lose all my flexibility and muscle tone in my injured arm."

"Can you get them?" Xerak asked. "Or at least one of them? I'd like to take a closer look."

"Sure," Vereez replied, and returned a moment later, carrying one of the slightly curved-bladed weapons in its ornate sheath. She pulled the blade out, revealing the shining pink-gold of what Teg knew was magically hardened copper. Wordlessly, Vereez handed the sword to Xerak.

Xerak inspected both the blade and hilt minutely. Then, with a quick glance at Vereez for permission, he unscrewed the glass ball at the pommel, slid off the haft, and inspected the tang of the blade.

"This sword is very like my staff," he said as he reassembled the weapon, and returned it to Vereez. "That is, it isn't magical as such, except that it is intended to channel magic—wind magic, lightning magic, specifically."

"That probably explains why the blades are copper," Meg said. "Copper and copper alloy are the chosen metals for lightning rods."

"Can I ask where you got those swords?" Xerak asked.

Vereez sheathed the bare blade. "From your mother, actually, shortly after we decided to go to Hettua Shrine. I'd gone by Fardowsi-toh's shop to wait for you, and your mother told me that she had a 'good luck' present for me. When she gave the swords to me, I figured my parents had told her I'd been studying twin sword style, but now I wonder if she thought these swords would suit me because she knew or guessed that I had magic similar to my mother's."

Xerak shrugged. "I can't speak for my mom. Maybe she was just feeling sentimental, but she's rarely sentimental about business, and these would have been an expensive gift. I wonder if your parents knew your affinity and told her? Or maybe Mom guessed based on what she knew about your mother's magic. Affinities often run in families—as do oppositions."

"Maybe." Vereez pinned her ears back and wrinkled her muzzle in a snarl. "One thing I'm sure of is that my parents didn't anonymously provide this gift. Fardowsi-toh made me promise that I wouldn't show the swords to Inehem or Zarrq. She hinted strongly that I should keep them under wraps until you and I were well away from Rivers Meet. I loved them right off, and was happy to agree. I was already pretty angry at my parents, so keeping the swords a secret was easy to do."

Peg broke the uncomfortable silence that followed. "The glass balls at the pommels may be more than ornamental. My second husband, Nash, collected antique yard ornaments, and I remember him saying that the glass balls on old-fashioned lightning rods were meant to shatter when the rod took a direct hit—an indication that the rod's grounding wires should be checked to make sure they hadn't been burned through. Maybe these are just decorative, but if they crack or break, I'd be sure to replace them."

"Glass is also highly nonconductive," Meg added, "so the glass balls may be practical—some form of insulation."

Xerak nodded. "The similarity to lightning rods makes sense. My spear is resistant to burning. That isn't to say that it wouldn't burn if I dropped it in a volcano, but..."

After learning the traits of Vereez's swords, Xerak incorporated their use into Vereez's training routine, showing her how she could store mana in the swords, much as he did in his staff.

The delay before their appointment at the Jaxine Museum repository also had the benefit of giving Vereez's wounded arm—as well as the smaller wounds suffered by the rest of the group—time to heal. Once Nefnet gave her okay, Vereez insisted on practicing swordplay as well, and Grunwold was happy to be her partner. Peg also joined in, saying that since there might be a chance she was going to need to use a sword again, she'd better stay in shape.

Meg and Teg found much to occupy themselves within the ruined Library, and although they decided to stay away from the repository, in case they encountered something even more dangerous than the acid bats, there were plenty of books, scrolls, tablets, data crystals, and the like to be sorted through. Emsehu usually acted as bodyguard when they ventured even a few steps away from the reception hall.

Grunwold wouldn't let either Xerak or Kaj lose themselves in their more sedentary occupations. Nefnet had shown them where the staff restroom had been located, and he was determined that before *Slicewind* departed in search of Uten Kekui, they would have cleared out at least this area, which included a shower and tub. Peg appointed herself head of the team, saying that she'd noticed that the inquisitors, children of wealth and privilege that they were, could be inclined to shirk on cleaning duty.

"You can't leave it all up to the abau," she scolded when Xerak protested at being asked to clean a toilet. "It's about time you acquired a few more practical skills, in any case."

Perhaps shamed by Peg's comment, Vereez offered to help, too, but Grunwold insisted that mucking around in dirt, grime, and who knew what latent magical hazards would not be good for her healing arm. Since Nefnet supported him in this, Vereez gave in.

Therefore, when not doing PT on her arm or practicing sword play or reviving her magical skills, Vereez did her best to make friends with Brunni, and to reconnect with the aunt she had thought was dead. Once Grunwold made clear to Brunni that he liked Vereez-toh "very, very much" Brunni seemed more willing to make friends. Once, briefly, she even wore the dress that Vereez had bought for her.

Even with teaching, researching, and outings for hunting, fishing, and foraging, as the days went by, Xerak grew increasingly tense, so Teg was relieved when the week that was only tomorrow in her home world concluded.

"I hope our plan works," she confided in Peg as they were getting ready to leave. "If it doesn't, I wouldn't put it past Xerak to decide he needs to go, break into Jaxine Museum, and steal the Nest himself."

"I know," Peg agreed. "Why do you think Grunwold started taking him out hunting? Xerak's practically crackling with nervous energy."

She and Peg went back a few hours early, so Peg could send e-mails and make a few phone calls. They picked a time when Teg's cat sitter, Felicity, was highly unlikely to come through, but Teg found herself thinking that maybe she should "make other arrangements" for Thought and Memory, so she could count on her house being vacant.

Of course, that would lead to other problems, like stopping the mail. She decided that making a decision could wait. Felicity was happy to be earning a little extra, and who knew how long Teg would be spending part of her life in another world? The Nest was the last part of Ba Djed of the Weaver they needed to find. Xerak's inquisition would soon be answered, and then—she guessed—there would be no need for the three mentors to keep going back and forth.

The inquisitors probably wouldn't even want us around. I mean, they're happy to have three old ladies hanging out now, because they need us, but why would they when they're no longer "held back"?

Teg put that out of her mind as well, aware that she had been doing a lot of that lately.

An hour before their appointment at the repository, she and Peg set out for the Jaxine Museum. As on the memorable night that Teg had brought Vereez through, walking seemed like the best idea and the February weather wasn't too terribly unpleasant.

"I think I've gotten in better shape," Peg commented as she walked briskly along at Teg's side. "But I don't think what we've been through is exactly a training program that can be recommended to the local gym."

Teg laughed agreement. "We've spent over sixty days there, but only nine have passed here. No... That would be really hard to explain, especially since even if our bodies' short-term demands seem to be tied to Over Where—meals, sleep, like that—for larger issues..."

"Like aging," Peg chuckled.

"Meg's request that we pick up her prescription has me thinking about things like taking medications," Teg said. "Originally, I'd decided to take about half of what I would, but after a while I backed off on mine even more. I have a feeling that—maybe it's only hope—that we're still on this world's slower timetable."

Peg nodded. "I know what you mean. My hair hasn't needed a trim or dye job, for example, but usually after two months—our timetable Over Where—I'd need at least a trim and tint."

Teg ran a hand over her own purple-dyed punk cut. "Me, too, and I didn't even have your foresight in getting my hair done right before we left."

"Well, whatever the reason," Peg said. "The time difference works well for us. If any of my kids ask about my new buffness, I'll enjoy coming up with an explanation."

"You would," Teg agreed. She pointed. "There's Jaxine Museum. Remember, this time, let me make the explanations."

"Aye, aye, Captain!"

Jaxine Museum was housed in a relatively new building across the street from the main campus of Taima University. The old museum building had been prettier, but was no longer suited for displays in the modern mode. Now the old museum's lower floors had been converted into classrooms, the upper into greatly coveted office space.

Most visitors to the stylish new museum appreciated the ample parking, the glass-walled atrium which housed a café that was rapidly becoming a destination in its own right, as well as the displays. Such visitors usually had no idea that below ground level an ultramodern repository occupied a series of rooms: some equipped with climate-controlled cases, some holding merely rank after rank of heavy-duty metal shelves.

Teg avoided the grand main entrance, leading Peg around to a much more utilitarian door near a loading dock. There she showed her ID and explained that she had an appointment. She'd just finished signing in both herself and Peg when a graduate student arrived to escort them. He introduced himself as Dan Reitz, and added that he was doing his dissertation on fabric curation and restoration.

Dan Reitz was probably older than Xerak, but something about his scruffy ginger beard and scraggly hair reminded Teg of the lion-headed wizard. From how Peg was trying not to giggle, she guessed she wasn't the only one.

After escorting Teg and Peg to a well-lit room with a conference table, Dan left, promising to return with the appropriate file container. The promised light box was already set up. Peg took out Teg's digital camera and a handful of junk from her purse, and did some practice shots. They were viewing these on Teg's laptop when Dan returned, rolling a dolly on which not only the box they wanted but also some others Teg had requested as cover had been stacked. Teg helped unload them, then thanked Dan.

"I'm sure you have research of your own to do. I'll call when we're done."

Sadly, Dan did not accept this dismissal. "I need to stay here. Sorry, it's one of the more annoying bits of museum policy."

"Must be since my day," Teg said, shrugging as if this didn't matter. "We used to take boxes home."

"Yeah," Dan said. "I hear that all the time from senior faculty and research associates. I think the policy was changed when the new museum was built. I guess they had to justify these fancy labs."

"No problem," Teg said. "Make yourself comfortable. We're going to be a while."

She and Peg both donned lightweight gloves, so as to not leave skin oils on the artifacts—and to avoid direct contact with the Nest. This done, Teg set out to deliberately bore their affable young guardian. At first Dan was eager to assist, doubtless believing he could speed them along. Initially, Teg encouraged him to help unpack items and line them on the table, although she was careful to make sure she took out any bag she thought might hold the Nest. Then she became pickier regarding the sort of shots she needed. After Teg made Peg take five pictures of the same spearhead, Dan obviously realized they weren't going anywhere soon.

When his phone buzzed, he excused himself to a seat at the far end of the conference table, took the call, then explained he needed to look up a few things for his caller, and pulled out a tablet as he did so.

"No problem," Teg said. She waited until Dan was well and thoroughly involved in whatever he was looking at, then opened the box that had been her goal all along.

The black jet Nest was wrapped in tissue, which had in turn been encased in a Mylar bag. Teg took it out, along with the arrowheads that had been her excuse for requesting this particular box. Using the light box for cover, Peg exchanged the real Nest for Kaj's forgery. Peg scooped up the "real" black tulip and slid it into her pocket with the confidence of an accomplished pickpocket. There was a slight clicking sound as she sealed the small enshrouding container she had placed there earlier.

I wonder which one of Peg's kids was into sleight of hand, Teg wondered. *Or maybe Peg learned that herself back in the days when she probably thought of the "squares" as fair game if she needed dough.*

As Teg continued to request photos, commenting for Dan's benefit that things were going faster now that she'd figured out exactly what angles she wanted, she was all too aware that, including travel time, the four or so hours she and Peg had so far spent on their heist amounted to over a day in the other world. Nonetheless, Teg didn't want to risk any suspicious behavior. If all went well, no one would open this box for years to come, and even if they did, no one should be able to tell that the "sculpted item, possibly pendant" wrapped and bagged and placed in the box had an origin much farther away than ancient Egypt.

Eventually, Teg and Peg took their leave, thanking Dan, who doubtless would complain about what a complete waste of his time their visit had been. They were almost to the exit when a man's voice said, "Excuse me, ladies. I'd like to speak with you."

⁂CHAPTER SEVEN⁂

Teg's heart leapt so hard that her hand flew to her chest. She couldn't keep from jumping a little as she turned. Excuses raced through her mind: "We didn't take anything. Check the box inventories." "We're in a hurry. If you don't mind . . ." "My friend's pocket? What are you talking about?"

She turned. A man who looked vaguely familiar was emerging from one of the side offices. He laughed uncomfortably.

"I'm sorry. I didn't mean to startle you. I thought I recognized you." He paused. "I remember! We shared an elevator ride a few days ago. You were taking an old lady home to her apartment in the same building where I live."

Teg mentally cursed that her darker skin and mixed-race features were distinctive among Taima's predominantly white population. She remembered how astonished the inquisitors, used to the variety of appearances Over Where, where even in the same family different animal heads were common, had been that such things as skin color would matter.

Of course, if you wanted to blend in, doing purple highlights on your hair wasn't exactly the best idea.

She forced a weak smile and put out her hand. "Of course! I remember. We held the elevator for you. You said you were a new resident."

The man beamed, obviously pleased to be remembered. "That's right! I've looked for you since, but hadn't seen you. What an amazing coincidence to meet you here."

Relief flooded Teg's system so intensely that her knees actually felt weak.

"Are you associated with Jaxine Museum?" she managed.

"Indirectly," her persistent acquaintance said. "I'm a new hire in paleo-osteology. Oh, I forget myself. I'm Heath Morton."

Heath Morton was clearly hoping to get her name, so, reluctantly, Teg said, "I'm Tessa Brown. Archeology. I'm on sabbatical this term. I stopped by to photograph some material for a possible paper. This is Peg Gallegos. She was helping with the photography."

Heath Morton shook hands with both of them, then Teg said, "I'm sorry, but I promised Peg I'd get her back before her next appointment. If you would excuse us?"

"I hope to see you again," Heath said. "Do let me know if you're coming back to do more research. I'd love to chat."

Teg made a few vague promises, signed them out, and prayed to high heaven until, at last, they were out in the brisk winter air. Her heart didn't stop beating overly fast until they were safely outside, and well into the walk home.

"I believe you have an admirer," Peg chuckled. "I saw him glancing at your hand, making sure there wasn't a wedding ring."

"Please!" Teg said, hurrying her steps a little faster. "Dr. Morton's new to town and probably lonely. I bet he hits on every woman he meets."

"I should have told him about the book club," Peg mused. "That's a good way to meet people."

"Don't you dare," Teg threatened. To put an end to the conversation, she lit up a cigarette. That reminded her to buy another carton, as well as treats for the left-behinds, when they picked up Meg's prescriptions. While Teg was in the drugstore, Peg went to the pizzeria next door and bought them each a large slice of pizza, which they devoured as they walked back to Teg's house.

"I wish we could bring some pizza back for the rest of them," Peg said, popping the last bite into her mouth, "but it's probably not a good idea. No microwave for reheating. Cold pizza's good, but I'm not sure that's the best first experience. Maybe I'll need to figure out how to make some. Difficult without a proper oven, and the one in *Slicewind*'s galley is just too small."

"Anyhow, based on what we just picked up, Meg watches her

cholesterol," Teg added. "It would hardly be fair to tempt her, right?"

She glanced at her watch. They had plenty of time before Felicity was due, but she'd feel better when this was over and they were safely back Over Where. And in any case, she was all too aware of the passage of time to relax. They'd been over here less than six hours, but in the other world over a day and three quarters would have gone by. Xerak was probably ready to come through after them, and that would never do.

Thought and Memory were asleep on Teg's bed when they came in. Thought opened a lazy eye and sniffed to check if they had pizza for her. When she saw no treats were forthcoming, she resumed her nap. Memory's only response was a hardly visible ear twitch.

Peg gave her phone a quick check, reassured herself that nothing catastrophic had happened in the half hour since she had last done so, and nodded to Teg.

"Let's go back Over Where!"

They stepped back into the other world to find everyone gathered around one of the long tables in the Library's entry area sharing a meal. Xerak leapt to his feet, nearly knocking his chair over backward.

"Did you get it?"

For answer, Peg put her hand in her pocket and came out with the enshrouding container holding the Nest.

"Everything went smooth as silk," she reported proudly.

A very few minutes were spent telling their tale, and even those were clearly too many for Xerak. He listened, pacing back and forth, ears twitching, tail snapping. Peg had clearly intended to use telling about their adventures to tease Teg some more about her admirer, but she took pity on the young man.

"What now?" Peg asked instead. "Do we put the three parts of Ba Djed together?"

"Wait!" Ohent shook her head vigorously, making the copper coins on her veil jangle to Brunni's dancing delight. "Do we know what will happen if we do that?"

Xerak replied, "I don't care. Sapphire Wind says it needs the full power it will gain from a reassembled Ba Djed in order to trace Uten

Kekui. The verse Teg recited when she and the other mentors arrived promised us the Library would be where we would find if not solutions to our inquisition, at least something of significant aid. This have proven true for both Grunwold and Vereez. At last, my turn has come."

"Verse?" Ranpeti asked. "I believe Vereez mentioned one, but I don't believe I've heard it."

Aware that Xerak was fuming, Teg recited:

Curing one ill who is not sick
Finding the victim of a cruel trick
Easing an ache that cuts to the quick

All of this and more you will find
After you pass through the doorways
Of the Library of the Sapphire Wind

"Mine is certainly an ache that cuts to the quick," Xerak said fiercely, "and has for over a year. Now, with the help of Ba Djed, Sapphire Wind may be able to help me find what will help heal that ache."

"Nonetheless, wizard lad," Ohent persisted, "that doesn't answer my question. What will happen when we reassemble this Ba Djed of the Weaver? Will the Archived suddenly appear among us? What sort of new powers will Sapphire Wind command? I don't think it's unfair or unwise to ask such things."

Meg's lips parted, but Sapphire Wind was the speaker. "I will not unarchive those I have stored until I have prepared for their coming. As for what powers I may gain? Why do you fear me so, Ohent? Did I not fail to stop you and your associates when you robbed me over two decades ago? Surely this is proof that I am neither omnipotent nor omniscient."

"You weren't pissed off then, either," Ohent replied tartly. "We slipped in under your guard, and you weren't aware of us until everything went wrong. Does that mean you resent us any less now? I don't think so."

"I could say that I am grateful to you," Sapphire Wind replied, "for showing me a weakness in my defenses. I assure you, should the

Library be reopened, should I continue as custodian, I will not make that mistake again. As for now, I have no desire to harm any of you, for you have been my benefactors. I am as eager as Xerak to see Ba Djed of the Weaver reassembled, for then I will be as I was always meant to be."

"I believe Sapphire Wind is speaking honestly," Meg added in her own voice. "It is both more and less complex than you may believe, but it is without human malice."

"Now," Xerak growled, "no more delays."

The lion-headed wizard drew on gloves, then removed the Spindle from its enshrouding container, and set it on the table. He snapped out his hand for the Nest in a fashion that reminded Teg of a surgeon demanding a scalpel. Peg spilled the Nest into his palm from the enshrouding container into which they had put it back at Jaxine Museum. Xerak threaded it into place on the Spindle, then held out his hand for the shining bronze Bird.

Ohent paused. "I wish I felt sure this wasn't going to create more trouble. If you'd had my dreams these last twenty-some years, you might feel differently about the wisdom of playing with this thing."

"I have waited long enough!" Xerak's words came out in a full lion's roar.

Chuckling to herself at some joke only she understood, Ohent reached into her bodice and pulled out the little brocade bag in which she kept the Bird in its container. She wrapped her fingers tightly around the bag, as if in a final embrace, then put it into Xerak's palm. With no hesitation at all, he took out the Bird, then threaded it on as a cap to bind Ba Djed together. Finality in every motion, he set the reassembled artifact on the table.

After Ohent's paranoid outburst, Teg fully expected something dramatic to occur. Sparks at least. Colored auras. Flames. But nothing happened. The assembled Ba Djed of the Weaver just sat there. Xerak spoke to the air.

"So . . . Here it is, Sapphire Wind. Three pieces reunited as one. Tell me where I can find my master!"

Peg looked at him. "Say, please?"

Xerak stared, his eyes so wide that the whites were visible around the gold. He leaned on the table, claws gouging the wood.

Peg raised her eyebrows. "Well?"

Xerak began to wheeze, then to laugh, a genuine laugh, hearty and full-throated. Then he turned to Meg and made a bow so low that the trailing ends of his mane swept the floor.

"Please?"

The smile was Meg's, stern yet approving, the smile of a librarian to a child who has remembered not to shout in the Quiet Rooms. The voice was Sapphire Wind's.

"Again, let us use the Font of Sight."

They trooped in, taking what were becoming their accustomed seats within the pearlescent sphere. Even Kaj drifted in to join them, leaning against the doorway. But Ohent's attention—as was everyone else's—was focused on the Font of Sight.

The image that took shape above the chalice was of a jagged rock formation set in the center of a powerfully swirling whirlpool. Above the rock formation, obscuring its peak, were dark clouds from which lightning crackled. After they had time to accept the unwelcoming fury of the location, the image pulled in for a closer view, showing that what from a distance had appeared to be natural breaks in the formation were actually the outlines of an irregularly shaped door.

"No wonder I couldn't find him," Xerak whispered. "That place doesn't exist!"

"Wait!" Sapphire Wind called into the uproar that followed. "Please. I have more."

Silence fell, broken only by Brunni, who whimpered, disturbed by the reaction of the adults. The image over the Font changed, showing a tall building, vaguely familiar. Teg realized that she'd seen it as an impressive landmark on the skyline during their visits to the city of Rivers Meet.

"That's the Spiral Tower at Zisurru University," Vereez said. "Uten Kekui-va can't be holed up there, can he?"

The image broke, dissolved. The next thing they saw was what looked remarkably like standard safe deposit boxes, if such were painted a flashy teal and elaborately ornamented with arcane glyphs, rather than being flat metal, painted drab grey. The boxes were ornamented with two different sorts of glyphs. The first type, inscribed slightly above the box itself, Teg's translation spell rendered into numbers and letters: clearly the code designating location.

"Xerak," Grunwold grumbled, "if you forgot to check your mail all this time, and there's a message from your master there, telling you he just went home to visit his sick mother, I'm going to hit you—hard."

Xerak shook his head. "That's not my mail box. That's a rental. Look!"

A ghostly collage of glyphs was becoming visible. Various glyphs began lighting in sequence. Xerak muttered a string of syllables the translation spell left unintelligible, but this time, rather than a spell, Teg fancied it was a particularly colorful profanity.

"So, all you need to do is push those symbols in order?" Peg asked hopefully. "I was always good at Simon."

Xerak ignored her, but Ohent replied, "I wish it was so easy. That's a wizard lock. Unless you can shape those glyphs, you can't work the combination. I'm no expert, but I can tell you that those are far above beginner grade."

Meg pulled out her journal and offered it and a pen to Xerak. "Here, copy those down."

Xerak nodded thanks and began doing so. Vereez helped, reciting the different glyph names and noting their colors. Fortunately, Sapphire Wind could "replay" the image, so at least they were certain that they had transcribed correctly. When they'd done a final check, Xerak let loose a gusty sigh.

"Thank you, Sapphire Wind, Vereez. That should do it."

"Are you going to explain what we saw?" Meg asked mildly. "Or is this some wizard's secret?"

Xerak looked curiously at her. "You don't know?"

"I don't. I am loaning Sapphire Wind my vocal cords. Sometimes I have flashes of insight that I suspect are the Wind's thoughts bleeding over into my own, but I am as ignorant as the rest of us mentors—and very curious. What did you mean about that place in the first vision not existing?"

Xerak moved as if to reach for his flask, then stopped himself. "It's a place I've only seen described, a place wizards seek if they wish initiation into the deepest of secrets. Most agree that it doesn't really exist, that it's a state of mind, not an actual place."

"So Uten Kekui-va went there?" Grunwold asked. "I wonder why he didn't tell you?"

Xerak shook his head. "I have no idea." But there was something odd in his tone that made Teg wonder if he had a suspicion.

Vereez said quickly, so quickly that Teg wondered if Vereez also wondered what Xerak might be hiding, "That second image looked a lot more attainable. We know where Zisurru University is. We can sail there in a few days."

"But can Xerafu Akeru work the combination?" Ohent asked, her tone not quite taunting. "Back in the days when I was an 'extraction agent' I learned about such locks. There is no way to get around them. Neither counter-spell, nor physical violence. Forget that lovely magical key you found. It won't work either. And failing to open the lock or trying to take shortcuts can have devastating consequences."

"Such as?" Peg asked.

Ohent laughed without humor. "Anything from killing the caster outright to draining all available magical energy to create curses, illness, disability, or idiocy in the one who failed to undo the spell correctly. The caster sometimes is permitted more than one attempt because, after all, even wizards can make mistakes. Sometimes, however, only one attempt is permitted."

"That's major," Grunwold said, awed. "Did any of your team ever learn to undo those?"

"Not a one," Ohent answered with finality. "The closest we came to beating one of those locks was a job where we physically removed not only the lockbox but also the wall surrounding it. Never did learn if the fellow we did the job for ever got it open."

Xerak had been absorbed in his own thoughts. Now he turned to Ohent.

"I don't know if I can open it. I certainly couldn't have a year ago, but my search for my master forced me to learn many things. During the first months following Uten Kekui's disappearance, I stayed in his home, immersed myself in study, thinking that his vanishing might be a test of my diligence. Even after I felt certain that I needed to seek him, not wait, I continued to advance my studies. I'm willing to make the attempt."

He looked at Grunwold. "Wanna give me a lift to Rivers Meet, pal?"

Grunwold grinned at him. "Sure. I mean, how could I miss watching you blow yourself up?"

"We're coming, too," Peg said. "I think this is part of the whole mentoring thing."

"Xerak, you helped me on my inquisition," Vereez stated in a tone that brooked no disagreement. "Don't you dare think you're leaving me behind. Besides, haven't you promised to help me learn magic? What sort of apprentice would I be if I abandoned my master when he was searching for his own master?"

"Not to be less comradely," Ranpeti said, "but if Nefnet and Sapphire Wind will continue to host us, Brunni and I will stay here."

"I will remain as well," Ohent said. "Even in the short time we have been here, Nefnet's treatments have done me a great deal of good."

"Mother," Kaj said, "you won't mind if I go with them?" He looked at the three inquisitors. "If you'll let me, that is. I—until I met you, watched you—I didn't realize it, but I'm held back, as well. I promise to follow orders and all that, just like I did when we went looking for Brunni."

Vereez froze, her lack of expression showing more intensity than any cry of welcome or refusal could. Xerak shrugged. Grunwold studied Kaj.

"If our mentors agree, sure. But don't try to pull anything stupid."

Kaj met Grunwold's gaze squarely. "Not stupid. Not opportunistic. Look... I feel that somehow, I belong with you three. Maybe it's because our parents were all idiots together, but I do."

"Yeah," Grunwold agreed. "We at least share idiot parents. That's true. Ohent keeps talking about what's owed her, but you've had it worse than the rest of us. We at least grew up in comfort and blissful ignorance."

Teg wondered at Grunwold's seemingly easy acceptance of his rival for Vereez into their company.

Does Grunwold love Vereez so much that he's willing to do anything to see her happy? Or does he realize that Kaj absent is a much bigger temptation to Vereez than Kaj present? Or does Grunwold really feel a bond with Kaj, reluctant as he might be to admit it? More than the others, Kaj and Grunwold share parents who have paid for years for mistakes made when they were too young to be wise.

The company left early the next morning. Brunni cried when

Grunwold gave her a farewell hug, brightened when he promised to bring her something pretty. Nefnet, Ranpeti, and Ohent seemed to have no regrets at being left behind. Teg wondered if Meg would have liked to join them. In some indefinable way, she seemed happier when they were at the Library.

However, Meg showed no tendency to linger when they went outside of the doors of the Library of the Sapphire Wind. The rickety ladder they'd used for their first several ascents and descents between the cleft into which the Library had dropped and what had been the main plaza had been replaced with two new, stronger ladders made from peeled saplings with the rungs lashed into place. Teg was reminded of the ladders used by the Pueblo Indians of the American Southwest.

And for good reason. Here, as there, the ladders serve two purposes: making it easier to go between elevations, and making defense easier, because the ladders can be quickly removed.

Slicewind rested on the plaza pavement, near the statue of Dmen Qeres, the Library's founder. As they approached the sky sailer, the eyes painted near the bow seemed to widen a bit, as if the ship had been drowsing, catlike, in the sun. Grunwold accepted a foothold from Kaj, then vaulted aboard and lowered a boarding ladder.

"All aboard for Zisurru University!" Heru squawked from where he was perched on the crow's nest. "Batten down the hatches!"

"Not a great idea, you idiot xuxu," Grunwold said affectionately, grunting a little as he hauled a bag of taga fruit, picked from a tree they'd come across when picking herbs. The fruit resembled grapefruit in size, Jackson Pollock's art in color, and were sweet-tart, more like lime than grapefruit. Vereez loved taga fruit juice, which was doubtless why Grunwold was going to all this trouble.

Peg took charge. "Okay, me buckaroos. All three boys in the bow cabin. You won't all be sleeping at the same time, so you can work out how to hot bunk it if you must. We mentors will keep the stern cabin. Vereez, you keep the little cabin near the mast."

"I'd be happy to share with one of you ladies," Vereez said almost too quickly, clearly asserting that her having the only single didn't mean she wanted Kaj to come calling. "Or if I'm on duty, and someone wants some privacy, I'm fine with the space being used for that."

Fleetingly, Teg considered suggesting that Xerak could bunk with Vereez, since he was uninterested in women and could chaperone as well, but decided against that; although Grunwold and Kaj were getting along well enough, it was probably not a great idea to push the relationship.

"Thank you for your offer, Vereez," Meg said. "It's not that I'm not very fond of all of you, but there are definitely times I would like to be alone."

After that, there was a flurry of activity as fresh fruit, herbs, and fish gathered during their layover in the vicinity of the Library were stowed. Peg recruited Xerak and Vereez to help cut up vegetables, then help assemble the shish kabob-style meal on a skewer they would cook above deck on a little hibachi-like grill for dinner that night. Xerak tried to slink away, but Peg was determined that the young people help with routine chores, and Xerak in particular was inclined to pay little attention to what he ate.

If he was a twenty-something in our world, he'd be the type of academic who eats cold condensed soup out of a can while leaning over the sink, his mind in the clouds.

Vereez simply didn't know how to cook, and had only gradually accepted that meals did not appear by magic. Teg decided to set a good example, and pitched in, so that, even with seven people to feed, the task was completed relatively rapidly.

After Peg put a couscous-like grain on to soak, she dismissed her assistants. Since the day was fine, everyone gathered above decks. The three mentors settled on the benches built over the stern lockers. Peg pulled out her knitting. Meg took out her journal. She'd already sliced out the pages showing the pattern of the wizard locks and given them to Xerak, who was now secluded in the bow, apparently deeply immersed in study.

Grunwold turned the wheel over to Vereez, so he could show Kaj what the various lines did, and teach him bits of nautical terminology, so he'd know what to do if called upon. Kaj was a good student, but from time to time Teg noticed him gazing at the surrounding sky in evident wonder.

Sky sailing is still new and wonderful to him, newer than to those of us who at least grew up in a world with airplanes.

Instead of resuming her notetaking, Meg spoke softly, as if half to herself. "Now that Ba Djed of the Weaver is intact, Sapphire Wind plans to try training one of the Library's guardian creatures to act as spokesperson: possibly an efindon, that is, a lizard parrot. Efindon seem to share with the parrots of our world a facility for imitating speech, although they are not actual speakers, such as xuxu, like Heru. In this way, Sapphire Wind will be able to talk with its new residents more easily. It's possible that I will be freed from interpretation duties by the time we return."

"Are you sorry?" Peg asked.

"A little," Meg replied. "It has been interesting. However, I won't mind being spared all the suspicious glances. Honestly! You'd think I'd been possessed by a demon."

"Weren't you?" Teg asked dryly.

Meg chuckled. "Well, maybe possessed, but not by a demon. Sapphire Wind is really very nice—especially given all it has been through. It has been like a soul without a body. Now it can begin to rebuild."

"Did it give you any sense of what it's going to do about the Archived?" Peg asked. "I don't suppose they can remain filed forever."

"Technically," Meg replied, "I believe they could, especially now that Ba Djed is restored and Sapphire Wind can draw on its power. Morally, though, that's another issue."

"And one that, I suppose, isn't our job to solve," Peg said. "Still, I feel as if the fate of the Archived is tied up in some way with what our inquisitors are doing, even if just as a loose end."

Crewing *Slicewind* was definitely easier with Kaj's help. He knew nothing about sailing, but those magnificent muscles weren't just for show. Teg tried not to shadow Vereez but, as far as she could tell, Kaj wasn't making a fresh play for the young woman. Indeed, he seemed to be trying his best to demonstrate his better qualities, including stepping in to help with the washing up and other such routine chores, something all three of the inquisitors—coming from privileged backgrounds as they did—constantly had to be reminded about.

Teg noticed that he often hung about while Xerak was putting his two apprentices through their training, and wondered if he had some latent ability or if he was simply bored.

After all, as I know all too well, when you're used to a full-time job, leisure time can get old. Kaj doesn't seem to be much of a reader, and he can only spend so much time carving. At least he's joined in weapons training. I wouldn't be surprised if before long Grunwold decides to show him some basic sword moves.

Rotations for night watch were shifted to omit Vereez, since she worked hard during the day both on PT for her wounded arm and magical training. Therefore, one night Teg found herself sitting beneath the stars with Xerak.

"I don't mind if you light up," he said.

Teg pulled out her pipe and rubbed her fingers over the elaborate carvings that turned the stone bowl into a representation of a peony-like flower. "I'm thinking about quitting smoking. I notice you've been cutting back on your drinking."

"Yeah..." Xerak checked their heading, spun the wheel, then set what Teg couldn't help but thinking of as the autopilot. "Hey, Teg, from something Vereez said, I've gathered you're good at keeping secrets. I have something I need to get off my chest."

"Is it something that will put someone else at risk?" Teg asked. "I don't keep that sort of secret."

"No. It's about what happened before my master disappeared. I've never told anyone—not even Kuvekt-lial or any of the others I asked to help me find my master. Maybe it's not important to anyone except me, but now that we might find Uten Kekui, and might at least have an idea what happened, I need to talk about it."

"Sounds like you'd better," Teg agreed. "I know you've been reviewing those glyphs and have them down cold, but that's going to be a dangerous spell to work. Better you don't have anything distracting you."

Xerak checked *Slicewind*'s heading again, then slouched down to sit on the deck. Even when he was comfortable, he didn't say anything, so Teg messed with getting her pipe lit, figuring the bit of business would make him feel less watched.

Eventually, his voice low, Xerak started talking. "Believe it or not, I wasn't always a drunk. I always liked a drink—I won't deny that. I started young. My parents were always entertaining both buyers and sellers, and early on I learned that while my parents couldn't be fooled, most of those they hosted didn't realize if their wine had a little water in it.

"I think the first time I got really trashed was with Grunwold, actually. A harvest festival. I still don't like beer much... That taught me about limits. But when I started studying magic, I also learned that there was another side to those limits."

"Hang on," Teg said. "I've been wondering about magical studies. From what you told Vereez, her parents may have actually led her to believe she had less talent than she does. Grunwold, on the other hand, accepts pretty calmly that he has no talent at all. Do they test you in school?"

"That's right. Magical ability is a lot like having another sense, but it's also a lot like... I don't know, physical ability? Basically, if you don't have it, you can't do it, but how it manifests varies a lot. Some people are great at running races but lousy wrestlers. Some have a great eye for shooting a bow but are fumble fingered with a sword. Like that, but different."

"You're extraordinarily talented, though," Teg said. "Right?"

"I am. Even when I was so young I could barely talk, I could see magical energies. By the time I was walking, I was beginning to manipulate them—clumsy stuff, hardly even worth calling spells, but my parents decided I'd better get training and soon. First a tutor, then classes as part of my regular education, then the plan was that I'd go to Zisurru University, probably as an early admission. But I met my master and everything changed."

"I don't think you've ever talked about how you met Uten Kekui-va," Teg said, wanting to learn as much as she could about this enigmatic figure, especially now that it seemed they might actually meet him.

"He came to my school to visit one of the faculty—a friend of his who taught language arts. I was late with an assignment and went by his friend's office to drop it off and make my excuses. Uten Kekui saw something in me. He asked his friend a few questions. That led to my being offered a chance to study with him the following summer.

"My parents were very pleased. Although he was pretty much a hermit, Uten Kekui had an amazing reputation. Even better, his fees were minimal, just enough to cover room and board. The class included me and three other kids my age.

"At the end of the summer, my master went to my parents and

asked if I could study full-time with him. He promised I would be taught all my subjects, not just magic. He implied that there would be other students but, in fact, there were very few, all older than me, the oldest being a girl who was going to enroll for advanced study at Zisurru University the following year."

Xerak glanced at the stars as Teg herself might glance at her watch, and sighed. "I'd love to tell you about those early years, but I need to skip ahead if I'm going to get to what's bugging me. Two things, basically. One, I learned that if I drank just enough to be almost drunk, my ability to read magical energies, and so manipulate them, jumped. Two, I fell in love."

"With your master," Teg said, voicing a conclusion reached long before.

"That's right. I wanted so much to please him, to be the best not only of his current students, but of any student he'd ever had, that I started drinking regularly. Uten Kekui wasn't a fool. He caught on and called me to his office to tell me that I had to stop getting drunk or he was sending me home. I was devastated. I told him that I loved him, that I was only doing it to impress him.

"He told me that he knew I loved him, but he didn't love me—not that way, as a son, maybe, but not the way I wanted to be loved. Then he reminded me of his ultimatum and dismissed me. I was crushed. And I was angry. I don't get angry very often, but when I do, it's bad."

Teg tried blowing a smoke ring. It came out pretty well.

"So I've noticed."

Xerak laughed. "Yeah. Well. So what did I do? I went to my room and got completely blitzed. I had a confused idea of working some sort of charm or setting back time, maybe both. I can't remember now. Eventually, I passed out. When I woke, I had the mother and father of all hangovers. That's why it was over a full day before I learned that my master had vanished."

"Uten Kekui-va didn't tell anyone else where he was going?"

"There wasn't anyone else there at the time. I think that's why he picked then to dress me down about my drinking. Leelee, that senior student I mentioned, came back first. She helped me search, and eventually insisted we report Master missing. After a week or so, the other students left. I stayed.

"First I quit drinking cold turkey and applied myself to my

studies. I was certain Master had left to make me show him what I could do. Stupid, I know, but how couldn't I believe that his vanishing didn't have something to do with our fight? Then . . . Well, you more or less know about how I spent something like a year searching for him before I decided to go to Hettua Shrine. On the way I teamed up with Vereez, then Grunwold. And here we are . . ."

Teg nodded. "I can see how believing your argument led to Uten Kekui-va's disappearing—especially now that we may be catching up to him—would distract you. How do you feel about your master now?"

"You mean, do I still love him?" Xerak sighed. "More than ever. It's stupid, but I can't let go."

"He didn't ever—encourage you?" Teg tried to put images of a younger, fluffier Xerak in the hands of a pedophile out of her head.

"Not by word or deed," Xerak replied firmly. "A couple of the girls had crushes on him, too, but I watched—he never did anything with them either. I think that's why I dared dream."

"You still hope, don't you?" Teg said. "That he was waiting for you to grow up or something like that."

Xerak's furred face couldn't blush, but the way his ears fluttered and whiskers curled gave much the same impression.

"You can't let thoughts like that distract you," Teg said. "If what Ohent told us about these fancy magical locks is true, losing focus at the wrong time could kill you."

"I know," Xerak said. "That's why I thought I'd better talk about this. I find myself hoping, envisioning our reunion. It's . . ."

"Vereez had similar dreams about Kaj," Teg said bluntly, "and look at her. There's a time and a place for romance and this most definitely isn't it."

Xerak nodded, then he asked shyly, "Have you ever been in love?"

Teg started to say, "A lot of times," then she shrugged. "I thought I was. Once I almost got married, but I called it off. I realized I was getting married to the idea that I should be married by that time in my life. I think my fiancé was relieved. Since then . . . Some flings but nothing that would have sent me searching for more than a year to find someone who told me flat out he didn't love me."

Xerak winced. "I deserve that. Thanks for listening, Teg. I think it will be easier for me to concentrate now."

"You're welcome," Teg said, getting up and stretching. "And don't worry, your secret is safe with me, but I bet the other mentors would understand."

Xerak laughed. "I know. Peg probably has a kid who had a love affair just as hopeless. Maybe that's why I didn't tell her. I want to hold on to the illusion that I'm somehow unique."

Since they didn't plan to remain in Rivers Meet any longer than was necessary for Xerak to try his hand at opening the locked safe deposit box and for Vereez to do some shifting of bank accounts, they didn't secure a hotel room. Instead, they flew directly to Zisurru University. This dominated a large area of land across the river from the portions of the city they'd visited in the past and, unsurprisingly, given that it specialized in magical lore, had an area for "parking" a peculiar variety of magical vehicles.

Grunwold opted for a riverside slip, both as less noticeable and as less expensive than an aerial one. Although no one talked about it, the threat offered by Zarrq and Inehem, especially here in a city where they had much influence, weighed on the company's minds. Even Heru seemed to have caught the mood, for the xuxu did not complain about being left behind on guard, although he did hint that treats would be appreciated.

Teg had the fleeting thought that maybe the reason Kaj had come along was because he hoped to make some easy cash by turning Vereez over to her parents, but as he made no effort to leave the group, she dismissed the thought as ungenerous—although she still kept an eye on him.

Xerak had stated that he didn't plan to visit his parents until after he'd opened the lock box, a statement Teg couldn't decide whether to take as an expression of confidence or of Xerak's concern that seeing his parents might weaken his resolve.

As she examined the campus from behind her lynx mask, Teg decided that the wizards' university was very much like the many campuses she'd visited during her varied career. The familiarity made the times when "real world" rules were violated all the more startling. Oddly, these violations of the norm had nothing to do with the student body.

Or I suppose it's more accurate to think "the variety of heads and tails and skin patterning on the students' bodies," Teg thought. *Actually, the variation is coming to seem so normal that when we go back home, I'm going to find just one type of head sort of bland.*

The administration building to which Xerak led them was one of the more outlandish campus structures, as if working in an exotic environment would compensate those who had to do dull work.

"Pixelated soft-serve ice cream?" Peg suggested, leaning back to look up at the multistory structure.

"Blue-raspberry flavor," Meg agreed, "with electric lime sprinkles."

Xerak grinned and shook his head. "I didn't understand much of that, but I'm glad you seem impressed and astonished. You're supposed to be. If you'll come this way . . ."

He indicated a swirl around the exterior of the structure, *Like,* Teg thought, *a hard candy coating applied carefully to only part of the ice cream. In violent lemon. Although I think Peg's analogy breaks down when you notice that people are riding the swirl.*

"We'll go up that way," Xerak said. "The 'will-call' boxes are near the top, since they aren't much in demand."

The ride up was a great deal of fun in itself. It also provided a terrific view of the sprawling campus. When they reached the top, a few sightseers were clustered on an outdoor viewing platform but, when their group passed through the entrance into the room holding the lockboxes, they appeared to be the only people on the entire floor.

The reason for the lack of sightseer interest became immediately apparent, for the room had no windows. The room was round, with no hint of the tapering structure of the building's exterior. Instead, the walls were lined floor to ceiling with banks of bright teal boxes painted with glyphs. The middle of the room was dominated with larger boxes, but these banks were only chest high, so it was easy to see in all directions.

Xerak walked briskly around to confirm that the room was empty, then said, "I'll put up a 'do not disturb' on the door to the outside, so no one will come in while I'm undoing the lock. Given how dangerous these locks can be, it's a common precaution." When he had done so, Xerak glanced at the notes he'd taken based on the vision in the Font of Sight. "The box we want is over there."

Peg asked, "Won't other people be annoyed if they can't get in to check their mail?"

Xerak shook his head. "Not really. These rental boxes aren't used that often. The main post office is in the student center."

In the empty room, their footsteps echoed on the polished stone tiles, and even their breathing sounded loud. Xerak paused in front of one of the small boxes and studied the top line of the glyphs, comparing them against his notes. As he did so, Teg realized that the collage of glyphs that had been visible in the Font's vision was completely invisible.

"This box is the one," Xerak said. "You all might want to sit down or something. This could take a while."

Implicit in his tone was that they should back up and give him some room. They did so, settling into a watchful tableau. Since Xerak had locked the door, Teg shoved her mask up on top of her head. Peg and Meg followed suit.

Xerak began etching the first glyph into the air, light following the tip of his index finger and hanging in the air, glowing a bluish white. The intricate shape reminded Teg of Celtic or Norse knotwork. However, it soon became apparent that while those designs existed in only one dimension, the figure Xerak was making existed in three—or more. Xerak's final gesture was a complex loop, concluded by his pulling his arm back.

Like the reverse of dotting a period on a written page, Teg thought.

As soon as Xerak gave the signal that he was done, a spark of light ran from the beginning of the figure, through the twists and coils. When it reached the end, the entire shape flared, then revealed itself in a gentle blue-white glow.

Xerak immediately started the next glyph. This one was a pale, yet still rich, violet. Its shape recalled elaborate intertwining arabesques. Once again, after Xerak signaled completion, a spark ran through the design.

Confirming he got it right.

Xerak was on his third glyph when Teg had a sudden insight.

These aren't just glyphs, they're elaborate three-dimensional mazes, and Xerak's sketching them from memory. If he gets even the slightest twist or turn wrong, then they'll blow. I wonder if one failure takes out all the rest?

By the time a shimmering gold glyph had joined the blue-white and the violet, Xerak was visibly sweating, damp patches soaking his tunic along his flanks. After indigo-touched-with-sky and sea-green-into-storm had been added to the sequence, Xerak was panting and leaning hard on his spear staff. Drops of sweat were running through the strands of his mane.

Poor kid. He's got the worst of both sorts of bodies when it comes to shedding excess heat. How many more? One, no, at least two. He's not going to make it! He's too young, too stressed...

Teg didn't even consider. She pushed herself up from where she'd been sitting on the floor and clapped her hand onto the side of Xerak's throat, feeling the light fur over the skin where his animal head merged with his more human body. His pulse was racing, jumping erratically.

"Easy, kid," Teg said. "I'm here. Don't worry. I won't let you fail."

She sensed rather than saw movement behind her, and a moment later Vereez's hand, cool and dry, lightly tipped with claws, touched Teg's own throat. Teg could feel the energy channeling into her and she concentrated on sending the enhanced mana to Xerak as she might have the sun spider amulet.

Fixing her gaze on the glyph maze Xerak was working—this one a glorious ruby red with silver sparks—Teg imagined her energy and Vereez's flowing into a current that flowed into Xerak and then out into the glyph. By the time Xerak began the final glyph maze—a psychedelic one in oranges, greens, and pinks...

...Like a Jefferson Airplane poster...

...Xerak's heart rate was no longer so crazy, and his breathing was evening out. While he still leaned on his spear staff, he no longer seemed about to fall over. Indeed, he finished the final curve and loop with a certain jaunty panache before pulling the "knot" tight.

When the final spark had run its course, the entire series of glyphs vanished and the door to the safe deposit box popped open. Xerak reached inside and removed a many-times folded and sealed piece of heavy parchment. Then he gave Teg and Vereez a little bow, and smiled, his whiskers curling.

"That, my dear friends," he said, almost purring, "is why so many wizards have apprentices."

Then he swayed, his eyes rolled up in his head, and he fainted, crumpling into a soft heap on the floor.

⁂ CHAPTER EIGHT ⁂

Sometime later, back on *Slicewind*, Xerak opened the folded parchment, scanned it, then began reading aloud. Only the fact that his voice was going faster than it should betrayed how nervous he was.

> *Dear Xerafu Akeru-va. If you're reading this, it's possible, just barely possible, that you might be able to reach where I am—which is also where Uten Kekui-va, your master, is. If you can complete the journey, then you will at last find him and learn why he departed as he did.*
>
> *If you cannot, then you will have been proven unworthy, and perhaps will have the sense to give up on a futile waste of your young life. I will give one hint. Your journey will be easier if you bring with you the heart of the Library of the Sapphire Wind.*
>
> *This letter will serve as a map to where your journey will begin.*

That was it. Not even a signature. Xerak handed the letter to Peg, who was nearest.

Peg turned it over, held it to the light. "I don't see any trace of a map. I suppose this is another of those wizard things?"

She handed the paper to Meg, who gave it a quick inspection before passing it along.

Xerak nodded. "I think it is. However, I'm beat. There's no way I could work the spell to activate the map now. In any case, we don't have Ba Djed of the Weaver with us—I'm sure that's what whoever wrote this meant by the 'heart of the Library'— so there's no benefit from my risking killing myself to awaken the map."

"Before we go back to the Library," Vereez said, "I need to go change the accounts my parents set up for us to some other bank."

"And we need to do some shopping for Nefnet, Ranpeti, and my mother," Kaj added. "Let's split up. Grunwold, why don't you bodyguard Vereez? I don't trust her parents not to try something if they think they can get away with it."

"Then let's both of us go," Grunwold said. "We'll handle the shopping on the way back, and the mentors can make sure Xerak actually rests."

Vereez nodded. "Sounds like a good plan. Peg, you have the list?"

"I do," Peg said, pulling it from a pocket on her knitting bag. "Let me come with you. I promise to stay in the background and keep my mask on, but I want to be there so I can check over any paperwork."

"I'd appreciate that," Vereez admitted, folding her ears into a soft puppy expression. "I learned a long time ago how to handle accounts, but I'd appreciate another set of eyes."

Xerak fell asleep almost as soon as the others left. Teg decided to rest on one of the benches in the lounge, since her own expenditure of mana had left her a little wobbly. She fell asleep and was awakened by the sound of the others coming aboard.

"It went well?" Meg was asking when Teg came on deck.

"It did," Peg said, dropping a few fabric-wrapped bundles on the deck. "Vereez handled the transfers like a pro. We all have nifty little bank books, too. I haven't seen anything like them since I was a kid. These are even real leather, not vinyl."

"Maybe we were too worried," Grunwold said, reaching to take a box Kaj handed to him from shore. "Maybe the threat of mange kept Inehem and Zarrq from trying anything."

"Maybe," Kaj said, bringing aboard the last of the shopping. "But I'd rather be too worried than trying to rescue Vereez."

"Me, too," Xerak said, hauling himself up the ladder and joining them on deck. He still looked wrung out, but moved with a bit more energy.

"Me, as well," Vereez said, "which is why I bought myself some new clothes while we were out, rather than going home to raid my own closet. I have permission, but it didn't seem worth the risk I'd be delayed."

"Then it will be back to the Library of the Sapphire Wind?" Grunwold didn't so much ask as state. "I hope Sapphire Wind doesn't fight us for Ba Djed. Or Ohent."

"If either of them does," Xerak said—even in his exhaustion, his determination made him fierce—"I'll fight back."

But Sapphire Wind didn't fight them, and Ohent actually encouraged them to take the reassembled Ba Djed.

"Truth be told, I'm glad to be rid of the Bird," she said. "Nefnet's medicines are helping me sleep and, without that thing in my charge, it's real sleep, not drugged unconsciousness. With the artifact farther away, I might even be able to sleep without any drugs at all. I'm feeling more—myself—although given that I spent as many years as custodian as I did before, I suppose that's ridiculous."

"Mother," Kaj said with a strange, stiff fondness, "you are always ridiculous."

Meg had been communing with Sapphire Wind. "Sapphire Wind would like Ba Djed of the Weaver returned, but it has stored sufficient power for now, especially since Nefnet agrees that waiting to release the Archived would be wise."

When Xerak held the Library's "heart" in one hand and the mysterious letter in the other, an image appeared on the back of the missive. It reminded Teg of the sort of simplistic map that had adorned boxes of Captain Crunch cereal when she'd been a kid. This map, however, didn't lead to a treasure chest filled with golden nuggets of oversweet cereal. It didn't lead to any final destination at all, but only indicated a direction into what otherwise remained blank paper.

"More details will show up as we need them," Xerak explained, folding the map and tucking it into his robe. "I'll keep checking but, for now at least, we have a direction in which to begin our journey."

"If we don't know exactly where we're going," Grunwold said, "our first stop should be the next town or city with a decent-sized market. I'd like to stock up before we go off into who knows where. Now that I have some extra money, I'd like to get another couple of bags of stored wind to replace the one we used when we stole *Slicewind*. We may well need it if we get becalmed."

Xerak frowned impatiently, then sighed. "You're right to plan ahead. Let's go back to Rivers Meet. It's not that much out of our way, and my mother has connections that just might get us a discount."

"I don't want anything chancy," Grunwold protested, "especially not something we'll be trusting our lives to."

"I trust my mother for something like this," Xerak said. "After all, if we find Uten Kekui, I'm likely to finally settle down."

"Not 'if,'" Peg said firmly. "When."

"When," Xerak repeated obediently, but Teg had grown enough accustomed to reading his expressions that she knew he was still very uncertain.

A few days later, they once again berthed *Slicewind* on one of the many rivers that gave Rivers Meet its name. After the four young people had gone into town to shop, Meg settled herself on one of the stern benches to write in her journal, and Peg drew Teg aside.

"We've assembled Ba Djed, sure, but I'm more worried than before. Everyone is being too cooperative. Were we right to leave Ohent there? She's a real wild card. Will she be a good influence on Brunni? What do we really know about Ranpeti, except that Vereez likes her? Our girl isn't exactly the world's best judge of character. Is Nefnet truly worried about what will happen if the Archived are set free or is she using this time to build a power base? Are she and Sapphire Wind plotting something?"

Teg shielded the cigarette she was lighting with one hand. "If so, what can we do? Should we do anything? This is their world, not ours."

"Huh!" Peg snorted in disgust. "I keep forgetting, you're from the disco generation. Self-obsessed. Focused on getting ahead."

"What did you idealistic hippies ever achieve?" Teg retorted. "How many of your heroes died from overdoses? How many went on to become rich stoners? At least my generation was honest—and hardworking."

"You're saying I'm lazy?"

"I'm saying I'm not buying that guilt trip," Teg replied tartly. "I'm fed up with hearing the eighties described as boring and materialistic. Whether you get stoned at Haight-Ashbury or Studio 54, it doesn't matter. Both are cop-outs."

"This from a woman who can't go two hours without a smoke!"

"At least I've gotten dirt under my nails and earned my own keep. I haven't relied on a string of husbands to provide me with alimony!"

"At least I'm not a commitment-shy antisocial hermit who . . ."

"Ladies!" Meg dropped her reading glasses on their lanyard onto her chest, and set her travel journal onto her lap. "You're scaring the youngsters."

She motioned with her free hand to where the four had just come up the gangplank, laden with boxes and bags.

Meg continued, "May I remind you, we mentors have not completed our mission. Until Xerak locates his master or at least learns something decisive about what happened to him, I believe we owe him our attention, not degenerating into trivial bickering."

Teg and Peg looked at each other uncomfortably but, for once, even voluble Peg seemed to lack words. Meg tsked at them, for all the world as if they were at the book club and had gotten into a heated disagreement over the relative merits of Agatha Christie and Dorothy Sayers.

"I believe," Meg said with a gusty sigh, "that the correct response would be saying something like, 'I'm sorry. I must have gotten out on the wrong side of the bed.'"

"Hard to do in that cabin," Peg grumbled. "But you're right. I am edgy. There's so much we don't know and every time we seem to have things figured out . . ."

Teg nodded and took up Peg's thought. "We learn something that puts everything we've learned before in a new perspective."

She might have added more but, at that point, Xerak chose to insert himself into the discussion.

"I've been thinking about whether your job might actually be done. You three humans—as well as Vereez, Grunwold, and Kaj—have helped me get me this far, but I'm not sure any of you can go the rest of the way. From what I know, the location we saw in the Font of Sight is restricted: a place for wizards only."

"Stop giving yourself airs, Raggedy Mane," Grunwold replied. "I'm coming with you until I can't go any farther. Then, and only then, do I plan on stopping. Even then, I'll wait to sail you home when you're done with whatever it is you're doing."

"I'm not leaving, either," Vereez said, words as incisive as swipes from her twin swords.

Kaj just folded his arms across his chest and glowered.

Meg smiled gently at the young wizard. "I don't think such restrictions may apply to the three of us. Who is to say whether or not we're wizards? Teg certainly seems to have some gift for magic. I have spoken with spirits, and Peg . . . who knows what surprises she holds?"

Peg grinned, her usual equanimity restored. "I'm full of surprises. That much is sure. Why don't we give coming along a try at least? What do we have to lose?"

Xerak sighed, but there was grateful resignation in the curl of his whiskers as he set his share of the shopping on one of the lockers. "According to lore, wizards who go to this place usually don't return. Those who do often have lost their power or are distorted in some way. Just warning you . . ."

"But," Kaj said roughly, "didn't you just say that none of us except you are wizards? By that logic, we have nothing to lose—or rather, what we have to lose is you."

"Well then," Xerak said, "if I can't stop you, I can't, but don't say I didn't try." He indicated a bag printed heavily with glyphs that was stirring sluggishly on the deck. "Let's get that into the locker before it decides to test its wards."

A few days later, Xerak tried again to ditch them.

Teg was on watch with Xerak when he attempted to jump ship. When, after the others had turned in, the young wizard offered her a glass of wine after pouring one for himself, Teg was immediately suspicious. Not only had Xerak been curbing his drinking since the successful rescue of Brunni had made his inquisition the group's focus, but once the Font of Sight had displayed the paired visions he'd been—as far as Teg could tell, and she'd been watching—completely dry.

With this in mind, as soon as Xerak was occupied making a course correction, Teg poured her wine over *Slicewind*'s side. She didn't think Xerak would try to poison her, so she assumed that if he'd put anything in the wine, it would be something to make her sleepy.

After she noticed Xerak covertly checking on her, she tested her hypothesis by stretching and yawning.

"I must have eaten too much for dinner, but those flying fish Kaj caught were amazingly tasty. He's a good cook." She yawned, and hoped the gesture wasn't too theatrical. "I'm *so* sleepy."

Xerak shrugged. "You spent a lot of magical energy when we were practicing earlier. That takes a while to rebuild. I thought you were overly optimistic about how quickly you'd bounce back."

"You seem fine," Teg said, stifling another yawn.

"I have a lot more practice," Xerak said. "Also, I channeled my energy directly."

"So did I." Teg had no trouble sounding offended. "I wrapped my hand around the sun spider amulet and used it as a focus."

Xerak glanced at the map, then made a minute course correction.

"Think of it this way. What you did was like shooting water from a hose. Directed sure, but with a lot of potential for spray once the 'water' left the pipe. What I did was closer to hooking one pipe into another pipe. Still used a lot of energy, but without the opportunity for waste."

"Hmm . . ." Teg yawned again, then flopped down on some folded sails, rolling onto her back and putting her feet up. "Makes sense."

She asked a few more questions about channeling magical energy, perfectly in keeping with her newfound role as sorcerer's apprentice. Letting the gap between questions get longer, she eventually "drifted off."

"Teg? Teg?"

Xerak set the autopilot, then came over, and laid a hand on her arm. Teg moved restlessly, as one might who was almost, but not completely, asleep. She heard Xerak sigh. He padded away, and Teg risked a glimpse from between her lashes. He was making adjustments to the elevation controls, shifting so that the ship would sink slowly. In this way, it was highly unlikely that any of the sleepers below deck would be alerted. Grunwold, in particular, had shown an amazing sensitivity to any alteration in *Slicewind*'s workings.

Teg fought the urge to "wake up" and confront Xerak, but she knew she had to delay until there was no way Xerak could make excuses for his behavior. Essentially, she had to wait until he was ready to jump ship, then hope she'd be able to stop him.

Xerak worked his adjustments with finicky patience, occasionally going to the rail to glance down for additional visual confirmation of whatever he was doing. Eventually, he grunted in satisfaction, took the map down from the post where they'd pinned it, and tucked it inside his robe. Next, he retrieved his pack from where it had been concealed within a coil of rope. Teg waited until he had shrugged it on, picked up his spear staff, and was heading for the rail.

Swinging her legs to the deck, she snapped authoritatively, "Xerafu Akeru, where do you think you're going?"

One hand still reaching for the side rail, Xerak stopped. He spoke without turning.

"To find my master."

"I thought you'd agreed we were coming with you?"

"I reconsidered. This is too dangerous. Moreover, it's my business. I'd never forgive myself if something happened to any of you because of my obsession."

Teg shook her head. "Sorry. I'm not letting you go."

Xerak turned to look at her. In the faint light from the on-deck lights, his eyes glinted golden amber. At that moment he looked far more lion than young man. "And how could you stop me?"

"I couldn't," Teg said. "But I could strike the alarm bell. Grunwold would be on deck before you could get clean away. Why don't we just skip the part where we have to chase you down, bring you back, then tell you how we're not letting you go anywhere alone until it's absolutely necessary?"

"Besides," said a deep voice from the hatchway leading belowdecks, "I'm not completely convinced that your search for your master is just 'your business.' I don't believe in predestination or any of that crap, but one doesn't grow up taking care of someone haunted by visions and nightmares, and not learn to recognize portents."

Kaj vaulted up onto the deck, closing the hatch behind him. "I sleep very lightly. A heritage of my peculiar childhood. I felt the ship begin to lose elevation. According to the course we reviewed earlier, there was no reason."

"But I put a pinch of tuatnehem on everyone's bedding," Xerak protested. "That should have made everyone highly receptive to the somnolence charm I worked right after coming on watch!"

"I recognized the smell," Kaj said.

"Properly enchanted, tuatnehem is almost odorless!"

"*Almost.* And I've used it on my mother, so I know what it smells like. I won't remind you about my peculiar childhood again. I'll start sounding like Peg and her two dozen children."

"Eight," Teg corrected automatically. She grinned at Kaj. "Though with the grandchildren and in-laws and ex-husbands, I bet we are up to something like two dozen."

Xerak sighed in resignation, slipped off his pack, and went over to the wheel. "I had the course set to resume altitude after I went over the side, but there's no need now." He glanced over at Kaj. "You sense portents? I'd like to hear more about that."

Teg nodded. "Me, too. I've had some thoughts about what we're facing, but I feel as if I'm too close to things. Kaj, you have the advantage of coming in late, and getting the Cliff Notes version of our earlier adventures."

Kaj seated himself on the coil of rope that Xerak had used to conceal his pack, then leaned back against the side of the ship.

"I think you're right, Teg. You both may be too close. What you see as one wide river, I keep envisioning as two streams running side by side, close enough to flood each other. I have a feeling that whatever these streams are goes back farther than our parents' shared crimes."

"What do you mean?" Xerak asked.

Kaj considered. "Well, let's start by focusing on you three inquisitors. When you first went to Hettua Shrine, you had no idea that there was any connection between your inquisitions."

"But there isn't," Xerak protested, "except that the Library of the Sapphire Wind was the best possible place for us to find answers."

"Really?" Kaj scoffed. "Take another look. In finding the first piece of Ba Djed, you get the story of Emsehu, of how he suspected that the Library hid something more than an amazing wealth of magical items and books."

"And it did," Teg said with a nod. "Ba Djed of the Weaver, the artifact that was broken when the extraction agents screwed up. The artifact that Sapphire Wind wanted reassembled."

"Exactly. Now, let's skip ahead, past my crazy mother, to what we learned when we went after Brunni. Not only did we find Brunni, but Teg and Vereez conveniently came across a mural that indicated that there may be another incredibly powerful artifact—the one that the Grantor used when he created the miracles that made his island nation famous. Doesn't that make you wonder about Ba Djed? Up until then, you'd all been thinking of it only as something created to perform the potent magics that enable the Library of the Sapphire Wind to function. What if powering the Library was only a side effect? What if the miracles that made the Creator's Visage Isles famous were only a side effect?"

"A side effect of what?" Teg asked.

"Of both Ba Djed and the Grantor's artifact being incredibly powerful," Kaj said. "When you light the stove to cook your dinner, you also heat the house. That's not the best analogy, but I think it works."

Teg nodded. "The intention is to have cooked food, not to provide heat, but you can't avoid having heat."

"That's it. What if Ba Djed and the Grantor's artifact were created for some other reason, and the power that Sapphire Wind draws on, that the Grantor of Miracles drew on, was a bonus?"

"That's a frightening thought," Teg said.

Xerak drummed *Slicewind*'s wheel with a claw tip. "Interesting theory. I'll admit, I haven't been thinking about anything other than that we needed to find the parts of Ba Djed to gain Sapphire Wind's assistance. I completely ignored any possible connection between Ba Djed and that other artifact."

Teg frowned. "I wish we'd had more time to study the mural, but Vereez was so strung out that I didn't like to make her stand by while I did."

Kaj grinned, sharp white teeth showing along the long line of his muzzle. "I did study it. When we were waiting to break out Brunni, I went for a walk."

"I remember," Xerak said. "I thought you were just edgy, needed to work off some tension."

"I was. Maybe to distract myself from thinking about the risks we were taking to rescue Brunni, I focused on how stumbling across an interrelationship between two incredibly powerful artifacts, artifacts that apparently most people had never heard of, was a bit much. I'm not saying I'm particularly intuitive but, much as I hate to mention it again, there's that peculiar childhood of mine. Some of what Vereez and Teg described made me remember some of my mother's weirder ramblings, the ones that I would have dismissed as her being strung out except that there were certain... themes, motifs, whatever you call them... that she'd return to time and again."

Kaj paused, looked very uncomfortable, then went on. "One of those themes seemed to have to do with my father. I believe Mother when she says she doesn't remember who he was, but... well... remember what I told you about how forced reincarnation works? How blood relation is an advantage? We know who Brunni's parents are: me and Vereez. I found myself wondering, whose blood is responsible for Brunni's relationship to the Grantor?"

Xerak held up his hand and started ticking off possibilities on his fingers. "If we look at Vereez's side of the family, we have Inehem and Zarrq. I know a little about Zarrq's family. Like him, they're not very inclined to magic so, even though Brunni resembles her maternal grandfather, she's not likely to have inherited magical ability from him—and because the Grantor's people would want their guardian to have magical ability, it's likely Brunni does."

"Point two," Kaj leaned forward and playfully bent over another of Xerak's fingers. "Inehem has magical ability, no doubt, but she and Ranpeti are full sisters. Ranpeti has some magical talent, although definitely not as much as Inehem. I heard her telling my mother that her parents put all their money into getting Inehem trained, since she had more potential."

"But lack of training," Teg cut in, seeing where Kaj's train of thought was heading, "wouldn't matter if the acolytes of the Grantor wanted a blood relative who had magical power. Ranpeti would do as well as Brunni—and given that she has ability, they'd probably overlook that she's an adult, so the Grantor's spirit would need to, well, share body space."

"The acolytes probably would have considered Ranpeti-toh a better candidate," Xerak agreed. "Ranpeti-toh would be a generation closer in relationship to the late Grantor, and with her magical abilities... Yes. I see where you're taking this, Kaj. You think the relationship to the Grantor is through you—specifically through your unknown father."

"I do," Kaj agreed. "My mother has visions and sometimes sees things that other people don't, but this isn't because she's inherently magical. The visions are because of her association with the Bird that is the top portion of Ba Djed. Me? I'm not certain. I have some magical aptitude—my early tests showed that—but my mother didn't want me to have formal instruction because she feared that, if I were trained, I would become susceptible to the Bird's aura, and she didn't want that."

"So," Xerak said, "you think that whatever talent you have comes from your father's side."

"I do."

Teg remembered how, when all three parts of Ba Djed had been assembled, Kaj had reacted along with Xerak, Vereez, and herself. At the time she'd thought this strange, but Kaj's theory now explained this—especially if Ba Djed and the Grantor's artifact were somehow related. No wonder he'd been watching the magic lessons.

"Why didn't the acolytes go after you then?" Teg mused. "Because Brunni was closer?"

"That's my theory," Kaj replied. "Remember how I told you that my mother had recurring nightmares? One of them had to do with her being pressured to bring something of tremendous value to some faraway place. She always fought against those impulses. Since I knew about her past history, I'd assumed that these visions were tied to lingering guilt over something she'd stolen long ago. Now though..."

"Do you remember when those dreams started?" Teg asked. "Or has Ohent always had them?"

"Those particular dreams started when I was in my early teens. I did some comparing and that's not too long after the Grantor died, then failed to be quickly reincarnated." Kaj's ears pinned back and he showed his teeth in a snarl. "I'll admit, I've spent a lot of time and energy over the years being angry at my mother for the deal she'd made, for the way we lived hand to mouth when her friends were wealthy. Now, though... Now I think I owe Mom an apology. I think she's been fighting for years to protect me, battling against trading my life away by keeping a low profile."

The long silence that followed this statement wasn't one of disbelief, but of pieces being shuffled about, theories tested. At long last, the silence was broken by Xerak.

"We know now that Dmen Qeres founded of the Library of the Sapphire Wind to both conceal and use Ba Djed. Now we suspect that the Grantor of Miracles—who could have been your father, although I guess he could have been an uncle or grandfather—was keeper of a second artifact. How do you think my master fits into this?"

Kaj shook his head. "I don't know. But I wonder about this person who kidnapped him. Could the writer of the letter be Dmen Qeres reincarnated? Did he know that stealing your master would set in place the series of events that would lead to Ba Djed being reassembled? Is that why you were told to bring it with you?"

Teg frowned. "I'd thought it was because Ba Djed is powerful— a fitting ransom for Uten Kekui-va—but when you think about it, the mural did show other artifacts, other custodians. Could the person who wrote that letter be one of these? Or could Xerak's master be somehow connected to them? Xerak, you did say Uten Kekui-va was extraordinarily magically gifted."

Xerak nodded, but his usual worshipful expression when his master was mentioned was muted as he worked through the puzzle.

"Powerful, yes. Ransom, yes!" In his excitement, Xerak was becoming less articulate. "But remember what the letter said? It didn't call Ba Djed by name or describe it—it only mentioned the 'heart of the Library.' If you didn't know what that was, you'd never think to bring it. I think even figuring out that much is some sort of test."

"Or simply more of the incredible caution we keep encountering regarding these artifacts," Teg countered.

"What other puzzle pieces are we missing?" Xerak mused aloud. "I still wonder why the third part of Ba Djed went into Teg's world. The fact that there's a connection between our worlds would explain why Vereez, Grunwold, and I were sent mentors from there—but what is the connection in the first place?"

Teg rose and started pacing. "There must be one. Absolutely. All of you here have physical traits taken from creatures that are common in our world, but otherwise unknown here. Moreover, I've been repeatedly struck by hints of shared artistic, linguistic, architectural and other elements that are harder to pin down—but I've kept reminding myself that similarity doesn't automatically indicate influence. Numerous cultures on our world have built pyramids or ziggurats, not because they share a root culture, but because the ziggurat—and its immediate descendant, the pyramid—is a stable form for a large structure, especially for cultures that lack the arch. Still, I feel certain there must be a connection beyond that of part of Ba Djed ending up in our world."

"I agree," Xerak stated.

Kaj stared hard at him. "Xerak, promise you won't try to leave us behind again—swear on something you value."

"How about on my power?" Xerak offered, clearly amused.

"How about on your master's life?" Kaj countered.

Xerak sighed. "Let's see. How's this? I swear upon my master's life that I will not try to leave you or any of my other companions—those commonly called Vereez, Grunwold, Teg, Meg, Peg, and Kaj—behind until or unless we reach a point where you cannot go with me. However, I don't swear that I won't try to convince you again that it's best for me to do this on my own."

In the morning, the others were informed of what Xerak had attempted, as well as Kaj's revelations and the theories that had been expounded. When those complex topics had been discussed and dissected, Meg turned to Kaj with interest.

"When you went back to look at the mural, did you learn anything more about the Grantor's artifact? Does it have a name?"

Kaj's ears did the sort of thing a puppy's do when embarrassed. "I did learn that, actually, and a lot more, but I was so caught up in how the Grantor might be related to me, I forgot to mention that."

"It's not too late now," Peg said encouragingly.

"When I started poking around, all the time I've spent in necropolises turned out to be useful," Kaj began. "I searched until I found a person I'd learned to recognize in the various religious institutions: someone with enough training to be an expert, but not enough seniority to be important. Those people like to show off. I told the one I found some of the truth, that I'd worked in a necropolis, and I was sure I'd seen a mural similar to the one that showed Ba Djed, but our mural was damaged, so incomplete. I acted as if I knew more than I did, and she . . ."

"She," Teg thought, amused. *Kaj doesn't just know about bored junior faculty, he knows he can charm anyone who likes a good-looking man.*

". . . was impressed that I knew the name Ba Djed of the Weaver, and was very pleased to demonstrate that she knew the names of the other two. The Grantor was holding Qes Wen, the Entangled Tree, and the third figure was holding Maet Pexer, the Assessor's Wheel. She didn't know anything more about Ba Djed or Maet Pexer, but since Qes Wen is associated with the local big shot, she knew a little more. It's very mysterious, and not of local origin. All their legends agree that a long-ago Grantor of Miracles brought it with her, might even have become Grantor because of it. Which came first has become muddled over time."

"Where is this Qes Wen now?" Meg asked.

"My acolyte didn't know for sure, but legend is that Qes Wen is hidden within the fiery heat of the volcano on Blinded Eye Isle, and that only the true heir of the Grantor of Miracles will be able to tap its power."

"Brunni?" Vereez said softly. "That's a hell of a lot to wish on a four-year-old. Ohent is one tough lady, and one third of Ba Djed nearly drove her mad."

"But," Xerak reminded her, "Ohent wasn't the true heir of Ba Djed. Emsehu's probably lucky that it was broken to bits before he could get hold of it."

Grunwold said, "This is all fascinating, but there's something I want to know that has nothing to do with any of this. Xerak, why did you try to jump ship when you did? Has the map shown you something new? Something that made you uneasy?"

Xerak forced a laugh. "Can we make that uneasier? More uneasy? If so, yes. I'll admit it."

He took out the letter, smoothed it so all could see the simplistic map, then made a quick gesture that Teg recognized as one of banishment or removal. Immediately, a long, complex series of glyphs, multicolored and impossibly ornate, appeared on the page.

Vereez had clearly recognized the nature of Xerak's spell as well. "You hid these! How long ago did those appear? What do they mean?"

"They appeared yesterday evening. I was checking the map shortly before Teg and I were due to take over from Grunwold and Meg. As for what they mean, I don't precisely know."

One didn't need to have been Vereez's friend from childhood on to recognize doubt in the hard stare she gave Xerak.

"Really," Xerak replied to the upspoken query. "I don't know for certain. What I do recognize is that this is a gateway spell. If it is performed correctly, it will open a passage to ... Well, that's the part I can't really make out. Somewhere else."

"You did say," Peg commented, "that the place we saw in the Font of Sight didn't exist. I suppose that could account for your lack of ability to figure out where this passage goes."

"Or he's prevaricating again," Vereez said. She turned to look at the three mentors. "Do you have a word for that? It's a nice way of saying *lying*."

"We do indeed," Meg said. "Several variations, in fact. However, I don't think Xerafu Akeru was prevaricating. I noticed a nicety in his wording ... What did you mean when you said 'If it is performed correctly'? I don't think that was just normal caution."

"I'd like to say that it was just me being appropriately modest," Xerak replied, "but it wasn't. Portal spells are inherently dangerous, since they involve violating the usual relationships between space and time. Most portal spells—including those that were employed to make the gate device we used to get from the Library of the Sapphire Wind to Sky Descry—take this into account. That's one reason you're more likely to find such travel done by means of a device than by a spell."

"And the other?" Peg asked with obvious interest.

"They take so much energy that they're likely to kill an individual caster," Xerak said. "Or at least knock him hard on his tail. Depends on the caster."

Grunwold shook his fist at Xerak. "And you, being an arrogant..." The translation spell broke down, probably because there was idiom as well as mere meaning in whatever Grunwold had just called the young wizard. "...figured that you could do the spell without it killing you, so you'd just ditch us all?"

Xerak huffed out his breath in an almost roar. "Well ... I thought it was better if only one of us, rather than all of us, ended up dead. That's what's likely to happen if I get the spell wrong."

"Teg and I helped you before, with the glyphs on the lockbox," Vereez said, suddenly shy, clearly recognizing the enormity of what she was suggesting. "Couldn't we help with this?"

"If I involved two barely trained apprentices," Xerak said, "in a spell of this magnitude, I would be in violation of just about every code of ethics I have learned. Even if I did find my master at the portal's other end, he'd be likely to beat me around the ears—hard—when he learned what I had done."

"What's the worst that could happen?" Peg asked. "We all die? I thought you people were absolutely certain you'll be reincarnated. I'd think that would make you less cautious about taking risks."

Xerak laughed. "We'll save the philosophical discussion as to how reincarnation makes us view our current lives for another time. To answer your first question—death itself is not the worst consequence. *How* we die is. If I get the spell wrong, who knows where we might end up? I, for one, don't like the idea of boiling to death in the heart of a volcano, or smothering in a bog, or falling into the ocean and drowning, or even appearing in the middle of city traffic and getting run over."

"He has a point," Grunwold admitted. "I can't say I'd like any of those things either. I guess, Raggedy Mane, you'll just need to get the spell right."

"And we'll help," Vereez said firmly. "Me and Teg and . . ." She looked sidewise at Kaj. "Maybe even Kaj, since he's so confident that he's the son of some mighty wizard."

"Maybe," he said without looking at her. "If Xerak thinks he can teach me what is necessary. Otherwise, I'll join Grunwold in the 'those also serve who stand and hit dangerous things on the head' brigade."

"The voyage won't be long enough for me to teach you much, Kaj," Xerak said, with obvious regret, "but I could start teaching you concentration and focus techniques."

Kaj nodded. "Definitely. I've been watching the lessons, but I can't quite get the hang of what they're doing."

"Can we do the spell anywhere?" Peg asked. "Or did the map wait to show you the glyphs because you need to be in a specific location?"

Xerak rewarded her with quick approving nod. "Good question. I don't think we should work the spell just anywhere. The map guides us to . . ." He tugged at a bit of his lower mane, as a man might his beard. "You don't have magic in your world, but you seem to have a lot of stories. Do any of them contain references to places where magical energies flow in greater concentration?"

"Absolutely!" Peg replied triumphantly. "Ley lines. Alpha vortexes. Planetary magnetic fields. Stonehenge. The Bermuda Triangle. There's a whole bunch of places that are supposed to have more magical power than others—or to have had that power once, even if they don't anymore."

She stopped. "Sorry. Got carried away there. The answer is 'yes.' Are we heading toward one of those sorts of places?"

"Yes, although our destination is known less as a source of power than as a place where many lines cross. This should make magical travel easier."

"Isn't a place like that going to be crowded?" Teg said. "It's one thing for us to take risks with ourselves, but I don't think we can endanger other people."

Xerak glanced at the map again. "Whoever sent us—well, me—these instructions seems to agree with you about involving others. The location it indicates is isolated enough that the difficulties involved in reaching it outweigh the benefits. For one, it's buried in the midst of a nearly impassable mountain range."

Grunwold frowned. "That shouldn't be enough to keep people away. After all, we're not the only people with a flying ship. What aren't you telling us?"

Xerak tugged at his mane again. "I've never been there myself, but legend says this particular vortex is protected by a very nasty guardian—or guardians. The details are vague."

"That doesn't surprise me," Grunwold said. "Knowledge makes it easier to plan an attack. Let's go scout the place out. If we need to go back to buy more gear, then we can."

He paused to inspect their strange crew. If his eyes narrowed involuntarily when he looked at Kaj, well, Teg didn't blame him. Vereez had remained jumpy, clearly uncertain if she wanted to spend more time with her former lover or avoid him entirely. Although they all found her shifting moods difficult, for Grunwold her indecision must be agony.

Grunwold continued, "If anyone wants to debark, we'll be passing over several cities with good transport networks."

But as they passed over plains and rivers, coming at last to where sharp-peaked mountains purpled the horizon, no one asked to leave. Teg didn't think this was from fear of being thought cowardly.

We all want to know whatever waits at the other end. Ostensibly, we're searching for Xerak's master, but we all know—even Xerak—that we're expecting to find something more.

❧ CHAPTER NINE ❧

Over the next several days, as they voyaged through the convolutions that carried them deeper and deeper into the mountain range, *Slicewind* bucked against erratic air currents made visible as the hosts of restless wisps of cloud. Eventually, they had to expand their duty watches to include three people: one at the wheel, one handling the lines, if necessary, and one up in the crow's nest. Only Grunwold was able to handle the ship on his own, but even he appreciated someone aloft, keeping watch for storm clusters. As the wind currents became more erratic, Vereez, who had a sixth sense for weather, took over high guard full-time.

They heard their destination—or rather the beginning of its defenses—well before they saw it: a strange, metallic vibration that drove every bird from the sky and set even the humans' teeth on edge. The shrieking wail came from the depths of a thick bank of mist that permitted no glimpse of the source.

Although the sound made the humans uncomfortable, the young people, each of whom were blessed—or in this case cursed—with more acute hearing, were miserable. Heru didn't make the situation any better by adding his own honks of protest to the din.

Peg shaped the four young people earplugs from soft wax. These helped for a time, but *Slicewind* had barely cut into the outermost edge of the mists before first Grunwold, with his large deer's ears, followed soon after by Vereez and Kaj, fled belowdecks. Xerak coped longer by using a charm that dulled his hearing, but eventually an odor he claimed was nauseating—but which the humans could detect only as a vague, rotten unpleasantness—bent him double with retching, and forced him to retreat below with the rest.

Peg matter-of-factly took *Slicewind*'s wheel. Meg carefully climbed up the mast to the crow's nest, binoculars slung around her neck, while Teg stood ready to reef or loose the sails if Peg so commanded. Heru soared around them, restless and uneasy, until Peg, in her capacity as captain *pro tem*, ordered the xuxu belowdecks.

"That sound may be warning us away," Peg shouted, one hand on a spoke of the wheel, another hovering over the elevation levers, "but the winds—I feel a strange spiral current. I think it's meant to drive ships away, but if we can surf on that . . ."

Peg worked the controls with expert concentration, aware of eddies that to Teg were only bumps. Intently focused, yelling semi-intelligible bits of surfer slang, Peg fought until *Slicewind* was riding the swirling vortex through the clouds, each rotation taking them a miniscule amount closer to whatever lay concealed within the mist. The mainsail belled out, and the lines hummed as if *Slicewind* was singing her victory over the winds that had so violently buffeted her a short while before.

As *Slicewind* cut through the muffling layers of fog and mist, the strange sound grew louder and more shrill. Teg thought about stuffing her own ears with wax, but didn't want to sacrifice her ability to hear Peg or Meg. She was still debating whether she should give in and use earplugs when the ship cut through the last of the shrouding clouds.

Suddenly they were under a blue sky, their destination revealed as a mesa-like formation, sheer at the sides. The flatness of the formation's top made it stand out among the surrounding peaks. Unlike these, which were snow and ice capped, the plateau was bare, without even scrub growth: just dirt or sand. As *Slicewind* swirled closer, a series of slender columns or pillars jutting from the top of the mesa were revealed as the source of the maddening shrieks.

From her perch in the crow's nest, Meg had the clearest view. Waiting until *Slicewind*'s around and around progress had made it possible for her to view the object from all sides, she called down her report.

"It's a series of slim, silvery-grey columns. Their bases are buried in the dirt. They aren't supporting anything and there's something odd about their tops." Meg raised the binoculars to her eyes and inspected the formation again. "It's possible that what I'd taken for painted accents or ornamental carvings may actually be holes. These 'columns' may be more akin to gigantic pipes than to columns."

"Pipes?" Teg asked, then understood. "Oh, not for smoking. Like for carrying water or chimneys."

"Or a pipe organ," Peg added. "That would explain the noise: the wind rushing through or over the pipes—sort of a tubular take on an Aeolian harp. Like when you blow on a beer bottle or over the top of a syrinx—panpipes, you know."

"The pipes look metallic," Meg began, then stopped herself. "No. That's not quite right. Plastic? But they don't have plastic here. Whatever the pipes are made from has been severely battered. And . . . Wait! No. Yes. Yes!"

Meg was hardly ever so inarticulate. Teg was about to risk leaving her place to take a look for herself when Meg resumed.

"It's moving! Yes! Definitely. The array of pipes is moving. Not very fast, but it's shifting—perhaps so as to use the wind more effectively."

Teg looked over the side in time to see the pipes in motion. Something about the gait reminded her of a centipede, as if the pipes moved on multiple sets of short legs rather than relying on only a few, longer limbs. After making a few fussy adjustments, the pipes stopped, angled slightly and the shrill sound changed, causing Teg to shake her head hard.

Peg cursed, then added, "And to think I was so proud that, unlike a lot of my hippie buddies, my hearing somehow managed to escape damage from speaker stacks. So that's where the noise is coming from. Any idea what caused the stink that chased Xerak below? It's getting worse."

"No idea," Meg replied. "We're still far enough out that fecal matter or the like would be hard for me to spot, even with the binoculars."

A shrill scream of—Rage? Protest? Warning?—cut her off.

"We're going to need to deal with that shrilling before we can venture closer," Peg decided. "I have an idea. Teg, go and check the water barrels. Waste, too, while you're at it."

Teg did so, reporting back. "Water's still mostly full. We tanked up only yesterday. Waste not so much. We purged at the same time."

Peg nodded. "Well, as much as I'd love to give that thing shit, that's probably not the best idea. Here's my plan. It's going to take pinpoint coordination, but I think we can pull it off."

Some minutes later, Teg was standing by the levers that would release the water stored in barrels strategically positioned around the ship where they served as ballast, as well as providing water for the crew. Since—as with hot air balloons—it was sometimes advantageous for the ship to be able to rise suddenly, the ballast was rigged for quick release. A side benefit was that this enabled the water to be completely dumped before restocking, thereby reducing the contamination that had plagued oceangoing vessels in olden times.

At a shout from Meg, Peg pulled *Slicewind* out of the vortex current, cutting directly across the top of the plateau. The screaming grew unbearable: loud and shrill enough that Teg had to resist an urge to sink to her knees and bury her head in her arms.

"Now, Teg!" Meg yelled. "Now!"

Teg pulled hard on the release lever, hoping that Meg had remembered to allow for the time needed for the hatch to open. Otherwise, their tormentor might only get splashed. Since *Slicewind* carried a finite amount of water, this attack could only be used a limited number of times.

She needn't have worried. The shrilling became a gurgle, then a sort of choked bubbling. *Slicewind* started to rise straight up, but Peg shoved the elevation controls with one hand, then hauled at the wheel with the other, bringing the sailing ship around so hard that the sails began to flap until they caught the wind again.

Thudding footsteps from below announced that the three inquisitors and Kaj had noticed the change. When they came up from below, Teg noticed that all of them wore scarves over their noses and smelled very strongly of something heady and floral.

To Grunwold's eternal credit, he didn't shove Peg from the wheel of his beloved ship, but instead tended to the sails. Vereez ran forward, taking charge of the small sail, while Kaj and Xerak grabbed the lines for the mainsail.

"Coming around for a second pass," Peg yelled. "Ready, ladies?"

"Ready!" came simultaneous replies.

"Now!" yelled Meg, and what remained of the whistling, whining, shrilling complaint ebbed into short fizzing burbles.

"Grunwold!" Peg called. "We're going to need to get down there and deal with that whatever it is before it clears the water from its pipes. Take the wheel!"

Grunwold loped over, managing to give Peg a one-armed hug as he grasped for the wheel. Peg hugged him back, then ran for the rail. Teg was already there, trying to figure out what the walking pipe organ was doing, but *Slicewind*'s erratic progress was such that she only could grab patchwork glimpses that were more confusing than edifying.

Meg made her way down from the mast to join them. Her pink-and-white complexion was flushed, and her blue eyes were snapping with excitement.

"Wonderful! Elegant! Perfect!"

"Not bad for three old ladies, eh?" Peg said with assumed nonchalance.

"I'm not quite ready for 'old,'" Teg mock protested, but she realized that until this trip she had been. Menopause had hit her hard, and so had the retirement of people she'd known for years.

Gradually, she was realizing that there was something to that trite saying "You're only as old as you feel." Sure, she couldn't do anything about hot flashes, needing reading glasses, getting tired after a day digging where once, after a brief rest, she'd have been ready to go hiking before bed. But she could stop selling herself short. Rather than thinking about what she couldn't do, she needed to think more about what she could.

Grunwold was shouting complicated directions about sail settings to Kaj, Xerak, and Vereez. He brought *Slicewind* around, heeling the vessel as tightly as if she were a race car. In the process, he also gave up some altitude, although he didn't bring the ship all the way down, but kept her hovering with her hull about ten feet above the surface.

Teg, Meg, and Peg crowded to where they could get a clear look at their—at least for the moment—vanquished opponent. The series of pipes were spitting out water, reminding Teg for all the world of a failed attempt at an avant-garde fountain. Water gushed out of both the tops of the pipes and from smaller holes along their sides. Apparently, the creature possessed some ability to breathe, so it wasn't completely reliant on the wind to make those horrible noises.

Any desire Teg had felt about figuring out just how the thing functioned was banished when she realized that it was moving—not with the centipede-like wriggle she'd glimpsed before, but with a rising and falling motion, as if it was doing a series of deep knee bends.

Then, with a mighty effort that flung clods of dirt every which way, the creature broke through the surface, revealing an ovoid body, something like that of a crab, but without a crab's long legs. The pipes that had so tormented the sky sailors were set along the creature's back shell, which was a similar silver-grey to the tubes, although with an underlying shimmer of blue the pipes lacked. Teg estimated that the creature was at least five meters from end to end, and perhaps three meters at its widest point.

As if the pipes were not weapon enough, the creature possessed not one, but two massive sets of claws—one set at each end of its body, the second claw replacing what would be the back fin on a crab. It was with its claws, rather than its legs—which were indeed centipede short and centipede numerous—that the creature had hefted the body from where it had "swum" below the sandy soil of the plateau. Clearly, this thing's joints were a great deal more flexible than those of a crab.

Like those of a crab, the creature's four eyes were on long stalks that were clearly capable of independent motion. One eye stalk darted back and forth, inspecting its immediate surroundings, while another gazed up at the floating ship. Another set seemed to handle directing the course of the creature's numerous feet.

With a discordant *brrapp* the creature shot forth water from several pipes, releasing at the same time quantities of noxious-smelling material, opaque and the color of spoiled custard. Teg felt her gut wrench. Perfumed bandanas notwithstanding, the young people gagged audibly. Kaj just managed to reach the side before he vomited.

"We've got to take that thing out of action," Xerak managed, sounding as if he were trying to speak without breathing. He began to make the now-familiar motions that led up to one of his fire spells.

"Wait!" Peg said, grabbing his arm with the hand that wasn't pinching her nose shut. "I think that thing has been hurt. Look! Some of the pipes have been jammed, the rest are partially shut. I bet that accounts for the horrible noise—and the stink."

"The stink?" Kaj, returning and wiping his mouth, looked both puzzled and interested.

"You can't have wiped as many snotty noses as I have," Peg said, "without being able to recognize a sinus infection. Somehow that thing has gotten its pipes clogged. I'd bet it's so sick it's gone crazy. If you can restrain it, I could maybe..."

In the wash of inarticulate protests that followed, two voices won through.

Meg said, "Peg, as much as I admire your desire to enact *Androcles and the Lion*, perhaps this is not the best time for mercy."

And Grunwold bellowed, "Restrain, that?"

But Vereez nodded. When she spoke, her words came in short gasps.

"Until it broke through... I didn't recognize it.... That's an oothynn... In the tropics they're... kept as pets. They're smart as draft lizards... create beautiful music. Though the... ones I've seen are a *lot* smaller."

Peg smiled at Vereez. "Will you help me, then?"

Vereez nodded. Grunwold gave a gusty sigh, and tightened his bandana.

"*Slicewind* doesn't need me at the helm if we're just hovering. I'll go with you so I can pull you out when you get yourselves in trouble."

Perhaps determined not to be outdone, Kaj wordlessly moved to join him.

Xerak rolled his eyes. "Well, this is my inquisition. I can't hang back."

Peg patted the lion-headed youth approvingly on one arm. "Now, my dears, here's what I want each of you to do."

Peg's plan called for two teams—Vereez and Grunwold, Xerak and Kaj—to approach the oothynn from opposite ends, rush in, shroud the claws with sail canvas, then use some of *Slicewind*'s ample supply of rope to bind the claws: "Like lobsters at the grocery store."

Once the claws were rendered ineffective, each team was to hold on and keep the oothynn from getting away. After the creature had been restrained, Peg and Meg would climb up on the shell and start clearing out the pipes.

"What about me?" Teg asked. "Am I on claw-binding or snot-clearing duty?"

"Neither," Peg said firmly. "Meg and I are mothers. We've dealt with worse stuff than that. You might blow your cookies."

"But..."

"Teg, you'll stay on *Slicewind*, where you will be above the action. You and Heru will stand watch. If something goes wrong, you can provide a distraction with your sun spider amulet."

"Peg, this is crazy. So much could go wrong! Let's just put the thing out of its misery."

Peg shook her head. "I can't. Even before Vereez told us these things are kept as pets, I had my suspicions. Look at the tops of the pipes. See those bands?"

Teg did. "What about them? Part of the shell."

"No. I don't think so. I think they're ornamental. My guess is that this thing was someone's pet. They put those on it, went away, almost certainly planning to return. But they didn't and, well, if this oothynn is like a crustacean, it grows by molting. It's managed, but just barely, and over time the rings have tightened."

Teg felt an unwilling pang of sympathy. She knew all too well the pain of a swollen finger caught in a ring. Water retention seriously sucked.

Xerak, who had proofed himself with a nose-plugging charm, borrowed a pair of binoculars and took a closer look.

"Peg's right. Those bands are artificial. They've been so scuffed and tarnished, I can't tell for certain, but they were probably enchanted to stretch, but even enchantment can only do so much. I wonder..."

He gagged as the oothynn sneezed out more slime. Apparently, the charm muffled, but did not eliminate his sense of smell entirely. The oothynn was starting to make noises—squeak toys to its earlier shrill screams, but a threat of what was to come.

"Later," Peg commanded. "If we're going to do it, let's do it!"

Had the oothynn possessed typical binocular vision, Peg's plan would have worked more smoothly, but the oothynn could turn its eyes in any direction. Again, had the young people not been sickened from the stench, Peg's plan would have worked more smoothly, but . . .

Teg looked on, acutely worried as Grunwold was buffeted back by one claw, flying through the air and landing on his tail. Vereez dropped her piece of sail canvas to come to his aid. Drawing her twin swords, she ran to cover Grunwold. She crossed her blades into an X just in time to catch the descending claw, but the force rocked her back. Grunwold struggled to his feet, ran to her, then managed to brace Vereez's arms with his own so the X didn't break.

Heru soared down, honking and snapping at the oothynn, distracting it sufficiently that Vereez and Grunwold were able to regroup.

On the other side, Xerak and Kaj had managed to get sail canvas over their designated claws, but neither had a sufficiently firm grip to let go long enough to get the rope around the pincher. Kaj was attempting a sort of horseman's mount over the section of the claw directly behind the pincher, but since the claws opened up and down, not sideways, he wasn't going to be able to hold them shut even with those muscular thighs.

And if he makes even a little mistake, Brunni isn't going to have any little brothers or sisters. Teg clenched her fingers around the sun spider amulet. *I wish the spider silk was strong enough to bind those claws, but that's out.*

She had a fleeting memory of Xerak saying that it was possible that the sun spider amulet might be used to summon real sun spiders.

But I don't think I could do that, and even if I did, how am I to know if they'd be big enough to deal with a cross between a pipe organ and a crab? What if I summoned sun spiders and they attacked us? No . . . here's got to be something else.

The idea that came to her was of a sort that she was familiar with from her work, a flash of inspiration that seemed unconnected with anything else, although later, she might be able to figure out the links.

If the oothynn couldn't see, then . . .

Teg didn't let herself think about everything that could go wrong. Instead, grasping the sun spider amulet in what frequent practice had made a familiar grip, Teg concentrated, first on focusing her energies as Xerak had taught her, then on envisioning the sun spider shooting forth a gob of silk to cover one of the eyes on its long stalk. Breathing in through her mouth, she forced her breath out in a pursed-lipped gust that left her lightheaded.

Now!

She could have sworn she heard little giggles from the amulet, as if it was amused by the idea of incapacitating the much larger creature.

One eye! Two! Three! Now for the last! Teg's head swam, but she gripped the side of the ship until the woozy feeling passed.

The oothynn forgot its attackers, trying instead to pluck away the spider silk without damaging its own eyes. Kaj and Xerak, each of whom already had canvas in place, used the distraction to get ropes over the claws and bind them shut. Then each sat astride their captive claw and exchanged spontaneous palm slaps.

Vereez and Grunwold had to run to reach their assigned claws before the oothynn could clear its eyes. Their job was made more difficult because the oothynn was trying to use those claws to clear its eyestalks, but between Grunwold's muscle and Vereez's agility, they managed to rope first one, then the other, and get them closed. When this had been done, the oothynn collapsed, overwhelmed and—at least for the moment—defeated.

A pathetic wail, like that of a disappointed kitten, made Teg suddenly feel sorry for it.

"I'm getting this gunk off its eyes," Teg said. "After all we went through to save it, I don't want to risk it being permanently blinded."

"We'll get to work on clearing its pipes," Peg said. "You kids did great, but you'd better back off. This is going to be a smelly job."

There was no protest and, after making sure that the ropes that held the claws were tight, most of young people went belowdecks. Grunwold alone stayed above, standing at *Slicewind*'s wheel, Heru on his shoulder.

After she'd cleared the spider silk from the oothynn's eyes, which, like those of a crab, seemed to be protected by a transparent bit of shell, Teg took a look at the bands that constricted the pipes.

"These bands look as if they have a seam. In fact, in a couple of cases, the band has actually broken, but the oothynn's chitinous shell has grown around them. I think I can manage to pry these loose. Could someone get me my dig kit?"

Ostentatiously holding his nose, Grunwold did so. Teg climbed up the rough shell and got to work. As she did so, she could have sworn she felt the oothynn purring.

Poor thing. If it was someone's pet, it must have been really confused. It must have a good heart, to trust strangers, rather than try and toss them off.

Only when she was done did Teg realize she was exhausted. She let herself be doused with water to remove most of the stink, then collapsed into a deep and thankfully dreamless sleep.

Teg awoke to the sound of a woman singing "Amazing Grace."

"You're awake?"

The voice was Kaj's. She felt strong hands lift her head and torso, then a cup of something was put to her lips. She drank thirstily. The lightly salted broth tasted wonderful.

"Enough for now," Kaj said, taking the drinking bowl away. "Do you want to lie down again or sit up?"

"Sit."

Teg felt herself propped against something soft but firm. Probably more of the sail cloth. Until this voyage, she'd never realized how often sails needed to be mended or replaced. Kaj's arm pulled away, and Teg relaxed, listening to the music. As an afterthought, she realized she could probably open her eyes.

When she did, she discovered that she was on the ground. *Slicewind* hovered at anchor, providing shade for an impromptu camp. She wondered why they weren't on the ship, then she saw Peg and understood.

Peg was standing on the oothynn's upper shell, singing. The oothynn's claws were still shrouded in canvas and rope, but it held them crossed in an "at rest" position. The creature's outer shell had been thoroughly cleaned, and the surrounding area was perfectly dry. Teg wondered how long she'd been out, then she realized that the oothynn had been convinced to move away from the putrefied area. That was still damp, but fresh sand had been dug and thrown over the worst of the snot and slime—Teg suspected by the creature itself, since it would take even a team of skilled diggers at least a day to do the job.

The oothynn's four eyes were focused on Peg with what Teg

recognized as pure adoration. When Peg sang a passage to it, it strove to imitate. When it failed—probably because its pipes were still bent from having been bound for so long—it would give a dissatisfied honk that reminded Teg of seals at the zoo, then try again.

"The oothynn is capable of using different pipes to make the same sound," Meg spoke from one side. Teg glanced over and saw that Meg was sitting on a campstool, a bowl of tea in her right hand, her notebook balanced on one knee. "Rather as a violinist can duplicate the same note with different fingering on different strings. Peg said she wanted to show it that it's going to be okay, that it can go back to singing."

"Seems to be working." Vereez padded over and crouched down next to Teg. "How do *you* feel? You saved the day, first with the blinding, then getting those bonds off the pipes. It really calmed down when the last of those dropped off. Peg's singing is doing the rest."

Peg had noticed that Teg was awake. After singing a quick line of notes that sounded vaguely familiar, she patted the nearest pipe, then jumped down off the oothynn's shell to come hurrying over.

"How do you feel?"

"I feel a mega headache coming on," Teg admitted. "If someone would grab my pack, I have some aspirin there." As Vereez hopped up and scrabbled up the ladder into the ship, Teg continued, "So, Peg, have you turned Disney Princess now? Singing to monsters?"

"Well, music does have charms to soothe the savage beast," Peg said.

"The actual quotation is 'savage breast," Meg commented mildly.

"Maybe, but Grace is definitely a beast, and not a mammal, so 'breast' is completely wrong."

"Grace?" Teg asked.

"For Grace Slick," Peg said cheerfully. "At her best, she had the ability to make her voice sound like instrumental music. I think when this Grace is well, she's going to be able to make music that will sound like words."

"Grace Slick?" Teg frowned, then nodded. "I remember. Jefferson Airplane. That song about the white rabbit. And wanting someone to love."

"Yeah, my old rival," Peg said reminiscently. "Well, she may have beaten me out for the place in the band, and gotten Paul Kantner, but I did have my thing with Marty Balin. She never managed that, though we did both have our times with Jim Morrison."

She smiled, looking so sexy and wicked that Kaj, coming to bring Teg fresh broth, halted in midmotion. Peg didn't notice. Or at least she pretended not to notice, but her grin became a little wider.

"I also wanted a name that would translate completely. After poor Grace's horrible sinus infection, Grace Slick seemed, well, appropriate in so many, many ways."

"Peg, you are one wicked woman," Teg said, downing two aspirin, and nodding thanks to Vereez, who was staring at Kaj, clearly puzzled. Teg wondered idly if Kaj smelled like a blush or something.

She fell asleep soon after, and when she awoke it was the next morning. The mountains visible over the mist surrounding them might have been rimed in snow and ice, but the plateau was comfortable—not warm, precisely, but somewhere in the midseventies.

More proof that this world doesn't follow the rules I know. Teg sat up and looked to where Peg was teaching Grace Slick to play "The Sound of Music" from the eponymous musical. *As if I needed a reminder.*

Xerak came over, saw Teg was definitely awake, and, without being asked, poured her a bowl of poffee.

Teg thanked him and, after taking a satisfying slurp, asked, "I was too out of it last night to ask, but why are we camping down here, not sleeping on *Slicewind*?"

"After your brilliant attack on Grace, over there"—Teg's ear heard that he had spoken the name in English, so apparently the translation spell was continuing to not translate names—"Grunwold worried we would run short of water. Peg didn't want to leave Grace, so we set up camp. Then Vereez, Grunwold, and Kaj sailed to where they could siphon up a fresh supply from a mountain lake."

Teg chuckled. "Oh, that must have been a fun voyage. Do you think Vereez is going to make a play for Kaj? Or will she realize that he's not interested—or if he is, it's for the wrong reasons?"

Xerak shook his head. "I have no idea. Vereez isn't confiding in me. I thought she might have said something to you."

"Not to this point. I think she figures we're all rooting for Grunwold."

"You're not?"

"I'm not rooting for anyone but Vereez. That young woman needs to get it through her pointy-eared head that she's her own person first, not who she is because she has caught some guy. Kaj messed her up big time by screwing her when she was just a kid. I'm not saying I blame him for not realizing how young and vulnerable she was—he was a kid himself—but I'd like Vereez to realize that she's got to be able to live without a man . . . or a woman . . . or whatever. In the end, the only person who won't leave you is you."

Xerak blinked. "That's bitter. Were you left?"

Teg forced a laugh. "Not really. If I have a problem, it's the reverse. I'm what my culture calls 'commitment shy.' I've never found anyone who I trusted enough, I guess. And the experiences of most of my friends—including Meg and Peg—well, they don't exactly scream 'Try this.'"

Heath Morton's smiling face flashed into her memory, but she shrugged it away.

"Meg seems to have liked her husband," Xerak said cautiously.

"I think she did, but it was a very"—Teg brought her hand down in a cutting gesture—"partitioned marriage. Meg's from a time when, in our culture, a woman's role and a man's role—even to the sort of jobs they could hold—were clearly designated. Peg's generation shook that up big time. Mine? Mine's still dealing with the fallout. Or that's what I tell myself. I wanted to go into archeology. It's a physically demanding profession, so I had to prove myself as good as any man—and be able to boss them. I wasn't the first to do that but, the older I got, more and more of the women who'd started in archeology when I did dropped out to raise families, take a job with less travel, because they didn't want to leave their husbands and kids, stuff like that. I found an easy way to avoid that."

"No husband," Xerak replied, nodding. "No family. You know, Teg, I don't think I've ever heard you talk so much about yourself at one time."

This time Teg's laugh was genuine. "Maybe I'm talking because each of you inquisitors has been forced to tell your story. Maybe I'm realizing that, in my own way, I'm a holdback, too. It's a scary thought, especially at my age."

"Because you didn't find a partner?"

"No. Because of *why* I didn't find a partner. Does that make sense?"

"I think so . . ." Xerak reached for the poffee, refilled Teg's bowl, and, after waiting to see if she was going to say more, asked, "How are you feeling this morning? Up to trying more magic?"

Teg ran a mental inventory of herself. "I feel fine. Actually, I feel great. Headache is gone and I don't have any of that hangover feeling I've had after doing a magical working. I guess I got enough sleep."

"That, and since this plateau is a vortex of lines of energy, it also helps wizards to regain spent mana. Now, my dear apprentice"— Xerak's ears quirked a half smile—"*Slicewind* has taken on replacement water. You and Vereez are ready. I'd like to try the spell this morning."

"Absolutely," Teg said. She drained her bowl of poffee, then got to her feet, extending her arms in a joint-popping stretch after she did so. "Give me time for a shower and to eat something more substantial than broth, then I'll be ready, teacher."

When Teg came up on deck, clean, dressed in a set of her "real world" clothes, Peg was coming back aboard. In the near distance, Grace—her claws now unbound—was doing a very convincing series of bird calls, doubtless meant to lure prey.

"Xerak's waiting for you and Vereez down off the prow," Peg said. "He didn't want to try the summons up here on the ship, just in case magical fields interfere with each other, or something like that."

"Your buddy"—Teg gestured with her head toward Grace— "seems a whole lot better."

Peg beamed. "She is. After a molt or two, most of the damage should be healed, and that will finish the cure. I wonder if we'll ever know how she came here?"

"Maybe someday," Teg said. "I'd better go join Xerak. Is Vereez ashore already?"

"She just went down. Grunwold, Meg, Kaj, and I are to stand by to sail *Slicewind* through whatever opening you create, if possible. If not, we'll grab supplies"—she gestured to neatly arrayed packs set on the deck—"and beat feet through."

Teg nodded. She could think of dozens of problems with that plan, but she was also certain the others had discussed them—probably while she was sleeping off her mana crash—and that this was the best plan they could come up with. She'd just need to trust them. Peg, in particular, was showing how her lifetime as "mother of many" had made her into something of a tactical genius.

When Teg reached her assigned post, Xerak had just finished using his spear staff to draw a grid of various-sized rectangles on the sand. Vereez held the letter map in her hand and was apparently double-checking some detail.

"The locks we undid at Zisurru University," Xerak said, explaining before Teg could ask, "were relatively simple compared to this. I've drawn a grid to help me keep track of the various glyphs and their relation to each other. An added bonus is that those aboard *Slicewind* will be able to estimate our progress."

"Sort of a visual checklist," Teg said. "Good idea."

"When I start the incantation," Xerak continued, "I want you and Vereez to stand behind me and put a hand on the side of my neck. Slide your hand up under my mane, where you'll have skin contact. Then give me what mana you can spare, but don't overdo. If I feel you getting unfocused or weaker, that will distract me, which would be a far bigger problem than my lacking mana. Got it?"

Remembering the destructive potential of the glyphs, Teg nodded.

Vereez stretched up on tiptoe to press her nose leather to Xerak's in a sort of friendly kiss. "Absolutely! Let's do this thing. I can't wait to finally meet this master of yours."

Xerak looked momentarily worried, as if wondering just what the feisty young woman might say to the long-absent Uten Kekui, then managed a quick whisker twitch of a smile. He turned, faced his grid, then, raising his spear staff, began to sketch the first glyphs. Teg knew she had achieved concentration when the sound of Grace's whistling faded, and she saw the building spell as clearly as if she were looking directly at it, instead of into the tangle of Xerak's mane.

Teg could feel Vereez's presence as well, a rush like a driving wind, while Xerak was flame mingled with something pepperminty and focused that reminded her, oddly enough, of Meg.

Is that the scholar in him, the element that has balanced his passion?

Teg wondered what she felt like to the others. Heard a soft

voice—Vereez?—whisper: "Stone cold, stone hot." And Xerak's wordless agreement, linked with an irritated match-strike reminder that they *must* focus. Teg did, soon seeing only the spell, feeling only Xerak's workings, Vereez's careful trickle of energy, a trickle that met with Teg's own, intertwined, then fed into Xerak's much greater flow.

As the spell built, character by character, glyph by glyph, Teg understood its complexity, as she had understood what the various instruments contributed to a complicated piece of music, an understanding that did not mean she would be able to duplicate the working, only to appreciate it as something other than intricate "noise."

Xerak filled the first line of his grid. Moved to the second. The third. Colors washed and danced, brighter than the eye could bear, improbably vivid. To the new sense that Teg was learning to use, these "colors" were beautiful, compelling, enticing. Teg had never wanted to study painting or drawing, but seeing these colors she craved the ability to manipulate them as her child-self had craved the crayon box with 120 colors and the built-in sharpener that promised infinite rejuvenation.

As Xerak entered the final line of the grid, Teg was aware of being tired, but didn't think she was in danger of collapse. That is until, as if sensing completion, the various parts of the spell began to reach for each other, interweaving, tapping power far beyond what any of them—even Xerak—had to give.

She felt Xerak's dismay. The spell was not supposed to begin to draw power until the final character had been worked, the one that would enable the spell to tap into the crisscrossing ley lines and use them to find the destination indicated in the spell.

Apparently, they had not provided enough mana. Rather than falling apart, the spell—like a plant questing after water—had sought an additional source. However, without the destination indicated, it was reaching every which way—and trying to take them with it.

Xerak struggled to lift his spear staff, to slice the tip through the glyphs he'd drawn and so break the spell—although Teg was aware of his fear that the spell would not break, but would take him over, using his staff as a conduit. Complex spells were like that, possessed of an impulse to "be" that made them like living things—close kin to annual flowers, which grow with no less vitality for all that their lives will be bounded by a few short months.

Teg felt Xerak try to shove out from under his connection to herself and to Vereez, determined that if he was going to be consumed, they would not be as well. She was equally determined to hold on, to send more mana, to strengthen him.

You can do it! she thought, throwing all her passion as a mentor into the assertion. *We can do it! Don't break the spell. Take back control.*

She thought that last with the force of an order. Then, riding on the heels of that command, she opened herself to the ley line, attempting to channel more of the area's passive mana. She felt Vereez's own blast of determination, but knew that neither of their offerings were going to be enough to enable Xerak to wrest back the distracted spell.

Suddenly, a new element entered the contest. A rush of energy, fresh and powerful. If Vereez felt like wind and Xerak like fire, this was not merely water, but flood. It came to them wrapped around Vereez's line and Teg recognized it as Kaj. Somehow, he'd managed to exploit his connection to Vereez, to the baby she'd carried that had mingled both of their bloods, then used it to bring his barely tutored but undeniable power into the matrix.

With that, the balance changed. Xerak grabbed onto Kaj's newly offered mana, used it to direct the spell before it could go further astray. He squeezed the mana it had stolen back into the glyphs, then set about drawing the final characters.

Teg pulled back her additional contribution, knowing that it would be catastrophic for Xerak if she were to collapse. She sensed the same awareness from Vereez, but Kaj only intensified his contribution. There was a wild delight in his new connection to a part of himself that he had long suspected, but never been sure of, that made Teg wonder, fleetingly, just what it would be like to fuck— there really was no other word for it, for love had nothing to do with the craving—this young man.

No wonder Vereez is obsessed, she thought, tamping the thought with every bit of her will, concentrating until her associates were nothing but streams of raw mana, mana enough to reshape time, to resculpt space, until a door was ripped into the web work of reality as she knew it, forcing it to become reality as Xerak desired it to be.

The recalcitrant glyphs fell into place, as eager to obey now as they had been to break free. They rippled through the air in front of Xerak, linked to the ley lines, created an elongated diamond that pulsed invitation.

That's going to be big enough to sail the ship through, Teg thought gratefully. Then she collapsed onto her hands and knees, and thought nothing more.

﷽CHAPTER TEN﷽

Coming around with a definite sense that time had passed was becoming a habit. This time, however, it wasn't Kaj who held a bowl of broth to Teg's lips, but Meg.

"How are you feeling?"

Teg managed a few sips and a groan. Her head was buzzing—then she realized that at least some of the buzz came from Thought and Memory, who were lying on either side of her head and purring comfort.

"Aspirin, right?" Meg efficiently nursed two tablets, one at a time, into Teg's mouth, making sure she swallowed a liberal amount of broth between each. "Here's an update. You four opened the gate, though you and Vereez collapsed in the process. Kaj and Peg dragged you and Vereez on board, then Grunwold piloted *Slicewind* through before it closed. As to where we are . . . We're not certain. Grunwold's compass is spinning in all possible directions."

Teg managed, "Xer? Ver? Kaj?"

"Xerak came around about an hour ago and, despite Peg's and my protests, has dragged himself up on deck to confer with Grunwold. Vereez is just coming around. Kaj held up until the crisis was over, but he's out cold. However, he is breathing steadily. He looks oddly content. It is perhaps not strange. Xerak says that Kaj is definitely a wizard—and one with solid potential, at that."

Teg tried a nod. She wanted to say something about hoping Kaj would use his power for good, but it was too much. She considered drinking more broth but, instead, her thoughts muffled in cat purrs, she went back to sleep.

When Teg woke up, she didn't feel great, but she felt capable of more or less falling out of the bed in the stern cabin and getting to the head. Thought and Memory were gone, so either they had gotten bored or it was feeding time back home.

When Teg emerged from using the toilet and washing her face, Peg was waiting for her.

"Lounge or more sleep?"

"Lounge. Food! Time?"

"You've been down and out for about eight hours."

When they reached the galley, sliding onto the bench behind the table pretty much exhausted Teg's store of energy. Peg filled Teg's favorite poffee bowl, then set about preparing a simple but nourishing omelet. After confirming that Teg's headache was no longer so severe that it made listening painful—Peg also dished up the latest news.

"The good news is that we now are pretty certain we know where we are. The bad news is that it's not where we hoped to be—or not quite. Remember the stormy peaks we saw in the Font's vision? We're near those. If we go closer, the lightning develops intent. Actually, it turns into something like dragons. And tries to eat us. Right now, Xerak and Grunwold are attempting to figure out how to deal with that. Meg's with Vereez, who is in the middle of a major crying jag. Kaj woke up long enough to drink about a quart of broth, then he passed out again."

The poffee tasted great, but it also made Teg's stomach queasy. She tried a few mouthfuls from the omelet Peg slid in front of her. These tasted excellent, liberally flavored with butter, and Teg's stomach rapidly agreed to let her eat more. Teg was augmenting eggs with bites of a light, fluffy biscuit, and Peg was cleaning the pan, when Meg came in.

"Glad to see you're doing better, Teg. Peg, do we have hot water?"

Peg motioned to the kettle set on a warmer, and Meg set about brewing something in a small cylindrical cup.

"For Vereez. She's a wreck, poor child, and I can't say I blame her. Apparently, her contact with Kaj was very much like sexual intercourse. He made his link into your magical workings by exploiting their previous connection and, since that was sexual, that's what he used."

"He'd raped her?" Peg asked, outraged.

"Not in the least," Meg said primly. "The connection goes back to when they were lovers. On some levels, Vereez still wants them to be lovers. Surely, you've heard of divorced couples—even acrimoniously divorced couples—who fall back into bed again, sometimes repeatedly."

Peg suddenly became very intent on scrubbing the frying pan.

Meg went on. "If Kaj committed a fault, it was that he exploited Vereez's desire for him, but even Vereez admits this wasn't intentional. Kaj saw the spell was failing. He sensed a link—and he used it. What has Vereez so badly shaken is that, as the spell was breaking apart, she realized this—and realized that while Kaj has a sort of mild affection for her, he does not care for her at all, not even, particularly, as a sexual partner."

"Ouch!" Teg said. "That's rough."

"Xerak gave me something that should calm her," Meg said, lifting the tea she'd been brewing. "Although he was reluctant to do so. He says all of us need to be alert."

"Well, Xerak's just going to need to be patient with Vereez," Peg said bluntly.

Teg nodded. "I felt Kaj's aura, I guess you've got to call it. He's sex: sex and rock 'n' roll. He didn't just connect to Vereez because they were lovers, though. It was because she carried Brunni—basically, his 'blood' and hers mingled in a creative fashion. Vereez is probably shaken by that, too."

"Because there is a link that cannot be denied?" Meg mused. "Yes. I can see that. Well, let me bring her this tea. I'll sit with Vereez until she goes to sleep and maybe after, in case she has nightmares."

"I'll spell you," Peg said. "I have knitting to keep me occupied. Maybe I'll try singing to her."

"That would be lovely. Get Teg fortified first." Meg paused and patted Teg gently on one cheek. "You did very well, my friend. I'm immensely proud of you."

Teg blinked, confused, but waited until Meg was out of hearing before asking, "Proud? Of me? Why?"

Peg chuckled. "Oh . . . Maybe because Miss Commitment Shy of the Century—and I may extend that back into the twentieth as well as into the twenty-first—has shown she can make a life-or-death commitment if she chooses. Maybe just because you looked so cool down there."

Teg laughed uncomfortably, but she felt pretty good as well. After a second bowl of poffee, she hauled herself up the ladder to where Grunwold and Xerak were conferring near the wheel.

Slicewind hung "at anchor," a light breeze rippling the sails. In the distance, the lightning-shrouded peak was doubly dramatic—the only visible feature in a vista that was otherwise a deep void of starless indigo into violet skies.

"Salvador Dali would approve," Teg said, by way of greeting.

"Peg said something similar," Grunwold agreed, "and also something about the scene looking like an 'Affirmation cover.'"

"Affirmation?" Teg chuckled as she lowered herself onto the nearest bench. "Oh! I bet she meant 'Yes.'"

"Isn't that what I said?" Grunwold asked, then shook his head. "Translation spell must have missed something." He lowered his voice, although there was no real need. "How's Vereez?"

Teg shrugged. "Meg just brought her Xerak's brew. Xerak probably knows better than I do."

"If Vereez drinks it, she'll sleep," Xerak replied, pushing a stray strand of mane out of his eyes. "How she'll be when she wakes up, though … That's up to her. And if she doesn't want to be all right, that's a problem because, well—we need her."

Teg reached for her cigarette pack, realized she didn't have a craving except for something to do with her hands, and settled for pulling out her pipe and starting to clean the bowl.

"Why Vereez specifically?"

Xerak sighed. Teg guessed he really wanted a drink, but he wasn't going to take one. As a gesture of wordless solidarity, she put her pipe away and gave him her full attention.

Xerak gestured toward the distant mountain. "Grunwold and I have confirmed that mountain is indeed the location we saw in the Font of Sight. You can't see them bare-eyed but, with a good telescope, you can even spot the doors."

"The problem," Grunwold said, "is that we can't get around the lightning shadows."

Teg listened and heard a word that sounded something like *oehenserit*, although her brain insisted Grunwold had said "lightning shadows."

"Lightning shadows?"

Grunwold nodded. "Don't you have them in your world? They're creatures who live in electrical storms. Thunder is said to be the sound of their passing through the sky."

Teg thought about trying to explain about what thunder "really" was, realized she didn't quite know herself, except that it had something to do with how the electricity moved through the sky, and shrugged.

Maybe "lightning shadows" is a literal translation of what he's saying, a description that has become a name. Maybe that's why the translation spell let it pass.

"We have stories, lots of stories," Teg said, "that explain the sound of thunder, but I don't think anyone takes those literally. Are you saying that in this world there are actually creatures that are responsible for the sound of thunder?"

"Sure," Grunwold replied, looking at Teg as if she'd questioned the reality of trees or rocks. "They're hard to see, but they live in the heart of storms, breathe lightning, and produce thunder."

"Lightning shadows are very difficult to control," Xerak added, "as you might expect, but sometimes wizards use them as guardians or defenses. Attracting lightning shadows is most easily done in an area where—or at a time of year when—storms gather. The tops of mountains are prime nesting locations."

Grunwold gestured toward the floating mountains. "Xerak's guess is that the spell written on the letter was intended to carry us inside the defenses, maybe even through the door. But..."

Xerak interrupted him. "But I screwed up. Even after Kaj threw his mana into the mix—an incredibly stupid thing for him to do; he could have been killed—we could have broken off the spell and tried again. Or we could have come back after you all had more training. However, once I felt all that additional power, I tried to punch through. My 'fix' wasn't quite right. It opened a gate, sure, but that gate took us here—on the wrong side of the lightning shadows."

"Can we just go back"—Teg gestured vaguely to indicate "back"— "and redo the spell?"

"We need to do the spell all over again to go back," Xerak explained, shaking his head. "And right now, we don't have the mana. I'm not even certain the spell would work from this end. The way it was set up, the final step was tapping the vortex where the ley lines met, then using that to shove us through the gate."

"Is there a vortex here?" Teg asked.

"Sure," Xerak said, pointing with the tip of his spear staff in the direction of the floating mountain. "There. I can't imagine that the lightning shadows would hold still and politely watch while we went through the stages of a complex working."

"So, we're stuck here," Teg said, "until we find a way to deal with the lightning shadows."

Grunwold nodded. "So it seems. We could try sailing around this void and look for somewhere to port but, as you can see"—he indicated the limp sails—"there isn't a lot of wind here, and the strongest currents are..."

"Let me guess," Teg cut in, "near that floating mountain."

"I've been contemplating options," Xerak said, sliding his hand restlessly up and down the polished wood of his spear staff. "One option is for a couple of you humans to go back to your world, then try to return somewhere else in our world—the Library of the Sapphire Wind would be best, because we have allies there and it's possible the repository would have tools you could use. Meg would probably have the best chance of getting there, since she has a strong tie to Sapphire Wind. If the repository didn't have anything useful, you could then go to Zisurru University, explain the problem, and ask for help."

"That might work," Teg conceded, "especially if you went with Meg, since you're a wizard and could work travel spells if needed. You're also an accredited graduate of the university. But I'm guessing that you don't want to leave when you're so close to your goal."

Xerak nodded. "I'm also the most skilled wizard of our company. If I left, *Slicewind* would be at great disadvantage, both offensively and defensively."

"We could all leave this place via our world," Teg suggested. She saw Grunwold stiffen. "Except that you don't want to leave *Slicewind*. I can understand that."

"I'd do it," Grunwold said, although he sounded as if he was agreeing to having his antlers pulled off, "if that was our only option, but there are a lot of 'ifs' involved in using your world as an in-between point, including whether Meg could reach the Library if none of us were there, or even if, without one of us inquisitors to act as anchor, you mentors could get back to our world at all."

Teg considered. The one good thing about their situation was that they didn't need to worry about supplies. Thought and Memory showing up to check on her confirmed that the link between the three mentors and their home world was still available to them. Still ...

"Wait! When I first came up on deck, Xerak said something that made it sound as if he thought Vereez could solve some of our problems. What did you mean?"

Xerak stood and started pacing, his tail lashing back and forth. "When we were connected through the spell, I sensed that you were aware of me and Vereez as if we were other than the physical selves you see here."

"Yes. You felt like fire. Vereez felt like a wind. Later, Kaj felt like, well, floodwaters ..."

She and Xerak exchanged glances that said, "Among other things," but out of consideration for Grunwold, they didn't voice their shared impression.

"And you," Xerak said, "feel like earth—more specifically, like stone. It's overly simplistic to say that all wizards have an element that they are associated with. That's how the nonmagical see it. More accurate is to say that each and every wizard has an element that they can manipulate with greater ease. Mine is fire. Yours would be earth."

"Earth makes sense for an archeologist," Teg quipped. "I've manipulated enough of it in the course of my career." Then she sobered. "And Vereez's element would be air, wind ... lightning?"

"That's right," Xerak said. "If anyone in our number can convince those lightning shadows to let us pass, it's going to be Vereez. But when I checked on her earlier, I saw that something has caused her to pinch off her connection to her magic."

Teg frowned. "You know as well as I do what has made Vereez react this way. Stop protecting Grunwold. He's no idiot."

Xerak looked at his friend, but Grunwold cut him off before he could speak.

"It's Kaj," Grunwold said bluntly. "Or rather what Kaj did. I'm no wizard, but I saw him down there, holding on to her, pushing against her like he was mounting her standing. I ..."

He curled his hands into fists, bent his antlered head as if he wanted to batter through something, then sighed. "I would like . . ."

He didn't get to finish what he would like because, at that moment, Kaj's wild-dog head thrust up through the hatchway. He looked like the last day of a three-day binge, his eyes bloodshot, his reddish-brown and tan fur sweat-matted.

"I didn't know I'd mess her up so badly," Kaj said, struggling to get up through the hatch. Xerak went over and pulled him up. "I swear on whatever you'd like—my newfound power, my unknown father. Here's why I did it. I saw the spell trying to take over. I saw reality beginning to crack. Maybe you didn't, but that's what was happening."

"I believe you," Teg said.

Xerak nodded. Grunwold only stared.

"And I saw that Xerak was struggling to hold it all together, but he was going to lose it. I went over the side, meaning to grab onto him like Teg and Vereez were doing. Then I saw, felt, tasted—I don't have the words for what happened to me—that I could more easily send the mana through Vereez, because she was connected to him, and there was a connection between her and me. And there was no time to waste, and so I did."

Kaj slumped down onto the deck, put his head between his knees. "And I'm sure you all hate me and I don't blame you, but that's the real truth—at least as I saw it."

Teg repeated softly, "I believe you."

Xerak nodded. Then, realizing Kaj couldn't see the gesture, said, "I believe you, too."

He looked at Grunwold, clearly expecting him to say something scathing.

But although Grunwold's fingers tightened on the spokes of *Slicewind*'s wheel, his words were no more than usually gruff. "I believe you, too, Kaj. But that doesn't change that the damage was done. Vereez is—to borrow a word I bet's just all too appropriate—seriously fucked up right now. And she's the one we need if we're to continue on to find Xerak's master—maybe if we're going to get out of this alive."

Teg went below to brief Meg and Peg, both of whom she found sitting at the pulldown table in the lounge, near the galley.

"Vereez insisted on being left alone," Meg explained, "and I decided to respect that. At least she's no longer trapped in a crying jag."

Teg was just finishing bringing her friends up to date on what Kaj had said when there was a soft rapping and Vereez poked her nose around where the door to her room intersected with the galley.

"May I join you?" she asked shyly. "I heard you talking."

"Sure," Peg said, pushing herself up from the table and moving to get another chair. "Sit here, next to me."

"Thanks," Vereez said. "I'm going to get some poffee. Can I fill anyone else's bowl?"

"Sure," Teg said.

"I'm fine," Peg said, and Meg nodded that she was as well.

After Vereez had seated herself, Meg said, "You didn't drink Xerak's concoction."

Vereez shook her head. "I started to, but then I was reminded of Ohent, how she dealt with her problems by taking various potions. I didn't want to be like her, especially because Kaj . . ."

She stopped, lapped up some poffee.

"Kaj wouldn't think much of you?" Peg finished into the silence. "He seems pretty patient with his mother."

"I don't want him to lump me in with her," Vereez said.

Teg listened with dread for the note of hysteria to enter Vereez's voice, or for tears to pool in the dark-brown eyes, but Vereez's voice remained steady, her eyes clear.

"I'm sorry about how I acted," Vereez said. When Peg started to say something soothing, Vereez raised one hand to forestall her. "I know I had good reasons to lose it. Believe me. I've been doing nothing these last several hours but telling myself how abused I am, how nothing has gone right, not since, well . . ."

Peg grinned. "Since the three of us showed up at Hettua Shrine, rather than the ideal mentors you had imagined?"

"Well, yeah." Vereez managed a slight self-deprecatory smile, melting down her ears as she did so. Then she shook her head and perked her ears. "But that's completely stupid. It's obvious from everything that has happened that you three were somehow intended to be our mentors. At the very least, we would never have been able to retrieve the part of Ba Djed that was in your world, and that's really the least part of it. So, when I say I'm sorry, I mean it."

Meg replied, just a little primly, "Nonetheless, I understand your reaction. This was not how the story was supposed to go. You were supposed to find a mentor who would not only lead you to Brunni and Kaj, but help you to cause them to love you, to be impressed by you."

"Yeah," Vereez said softly. "Instead, Brunni has a 'mom' she really loves and trusts. At best, I'll be like an aunt to her, which is crazy weird, because her mom is my aunt. And Kaj . . . I've been in love with him since I was fourteen. He was supposed to love me, to be pining for me, and I kept hoping that was true but he was just hiding it, but after that . . . After he . . ."

She took a deep, ragged breath and managed, "After the connection we experienced during that spell, I can't fool myself. Kaj doesn't love me. Right now, he doesn't even like me very much. I'm everything he grew up despising: privileged, spoiled, indulged. You know what's the worst part of it?"

The three mentors waited for her to speak.

"My being in love with him is the thing Kaj likes least about me. He thinks I was stupid, that instead of making up involved romantic stories to excuse his not answering my letters, not trying to see me, that I should have gotten on with my life, used all the advantages I was handed at birth to make something of myself. He's not even sure he believes I wanted to find Brunni for herself. He thinks it's just part of this complicated romantic epic I've created to justify my stupidly throwing myself at him."

Again, when Peg started to say something, Vereez held up a staying hand.

"And the worst thing is, he's probably right. That's what hit me so hard. Not the mana depletion after the spell, not even his not loving me. It's that the last five or so years of my life have been a lie I told myself so I could accept that I flung myself at a hot guy and got knocked up. That's it."

"I think you're being a bit hard on yourself," Peg said, "but that's acceptable, especially if it serves as a starting point to moving past what's been holding you back. The real question is what are you going to do with yourself now?"

Teg added, "How much of what I told Meg and Peg did you overhear?"

"Just about all of it," Vereez admitted, looking more sheepish than someone with a fox's head should be able to do.

"So, you realize that Xerak thinks you're the only one who can get us around the lightning shadows."

Vereez shook her head, not rejecting that she'd heard, but rejecting Xerak's assessment.

"I think Xerak's underestimating himself. I'm not saying I don't have an affinity with air. That would be denying what's obvious but, when I was in school, our teacher stressed that too much importance was placed on affinities, that a trained wizard with no affinity at all was often far better than someone with an affinity, even after training. People with affinities too often cut corners, take shortcuts, trust to instinct."

Peg's lips shaped a cynical smile—or maybe she was just counting stitches. Once Vereez had settled at the table, she'd pulled out her knitting.

"This is the same instructor who downplayed your own magical gift?" she asked too sweetly. "Perhaps this person's testimony is not to be trusted."

Vereez's ears flickered, as if hearing an unexpected sound. "Xerak hinted at something similar, but I wasn't in the mood to listen. You mean, my tutoring might have been meant to keep me from exploring my potential magic?"

"Was he a private tutor or someone giving group lectures?" Peg asked.

"He was the general lecturer at my academy," Vereez said, "but my parents hired him as my tutor as well."

"Then I'd definitely take whatever he said with a healthy dose of suspicion," Peg said. "Although I suspect there is some truth in what he said. It's true of most things. Those with raw talent often do take shortcuts, and sometimes that's to their detriment later on. But we're getting off the subject."

Teg cut in. "Vereez, I think there's something else you need to consider before you completely reject taking charge of getting us around the lightning shadows. You keep talking about Xerak as if he's perfect. Did it ever occur to you that maybe he doesn't trust himself to manage this?"

"But Xerak's incredibly talented!" Vereez retorted. "Maybe you don't realize how amazing it is for someone of his age to have been fully accredited as a wizard."

Teg found herself getting unexpectedly angry. "Xerak is also badly shaken by his failure to get us where we were supposed to go—even with the power of three others and the vortex to bolster his spell. Add on to that how he's within reach of the master he's been searching for for over a year, and he's about to fail. Xerak hasn't started drinking again, but I think that's only because he's worried what will happen to the rest of us."

She bit her lip before the next words—about how maybe Kaj was right and Vereez was nothing more than a spoiled, indulged daughter of wealth and privilege. Perhaps anticipating those unspoken words, Meg put a warning hand on her arm. Peg's needles stopped in their rhythmic clicking.

Vereez's ears flattened to her skull, then slowly perked erect. "I get why you smell so angry. I was only thinking about how I'd feel if I failed. I wasn't thinking about how Xerak must be feeling. I'm still not sure I can figure out how to manage the lightning shadows myself, but then again—I don't need to, do I? Xerak wasn't ashamed to ask for help. That's what I need to do—ask Xerak how I might help us to handle these lightning shadows."

"Good girl," Peg said resuming her knitting. "Why don't you run up topside and tell Xerak that? I'm sure he'll be relieved beyond belief. Teg, you go with her. I wouldn't be surprised if a conclave of you wizardly types will be convened."

Vereez dashed away with a speed that showed how much she feared that delay would give her indecisiveness an excuse to return. Teg pushed herself to her feet to follow.

"Thanks, Meg."

"For what?" Meg looked up at her, eyes all pale-blue-crystal innocence, lips a light rose bow that shaped just the faintest smile.

"For being so cool . . . and for helping me keep mine."

The conclave of "wizardly types," rapidly morphed into a general counsel with all hands on deck.

"The lightning shadows get agitated when we're about two tenths of a mile away," Grunwold explained, indicating the distant activity with a wave of one arm.

He'd turned the wheel over to Peg and was standing in *Slicewind's* bow with Vereez, using the ship's most powerful telescope to inspect the insubstantial creatures. Xerak stood nearby, alongside Kaj, who was within easy hearing distance, but very obviously taking care not to crowd Vereez.

Teg had studied the lightning shadows through both *Slicewind's* telescope and various sets of binoculars, but she still couldn't decide what they looked like. They were dark—not black, but that deep indigo-violet that is somehow darker than actual black. There was something feline/lupine about them, but that was more the fluidity and strength of their motion. Dragon? Maybe, but, if so, the Chinese type—possessing a raw ferocity that those usually lacked. These creatures elongated and contracted like shadow did, shapeshifting in motion as if reacting to a light that shone on them, but nowhere else.

"The lightning shadows start stalking toward us when we get to about a tenth of a mile out," Grunwold continued.

"And if we back away?" Vereez asked.

"They do, too. But they keep watching until we're about a quarter mile out. Then they—well, it's hard to say 'relax' about creatures that spit lightning and shit thunder—but they stop being as focused on the ship."

"I can feel the storm," Vereez said, closing her eyes and breathing evenly.

"What do you feel?" Xerak asked.

"You can't tell?" Vereez asked, apparently not certain if he was humoring her, or prompting her, teacher style.

"If you mean, 'Can I feel what you feel?'" Xerak replied with the edge of a growl to his voice. "No, I can't. Not unless we're tied into a spell, and then only when you're providing me with mana. If you mean, 'Can I feel the storm?' No. I can't, not this far out. It's very contained, centered on that mountain peak."

"Sorry," Vereez replied. "I'm having a hard time accepting that a sense I've taken for granted all my life isn't something like—well, seeing or hearing or tasting."

"It isn't," Grunwold said, bopping her lightly between the ears with two fingers. "But it does explain why you always managed to get in ahead of the rain, leaving me and Xerak to get soaked. So, spill.

What does the storm feel like? Any thoughts as to how we can get through it?"

Vereez elbowed him, then ducked out of reach of an ear tug. "If you promise not to laugh at me or say 'Are you sure?' I do have an idea."

Grunwold rolled his eyes, but Teg thought he was enjoying himself. "Promise."

Vereez moved to where Meg had seated herself on a coil of rope, since the bow area didn't have as many benches as did the area behind the mast. "Can I borrow a blank page of your journal and a pencil?"

Meg handed over the entire journal, inserting a pencil to bookmark a blank back page. Vereez sat cross-legged on the deck, then spent a few minutes sketching, erasing, and sketching again. When she was satisfied, she handed the journal to Meg, who glanced at the drawing, nodded, and passed it to Grunwold, who passed it to Peg, taking the wheel back from her in the process. When everyone had a chance to look at the sketch, Vereez accepted the journal and held up the sketch as she talked.

"What I've drawn there is the storm as I see it—except 'seeing it' is a poor way to explain. Still, it's best as I can do right now. Since the rest of you can't see storms, I'd better start by saying that this formation isn't normal. Storms don't coil like springs around mountains. See how I've drawn the winds as dashes of different lengths, rather than solid lines? That's the only way I could think of to show how various air currents have been forced into place."

"So that's not a solid wall of wind," Xerak said, "no matter how it feels to us when we try to take *Slicewind* in."

"That's right," Vereez replied. "I think that I might be able to force the 'spring' apart along the dashes. If I did that, then Grunwold could slide *Slicewind* through the gap. But there's the small problem of the lightning shadows."

At her mention of "small" Grunwold started to snort derisively, stopping himself with such violence that Teg half expected the air to come puffing out his ears.

"Any insights as to how we might handle them?" Xerak asked. "Whether or not the lightning shadows cause thunder is moot. We've been watching them long enough to confirm that their primary attack is a controlled lightning bolt. *Slicewind* couldn't survive many of those—and her passengers couldn't handle even one."

Grunwold nodded. "*Slicewind* is fitted with a lightning rod on the mast. Don't ask me how it works, because I don't know, except that if it's hit, the lightning is somehow dispersed through the hull and is then discharged. However, I don't think the lightning rod will hold up to repeated strikes so, if those lightning shadows can direct their force, we're screwed."

Vereez muttered something in a very soft voice, but although Teg bet no one—not even the sharp-eared locals—understood a word, it was enough to draw all attention to her.

"Excuse me, dear?" Meg asked. "I didn't quite catch that."

Vereez squared her shoulders. "I think I can do it. I think I can catch the lightning bolts and throw them back—or at least divert them."

Everyone stared at her, then Peg managed a somewhat strangled sounding, "That would be lovely, dear. Could you explain in more detail?"

"Hang on. I'll need my swords." Vereez ducked below decks and emerged wearing the belt from which hung her twin swords. As she slid one from its scabbard, Teg was struck anew by the burnished copper of the blade.

"With these," Vereez said. "I think I can do it with these. I think that they're meant for this sort of work."

Grunwold interrupted her. "I know I said I wouldn't say this . . ."

Kaj cut him off. "So I will. Vereez, are you really suggesting that you'll go head on with those lightning shadows?"

She looked squarely at him. "Do you think that makes me as crazy as Ohent?"

"I am becoming less convinced my mother is crazy," Kaj countered. "Sleep deprived, beset by visions, but not crazy. Leaving her out of it . . . No. I don't think you're crazy, but I do think you're being brash. You've only had those swords a few months. Now you're going to use them to parry bolts from lightning-spitting monsters?"

"If no one else has a better plan," Vereez shot back. "That's exactly what I was going to suggest. I'll stand in the bow, right at the front. The lightning shadows seem to have distinct territorial boundaries. When they come at us, I'll intercept their attacks. One reason I drew that picture is that I was hoping that if I was occupied with the lightning shadows, Xerak might take on the task of pulling apart the wind veil so *Slicewind* can squeeze through. If Xerak's guess is correct, the lightning shadows have been told to protect against intruders. I suspect that once we're inside, probably within that same two tenths of a mile limit, then we'll be safe. Otherwise, the summoning spell dropping someone inside the ward wouldn't be of much use, would it?"

Silence, then Teg heard herself saying, "We could pick an area where the lightning shadows are more thinly clustered for our entry point. Even better, we could divert them by coming in close on one side of the mountain, then pulling back, and coming in fast on the opposite side. In that case, Vereez would only need to deal with a couple of attackers."

"After the lightning shadows have clustered, they do take a while to spread out again," Grunwold admitted. "But I'd feel better about this plan if we had some evidence that Vereez can actually catch and parry lightning."

Xerak stroked his chin. "I can help with that. I know a minor lightning spell—it's meant for nudging creatures you don't necessarily want to hurt permanently. It's low enough power that, if any of the charge gets through, it'll just frizzle her fur a bit."

Grunwold nodded. "I remember that spell. You used it on the draft lizard we disturbed that night when . . . Well, anyhow. You used it on the draft lizard. It isn't anything like the force those things are throwing, but if Vereez can't parry even your little bitty bits of lightning, we can make another plan."

"I'm game," Vereez said with a show of bravado. "Let's try."

"Not," Meg said firmly, "today. You, Teg, and Kaj are barely recovered from your last magical excesses. Xerak is doing better because he has a lot more training. We've had a busy day. Tomorrow will be soon enough."

Her words were so sensible that no one argued, although Xerak looked as if he wanted to.

Early the next morning, they cleared a portion of the foredeck for the experiment. Xerak rattled off a rapid incantation, then something blue-white and about the size of a golf ball shot from his cupped hand toward Vereez's chest. Vereez parried with ease, rolling the ball lightning down the blade, where it vanished into the metal.

"Excellent!" Xerak said, after they'd repeated this routine several times. "This time, see if you can throw the lightning back at me. Don't worry about hurting me, just do it."

Vereez flattened her ears in concentration. "Ready, coach!"

Xerak tossed another blue-white sphere. After catching the glowing golf ball, Vereez snapped the blade at Xerak, as if trying a conventional sword strike, although he was well out of range. A marble-sized ball shot back toward Xerak, who stabbed it to frizzle away on the tip of his spear staff.

"So, both defense and offense," Xerak said. "Very useful. How do you feel?"

"Wobbly. Excited. Like I want to do it again."

"Fine. Let's keep practicing," Xerak said.

"Won't doing that spell wear you out?" Vereez asked. "Remember, my plan was to have you handle creating an opening for *Slicewind*. You can't do that if you're beat."

"That's why we practice now," Xerak said. "I'll be fine. This isn't even touching my reserves."

Grunwold took advantage of the interruption to cut in. "I like Teg's idea about diverting the lightning shadows away from where we're actually planning to attempt to get through. I suggest we choose the side of the mountain opposite from the door. I'll sail *Slicewind* over and make a few feints so the lightning shadows think—if they do think—that's where we're going to punch through. Meantime, you two practice until one of you falls over. While you sleep, Peg can take the helm while I rest. Then we make our attempt when we're all . . ."

"Except for me," Peg quipped.

". . . rested."

"Better than letting Vereez try something so dangerous without any practice," Kaj said, "though what she's planning to try is still risky."

Teg leaned to punch him on the shoulder. "Then, fellow apprentice, maybe you and I should figure out what we can do to raise the odds in our favor."

* * *

"Closing to three tenths of a mile... Two tenths... One." Meg's voice, calm and controlled, despite the fact that she had to shout to be heard over the omnipresent thunder, provided updates from her vantage in *Slicewind*'s crow's nest. "The lightning shadows are reacting as anticipated and gathering into a tight cluster."

At the helm, Grunwold made finicky manipulations to the wheel, slowly bringing *Slicewind* around so her side, rather than her bow, faced the approaching lightning shadows. His task was made even more complicated because he was also maintaining the ship's position at the very edge of the sensitive reaction boundary.

Vereez waited poised in the bow. The rest of the ship's crew were scattered at various posts on deck, waiting for the race against light and shadow to begin. Teg and Kaj held the lines for the rarely used secondary sail.

Meg shouted, "Grunwold! The lightning shadows in the lead are heading toward us!"

Teg tightened her grip on the line. Behind her, Xerak held a sack holding one of their stored winds. At his nod, Peg ripped open the release, while Xerak spoke a few pungent syllables that directed a steady stream of wind into the sails.

Teg was glad she had grabbed hold before because, even with Kaj's muscular arms bulging as he steadied the sail for maximum effectiveness, the line still slipped through her gloved hands before she tightened down and got a solid hold. Spinning the wheel with careful control, Grunwold brought *Slicewind* around, driving the ship outside the two tenths of a mile limit, so the lightning shadows wouldn't be compelled to chase, skirting the invisible whirlwind that bordered the floating mountain, racing them on an invisible track to the far side.

Slicewind cut through the air with incredible rapidity. Even so, even with the care they had taken to lure the majority of the lightning shadows away from their projected point of entry, when Grunwold brought the vessel in, some of the rearguard of the—Herd? Flock? Host? Was there even a collective noun for such things?—lightning shadows were reorienting, cutting through the air to intercept the intruders.

Teg was all too aware that the only thing that stood between the *Slicewind*'s crew and disaster was a messed-up, gap-year kid who stood, apparently frozen, in the bow, her arms crossed, hands resting on the hilts of her swords. The time to show Vereez was an adult in more than law was coming up really, really fast.

Now that the burst of speed was ended, the secondary sail was no longer needed. Once it was lowered, Teg wrapped her fingers around the sun spider amulet. She didn't know if its power would work on creatures that seemed to be made from nothing but pure energy, but better to be ready.

She could feel Kaj tensing beside her, ready to loan her mana, if needed. They had all agreed that it would be best if Vereez did not have contact with Kaj again. However, while Teg had a shown an unexpected gift for the magical arts, she had the least mana to contribute. The plan was that she would serve as a funnel to supply mana to Vereez, hopefully muffling Kaj's signature in the process. They couldn't count on Xerak to help, because he was opening up a segment of the whirlwind, as well as standing by to help with ship defense, if needed.

The lightning shadows raced closer. Darkness upon darkness... (Something in Teg's memory said, "*Tao Te Ching*?" and she wondered if she was right.) The nearest lightning shadow raced closer. It was nearly upon them. It opened a maw that coruscated with ball lightning and spat.

Moving with such speed she seemed to be one of the lightning shadows herself, Vereez parried. Her copper blades flashed, liquid fire in the weird, indirect light. The lightning shadow swerved toward the motion. Vereez reoriented, cutting at the approaching monster.

Is she attacking too soon?

But Vereez's acute awareness of these creatures of wind and wind's fire—the lightning—didn't fail her. To those watching, it seemed as if the lightning shadow had not yet reached *Slicewind*, but Vereez's parry—for from the way the lightning shadow reeled back, she had struck something invisible to the rest—was successful.

Having parried the lightning shadow's attack, Vereez followed through. She sliced down with one blade, up with the other. What she caught between those sharp-edged strokes became visible as an LSD-dosed spider's web of crackling energy, the shape compact yet deep with complexity. Vereez caught the violent energy with her blade, then rolled it into to a compacted ball of force that she shot back to crash into the lightning shadow's writhing torso.

The creature fell back, but another lightning shadow was approaching, undeterred by what had happened to its host-mate. Teg looked for any indication that Vereez was becoming weary, but the young woman was, if anything, invigorated by the contest. Her fur crackled, giving off multicolored sparks that spat defiance at her opponents.

Nonetheless, Teg nodded to Kaj. He stood behind her, placing his hands on the bare skin of her neck. Teg breathed in the raw lust the young man's touch inspired, reminding herself that this was just a boy, at least as messed up as the rest, and she was no predator. Along with her awareness of Kaj, she took the mana he was offering her, filling in the reserve she had been learning to build in her lessons with Xerak.

When Teg came back to full awareness, Vereez was still going strong. She was laughing now, catching the lightnings and batting them back with her blades. Grunwold had brought *Slicewind* through the first ring of the defense—and was guiding them within that two tenths of a mile border. The stored wind was ebbing now, but there was enough that they should be into the hoped-for safe zone before they lost speed.

Meg was calling out again. "I think we were right. Most of the lightning shadows are beginning to show less interest. Only the ones who are actively engaged with *Slicewind* are still following us. Vereez! Vereez! I think if you shift to defense..."

Meg let the words trail off, for it was suddenly apparent to them all that Vereez could not hear them. Teg guessed what had happened. Vereez was drunk on the energy she had been absorbing from the lightning shadows. Vereez might not even be aware that her own resources were exhausted—and why should she be? She'd replaced them with something that probably felt a whole lot more potent.

At that moment, Vereez was playing with a lightning shadow, taunting it, then slicing into it when it drew close. Her laughter sounded like a high-pitched echo of the thunder. Teg dashed forward, suddenly aware Vereez was in danger of more than just overdosing on alien mana. She felt rather than saw Xerak running next to her.

"I'll hold back the lightning shadow," he said. "You grab Vereez.

Haul her back. Insulate yourself. She's half-gone into becoming one of those things herself."

Teg was short enough of breath that she could only grunt her reply, but Xerak seemed to understand. He roared, then darted between Vereez and the lightning shadow, shoving Vereez with the butt of his spear staff while exhaling fire at the lightning shadow. It was an impressive performance, but Teg didn't have time to admire.

Insulate myself. Insulate myself. How do I . . . ?

She drew on the sun spider amulet, channeling her and Kaj's combined energies through it, envisioning liquid rock, cold and nonreactive as glass, but with the flexibility of molten lava. The sun spider liked the contradictory concept of molten yet cool. Teg heard it giggling as together they guided the liquid stone up and over her hands, continuing past her elbows. The sun spider took over guiding the insulating process, for Teg's attention was needed elsewhere.

The maddened air mage was about to bring her blades down against Xerak's unprotected back. Clearly, in this moment, Vereez saw Xerak not as a friend from childhood, but as an impediment between herself and the next infusion of the element that was now singing in her veins. Teg used her glass-gloved hands to grab both of Vereez's arms before the swords could land.

Vereez screamed protest, flung back her head and snapped at Teg with her long fox's jaws, teeth closing so close she caught Teg's short hair between her jaws.

Teg knew she had to restrict Vereez's ability to use her blades, while keeping her from moving her head around for a second snap. Trusting in the breastplate of insulation the sun spider was building over her chest, Teg embraced Vereez in a tight hug, pinning the young woman's crackling arms to her sides. For a moment, there was a question as to whether youth would defeat muscles built from years of hard labor on archeological digs, but Teg managed to keep Vereez in a tight hold.

The copper blades were awkward to use at this close range, but Vereez would soon have managed to score at least one clumsy cut in her captor's lower body if Grunwold, muttering apologies, hadn't walloped his would-be lady love in the gut. He wore heavy leather gloves but, even so, he shuddered, caught by an electrical jolt. Sparks erupted from his antlers.

At Grunwold's blow, Vereez gasped, loosening her grip on the twin swords enough that Grunwold could knock the weapons from her hands. Teg continued to hold Vereez as the younger woman kicked and screamed, spitting out invective in a voice of thunder. Then Xerak was with them, also gloved, and the three of them managed to restrain Vereez until, cursing and spitting sparks to the end, she collapsed in something that looked less like a faint than the quiet that follows a violent storm.

※「CHAPTER ELEVEN」※

Peg had taken over the helm when Grunwold had raced to Teg's aid. With Meg serving as navigator, and Kaj trimming the sails and fending them off the mountainside with a boathook, she brought *Slicewind* to rest in front of the intricately carved door in the side of the floating mountain.

Heru fluttered down from the mast and trumpeted, "We're here! Where's here?"

The lightning shadows had retreated, and were now no more threatening than distant thunder. Vereez had come around, nauseous and bruised, but in far better shape than anyone had dared hope.

"I'd stored scraps of Xerak's energy in my blades when he and I were practicing," she explained. "I drew upon that until I had the lightning shadows' own power to use. Then I had enough, and more than enough. After that, I'm not quite sure what happened."

Xerak sighed. "I know what happened, and it's really my fault for not warning you. There's a danger to having an affiliation with an element. You can use it, but if you take in too much of the mana—especially from a living source—then you are in danger of being dominated by that force. I didn't think you'd be absorbing the lightning shadows' energy, so I didn't warn you. I'm sorry. I've been a very poor teacher."

Vereez reached out and tugged the edge of his mane. "You taught me a great deal in a very few hours. I was the one who overreached myself. I did mean to just bat the energy back, as we'd done in practice, but when I got a taste, I found I wanted more."

"Like cocaine," Peg said, "or especially heroin. I always avoided both of them, because I heard too many times that the first high was the best. Later, you just keep chasing, trying to get that first high back. You've learned a valuable lesson."

"And Teg," Vereez asked anxiously, "are you all right? Did you drain yourself too badly?"

Teg shook her head cautiously, so as not to release a lurking headache. "Not too badly. I'd stored some extra mana myself, thinking I might need to come and be your supplemental battery, like we were for Xerak. The sun spider amulet helped, too."

She looked at it thoughtfully. "It's more alive than we guessed. A great deal more. And I think it's come to sort of, well, like me. Or maybe," she said, laughing, as Thought and Memory suddenly leapt up into her lap, "it likes my cats. In any case, it seemed to know what I needed and helped me shape it."

"So," Kaj said, "if we're all more or less well, there's no reason for us not to see what's behind those doors. Let's get Xerak to wherever in the flaming torture space it is he's going."

"Teg, can you read any of what's carved on this door?" Meg asked some time later. "The translation spell is proving of little help."

Meg moved aside so that Teg could make a closer inspection. The stone portal was round, rather than rectangular, and heavily covered with ornamental carvings. They'd already tried to open it, but it could neither be pulled nor pushed, nor slid side to side or up and down. Teg had been itching to get a closer look but, remembering how the others had reacted to her methodical archeological approach back when they had been seeking the entry to the Library of the Sapphire Wind, she had restrained herself. Now she moved forward with alacrity.

The carvings were deeply inlaid with grime, so Teg blew on them, which helped only a little. "These are really filthy. It's possible we're missing parts of the inscription." She pulled out a handkerchief, spat on it, and gave an experimental scrub.

"Here," Vereez said, extending a rag and a bottle of water from the kit Grunwold kept for shining the brasses. She still sounded a bit chagrined. Everyone else might be willing to overlook her excesses when battling the lightning shadows—even be grateful, since she'd saved their lives—but she was still troubled by this latest evidence of her inclination to emotional extremes.

"Thanks," Teg replied. "What I'd love to have is a soft brush . . ."

A fleeting image from a long-ago watching of Walt Disney's *Snow White* came to her, and she had to fight back an impulse to ask Vereez to dust off the door with her fox tail.

A short time later, Heru glided up, a burlap-wrapped bundle gripped in his long pterodactyl's beak. He dropped it in front of Teg.

"Grun send these. Your dig kit. He say you'll ruin his stuff."

"Thanks, Heru. You're a prince among xuxu."

Heru played a cascade of cheerful notes on his crest, but Teg, excited by the lure of new discoveries, hardly heard him. After using the rag as a duster, she continued cleaning with the brushes from her dig kit. Some areas were already partially cleaned from their earlier attempts to move the stone slab, so within a short time she had a sense of a design. She found the apparent center, then worked out from that. The others were peering around her, making guesses as to what might be depicted, but she shut out their comments, focusing on the image taking shape before her.

It was a spiral or rather a series of spirals, beginning from a central core and becoming multifaceted as they expanded. The innermost spiral began as nothing more than a line, then became pictographs. These were so stylized that they were difficult to interpret as other than "figure on two legs," "figure on four legs," "figure with three legs?" Or was that third leg a staff or spear? It certainly wasn't central enough to the body's "fork" to be the sort of optimistically large penis that wasn't uncommon in prehistoric art. There were other simple drawings that probably represented neither animals nor humans, but indicated shelters, tools, plants, and the like.

As Teg continued working outward, that first spiral ended, or rather it became intertwined with a second spiral that wound around it, gradually taking precedence. At first these pictographs bore a slight resemblance to the earlier ones, but they diverged, becoming more and more abstract. The final abstract forms were something like elongated triangles interspersed with straight lines. Even as Teg recognized what they were, she found herself thinking how curiously modern they looked: like circuit diagrams or something.

No one interrupted her, so Teg kept working, wanting to see what the next shift in style would be before she verbalized any conclusions. Interestingly, in the new spiral, the previous evolution was not superseded, but rather developed in parallel. Once again, pictographs became a form of writing, this one so easy to identify that Peg cried out in surprise.

"Are those Egyptian hieroglyphics?"

"Hieroglyphs," Teg corrected automatically. "And yes. They are. Absolutely. These"—she pointed to the "circuit diagrams"—"are cuneiform. These here that seem to be roughly colinear look a lot like the earliest Chinese forms of writing. I never studied any of these scripts in anything but a basic Introduction to Linguistics course, but if I remember correctly, they all evolved from pictographic writing that was later simplified, and eventually became representative of sounds."

"But those forms of writing originated in our world," Peg protested. "But they're here. Here in this world. Here on this door."

"That's right."

Meg mused. "I wonder if the translation spell is not helping us make sense of what is written here because these are ancient languages, or because the languages did not originate in this world— or is it simply because the door itself has been enchanted to prevent translation spells from working?"

"We'll probably never know," Xerak said. "I just hope we can get through."

To a backdrop of fascinated silence and occasional muttered comments, Teg continued cleaning, working outward. She noticed that no one linguistic approach was abandoned in form of another. Indeed, the spirals with pictographs were multiplying, even as their styles varied subtly. She wondered if they represented numerous cultures that hadn't evolved a formal written language. She finished cleaning a line of what she was certain were Mayan glyphs before speaking again.

"Xerak, you're the formal scholar of this group. Do any of these lines of writing look like anything you're familiar with from this world?"

He replied promptly. "The pictures are similar, although it's weird how so many of those images have round heads, and only a few have ears or tails. However, when the pictures change into writing, no, not really. Every so often I've seen something that looks familiar but it never carries through."

"Thank you. How about you, Kaj? You must have seen a lot of different sorts of writing when you were living in the necropolis. My experience is that religions hold on to older forms of writing longer than any other aspect of a culture. Anything?"

"It's like Xerak said," Kaj replied, after taking time to give a careful inspection, "sometimes a few bits are similar—especially in that one Peg called 'Egyptian,' but that could be because it seems to have stayed closer to picture writing than some of the others."

By the time Teg had the door cleaned, she was certain that what was represented was writing from many cultures of the ancient world. There was Linear B, Indus Valley writing, the very early proto-Elamite, and others she knew she had seen but couldn't put a name to. Somewhat more recent scripts were represented as well. The so-called Latin alphabet was there. She recognized others that were similar, but subtly different. However, the modern alphabet was not there, and she was willing to bet that the modern versions of the other forms of writing were not as well.

After she summed up her analysis, Grunwold said, "So this means?"

"I have no idea," Teg said, "since I am an archeologist, not a linguist. I speak English, and enough Spanish to get by. That's it. I read a bit more fluently in a couple other languages, but usually with a dictionary in hand. Meg? Peg?"

Peg shook her head. "I'm even less qualified to judge. Some Spanish, mostly spoken. About three words in Gaelic. No, wait, if you count the insults, a few more. My parents were of the assimilation immigrant type."

Meg frowned thoughtfully. "I'm not a linguist either, but I do have a slight reading knowledge of several modern European languages. About all I can add is that not every character in the Latin alphabet is English—even of the 'Old' type. I suspect this is an even older form."

Grunwold listened, ears twitching in a manner that meant he was confused, but resigned, and then repeated, "So this means?"

"It's confirmation of what we've suspected for a long time—that there is a connection between your world and ours," Teg said. "Beyond that... Well, in many cultures, spirals indicate a journey—especially one of discovery, rather than between two known points."

She rose a little stiffly from where she'd crouched to clean the lower panels, then brushed off the knees of her cargo pants. "And since we hope to begin a journey, then I think we should start..." She pressed her right hand, then the entire weight of her body on the center of the spiral design and felt something give just a little. "...here." She moved her left hand to the beginning of the secondary spiral. "And continue here... and then..." She used an elbow. "Here..."

At her third push, there was a grinding sound, then a light—beginning as a speck of dark glowing shadow, then moving through the spectrum of the rainbow—began racing through the manifold spirals, and, like magic... *Almost assuredly magic,* Teg found herself thinking... the door began to spin, faster and faster until it became an invisible blur, and they could glimpse a large area beyond.

"After you?" Teg asked, motioning for Xerak to lead the way.

Xerak gripped his spear staff tightly in his hand, gave Teg a nod that was halfway to a bow, and walked into the doorway. His shoulders were tight, as if he fully expected to be hit by the spinning stone panel, but he passed through the blur without difficulty. One by one, the others followed, Teg last of all. After she had stepped through the spinning door slowed, became visible once again, the blur thickening until a solid stone slab stood between them and the outside world.

The space they were in felt like a cathedral, although Teg decided, as her eyes adjusted to the dim light, it looked more like the interior of a basket. Vereez played the concentrated glow from her magical flashlight over the walls, revealing the basket weave for what it actually was.

"Tree roots?" Peg asked. "But there was no tree, only a mountain."

"You stand," came an unfamiliar voice, masculine, deep, and resonant, "at the roots of the world. The roots of more than one world, to be precise. You are welcome here."

"Master?" Xerak's voice broke, making him sound young and afraid. "Master? Where are you?"

"I am here, Xerafu Akeru. Focus your gaze carefully, even as I have taught you, and you will find me."

Xerak had been looking wildly in all directions. Now, with great effort, he stilled himself. Centering his staff in front of him, he closed his eyes and bent his head slightly forward.

Recognizing the attitude as one of those Xerak used when focusing his power, Teg grasped the sun spider amulet, then closed her own eyes. As she ran her fingers over the swirls and convolutions that the journey through the heavens had etched into the surface of the meteor that was the sun spider's body, she became aware of a glow, taller than it was wide, that gradually resolved into a faint, ghostly figure of a broad-shouldered man with the head of a bison.

Teg waited, expecting the figure to resolve into something more solid, but he remained a ghostly wisp. Opening her eyes, she looked in the direction in which her magic had shown her the insubstantial figure, but all she saw were the tangled tree roots.

"Master," Xerak said. "I see you—or rather I see your spirit. You're still alive, aren't you?"

"I live, but I am a prisoner. I . . ."

The words were cut off by a second voice, this one female, holding a certain long-suffering note beneath the words.

"You are your own jailer, Uten Kekui. There is a path away from here that has been open to you since soon after your arrival. You are the one who has chosen not to take it."

Uten Kekui chuckled dryly. "That is true, as you see matters. Less so as I do. Will you let me go to my apprentice? I would explain my situation to him. His fidelity in seeking me out deserves nothing less."

"I will permit this. Only one form of escape is open to you, and you know that all too well." The female voice "turned," as if she now faced Xerak and his allies. "Before I let Uten Kekui come to you, let me make certain matters clear. I do not so much control this place as that this place and I are aligned in our goals. Uten Kekui cannot leave here unless certain conditions are met. Should you attempt to take him, even by force, I assure you that your efforts will be for naught. I do want Uten Kekui to tell you his tale. Perhaps you can persuade him where I cannot, but I do not wish to raise any false hopes."

"If you wanted him to report what had happened to him," Xerak said angrily, "why didn't you let him write me—or if not me, one of his associates?"

"Because only one who could find him might—and I stress

'might'—be able to set him free. You have come here. Therefore, you have earned the right to understand what Uten Kekui has done to bring him to this impasse."

Grunwold had made an "oh, yeah," sound when the disembodied voice had stated that efforts to free Uten Kekui were foredoomed to failure. Now he stepped shoulder to shoulder with Xerak.

"So, if we're so helpless," he said truculently, "why don't you come out along with Uten Kekui-va? I'd like to get a look at someone who could hold such a powerful wizard prisoner."

"Thinking to free him, perhaps by taking me hostage?" The female voice sounded amused. "Even if you should manage—and you would be many against my one—even that would not free Uten Kekui. Even holding a knife to my throat or cutting off my fingers one by one would not cause him to be set free. A more powerful force than any I command is what holds him here."

"Maybe," Grunwold countered. "But maybe you're just trying to intimidate us."

"Cerseru Kham does not lie," Uten Kekui said. "Nor does she misrepresent the situation. She brought me here, but more complex elements keep me prisoner. I will explain."

Xerak nodded. "I'll listen." He turned to Grunwold. "Please. I appreciate the support, but this seems to be our only option. All right, Cerseru Kham-va, if that is what you are called. Let Uten Kekui..."

"Wait!" Meg's voice cut through, silencing Xerak. "If the members of our group remain to hear Uten Kekui-va's tale, are we also fated to become prisoners? From where we come there are tales of such a price being exacted."

"No," came the woman's voice. "You will be free to go, even to speak of what has happened to Uten Kekui. Although, as to the latter, you may decide that it is wisest not to do so."

"Fair enough," Meg replied. "Please, go ahead then."

As soon as Meg agreed, the room began to change. Several of the thicker roots interwove to become a long, narrow table of the "conference room" type, although best suited, Teg thought, for a conference of wood elves or Ents. Rocks rose from the dirt underfoot, then shifted, shaping an array of open-backed chairs around the table. Lastly, directly from the top of the table, sprouted a miniature tree covered with ripe fruit.

Teg was surprised to recognize many varieties of fruit from the "real" world, such as apples and pears, as well as the pa-pas and proggies she'd become accustomed to eating Over Where, all perfectly recognizable, although the fruit themselves were rarely larger than a golf ball.

At the far end of the chamber, the roots swayed and parted, admitting first Uten Kekui and then a woman with the head of a creature with big ears like a deer, but striped, rather like a zebra. Teg felt triumphant when she remembered the name of the creature.

An okapi, related to a giraffe, but with a short neck. Actually, really pretty.

Both Uten Kekui and the person with the okapi head, presumably Cerseru Kham, wore wizard's robes, similar to those worn by both faculty and students at Zisurru University. The okapi-headed wizard made a sweeping gesture with her right hand, and the chairs at the head and foot of the table moved back, indicating where she intended for herself and Uten Kekui to take their seats. Ignoring the implicit suggestion, Uten Kekui walked straight to Xerak and offered him an open-armed embrace.

"You've grown," he said in that tone of voice adults use when they know they're speaking an obvious truth, and feel a little dumb about it, "and put on a lot of muscle."

"I've spent over a year travelling," Xerak said. He had accepted the offered embrace, but with a great deal more restraint than might have been expected, given the intense mixture of emotions that had driven his search. "Mostly on foot, looking for you."

"And now you have found me," Uten Kekui said, "and I must explain myself."

He'd been sneaking glances at the three humans, although Teg felt with less astonishment than they'd encountered before.

Uten Kekui knows about humans. He believes in humans. Teg thought. *For him, seeing us is like seeing an elephant the first time. Interesting, even astonishing, but not surprising.*

"May I be introduced to your companions?" Uten Kekui said. "I would like to know who will be bearing witness to our reunion."

Xerak nodded stiffly. "You've heard me mention my lifelong friends, Grunwold and Vereez. This is Kaj . . . He's the son of friends of our parents, and has joined us for reasons too complicated to go into now. These are Meg, Peg, and Teg—mentors granted to us when we went to Hettua Shrine to seek guidance."

Uten Kekui offered the entire group a deep and dramatic bow, then bowed again, even more deeply, to the three humans.

"I owe Xerafu Akeru's coming here to your involvement," he said. "Thank you."

"You owe Xerak's coming here," Peg replied tartly, "to the fact that Xerak is so stubborn he should have a bull's head, rather than a lion's. I hope you appreciate him."

"I do. How much I value him, well ... But I get ahead of my tale. It is a long one, stretching back through more than one life. Avail yourself of refreshments. You may be assured that no harm nor geas nor restriction of any sort will come to you by doing so."

Uten Kekui gave Xerak a fatherly pat on the shoulder, then moved to take the seat at the foot of the table. He gestured to the okapi-headed wizard, who had seated herself at the head.

"This is Cerseru Kham. Who she is and why she brought me here will be explained in time. However, for you to understand the whys, I must begin well before the day a dragon landed near my hermitage, back to before the building of the Library of the Sapphire Wind."

"In my last life," Uten Kekui began. "I was called Dmen Qeres."

"Dmen Qeres?" Kaj blurted. "As in the founder of the Library of the Sapphire Wind?"

"One and the same," Uten Kekui agreed. "However, although founding that great research institution is a claim to a certain amount of fame—or perhaps I should say 'notoriety'—even in that life, perhaps especially in that life, I was prouder of another role. It is only stating facts to say that as Dmen Qeres I was both powerful and versatile. I was also highly inquisitive. These traits led me over time to discover a secret—Society? Organization? I am not certain what to call it, for it was neither social nor rigidly organized."

"Association," suggested Cerseru Kham. "Now, stop stalling. You always get pedantic when you try to remember being Dmen Qeres."

Uten Kekui inclined his head in mute acknowledgement of the truth of this statement, then continued. "Association then. What associated the members was that each one was the trustee of a powerful magical artifact or one of those who might someday become a trustee."

"We may have come across a reference to those trustees," Xerak said. "Or at least to some of them. Are they depicted in an ancient mural on the island of Sky Descry?"

"Very good." Uten Kekui nodded approval. "What you may not have learned is that those artifacts are key to the continuation to life as we know it."

He spoke as if expecting his words to have a dramatic impact on his listeners. However, although glances were exchanged, the only one who made a sound was Meg, and she merely sighed in the tones of one whose guesses have been confirmed. Uten Kekui looked at Meg, as if wondering if she would say something but, when she simply smiled one of her gentle, enigmatic smiles, he went on.

"I was not the first trustee for Ba Djed of the Weaver, nor was my life as Dmen Qeres the first time I had been entrusted with this duty. However, as Dmen Qeres I made a choice that haunts me to this life. For various reasons that I will not enumerate now, I became convinced that I was the best person to be trustee of 'my' artifact. Therefore, I took steps to assure that the artifact would not pass into another's hands, but would be waiting for me when I reincarnated. In short, I created the Library of the Sapphire Wind."

"You created an entire research facility library to conceal one magical item?" Grunwold's voice was incredulous.

"One highly important *artifact*," Uten Kekui said. "Yes, that's right. As I am sure Xerafu Akeru has told you, although it is possible to use magic to search for magic, the more complex and confused the signature, the less effective such a search would be. I already had a considerable collection of magical materials myself—especially books. What I hadn't anticipated was how many of my associates would wish to donate their own materials. There came a time when I had to charge a fee for archiving and care . . ."

Xerak made a tightly contained but clearly impatient gesture, a motion that said, "Get on with it!"

Uten Kekui frowned, not so much in anger as in confusion.

Teg didn't bother to hide her smile. *You thought you could abandon Xerak for over a year and find him unchanged in his adoration. Maybe at first that was the case, but these last few months have been a crash course in the difference between earned and unearned loyalties.*

"Eventually, I died," Uten Kekui continued, "after a long life. My death came from the natural failure of my body. However, at my death, my plans went awry. Cerseru Kham, you know this part of the story closer to firsthand."

Cerseru Kham nodded briskly and set aside the miniature pear she'd been about to bite into. "I was alive when Dmen Qeres died, and a member of the association of which he spoke, although I had not yet become a trustee. I was preparing for that role, however, and knew much of the lore associated with the role of trustee. When Dmen Qeres died, my own master waited for the signs and portents that would indicate that Ba Djed of the Weaver had been passed to a new trustee. When several years went by and these auguries remained mute, she began to actively investigate who might now hold Ba Djed."

"You must have gone to the Library of the Sapphire Wind," Peg said. "Didn't you sense that Ba Djed was there?"

"We did," Cerseru Kham replied, "but 'sense' was all we could do. Dmen Qeres had hidden Ba Djed very well, and we could not pinpoint its location any more closely without arousing suspicion."

"Didn't your artifact—or rather the one your master held in trust—sense its associate?" Vereez asked.

"Other than confirming our suspicion that Ba Djed was still concealed within the Library of the Sapphire Wind, no, it did not," Cerseru Kham replied. "You must understand, the great artifacts are not pieces of one artifact, but separate." She placed her right hand upon the elaborate many-dangled necklace she wore. "The great artifacts are like the pendants on this necklace—associated but wholly independent."

"Why did you need Ba Djed so badly, then?" Peg asked, her knitting needles clicking busily. "You said they're independent."

"Independent but associated," Cerseru Kham repeated. "If one of these pendants were removed, the necklace would be unbalanced. Lack of balance can be tolerated for a time, but in the end, it causes problems."

"But . . ."

Cerseru Kham made an abrupt motion. "Please. As much as I

appreciate your interest in these arcane matters, let me finish my account. Besides, Xerafu Akeru is growing impatient. He has searched long and exhaustively for his master, and still does not know the full reason why Uten Kekui vanished."

Peg had the grace to look embarrassed. "Sorry. I apologize. To you, too, Xerak."

The young wizard forced a smile, but his aura of tension didn't abate. "That's all right, Peg. Now, Cerseru Kham-va, please go on."

"As I said, the hypothetical 'necklace' of great artifacts can function with a piece missing for decades. However, when I learned that Ansi Abzu, the trustee who held the second of the triad of artifacts—Qes Wen, the Entangled Tree—was nearing death, I began a serious search for the one who would be Dmen Qeres's heir. By then, I had come into the role as trustee of Maet Pexer of the Assessor's Wheel. However, even with it to draw upon, all I could learn was that Dmen Qeres had indeed been reincarnated, and all the signs indicated that he would continue as trustee in his new life. Making matters more complicated was that in the interim the Library of the Sapphire Wind had been destroyed. If we had not been able locate Ba Djed when the Library was intact, we had little chance of finding it among the ruins."

She looked over at Uten Kekui, and he resumed the tale.

"I have no sure knowledge as to why I was reborn without any memory of my past lives. Cerseru Kham and I have discussed this at length, and our best theory is that my—Dmen Qeres's—very arrogance in assuming that he/I was the only one who was capable of caring for Ba Djed was the precise reason that I lacked a memory of my past incarnations. In a sense, by assuming I was the only fit trustee, I violated the terms of my role."

"But . . ." Peg dropped her knitting and slapped a hand to cover her lips. "Sorry."

"Although each artifact has its own traditions," Uten Kekui went on, "as Cerseru Kham mentioned, there is a need for balance. It's highly likely that the difficulty that Sky Descry has had in finding a new Grantor is also a result of my actions, because for many years the Grantor and the trustee of Qes Wen, the Entangled Tree, have usually been the same person, and the disturbance I created flowed into the associated succession as well."

"They would have taken my little girl's body as a vessel for their Grantor!" Vereez snarled, her ears pinned back, her eyes narrowed and fierce. "Your 'association' has a *lot* to answer for."

Uten Kekui closed his eyes and looked impossibly weary. "More than you can know, child. Apologies are empty air, I realize, but still—please accept mine."

Vereez continued to snarl, leaning forward as if she would snap at him, but Xerak put a hand on her arm. "Please, Vereez. I've waited . . ."

She immediately looked apologetic, her ears melting into a less hostile position. "Right, Xerak. It's your turn. We've saved Brunni. I'll concentrate on that."

But the look she cast at Uten Kekui was anything but forgiving.

Cerseru Kham took up the tale. "When I became certain that Dmen Qeres had not reincarnated and then hidden his identity— perhaps while he sought to regain possession of Ba Djed—I changed how I was searching. Rather than looking for Dmen Qeres or someone who resembled Dmen Qeres, I began to look for someone who had tremendous magical power, but no previous life to explain it. I had already researched what was known about Dmen Qeres's past incarnations—often there is a similar interlude between incarnations—and in this way I narrowed my search."

"As for my side of the matter," Uten Kekui said, "I had wondered why, despite my considerable magical abilities, I had no memory of my past lives. Wizards are usually among the first to remember at least elements of their past lives, usually sometime in their thirties. By all indications, I should have remembered already, but other than occasional flickers, I did not.

"From my childhood onward, I had been solitary in nature. Now I began to force myself to take students, hoping that in teaching others, I would learn more about myself. Then Cerseru Kham contacted me. She said she had something of great importance to discuss with me. I shied away from her. Perhaps I knew that I would not like what I would learn."

Cerseru Kham's okapi ears flicked back in remembered exasperation. "Since Uten Kekui kept avoiding me, eventually, I kidnapped him. Doing so was not as difficult as it could have been. I think that, on some level, Uten Kekui wanted the truth—even as he feared it. I learned his routines and, one day when he was out for his usual walking mediation, I took him."

"No one saw . . ." Xerak began, then he shook himself. "But I forget. You are trustee of yet another of these great artifacts. We know very little about what Ba Djed can do, but the artifact associated with the Creator's Visage Isles is used for granting miracles. Seizing even a powerful wizard would be simple for you."

"I wouldn't say 'simple,'" Cerseru Kham replied, "but, as I said, I think on some level Uten Kekui wanted to be forced to confront the truth, to confront his past self. I thought that once I had explained matters to him, he would agree to go through the initiation that strengthens and educates trustees regarding their task, then, together, we could go to Sky Descry and straighten out matters there."

"When Cerseru Kham brought me here," Uten Kekui continued, "and I learned about who I had been and what I had done, the more I realized, the more horrified I became. In our efforts to discover what had happened to Ba Djed, we uncovered hints of Emsehu's role in the destruction of the Library of the Sapphire Wind. However, this did not lead us to Ba Djed."

Xerak said, "Because not only was Ba Djed broken into pieces, one third of it wasn't even in this world."

Peg looked at Xerak for permission to ask a question. When he nodded, she said, "Uten Kekui-va, did you—or maybe Dmen Qeres—realize that Emsehu was your son? He believed you did, and that, despite knowing, you still denied him."

"No. I didn't. In believing I deliberately denied him, Emsehu was wrong. However, when I considered how Dmen Qeres had treated his offspring, how I had behaved in my life as Uten Kekui, my belief that I was unsuited to be a trustee grew. Even without any memory of my past selves, I had continued as a self-absorbed, self-centered individual. In my current life, although gifted with considerable magical ability, I had chosen to be a hermit rather than join some larger organization. Clearly, I was no less self-centered in this life than in my former. Even my reasons for taking on students were selfish. So, despite Cerseru Kham's prompting, I have refused to undergo the initiation and accept trusteeship of Ba Djed, if and when that artifact could be found."

Cerseru Kham sighed so deeply her large ears trembled. "And no matter how I argue, I can't budge him from this opinion. The roots of the world are trembling, but Uten Kekui will not assume the role he himself claimed in his last life."

Meg's voice was cool and analytical as she asked, "Cerseru Kham-va, do you think it was a coincidence that your kidnapping Uten Kekui-va indirectly led to the restoration of Ba Djed?"

Uten Kekui took it upon himself to reply, speaking with the swift eagerness of one who raises a familiar argument. "Ba Djed was split into parts as a direct result of my self-centered behavior. Although many decades went by, and people ranging from Cerseru Kham and Ansi Abzu to Emsehu to random treasure hunters searched the ruins of the Library of the Sapphire Wind, Ba Djed remained in three parts until the one positive connection I had made in all my selfish existence began the search for me. Then the pieces were reunited."

Teg frowned. "I've been wondering about that." She turned to Cerseru Kham. "Once we started finding the pieces of Ba Djed, why didn't you try to claim them?"

"I considered doing so," Cerseru Kham admitted frankly. "When you six found the Spindle, and I felt its pulse out in the world again, I began searching for the remaining pieces. I spied on you, learned where you were heading, and made my own search in the necropolis. I located the Bird that was in Ohent's charge, but I could not find any trace of the final segment, so I left it with her."

Uten Kekui cut in. "I encouraged Cerseru Kham to let you continue your search. I suspected that it was not a coincidence that your mentors were no one of whom we had ever heard, and of mysterious origin—for that much we could learn, although we did not know until you came here that the three mentors were humans. To get Cerseru Kham to agree to leave the search in your hands, I had to promise that if you did not find all three pieces and then make your way here, I would agree to do what she wanted. But you are here . . ."

"And what does she want you to do?" Xerak said. "Somehow, I sense that it is more than merely taking custody of a powerful artifact."

Does Uten Kekui hear the scorn in Xerak's voice? Teg wondered. *Does he realize how tremendously he's disappointed that young man?*

"There is an initiation," Uten Kekui explained. "It protects the initiate from the force of association with the tremendous power of one of the great artifacts. A side benefit is that it enables the initiate to draw on the artifact with some degree of safety."

"And?"

"The difficulty is that it connects the initiate with his or her past selves. As I have said, I do not think that the person I was handled the trust well or responsibly. I do not think he—I— should have another chance. Moreover, I felt certain that the elements of me that were Dmen Qeres would agree when he/I saw what had happened as a result of our selfishness."

"And so?"

"And so, I want you, Xerafu Akeru, to attempt the initiation and become the new trustee of Ba Djed of the Weaver."

"What!"

The roar of protest was nearly universal. The only ones who didn't participate were Xerak and Cerseru Kham. Xerak's expression became so immobile he looked taxidermied. From the cant of her ears, Cerseru Kham was resigned.

She, at least, knew this was coming. Did Xerak suspect it was?

Grunwold's bellow dominated the assembly.

"Hey, I'll be the first to admit that Scraggly Mane here is ferociously talented, but even if he's the youngest to be certified a full wizard in however long, he's still a scrawny-assed kid. If you can't handle this sort of power, Uten Kekui-va, what makes you think he can?"

"I am his teacher. I know better than you do what incredible potential Xerafu Akeru has. When I left him somewhat over a year ago, he was promising but so lacked discipline that his raw talent was more a handicap than a benefit. In the last year, his promise has gone from bud to blossom. He has demonstrated perseverance and loyalty. I would not suggest that he undergo the initiation if I didn't think he could succeed. Ask Cerseru Kham her opinion of Xerafu Akeru's ability."

All eyes turned to the other wizard. She flapped her large ears once, but otherwise maintained her poise of superficial tranquility as she spoke.

"The glyphs sealing the safe deposit boxes at Zisurru University took a master's skill to undo them. Revealing the stages of the map was, once again, a master's task. However, working the transport spell—that took a grand master. Despite having just done such a great working, here is Xerafu Akeru, alive and—judging from the power nearly crackling from him—with mana to spare. I will admit, when Uten Kekui told me that Xerafu Akeru would be a fit successor, able to handle the rigors of the initiation, I did not believe him. Now... Now... I must say, Uten Kekui may be right."

Xerak shook his head so hard that his mane swept into his eyes. "You don't understand. I didn't meet those challenges alone. If Teg, Vereez, and Kaj hadn't helped me, I couldn't have worked a single one of those spells. And that's really the least of it. I've needed help every step along the way. As long as I searched alone, I got nowhere. It was only when I decided I needed help that I got anywhere."

Uten Kekui nodded, pride evident in every line. "And so you proved yourself far wiser than I have become. In my life as Dmen Qeres, I decided that no one but me could be trusted with Ba Djed. In my current life, I chose solitude—a version of the same arrogance, for once again I chose to stand alone. You, though, you have proven you can work with others, take a turn as leader, a turn as follower, even sublimate your private passions to the needs of those around you—as you did when you allowed first Grunwold's, then Vereez's inquisitions to come before your own. As you have surpassed me in these things, so I believe you can at least match my past selves and take over as the trustee for Ba Djed."

Xerak stared at his long-sought master with anything but adoration. "Would I be permitted to take the others with me on this initiation quest?"

"Of course. Isn't that what I just said? One of the ways in which you surpass me is in your ability to work with others."

Xerak kept speaking, as if he hadn't heard Uten Kekui. "I mean, if they would go . . ."

"Of course, we'd go, Xerak," Vereez snapped. "You helped with our inquisitions. It's only right we stick with you through yours."

Grunwold grunted a laugh. "I may not have magic, but you'll need someone to guard your back while you wear yourself out with the arcane nonsense. Heck, you'll all need me to assist you, now that you've turned Vereez, Kaj, and Teg into wizards. Can't expect Meg and Peg to drag your carcasses around by themselves when you fall over."

Peg laughed. "Don't underestimate us two old ladies. We might surprise you. Anyhow, Grunwold, if you're dragging exhausted wizards around, you'll need someone to protect *your* back. Don't forget that."

Kaj raised and lowered his broad shoulders in an eloquent shrug. "I pushed myself into this inquisition. I'm not about to back out now."

"We're in this until your search is complete, Xerak," Meg said firmly. "We made that promise at Hettua Shrine, and I don't think we're about to quit now."

Teg only smiled and tapped her pocket where the sun spider amulet rested.

"Thanks, all of you," Xerak said. Then he turned to face Uten Kekui. "You've heard them. Now listen to me."

"Yes?"

"I refuse."

Uten Kekui's mouth hung open in complete astonishment. Looking at him, Cerseru Kham began to laugh, a deep unaffected sound that made Teg suddenly like her.

"I'm sorry, Master," Xerak said, "but you're all wrong about how you're handling this. As Dmen Qeres you took too much upon yourself. As Uten Kekui you tried to take on too little. Neither course of action has worked. You're going to need to accept your responsibilities. Dmen Qeres may have been wrong in trying to pass Ba Djed on to himself, and himself alone, but that doesn't change that he named his heir—and that you are that heir."

Cerseru Kham started to say something, but Xerak halted her with a gesture.

"I'm not finished. I'm willing to assist you, Master. After all, my inquisition was to find you and, if you lived, to return you to where you belong. I've found you. Now I know where you belong. If you will accept my aid, then you will have it."

This time Cerseru Kham remained silent. For a long time, the only sound was the clicking of Peg's knitting needles and the occasional murmur as she counted off stitches.

Uten Kekui balled his fists and glowered at his apprentice, bending his head as if he were considering bringing his bison horns into play. He stood there for so long that Teg glanced over at Cerseru Kham, wondering if she'd cast some sort of spell of immobility on her colleague, but the thoughtful concern she could read in the okapi's features—*like but unlike Grunwold's*—reassured Teg more than any words that Cerseru Kham had not interfered in this battle of wills.

At the point when Teg was wondering if anyone would care if she pulled out her pipe, Uten Kekui stirred, lifted his head, and focused on Xerak, as if there were no one else in the room.

"Very well. I'll do it." He gave Xerak a hard look. "But I'll do it on my own. Not because I'm rejecting your help, but because you're right. Once upon a time, I believed that I was the one and only person capable of acting as Ba Djed's custodian. There must have been some basis for that. If I've lost the ability to trust in my own abilities, what sort of custodian would I be?"

Xerak looked worried. "I never meant for you to do this alone."

"I know. Nonetheless, Cerseru Kham believed I could pass the initiation without aid. Dmen Qeres believed he—I—could do this. Time to convince myself that I am worthy. If I accept your help, I would forever doubt myself."

Cerseru Kham opened her mouth as if she were about to say something, then stopped. Uten Kekui rose to his feet, then looked in her direction.

"Embarrassing as it is to admit, I don't know what I'm supposed to do. Could you point the way?"

"Doing so would have been much more difficult without the presence of Ba Djed," Cerseru Kham replied. "I would have needed to go with you. Then, together, we would have used my bond to Maet Pexer and your presumed bond to Ba Djed to create a link to Ba Djed. After that, you would have been able to pull the physical artifact, even if it was in parts, back to you. However, with it here, with it intact, Ba Djed of the Weaver will direct you to where you need to go for your initiation."

"That easy?" Uten Kekui said. Wordlessly, Xerak held out to him the enshrouding container that held the reassembled Ba Djed. "Well, then, I had better be at it."

He picked up the box, opened it, and touched one finger to Ba Djed. The cavernous space vibrated with a hum Teg felt in her bones, rather than her ears. The roots that walled the cavern moved restlessly, then parted, creating a tunnel. The inference was plain.

"I'll hurry back," Uten Kekui said, closing the enshrouding container and holding it firmly in one hand. Then, with an almost jaunty wave, Uten Kekui moved forward and was gone.

▌{ CHAPTER TWELVE }▐

"Now what?" Grunwold asked.

"We wait," Cerseru Kham replied. "To make the wait more pleasant, let me supply more substantial refreshments." She waved one hand and a laden buffet appeared to one side of the conference table. "Avail yourself of them. Or you may return to your ship. The lightning shadows will not trouble you, even should you try to depart—only if you should try to return."

Grunwold and Kaj beelined toward the refreshment table. Xerak didn't even seem to have heard the invitation but sat, unmoving, staring where his master had vanished.

"I have several questions," Meg said. "Perhaps, now that we must wait, you could answer them."

"I will answer what I can," Cerseru Kham replied. "Some mysteries are restricted to the initiated."

"Such restrictions are traditional in our world as well," Meg agreed mildly. "We," she indicated herself, Teg, and Peg, "have been troubled—perhaps tantalized is a better word—by links between this world and the one from which we came."

"Such as?"

"Echoes of language, similarities of art or symbolism . . ."

"The fact," Peg interrupted, "that from what we've seen, you people have characteristics—most obviously heads and tails—of creatures that are common in our world, but apparently don't exist here."

"I was getting to that," Meg commented, arching her eyebrows in mild reproof. "However, it seemed impolite to rush in to such a very personal element."

"But it's the most obvious link," Peg countered. "The others could be explained away on anthropological grounds. Right, Teg?"

"Some," Teg agreed from where she'd followed the boys over to the buffet. "Symbols such as star shapes, spirals, masks, even pyramids, dragons and other winged creatures aren't restricted to any one culture. Sounds also recur, whether because of common linguistic roots or plain old coincidence."

"Like Ohio is the name of a state," Peg put in helpfully, "but also how to say 'good morning' in Japanese."

"Like that," Teg said. She looked at Cerseru Kham. "So, now that Peg's been blunt and rude, can you explain why it seems like this world holds so many echoes of our world?"

"Or yours of ours," Vereez put in from where she was—without being asked—preparing poffee and tea for Meg and Peg. "I've been there, remember. I've seen how people who look like us constantly show up in your art."

"You've been there?" Cerseru Kham's eyes widened. "That's amazing!"

"I brought her," Teg explained worriedly. "The boys, too. I hope I didn't break any rules."

"No, you didn't. At least not any rules I know, but your inquisitors may be the first people from our world to go to yours in several centuries. And, as far as I know, you three are the only humans to ever visit this world—at least as humans."

Cerseru Kham rose and trotted briskly over to the buffet, poured herself a tall glass of pa-pa juice, and put a few nibbles on a small plate, which she carried back to her seat.

"Much of what I am going to tell you is usually reserved for initiates but, given how unusual this entire situation is, I am going to break silence. I hope that when I am done, you will understand why this information is usually kept secret."

She looked at them as if hoping someone might promise in advance, but no one did.

"Sorry," Grunwold said, sniffing various pitchers and bottles before settling on a dark ale that frothed as he poured it into a drinking bowl. "We've had too much of secrets lately. They're beginning to taste a lot like lies."

"Tell us your story," Meg said encouragingly. "We are not

unreasonable, and we have all, humans and denizens of Over Where alike, had to learn to accept a great deal that would have seemed beyond reason."

Cerseru Kham nodded. "Being capable of accepting what seems beyond reason may be useful in understanding what I am about to tell you."

She waited until everyone had refreshments and had taken seats. Xerak remained cross-legged on the floor, facing the section of tangled roots through which his master had walked, but the cant of his head made clear he was as attentive as the rest. He even gave Vereez a smile when she set a bowl of poffee down next to him.

"Long, long ago," Cerseru Kham began, her cadence that of a storyteller, "our ancestors lived on your world. Magic flowed more freely then, and those who could use it often served their communities as teachers and leaders. Even in those early days, when people lived in small family groups and everyone knew everyone, those who were especially talented in the ways of magic were often taken as gods.

"Whether as gods or priests serving gods or mystics, as human society evolved, wizards were highly influential. To mark themselves out from the general population, they often adopted shapes that blended human characteristics with those of animals that were considered particularly important in one way or another.

"Time passed. Humans prospered. Eventually, the first great city-building civilizations developed. Wizards remained influential, often serving as advisors to those who did the actual ruling and administration. Over time, debate arose within the community of wizards as to how best to influence their societies. The first rulers of these larger communities had been those with personal influence—whether those with magic, those who excelled in the hunt or in war, or those with some other value to the community.

"As communities grew in size, a new ruler arose. This new ruler was not human. It grew to power in stealth, gaining in prominence even before it was proclaimed. This new ruler was the domination first of custom, later of law, for law is custom codified. In time Law came to hold power over even those who were lawgivers. Law became the means to challenge the rights of even the most powerful warlord or arrogant plutocrat. Law allied itself with punishment, and through punishment with death. Thus, death, which before had been seen as a part of the natural cycle, came to be seen as the enemy of life.

"While many wizards were uncomfortable with the rise of Law, seeing it as inflexible and impersonal, some wizards saw Law as the means to bolster their own waning influence for—and no one has ever settled on what the reason was for this—since the rise of cities, the power of magic had been ebbing, and with it the influence of those who wielded magic.

"From being seen as gods, many wizards had fallen to being seen as servants of gods, and weak servants at that, for the working of magic drains the user. But what if Law could be transformed from a code that had evolved from a society's needs into something given by the divine? Then the gods and the servants of the gods would have influence to compete with—even to surpass—that of those who commanded armies.

"So it was that those who sought to use Law to preserve their own power banded together. But not every wizard agreed with this choice. Some had been studying the ebbing of magical power, and had come to the conclusion that the reason there was less magic was that people had forgotten that death was not an ending, but was simply one element in the soul's journey. Death was coming to been seen as—at worst—a cessation of existence. At best, death was seen as a passage into an afterlife separate from this life's cycle.

"When some wizards argued that magic could be rejuvenated by teaching people how to connect with their past selves, those who had embraced the ideology of Law protested. Humanity did not need more magic, they said, it needed more order. To encourage the belief in a reincarnating soul was to remove the sting of death that lies behind so many punishments—especially as many religions were teaching of an afterlife that included rewards for those who adhered to Law and punishments for those who did not.

"So it was that from the single seed of magical ability, two trees arose. One was the Tree of Law. One was the Tree of Life. Eventually, those who chose to dwell beneath the shade of the Tree of Life decided to leave the world where magic had become twisted and perverted into a means of control—of limiting potential, rather than expanding it.

"They sought—some say created—another world where they

could begin again, without coming into conflict with their rivals. Reaching back to their most ancient roots, they chose to reshape themselves into creatures other than humans. This was because, increasingly, the wizards of Law had preached the primacy of the human form. By choosing a wide variety of nonhuman traits, the advocates of Life made a statement as to their oneness with the variety of all living things.

"The advocates of Life are this world's first ancestors, although not our only ones. The story goes on to say how not all of this tradition left the world of origin at one time. Many users of magic remained on your Earth, thriving for centuries, even millennia. However, eventually the rule of Law spread—encouraged, so some say, through the sheer force of the long-ago city-builder's tradition. Each time Law won out over Life, a new wave of immigrants found the Tree of Life and joined us here. The one thing that binds us is the knowledge that the soul is immortal and will repeatedly take different living forms."

Cerseru Kham folded her hands in her lap and bowed her head, indicating that her tale was done.

"Wow!" Peg said. "That makes a curious sort of sense. I can see why, in the variation of the story that we have, Adam and Eve aren't supposed to eat from the Tree of the Knowledge of Good and Evil. Knowledge of something, rather than blind adherence to—even fear of—a code of laws is a big difference from blind obedience. Basically, choosing obedience over knowledge is accepting the law, but leaving the understanding to someone else."

Teg added, "The story you told us, Cerseru Kham-va, does explain why the mythologies of so many cultures in our world include a 'before' time, a time when gods walked the earth and miracles were commonplace. Usually, anthropologists explain this as wishful thinking, but I've always wondered why so many cultures should wish for the same thing, why they should be content to view themselves as fallen from an age of gold to one of mud. You'd think they'd want the reverse—a sense of progressing toward perfection."

Meg nodded agreement. "Cerseru Kham-va's story also explains why there are many stories of a time without sin, because the concept of sin in the abstract belongs to Law."

Meg turned to Cerseru Kham, a light of challenge in her pale blue eyes. "When you were chiding Uten Kekui for his refusal to take up his responsibilities, you spoke of the roots of the world trembling. Now that we understand that your world has its roots in ours, tell me, do the great artifacts have some part in this story?"

Cerseru Kham nodded. "When our ancient ancestors left their world of origin, they did not close the way to eventual reconciliation. However, those we left behind remained frightened of us. Perhaps because we did not embrace their right to rule us, they felt we would someday seek to undermine them. Because of that fear, they blocked our return. In doing so, whether knowingly or unknowingly, they also blocked the ability of our souls to follow us after death into our new home."

"What?" "How?" The exclamations were general.

Peg murmured, "The angel with the fiery sword barring the way into the Garden of Eden."

Cerseru Kham continued, "It seems that our souls 'belong' in some sense to the world of their origin. We learned of the consequences of this obstruction early in our migration: if blocked, the soul cannot be reborn. Since we still had many who shared our priorities back on the world of our birth, we worked with them to create a structure called the Bridge of Lives over which our souls could continue to cycle. The great artifacts are what maintain this bridge. With only one—my Maet Pexer—currently working fully, the gap is decreased. I am aware of a . . ."

She gestured, swirling her hands in the air as if physically reaching for an idea. "There isn't really a word for it. A pressure? In any case, a sense that the passage of souls from past life to rebirth is being constrained."

"I see why you're worried," Meg said thoughtfully.

"Are there no new souls?" Peg asked. "Or are you all descended from the rebel angels?"

Apparently, the translation spell was able to handle Peg's wording, for Cerseru Kham replied, "There are new souls, but these are only created when there are not sufficient souls to animate the bodies of those newly born. This happens from time to time, but globally our population is very stable."

Grunwold said, "I don't understand. If all of us are descended from wizards, why don't all of us have the ability to work magic?"

"All of us are not descended from wizards," Cerseru Kham replied patiently. "Many of those who chose the way of Life rather than Law were not wizards. However, even a wizard's soul may lose the ability to perform magic for a lifetime or so—most often if he or she is working through a personal conflict and chooses not to remember some key aspect of his or her past lives."

"My master," Xerak challenged, his gaze still fixed on where Uten Kekui had vanished, "lost his memory, but retained his power."

"Your master," Cerseru Kham said, a note of asperity in her voice, "may have remembered more than he is admitting."

"Speaking of Xerak's master," Vereez said. "How long before we can hope for Uten Kekui-va to come back? Is this initiation journey something that might take days?"

Nice of her to ask, Teg thought. *Xerak is clearly beginning to worry, but he doesn't want to sound as if he doesn't believe that Uten Kekui can handle whatever challenge Ba Djed will lead him to.*

"The amount of time needed to fulfill the challenge can vary," Cerseru Kham replied. "Let's give Uten Kekui somewhat longer before declaring his effort a failure, shall we? After all, although my tale embraced the events of millennia, still, not all that much time has gone by."

Xerak grunted agreement.

"I would like to hear about this Garden of Eden you mentioned," Cerseru Kham said, looking at the three humans.

"Me, too," Vereez said. Grunwold and Kaj nodded. Xerak cocked one ear back, but otherwise remained focused on the tangle of tree roots.

Peg obliged. "I can't promise to get the story perfect, because there are so many different retellings, but I'll do my best."

When she finished, Meg said, "Nicely done. A little Milton, a little Sunday school, but mostly Biblical. As you were telling the story, I found myself thinking how interesting it is that, in some versions of the tale, the serpent ate the fruit of the Tree of Life and so gained the immortality denied to the descendants of Adam and Eve."

"Something similar happens in the *Epic of Gilgamesh*," Teg said, "except that a serpent eats the flower Gilgamesh is bringing back to the world of the living, rather than a piece of fruit, which is why snakes, rather than humans, are immortal. Interesting how the desire to live forever is repeatedly given a negative slant."

"I wonder," Teg went on, "how the various flood tales fit into this. It's interesting that one of the earliest—the Sumerian tale of Utnapishtim in the *Epic of Gilgamesh*—is also tied up with the search for eternal life. You'll recall that Gilgamesh . . ."

From the *Epic of Gilgamesh*, they went on to discuss other flood tales from around the world, including how in many the Earth is remade after the flood. Vereez listened avidly. Grunwold stretched out and at least pretended to nap, Heru nested down next to him. Kaj also listened, occasionally asking questions. Xerak sat, stiff backed, his spear staff across his lap, gaze unwaveringly fixed on the spot where his master had vanished.

It was Grunwold who broke the increasing tension.

"I may not be a wizard," he said, rolling to his feet and stretching, "but I do have a good sense of time. Cerseru Kham-va, how much longer before you do whatever you do to figure out if Uten Kekui is in need of assistance?"

"I suggest we give him at least a day," Cerseru Kham replied. "I suggest that you all spend at least some of that time resting. If you do need to help him—something that I think is highly unlikely—you will do neither him nor yourselves any good by being exhausted. This cavern is not equipped with sleeping quarters, but I swear on Maet Pexer that you will be able to return here if you leave to go to your craft."

"She has a point," Peg said. She put down her knitting and went over to Xerak. "Come on. Be sensible. You've worked some major magics over these last several days, your nerves are shot."

"C'mon, bud," Grunwold echoed. "You know Peg's right. If you won't come on your own, I'll drag you."

"You and whose army?" Xerak growled, a deep rumbling thing, close on a roar.

"Me." Kaj stood beside Grunwold, his magnificent muscles rippling. "I've seen the results of sleep deprivation all too often. And I'm not as confident as Cerseru Kham-va that we're not going to need to go after Uten Kekui."

"Give in, Xerak," Teg suggested. "Me and Vereez and Kaj, we're all your apprentices, right? And we have your example of stubborn devotion as our model. How about making this easy on all of us?"

At that, Xerak started shaking, Teg thought at first with rage.

Then she realized that he was trying to hold in laughter. When it bubbled out, it started the rest of them—even Cerseru Kham—laughing as well.

"All right. I'll go get some sleep." Xerak pushed himself to his feet. He looked hopefully over at Peg. "Dinner first? All that Cerseru Kham-va so kindly supplied is tasty, but suddenly I could use some of your Irish stew."

"Easily done," Peg said. "I have some in the larder. It only needs warming." She looked at Cerseru Kham. "We'll send you a bowl. It's not quite right, since I had to use domestic kubran rather than mutton, and substitute different root vegetables for the onions, potatoes, and carrots, but it's pretty good."

Cerseru Kham showed her teeth in a wide smile. "I would be honored. There are times I grow quite tired of my own cooking."

Despite Cerseru Kham's confidence that Uten Kekui would succeed in his initiation, when they re-entered the cavern beneath the roots of the world some hours later, she was its only tenant.

"Uten Kekui hasn't come back," she said without waiting to be asked. "Worse... I believe something may be seriously wrong. Remember how I told you that since Ba Djed and Qes Wen lost their custodians, I have been aware of an increasing sense of pressure?"

No one spoke, but ears of various sizes and shapes perked to indicate agreement. The humans had to settle for nodding.

"Sometime during your rest period, I became aware of fluctuation in that pressure. At first it became less, which I took as a good sign—an indication that Uten Kekui had retaken his role as trustee and the bridge was strengthening. Not long ago, I felt the pressure increase again, becoming—if anything—more intense than it had been."

"So, what's happening?" Grunwold demanded.

Cerseru Kham looked directly at Grunwold when she replied. "Yesterday you said something that indicated you believed that I could somehow see Uten Kekui and monitor his activities. I didn't bother to explain then—because I thought Uten Kekui would have returned by now and the point would be moot—but I am unable to check on him. He has gone where one might follow, but none can see."

Xerak made a choking sound, but otherwise couldn't seem to form words.

"One?" Grunwold retorted. "Is that poetical phrasing, or are you saying only one of us can go after him?"

Cerseru Kham smiled. "Poetical. If all of you wish to go, you are welcome to share the risk. I, however, will not be going. As the one remaining custodian of a great artifact, I cannot in good conscience do something so irresponsible."

"That makes sense," Grunwold agreed gruffly. He looked at the others. "Anyone want to stay here to protect our backs?"

"Or be ready to come pull you out if you fail?" Vereez said, trying to sound as if she were joking and failing entirely. "Honestly, I think we all should go."

Xerak started to say something and she held up one black-nailed hand.

"Xerak . . . Stuff it. We're not letting you go alone."

Xerak rubbed a rounded ear. "Actually, I was going to say that if Uten Kekui has come up against something he can't deal with, then I'm not certain I could deal with it alone. I'd appreciate some help. But Grunwold does have a point. It might be wisest for a backup team to wait."

Kaj shook his head. "We're too small a group. How would we split our numbers to leave an effective backup? Four and three? Five and two? Two and five? However we do it, we either start with or leave behind a weaker band—and it's not as if our abilities are interchangeable. Xerak is the only qualified wizard in our number. He will definitely want to be in the first group. Any group without him will be without a wizard—less able by definition."

Teg fought down a sudden impulse to claim she could serve as backup wizard, uncertain as to whether what fueled it was overconfidence or a desire to have an excuse to stay behind.

Instead, she said, "Kaj's made a good point. Cerseru Kham-va is remaining behind. If we also vanish, after a suitable time, she can arrange a rescue party."

"I would and will," Cerseru Kham agreed. "No matter what lingering doubts you may have regarding my ethics, you can believe that I will arrange a rescue. After all, Uten Kekui took Ba Djed with him, and that must be retrieved at all costs."

"Enlightened self-interest," Meg said, with a close-lipped smile that robbed the words of any sting. "A believable motivation."

"Since we're looking for my master," Xerak said, "I think that rather than attempting to retrace his steps, the best thing would be to create a search centered on him specifically. Cerseru Kham, can you show me how to make the ritual understand that?"

"I can try," she replied. "It's a sensible enough request."

Moving to the vicinity where Uten Kekui had departed, she reached up and wrapped her hands in a cluster of dangling tree roots, then shut her eyes and began to chant under her breath. The tree roots began to move, twining down to stroke the sides of her face and fondle her large ears. Eventually, Cerseru Kham opened her eyes just enough to look out from beneath hooded lids. With a jerk of her head, she beckoned Xerak closer.

"Join me," she said, her voice distant. "Show the tree your intent."

Without hesitation, Xerak reached up to meet the grasp of the roots that were already reaching for him. They entangled his arms up past the elbows, lifting him off the ground with what seemed like indecent eagerness. More tendrils grabbed his head, twisting through his mane to caress the skull beneath.

Teg found her hand drifting to where the sun spider amulet rested, wondering if her rapport with earth magic would be enhanced here in this apparently subterranean realm, or if the gigantic tree beneath whose roots they stood was already using all available magic. Happily, Teg wasn't forced to find out. Well before she was tempted to experiment, the roots gently released both Cerseru Kham and Xerak. Xerak's boots hadn't quite come to rest on the packed dirt of the floor before he was talking.

"I think I've gotten the tree to understand that we want to go to where my master is. I felt as if the tree was trying to tell me something, but I couldn't grasp what it was. I think it was that Master has met with some sort of difficulty, but we already guessed that, right? So, I'm still going. Everyone who's coming, follow me."

Pausing to give Cerseru Kham the briefest of bows, Xerak started off at a jog-trot toward where—as on the day before—the dangling roots were separating, creating what was definitely a tunnel between here and . . . where?

Not long ago, Teg might have considered her actions more carefully. Now all she saw was Xerak's maned head, followed closely by Grunwold's stag antlers, and she started running to catch up because who knew what trouble those kids were going to get into if she and the others weren't there?

The tunnel through the roots didn't so much end as, all at once, they found themselves somewhere else. Teg didn't bother to look back to see if the tunnel remained open behind them. She knew it wouldn't be, and that didn't particularly bother her. What did was the vista in front of them.

Stretching side to side was a broad sweep of something varicolored green, simultaneously opaque and translucent. It took Teg a long moment to register that what she was seeing was a broad, mostly flat body of water. She looked up and saw a sky heavy with rain clouds. Little bits of light peeked out around them, silvering the edges of some clouds in a fashion that made the overall impression all the more dark and heavy.

"Lowering clouds," Peg said, pronouncing the word *lou-er-ing*, "or is that *lo-ering*, because they look so low? I've never known what's the right way to say that word."

"*Lou-er-ing*," Meg said, absently, "but the root word probably means 'to lower,' so you could justify either. The real question is, where is Uten Kekui?"

Xerak was standing at the edge of the water, looking out over the flat green sea. He grasped his spear staff tightly in his hands, his attitude one of intense concentration.

"Xerak's looking," Vereez said trotting back to join them, "or scrying or sensing or something. Where are we? This doesn't look like your world, does it? It doesn't look like anywhere I know in ours."

Teg wrenched her gaze away from that huge sheet of water. She had no idea why this body of water was so mesmerizing. She'd seen large bodies of water before: the Atlantic and Pacific Oceans, some of the Great Lakes, even the Mediterranean Sea. Why did this strike her as so impossibly vast?

Looking behind her, Teg felt a shock. While she hadn't expected to find a neat tunnel, offering retreat, she hadn't expected this. They stood on a shelf of material too gravelly to be called sand, too sandy to be pebbles. In a life spent grubbing around in the dirt, this was the most innocuous material Teg had ever seen. It reminded her of crusher fine gravel, but it was somehow even more boring than that most utilitarian of landscaping materials.

Beyond the crusher fine spit on which they stood hung a thick curtain of fog. Like the gravel, it was lifeless and flat. No wind rippled it; no light bounced off it. It was just there. Teg knew if she walked into the fogbank, sound would be muffled, her sense of direction would vanish. She'd be encased in nothing. The idea was hypnotically tempting.

Xerak turned around before Teg could give in to the temptation to walk into the fog.

"Master's out there." He pointed over the flat, green water, the tip of his spear as direct as the needle of a compass. "I can sense both him and Ba Djed. My awareness of them is faint but definite."

"Pity," Grunwold said, "we don't have *Slicewind*. I'd sail you right over to him . . ."

He broke off in midphrase as the green glass of the flat waters was suddenly interrupted by the intrusion of a very familiar shape. *Slicewind* bobbed slightly as it adjusted to its new undersurface, then steadied.

Grunwold started to run forward, then stopped. Wheeling around, he tried to face the others without losing sight of his beloved ship.

"I'm not hallucinating, am I? That *is Slicewind* floating there, right?"

"It looks like it," Kaj replied, deadpan. He tilted back his head and sniffed. "Smells like her, too. I catch the odor of the pancakes Vereez burned this morning."

Vereez tossed her head back and sniffed. "Kaj's right. And if I try hard, I get the smell of Xerak's socks."

Grunwold might have been expected to add something. This was just his sort of takedown match, but he only stood, staring at *Slicewind*. Then he turned to Xerak.

"You did this? Right? Or whatever you were communing with earlier knew we were going to need a ship."

Xerak shook his head slowly. "I think you did it, Grunwold. You've always gotten far more out of *Slicewind* than the rest of us. I thought you were simply a fine sailor, but now I think you also have something of a wizard's gift. Maybe, as with Teg and the sun spider amulet, you simply needed the right artifact to channel your abilities. Wind and water would be my guess as to your affiliations, but wood, too, or you wouldn't have been able to bind the ship so closely to you."

Anyone but Grunwold might have continued to protest, but his usual cockiness carried him through.

"Well then, as I was saying, I'll sail you to wherever it is you sense your master." Grunwold ran his fingers over the tines of one antler. "But first, can one of you give me a boost up to the deck so I can lower a boarding ladder?"

Teg decided that the wind that came from nowhere to fill *Slicewind*'s sails was a materialization of Xerak's desire to find his master. Peg thought it had more to do with Grunwold's will and his rapport with the ship. Meg refused to conjecture.

"What matters is that we are moving—and at a fair clip—over an ocean that remains still as glass although, overhead, the clouds are in motion."

Teg leaned back and looked up. The clouds were indeed moving, but their action was anything but normal.

"There's something wrong with those clouds. Look! They keep going back and forth, back and forth," she said.

"Like a giant's breathing, pulling and pushing," Peg offered. "In and out, in and out. You don't think there could be a giant somewhere, do you?"

She addressed her question to the company in general. Xerak, poised in the ship's bow, figurehead and compass in one, answered.

"It's possible. I think anything is possible. We're getting closer. Soon we won't need to guess. I hope everyone is ready."

"Ready for anything," quipped Grunwold from the wheel. Despite the uncertainty of their situation, he was almost insanely cheerful. He reached up to stroke Heru, who was perched on his shoulder.

No matter how good a face he put on it, Teg thought affectionately, *Grunwold didn't like being the only one of that trio without even a sniff of magic.*

Vereez called down from the crow's nest, although the curious stillness of the air meant she barely had to raise her voice to be heard. "No sign of land. Not even an island, but there's an odd cloud formation off in front of us, midhorizon. Do you see it? It seems uninfluenced by whatever is pushing the high-altitude clouds back and forth."

Everyone except Grunwold moved to where they could get a clear look at the skies, unimpeded by the sails.

"That can't be a thunderhead," Peg said, her inflection making the statement almost a question. "Maybe a pair of thunderheads?"

"With lightning?" Kaj asked from where he stood, one hand resting lightly on the port rail. "There's something bright toward the middle."

Then Teg experienced one of those sudden shifts of perspective that were so incredibly valuable to her as an archeologist. "Holy Mother of Mercy! That isn't a thunderhead. It isn't a cloud at all. It's an angel! Those 'thunderheads' are its wings. And the 'lightning' is the shimmer of its blade."

The angel was gigantic, a towering humanoid that bore as much resemblance to the angels of Christmas pageants as a bump in the bedding does to the mightiest of Himalayan mountains. Its features were those of a human only in that they were not those of a fox or a lion or a deer or any other creature, but their lines and planes belonged to an idealized concept of humanity, not to any of the races of the Earth. The eyes were bright yet somehow blind: eyes that had looked upon a light more brilliant than the sun, and saw only by what it remembered of that light.

In its right hand, the angel held a sword that could have cleaved *Slicewind* from bow to stern; the left arm supported a shield that could have roofed a city. It stood, apparently upon the water, legs braced, as if on guard. The motion of the angel's slowly fanning wings was the source of the wind that moved the highest clouds. Teg was trying to figure out what the angel was standing guard over when Kaj screamed, a howl raw with panic.

"Grunwold! Up! Take *Slicewind* up! I feel something moving in the depths!"

Grunwold didn't wait for explanations. At the first shout of "up," he hauled back on *Slicewind*'s altitude lever, raising his ship into the skies at an angle so steep that Xerak reeled back from the bow, only keeping from spilling overboard by sinking his claws into the mast. In the crow's nest, Vereez shrieked and gripped the basket's edge. On deck, the others clung to coils of rope and the edges of lockers. Heru sprang skyward, flapping his wings and squawking complaint.

Grunwold leveled *Slicewind* off well beneath the high-altitude clouds, but far above the now-roiling dark-green waters. Foaming white, these parted, revealing the gaping, many-toothed mouth of what Teg's brain, dredging up long-ago Sunday school lessons, offered a name: Leviathan.

To say that Leviathan could have swallowed *Slicewind* in a single gulp would have been the understatement of all time. The jaws that gaped beneath them were a vast cavern, bordered by row upon row of snaggling teeth, a cavern that yawned so wide that it could have engulfed a continent. The eyes that peered up at them were minute by contrast, flat pinpricks of coolly judgmental awareness.

"Gee," Peg said, her voice shaking even as she joked, "do you think someone doesn't want us to sail any further?"

Undeterred, Xerak staggered forward again. He leaned out over the bow, looking right, left, beneath, seeking an impossibly small figure in this landscape of giants. Teg ran forward to his side, pulling out her binoculars as she did so. Let Xerak use his internal compass to find Uten Kekui. She had a thought as to where he might be. She didn't like it but . . .

Below, Leviathan made the waters unnavigable. Teg had no doubt that should they try to take *Slicewind* higher, the wind from the angel's gigantic wings would make the skies too turbulent for sailing. Yet the angel did not come after them, but instead stood guarding something. What?

She found the angel's prize in the middle distance that was neither sea nor sky: a liminal space that she had nearly overlooked, taking the glimpses of shimmering color for mist or sea spume lit by the brilliance of the angel. However, now that she had located it, she could see that the angel stood upon an insubstantial bridge, lit with the brilliance of the aurora borealis. One terminus faded off into the distance to be swallowed by the massive bank of fog and mist. The other ended somewhere near where the angel's bare feet rested in the unnaturally still water. A slight turn of the head was enough to render this bridge invisible, but now that Teg had located it, she scanned along its span, looking for what she knew must be there.

Curled in a tight fetal position, not far from the angel's little toe, lay Uten Kekui. Whether or not he was conscious was open to question, but Teg had no doubt that he had wrapped his body around Ba Djed—protecting the responsibility he had first tried to claim for himself alone, then as desperately to reject—with every bit of strength left to him.

Apparently, the angel wasn't going to bother even stepping on him, but equally Uten Kekui could not escape under his own power. Beyond the angel, the aurora borealis span vanished into some impossible distance, presumably back into Teg's own world, so even if Uten Kekui was conscious, and they somehow distracted the angel, Xerak's master couldn't escape that way.

"Xerak, keep control of yourself," Teg said, touching the young wizard's arm and tugging one side of his mane to turn his head in the correct direction. "Look for the most improbable bridge you can imagine. One end is near the angel's feet."

She knew when Xerak caught sight of both the bridge and the one who lay upon it, for his arm went tight under her fingers, but to Xerak's everlasting credit, he didn't do anything impulsive or foolish. He whispered very softly, "Master," but that was all.

Teg became aware that the rest of *Slicewind*'s crew—with the exception of her captain, who remained at the wheel, his restlessly preening xuxu back on his shoulder—had come to join them.

"How can we rescue Uten Kekui?" Peg's question was so matter-of-fact that she might have been asking what sort of toppings they wanted on an after-book-club pizza. "Do you think the angel will let us go onto that weirdness of a bridge?"

"If it does, I could sail *Slicewind* over the span," Grunwold offered. "Then one or more of us could climb down, tie a rope around Uten Kekui, and haul him up."

"Me," Xerak said. The strain of keeping even a facsimile of calm was making him shake. "I'm going."

"I'd want at least two of us to go," Teg said. "I think your master is holding Ba Djed. We'd be in a real pickle of he dropped it and it rolled off the bridge. We'd be lucky if all it did was roll into the water. More likely, Leviathan would swallow it."

"I'm worried as to whether that bridge is strong enough to hold us," Kaj said. "It's sagging under only Uten Kekui's weight."

Teg raised her binoculars. Before she'd been mostly focused on

Xerak's master, but now that she looked at the bridge itself, she saw what Kaj meant. Initially, she'd believed that the span was difficult to see because—well, because it was nothing more than light and mist. Now she realized that it was very, very slowly fading. Ghost images at the edges showed that once the bridge had been wider. Doubtless it had been more solid as well.

"The bridge might be weaker than usual," Kaj suggested, "because only one of the great artifacts has a keeper. As long as all it had to support were reincarnating souls, it could manage, but a grown man is too much for it to bear. It's dissolving under the pressure. If we step on it, we'll finish the job."

Teg expected Xerak to take offense on his master's behalf, but clearly the danger Uten Kekui was in made trivial any arguments as to whether the wizard was responsible for his own plight.

Peg went over to one of the coils of rope and began industriously sawing off a piece. When she was done, she held the length of rope against an astonished Xerak.

"What *are* you doing, Peg?" The young wizard was astonished enough to stop shaking.

"Making a flying harness to put around whoever we lower down. It's possible that we can move Uten Kekui to one side. Then we can get Ba Djed, and haul up your master."

"Make a second harness," Xerak suggested eagerly. "If we can get one onto Uten Kekui, maybe we can pull him up without anyone having to walk on the bridge."

"I am going to make two," Peg said, "but Uten Kekui is going to have to do with either a rope tied firmly around him or someone who can grab hold of him and hang on while we haul them both up. We'll need at least two people to go down—one to grab Uten Kekui, one to get a firm hold on Ba Djed. I'd suggest you and Kaj. You're attuned to the artifact. He and Grunwold are the strongest of the lot, but Grunwold's going to be needed at *Slicewind*'s helm. It's too much to expect that the angel isn't going to make a try for us."

"Let me help you, Peg," Vereez said, hurrying over. "I'm actually pretty good at knots."

"Excellent. Many hands make light work, and mine aren't as strong as they used to be."

"I'm not bad with knots, either," Teg said, lowering the binoculars.

"You measure Kaj," Peg said. "I trust you to be accurate, even if you do need to work fast. We'll need around his waist, then over his chest..."

She rattled off a series of measurements. Kaj obediently raised and lowered his arms while Teg got the measurements she needed, then he hurried over to inspect the cargo winches. Luckily, for their purposes, there were two. Grunwold clearly wasn't thrilled about having Kaj tinkering with any aspect of *Slicewind*, but he needed both hands for the wheel, since the gusts were becoming increasingly erratic. Instead of complaining, Grunwold used the time it took to knot the harnesses together and get them fitted on Kaj and Xerak to test the angel's reactions, much as he had done with the lightning shadows.

"I'll bring *Slicewind* in as close to that winged guy as I can," Grunwold said when Kaj and Xerak were ready to go over the side, "without seeming to challenge him. I'll angle for a broadside pass, so as to place you as near to Uten Kekui as I dare but, even so, you may need to run a few paces on the bridge."

"Try to let the rope take most of your weight," Peg suggested, "while you just provide the horizontal motion."

Meg had taken over the crow's nest, and now she called down. "I finally remembered what that bridge reminds me of: it's a more vibrant version of the span created when Inehem's transport spell and ours were in conflict. Expect the footing to feel odd—as I recall, Inehem's version almost felt rubbery."

Xerak flashed Meg a smile. "Thanks. Oddly, knowing this is like that makes me feel better. One less strangeness."

With Grunwold needed at *Slicewind*'s wheel, and Xerak and Kaj going down, the winches were left to Vereez, Peg, and Teg. The two humans were teamed on one winch, while Vereez took the other—reminding them tartly that though she might not be a bruiser like Kaj or Grunwold, daily practice with her twin swords had left her far from weak.

That spared Meg for the highly important post of spotter, since Grunwold would only be able to estimate when *Slicewind* would be in position, and the winch teams would also need help knowing when to play out or haul in their lines.

There was no time for rehearsal, not with the aurora borealis span thinning more and more with every passing moment. Grunwold brought *Slicewind* around. The angel's flat, all-seeing, unseeing eyes tracked the ship's motion, but otherwise the angel did not move, not even to the rippling of a gargantuan muscle or the pulsing of a wing.

"Based on Winged Boy's lack of reactions, I could probably take us in closer," Grunwold said as he glided *Slicewind* in less than ten meters away from where Uten Kekui still sprawled in apparent unconsciousness, "but I'm not going to risk it."

"Good," Teg responded nervously.

Grunwold might not be worried, but this close the angel looked more monstrous than ever. Its basic unreality was emphasized by how its skin lacked even the tiniest blemishes, such as visible pores or the fine down of hair that adorned even "naked" human skin.

"Winged Boy looks plastic," Peg commented. "Like the universe's largest tree topper."

She might have said more, but Meg called, "Almost in position. Three, two, one . . . Go!"

❦ CHAPTER THIRTEEN ❦

At Meg's command, Xerak and Kaj, who had been crouched on the rails, dropped over *Slicewind*'s side, their lines trailing smoothly behind them. The winch teams watched Meg's hands. Rather as if she was conducting an orchestra, she provided nonverbal commands for when they should tighten or loosen the lines.

Meg was giving the sign for them to "hold" when the angel moved at last. His sword swept down in a calm, smooth strike that nonetheless was frighteningly swift and dangerously precise.

"Reel in!" Meg shouted as soon as the blade began to move, her usually calm voice shrill and cracking.

Peg and Teg were doing so, aware anew just how solidly Kaj was built, when Vereez screamed and the wildly spinning winch handle was ripped out of her black-clawed hand. She toppled back, hitting the deck hard.

Teg had a moment to think, "Xerak's line must have been cut!" when their own line became impossibly heavy, sagging under added strain. The rope they had already coiled in began to unwind, lowering its burden slowly and inexorably toward Leviathan's gaping maw.

"Kaj caught Xerak!" Meg shouted.

Grunwold yelled, "Peg, take the wheel!" then took her place at the winch handle. Vereez sprang up from the deck, shoved Teg out of the way, and joined him. Teg, aware that only so many people could effectively work the winch's handle, ran to the side of the ship to see what she could do to help.

Dangling below, Kaj held Xerak beneath his armpits. Xerak hung limp, blood dripping from the top of his head, matting his fur. The line of his harness had been neatly sliced through and trailed behind him like a second tail.

Teg glanced at the angel. The towering form had returned to its former impassive stance, watching, but not acting. Below, on the aurora borealis span, Uten Kekui still sprawled unconscious. Beside him a single boot-shaped print had worn the surface to translucency.

Peg was slowly sailing *Slicewind* out of the angel's reach, but she didn't dare go too quickly, not while two of their companions still dangled over the side. When Kaj and Xerak had been raised within reach, Grunwold set the brake on the line.

"Teg, take my place on the handle in case we need to play out or take in line. There's no way you can haul Xerak and Kaj over the side."

"Aye, aye, Captain," Teg said, with complete sincerity. "Vereez, you go help Grunwold."

Xerak was pulled aboard first, then Kaj. Xerak was fully conscious, although obviously in shock. The angel's sword had cut the tip of his ear, an injury that had bled copiously but was not in the least life threatening. The sword had also cropped a good bit of Xerak's unruly mane so he looked extremely lopsided.

"Grunwold hurt me worse when we fought as kids," he said, when Vereez came rushing over with the first-aid kit. "You didn't fuss like that then."

"Then," she retorted, "I wasn't trying to reassure myself that your stupid head was still on your stupid, stupid neck."

Grunwold gave Xerak a rough hug. Then he grinned at Kaj—a true smile, full of appreciation for Kaj's heroism. He started to offer his hand, then impulsively hugged Kaj, too.

"Kaj, you win the prize," he said. "Thanks for keeping Xerak out of that sea monster's toothy jaws. What happened?"

Xerak replied, "As soon as I put my foot on the bridge, that winged thing—'angel'—swung at me. If my foot hadn't slipped or the bridge's surface hadn't given or something like that, the sword would have taken my head off."

Kaj added. "I hadn't actually touched the bridge. I was bending to see if I could lift Uten Kekui, when I heard this shrill hiss—the sword cutting through the air, I think. Then Xerak was falling and, well, I grabbed him. Meg yelled and I was hanging on, then you reeled us in."

"The angel didn't continue its attack once you were off the bridge," Peg mused. "That's interesting."

"I was watching it pretty carefully," Xerak admitted, "at least after I realized that Kaj had caught me and I wasn't going to be fish food. You're right. As soon as we were off the bridge, it went back to its guard stance."

Meg had been studying the angel and its surroundings. When she lowered her binoculars, her expression was thoughtful. "The angel might let humans onto the bridge."

"Why you and not us?" Vereez snapped, her tone aggressive, her ears telegraphing shame.

Teg suspected the young woman had been getting ready to volunteer for the next attempt, and couldn't decide whether her spontaneous feeling of relief meant she was actually a coward at heart.

"Because," Meg replied in the practical tones she might use to direct a researcher to the appropriate aisle and shelf, "I think the angel is meant to keep those of this world from crossing in the wrong direction—that is back into our world. Like most legalists, I don't think he's much of a freethinker. We are not of this world, so we should not be perceived as violating the Law."

"I'm willing to try," Peg said.

"Me, too," Teg agreed.

"I wouldn't have suggested it," Meg said, "if I wasn't willing to take part in an attempt. We'll need a somewhat different division of labor, though. Xerak was going to take charge of acquiring Ba Djed, since he already has some rapport with it."

"I can try," Teg offered. "We have spare enshrouding containers. I'm pretty good at delicate manipulation. I think I can get the artifact into the box without touching it, at least not for more than a nudge or two."

"Then Peg and I will take charge of getting a rope around Uten Kekui," Meg said. "That process, however, will inevitably involve some contact with the bridge. I am in very good shape for a woman of my age, but I don't think I can lift an unconscious man while hanging in midair from a rope harness. At least not for very long."

Peg sighed. "I'm not Kaj. Even when I was into weightlifting—my third husband, Irving, went through a personal-trainer phase—I never *was* built like Kaj. And while those flying harnesses are solidly knotted, they do cut into one—deeper the more weight you're holding."

Kaj gave a dry chuckle and lifted his shirt so they could see the deep grooves the harness had cut into his skin. "Tell me about it. I agree. You should plan on resting at least some of your weight on the bridge."

"Sorry, Kaj," Xerak said. "I . . ."

"Forget it. Come up with a miracle for us, wizard."

Xerak rose to the bait. "I could try to strengthen the bridge. I have some rapport with Ba Djed. If it could be retrieved, then I could draw on its connection to the bridge, as well as use it as a source of additional mana."

Vereez paced restlessly. "But that's the problem. We can't retrieve Ba Djed without going onto the bridge, and taking it away from Uten Kekui. But even the humans shouldn't go onto the bridge without the assurance that it won't dissolve under them. And I don't think we should plan on repeat visits. Have you seen the mark Xerak's boot left? It practically dug a hole, and he was only on the bridge for a few breaths."

"Good assessment," Kaj responded. It said a lot for Vereez's state of mind that she only nodded, accepting the compliment as if any of the others had spoken, rather than her first and only love. "Xerak, can you commune with Ba Djed from here?"

"I can try," the young wizard said dubiously, running his hands up and down the shaft of his spear staff as if anticipating the attempt. "If it was aligned with fire, I would feel more certain, but I had to prove I could work all four elements to graduate. Yes. I can try to do something."

"If you're willing to try to establish contact"—Kaj went to stand next to Xerak and put a hand on his shoulder—"I'll stand by to give you whatever mana I can."

"Me, too," Vereez said. "After all, you're our teacher, right?"

Grunwold interjected, "One problem. If the three of you are doing magic, I'm manning *Slicewind*'s wheel, and all three humans are going over the side, who's going to handle the winches?"

Silence, then Peg said, "Good point. Change of plans. Meg and I are the least useful regarding anything to do with either brute strength or magic, so we'll go down and leave Teg here. Teg wasn't planning to use her magic to retrieve Ba Djed, just her delicate touch. We're not useless in that department. Mothers are good at delicate jobs."

"From diaper pins to dyeing Easter eggs, to combing tangles out of hair, to . . ." Meg chuckled. "Yes. I think Peg and I can manage, especially if Teg will loan us a few of the brushes from her dig kit."

Teg nodded. "I suppose you want me to serve as Xerak's battery, right? That would free up Vereez and Kaj to handle the winches. Who will be the lookout? Meg was crucial to our success last time."

Peg nodded. "Once Grunwold pointed out the shortcoming of my plan, I started thinking about that. I think I'm going to need to go down alone and leave Meg on high guard."

Several people tried to protest at once, but Peg waved them down.

"It will be dicey," Peg said cheerfully, "but if Xerak and Teg can keep the bridge from fading out, I think I'll be able to manage both getting Ba Djed into its box and tying a rope around Uten Kekui."

Silence, broken by an explosive curse from Xerak that the translation spell didn't even attempt to make sense of.

"Peg's right," he said. "The only other option is not doing anything to strengthen the bridge, and I don't think we can take that risk."

Reluctant nods all around signaled agreement.

"Let's do it," Grunwold said, moving to the helm, "and everyone try not to die."

As Grunwold brought *Slicewind* around for another pass, Peg set about strapping herself into Kaj's flying harness. Since Peg was much smaller than Kaj, Teg knotted off the trailing ends to assure a snug fit. While they waited, Vereez, Grunwold, and Kaj started discussing contingency plans until Peg interrupted them.

"Stop fussing. If there's anything I've learned from raising eight kids, it's that the more complicated a plan gets, the less likely anyone is to remember what they're supposed to do when the shit hits the fan. So, let's keep our priorities in mind. We want to retrieve Uten Kekui. That's first. Second, we want to get Ba Djed."

"No," Xerak said. "First priority: we don't want to lose a single member of our crew."

Everyone stared at him.

"I know," he said, his rueful expression and angel-cropped hair combining to make him look rather pathetic, "I'm the fanatic who has been chasing after his master for over a year. I know. However, Master chose to go alone, even when he could have had us as a support team. He's still making the same mistake he's been making for lifetimes. I refuse to let any of you have your lives cut short trying to rescue him. So, whatever we do, if it looks as if we're in danger of losing someone, then we retreat. Maybe we'll get another chance to rescue Master. Maybe we won't. But I don't want any regrets that I have him, but I lost someone else. Got that?"

"Got it," Peg said. "And good for you. I have a feeling Uten Kekui would approve. Now, who wants to help me over the side?"

In reply, Kaj moved silently over to her, lifting her sturdy form as if it weighed nothing, and resting her behind on the rail. He glanced over to see if everyone was ready.

"Peg, Kaj, give me a moment to get myself composed," Xerak said as he sat down on the deck, his spear staff over his knees. He closed his eyes and began the breathing exercises he used to build his focus.

Teg sat facing him, cradling her sun spider amulet in both hands. Closing her own eyes, Teg forced her breathing to match Xerak's cadence. She imagined Xerak as a fire, herself as coal crystalizing into diamond, feeding that fire. She felt the sun spider amulet helping her, approving this fascinating new venture.

At what seemed like a great distance, Teg heard Peg being lowered over the side, the winch turning. Sound had slowed, altering so that the voices and creaking of the ship became groaning and deep, like the sound a spinning vinyl album made when you put your finger on it, forcing it to turn very, very slowly.

Fire blossomed hot, sent out questing tendrils anchored in Teg's coal. Threading through, together they quested down below *Slicewind*'s hull, dropping lower, lower, lower . . .

When nothing seemed to happen, Teg wondered if Xerak had failed to link to Ba Djed. Then there was a hiss as if fire had met water. Mist rose and was lit by focused fire, the combination emanating rainbows, rainbows that Xerak now guided to interweave with the shimmering light of the aurora borealis bridge. The rainbows flowed in, currents of color intertwining with the weakened blues and greens and purples of the original bridge.

Contact with the bridge became contact with what rested on the bridge's span. Peg could be seen, not as a woman, but as the strong, multifaceted, adaptable essence that she was. Teg realized that what she was seeing was that uniqueness that some would call the soul. Uten Kekui, too, became visible, his essence weakened and defused. His many lives were evident in the complexity and depth of his soul's image.

Then, like a punch in the gut, ice down the back of the neck, there was Ba Djed of the Weaver. Whereas the living things were complex twistings of what must be termed colors or tastes—because metaphor is useful when there are no words—Ba Djed was violently present because of its sheer lack of complexity. It *was* and it *was* for a purpose. With that purpose thwarted, all of its *wasness* had become contained, compacted, the pressure all the more terrible because at some level Ba Djed *knew* that the means for its fulfillment was close by.

Images flickered through Teg's thoughts as her metaphor-making mind sought a comparison. The desperate need to pee. Or sneeze. Or breathe. Ba Djed needed release. When it had been in three separate parts, it had channeled that intensity into a desire into be reunited. Now, it needed but one thing more—the body that would let it fulfill its mission, release the pressure, flow forth, explode...

Whoever activates that thing is going to need to be careful. It's going to be like getting hit in the face with a firehose.

Suddenly, while the force of the intensity did not diminish, it was dampened. Teg felt her shoulders sag, only then realizing that she'd been braced as if walking against a powerful wind.

Peg has stuffed Ba Djed into the enshrouding container. The thing's so powerful its energy is still leaking out, though. Time to worry about that later. We've got to hold the bridge together while she gets Uten Kekui into his harness.

Speculations as to what had brought Uten Kekui here, how he had come to collapse, danced distraction at the edges of Teg's imagination, but she forced herself to concentrate. Xerak continued reinforcing the bridge so that it did not rip apart under the strain of holding Peg as she moved about, but what he was doing was akin to lighting one cigarette off another. He didn't so much create strength as provide a new material to be destroyed. Xerak needed the mana Teg was feeding him if he was to control the mana he was tapping from Ba Djed and feeding back into the span. Making his task harder was that Ba Djed was trying to tap *him*, to use him for whatever arcane purpose it felt was being neglected.

They both felt when Peg and Uten Kekui lifted from the bridge but, although they ached to be free of Ba Djed's probing, Xerak and Teg maintained the bridge. Too clear in Xerak's mind was the image of the angel's blade slicing his line, of falling, only to be caught by a hand that barely grasped the back of his harness, of the terrifying moments as Kaj shifted to get a better grip, the tiny jerks at each stage as they were winched aboard, of the dank, sucking wind of Leviathan's breath beneath them as the monster eagerly anticipated the feast.

No. Xerak would not let the bridge return to its tenuous state until he knew Peg and Uten Kekui were safely aboard *Slicewind*, and the vessel had turned toward—if not home—at least to a refuge. When they arrived, Cerseru Kham could straighten out what had gone wrong for Uten Kekui. Everything would be . . .

A furious wail that was precisely the sound lightning would make if thunder didn't make such a fuss tore both Teg and Xerak from their shared trance. Teg forced her eyelids open. Kaj was lifting Uten Kekui over the side rail, while Vereez was helping a sweat-soaked Peg to climb aboard. A tangle of ropes littered the deck.

The wail had burst from between the angel's perfect lips. As the gigantic head turned to orient on *Slicewind*, for the first time Teg felt as if those eyes were really seeing them. Before, when the angel had swung its sword at Xerak, the level of awareness had been that of a man swatting at an insect that prickles the back of his neck.

Now the awareness was so acute that Teg wanted to crumple to her knees and hide in the darkness behind her eyes, hide as she had when her grandmother would get drunk and begin throwing insults around like ice grenades: hard and cold and cutting. Xerak also began to crumple, but grabbed his spear staff, and shoved the butt against the deck so he could stand tall.

Teg made herself get to her feet as well, gripping the sun spider amulet with one hand, bracing the other on the nearest rail. She wanted to meet the angel's gaze, stare back defiantly, but it was impossible to meet eyes that huge.

People always talk about getting lost in someone's eyes, Teg thought irreverently. *You could definitely drown in those baby blues.*

At the angel's wail, the others had also turned, although none of them looked quite as shocked as did Teg and Xerak.

Probably because we were tuned in to other senses than the classic five. We're not just hearing with our ears, seeing with our eyes, but catching something on the magical frequencies as well.

Then Teg realized that one other was reeling back, perhaps the last person she would have expected to be so hard hit: Kaj. His ears were pinned against his skull and the dark brown of his eyes showed white all around. He staggered back a few steps, then stumbled and halted beside Teg.

"Ooh, boy!" Peg exclaimed, her entire person wild with the adrenaline of a danger met and matched. "I think Winged Boy realizes we got its toys away from it. Can you get us out of here, Grunwold?"

Grunwold was struggling with *Slicewind*'s helm. Certainly, there was wind enough, but no matter how he shifted the masts or angled the craft, the gusts refused to fill the sails.

"Emergency wind?" Vereez offered, moving toward the locker in which the precious stuff was kept.

"Not yet!" Grunwold said. "Something's wrong with the controls. They're not responding as they should. I'm going to need to take us down to the water."

"But that huge fish," Vereez began, then Meg cut her off.

Meg called out, "The angel is leaving its post. It's launching into the air and flying right for us." More softly, she added, "I'm never going to be able to look at an angel tree the same way. That thing brings the *awe* back to *awesome.*"

"I hadn't forgotten the fish, Vereez," Grunwold said. "Let's just hope it stays to guard the bridge, since Winged Boy is heading for us."

Kaj tore his gaze away from the approaching angel. "Teg, Vereez, it's got to be us who stops that thing. Xerak's blown. Uten Kekui is out cold. I've an idea . . . Can you help me?"

The angel was circling them now, close enough that each beat of its massive wings made the sails flap and cut whitecaps on the waters. At least for now, there seemed no need for Leviathan to assist. The angel was doing a great job of supplying tempest without any useful wind.

"If I can," Teg said firmly, "I will."

Vereez didn't speak, but she took a few steps toward Kaj to show she was listening.

"Don't leave me out," Xerak said, staggering over to join them. "Peg, give me the enshrouding container holding Ba Djed."

Peg did, and Kaj didn't waste time arguing, but started explaining his plan, words tumbling over each other in his haste.

"I don't think that Winged Boy is supposed to be able to come this far away from the bridge. Don't ask me why. A feeling. Winged Boy can come here because only one of the three great artifacts is working right."

The tense group of listeners didn't even nod, just waited, all too aware of how *Slicewind* was rocking on the suddenly choppy sea.

"I can feel Qes Wen," Kaj continued. "The awareness started after we came through the tunnel, but I had no idea what it was. I only realized what it was I'd been feeling when Xerak and I were dangling over the bridge. If you help me, I think I can claim Qes Wen, direct it. Or maybe, it'll direct me. It's already reaching into this area, but it's crippled. Like Ba Djed, it needs a living person to work through."

Teg remembered what she'd felt before Peg had boxed Ba Djed: that urgent need to do something, the frustration of being unable to do so.

"Kaj, you've had even less training than I have. Can you handle something that powerful?"

Kaj shrugged. "Qes Wen is conditioned to being used by someone of my father's bloodline. If Brunni would have done, I should do better. Besides, right now I'm not worrying about long-term damage, not when the alternative is us getting drowned or chopped to bits."

"So what . . ." Xerak began.

"We don't have time for complex plans," Peg interrupted. Her mad gaiety had vanished, but her intensity remained. "Kaj, what do you want us to do?"

"Like I said, I think I can connect with Qes Wen, but I'm going to need some time. Can you keep that 'angel'"—he used the English word—"back while I do?"

Vereez looked at Teg. In answer, Teg raised her sun spider amulet.

"Vereez and I will handle distracting the angel. Xerak, you be ready to use Ba Djed to help Kaj link with Qes Wen." She shook her head when Kaj would have argued. "No. I'm right in this. Trust me. You two help the great artifacts do whatever they're supposed to do. Me and Vereez will be fine."

Grunwold asked, his tone just a little mocking, although who that mockery was directed at was anyone's guess, "And the rest of us?"

"You keep *Slicewind* from flipping," Teg snapped impatiently.

Peg trotted over and gave Grunwold a one-armed squeeze around his trim waist. "Don't sulk. We're just as important as they are—more. Kaj might fail. Even if Vereez and Teg succeed in distracting the angel, you're the one who can sail *Slicewind* out of this weird place."

Grunwold snorted, but his grip on the wheel tightened and he leveled his gaze on the circling angel. "First thing I'm going to do when we're home and settled is get some weapons mounted on this boat."

His words sparked an idea. Teg turned to Vereez.

"Remember back when we first stole *Slicewind*? How Xerak used fireballs? Can you do something like that—air balls or directed gusts or something?"

Vereez grinned. "How about arrows? I can envision those more easily than spheres. A creature that flies isn't going to like anything that disturbs the air."

"Aim your shots for the angel's wings," Teg suggested. "We don't need to injure it, just make it unstable enough that it'll retreat."

"That'll be easier," Vereez said. "I was having trouble thinking anything could dent that hide. It looks so . . ."

"Don't think about it," Teg said. "That kind of thinking will only get in your way. Concentrate on making your arrows."

She moved to stand slightly behind Vereez, close enough that she had to widen her stance so she didn't pinch the young woman's bushy fox tail. Placing one hand on the side of Vereez's neck, the other on her sun spider amulet, Teg matched Vereez's breathing, closed her eyes, and envisioned herself as a sort of quiver from which Vereez could draw upon at need.

Vereez liked the image. Teg felt the equivalent of a quick grin through their bond. Then Vereez was stretching, one hand held as if it gripped the shaft of a bow, the other pulling back an invisible string. The index and middle fingers of her right hand were slightly apart, as if an arrow butt was balanced between them. When Vereez released the invisible shaft, Teg glimpsed it soaring forth, visible only as a current in the air.

Whether the angel didn't see Vereez's shot, or if it saw it and disregarded it, Teg wasn't sure. However, it could not disregard the narrow bolt that passed through one wing, sending feathers flying.

Somewhere in the distance that was the world outside the spell, Teg was aware of Peg cheering. She kept her focus tight on Vereez, feeling the younger woman's anger and resentment directing her to aim the next arrow at the upper edge of the wing, doubtless with the hope of hitting bone. Teg soothed the younger woman, reminded her that they didn't have either time or energy for tricky shots. The angel must be distracted until Xerak and Kaj did whatever it was they were trying to do.

Vereez settled down and concentrated. As the angel realized that someone was attacking it, it began to move around, not so much dodging as avoiding irritation.

Meg assigned herself the role of spotter. "Next shot further to the right, Vereez. Good. Now up a bit. Ah! Feathers flew that time. The angel is shifting to the left now."

On the edges of her attention, Teg felt Kaj's attempts to orient the flailing Qes Wen on himself. No matter that the great artifact was clearly aware of him, connecting wasn't proving quite as easy as, say, pulling a sword from a stone. Xerak was advising Kaj, but couldn't intervene. Not only did he need to reserve most of his own strength for when he'd need to open the enshrouding container and deal with the unruly artifact contained within, but it wouldn't do to confuse Qes Wen. Powerful the great artifacts might be; brilliant they were not.

Vereez was beginning to flag. Teg—who had not long before channeled mana to Xerak—started wondering if it would be better to burn herself out completely or hold back and be prepared to get the baptism of all time when the pissed-off angel sank *Slicewind*. Then, something changed.

As so often was the case with magic, Teg struggled to find words. Can you hear sunrise? See the odor of peppermint crushed with rock salt? Taste jubilation?

Something like that was what crashed into her and Vereez when Kaj finally got Qes Wen to perceive him. Teg's skin shivered beneath the touch of indigo; her ears heard the cry of riced watermelon. Her eyes were already closed, but Teg saw as clear as day when Xerak opened the enshrouding container, preparatory to giving Ba Djed permission to claim him, so that the bridge between the worlds could be... respun?

Shedding feathers, the angel began to back away from *Slicewind*, not though, Teg knew, because she and Vereez had beaten it.

Kaj guessed right. The angel could leave its post guarding the bridge because the bridge was beginning not to exist. Now that Cerseru Kham and Kaj have taken charge of two of the great artifacts, the angel is being recalled to its duty. When Xerak does whatever he has to do to convince Ba Djed to acknowledge him, then...

Her exhausted mind was struggling to complete the thought, her relief intertwining with vague apprehensions as to what this might mean for Xerak. Would Uten Kekui be relieved or insulted? Would Xerak have a sufficient sense of purpose to control Ba Djed, especially now that their lives were no longer in impending danger?

Vereez let her bow lapse into air and slumped back into Teg. The two of them began a slow-motion crash onto the deck. Teg heard Peg's feet thumping across the deck toward them.

This is going to hurt, Teg was thinking, when Peg caught her, cushioning her fall.

"Thanks," Teg managed, but she wondered if she was starting to hallucinate for, at the edge of her line of sight, something large seemed to be rolling across the deck toward Xerak.

"Xerafu Akeru," the resonant voice bellowed, "stop!"

That's Uten Kekui's voice. And he's rolling because something's wrong with his legs.

Xerak stopped, his fingers just inches from Ba Djed. "Master?"

"Give me Ba Djed," Uten Kekui ordered. "I can do this. I must do this!"

Xerak's brow furrowed. He opened his mouth as if to argue, but new gusts as the angel began to move closer again reminded him there was no time. He tilted the enshrouding container, holding his own hand out, as if to let Ba Djed choose.

Uten Kekui's hand darted out, and he caught Ba Djed by its spindle. He pressed both palms together and began to rub the spindle between them. Although he had no wool to work, a thread began to appear, rising and covering the "Nest" portion of the artifact. The bronze bird dipped its head and began plucking at the threads in a rhythmic dip and rise, dip and rise. With each rise, a length of billowing fabric appeared, rapidly shaping into a floating net.

Xerak gripped Uten Kekui under his elbows and hoisted him so he could sit upright, leaning against Xerak's legs. Kaj stepped to stand beside the pair. He did not hold Qes Wen, but instead slowly swung a lasso, its rope of many colors, each distinct but blurring into white as he swung it into a loop over his head.

Cerseru Kham, ghostly but absolute in her presence, appeared. She held Maet Pexer high, spinning the wheel to generate a tangle of intent that enhanced both net and lasso so that they moved as if alive. The threat was clear. Kaj would catch and pin those proud wings. Uten Kekui would net Leviathan.

The angel, servant of the powers of Law whose enforcer was Death, was the first to break. It saw its own death and fled. Landing at the base of the Bridge of Lives, it resumed its watchful stance. Only the massive bulk of scattered feathers drifting on the now-stilled waters proved that it had ever left its post. Leviathan sank beneath the waves, the only evidence of its presence the roiling of the dark-green waters as it swam back to its place beneath the attenuated span.

"The bridge is still weak," Kaj said.

"Yes. We must respin the Bridge of Lives," Cerseru Kham agreed. "I will lead."

Maet Pexer the Assessor's Wheel stayed itself but became, somehow, also, a spinning wheel. Cerseru Kham reached out and grabbed Kaj's lasso and Uten Kekui's net. These became the raw fleece that she transformed into bright iridescent threads of purpose and commitment, of resolve, of a raw, arrogant assertion that death was not the end of life, only a stopping point, a breathing space, truly just a form of sleep.

Ba Djed began to turn like a top on Uten Kekui's palm, then

gripped the new thread and darted toward the Bridge of Lives. In the far distance, rising from the flat green waters, grew a tree.

Qes Wen of the Entangled Tree stood in for the roots of the world, anchoring one end of the Bridge of Lives. When, after long eons that might only have been seconds, the Bridge of Lives shone bright and strong, Qes Wen sank beneath those waves.

Ba Djed returned (had it ever been truly gone?) to Uten Kekui. When it did, Uten Kekui collapsed, crumpling to one side, his fingers relaxing as if to grasp Ba Djed, but his hand fell slack before he could take hold. Nonetheless, the artifact rose and balanced upon Uten Kekui's palm, at an angle ninety degrees to reality.

"It has accepted him," Xerak said, "and he it."

Cerseru Kham, fading now, said, "Come back now. I will hold the doorway for you. Heru will show you the way."

"I'm glad that big fish didn't join in on the attack," Grunwold said, as he spun his newly responsive helm and began to sail *Slicewind* in the wake of the green-and-orange mini pterodactyl. "It could have had us in less than a gulp. By the way, good job, Kaj. Good job all of you. I didn't think we were going to get out of there."

"Thanks, Grunwold," Kaj said. He looked somehow different. Teg thought that maybe it was because he didn't have that chip on his shoulder anymore. He'd done something. He was a hero in his own right, not just the rejected bastard of a nameless father.

"I'm beat," Vereez said from where she rested against Teg, who in turn rested against Peg. "But I feel good."

Before she could voice her own agreement, exhaustion choked the breath from Teg's lungs. She slumped back, aware of Peg's voice saying from somewhere far, far away, "Sleep. We'll take over from here."

⁜❦ CHAPTER FOURTEEN ❦⁜

When Teg came around, she was in the bed in the stern cabin aboard *Slicewind*. Other than a certain cottony dryness in her mouth, she felt wonderful. The lingering exhaustion that had soaked so deeply into her that she had ceased to feel it was gone. In its place was a curious buoyancy, the sort she hadn't felt since she was a kid waking on Christmas morning or her birthday.

She was tying her second bootlace when Peg poked her head in through the cabin door.

"You're awake! I just made a fresh pot of poffee. Want some?"

"Sure, but I want breakfast, more, or lunch, or whatever . . . What time is it?"

"Midmorning. You've been asleep for a day and some."

"Am I the last one to come around?"

Peg nodded. "Xerak said that was because you gave so much of yourself. He's been checking on you every hour since he came around himself."

"At least," Teg said, "he didn't say it was because I'm so old. How are the rest? Uten Kekui seemed to have something wrong with his legs."

"The angel got him with his sword," Peg said. "Cerseru Kham's patched him up, but it looks as if Nefnet is going to have another patient."

Teg pushed herself to her feet. "Where are we anyhow? Are we still in that weird place?"

"Which weird place?" Peg laughed, then waved her hand to dismiss Teg's reply. "I know what you mean. The one with floating mountains and lightning shadows. We're back in normal weird—where all the people have animal heads, ships sail through the skies, and magic works. Everybody but you is up on deck."

Teg stopped in the lounge long enough to gulp down a bowl of poffee, then Peg shooed her up topside.

"I'll bring you a proper breakfast. Go reassure the rest you're all right. I don't think everyone believed Xerak's diagnosis."

As Teg moved toward the hatch, Thought and Memory made one of their periodic appearances, twining around Teg's ankles, clearly thrilled to find her awake. Stepping carefully to avoid treading on the cats, Teg climbed up the ladder.

On deck, Teg found that "everyone" included Uten Kekui and Cerseru Kham. Uten Kekui looked a lot better than he had the last time she'd seen him, but then it didn't take much to improve on crumpled unconscious in a heap.

Cerseru Kham lounged on one of the stern benches. Superficially, she looked much the same, but something had changed. With a start, Teg realized that she looked relaxed.

No wonder. For something like ten years she's held all the responsibility for keeping the Bridge of Lives open. Now she'll have help again.

Vereez was the first to spot Teg. Arms open, she rushed over to hug her. The boys were more restrained—but barely. Even Kaj gave Teg's hand a squeeze and gaped his jaws in a wide canine smile. By the time the usual questions had been answered all around, Peg had arrived with a breakfast basket for Teg.

"You can even have a cigarette," Grunwold said from his post at the wheel.

"Maybe later," Teg said, realizing that, at least right now, the usual craving was barely an impulse. Maybe her pipe, but after she'd eaten. "Where are we going?"

"The Library of the Sapphire Wind," Uten Kekui replied. "Now that I've accepted my role as trustee of Ba Djed, I need to start dealing with the problems I created in my last life—and one of those is the Library."

Teg glanced at Xerak, wondering if he regretted giving up so much power to Uten Kekui, but the young wizard looked completely content. He'd even taken time to trim his mane, so he didn't look so lopsided.

Our boy... Saves the world, but just as vain as ever.

"Not only the Library. There remains the problem," Meg noted primly, "of all the spirits that Sapphire Wind archived."

Uten Kekui nodded. "I know. Either they're going to need to be brought back—and that's going to cause a host of problems—or moved on. And that," he said quickly, when several mouths opened in shocked protest, "is too much like murder. I do have Ba Djed and its power. Hopefully, I can use that to work something out."

Vereez said, "I want to stay at the Library for a while. I think I'm finally all right with Brunni having Ranpeti for her mother, but accepting that doesn't mean I can't be Brunni's friend, maybe even an 'aunt.' And the Library would be a good place for me to learn how to deal with magic. Eventually, maybe, I'll apply to Zisurru University, but right now I'm not ready to return to a city where my parents have so much influence."

"You're not going to try to avoid them." Peg's statement was almost a question.

"No. But until I'm a little more balanced, I'm not ready to confront them. When I do, I want to do so from a position of power—not be seen as a little girl who can be sent to her room."

"Good." The response came from Cerseru Kham. "I am drawn to you, Vereez. Perhaps we were linked in a past life. If you're interested in having more than one tutor, I would like to offer my services. Now that I am not pulled so thin, I would like to get involved with the world of the living again. Moreover, those of us who guard the roots of the world need to seek possible successors. Would you be interested in learning from me?"

Vereez's eyes widened. "I would! I would be very honored, Cerseru Kham."

"Excellent. We'll talk more. I also plan to stay at the Library for a time. Such a place should not be left vulnerable to looters now that it has been reopened to the world, and I think Uten Kekui should welcome assistance."

Uten Kekui looked startled. Clearly, he had been viewing the Library of the Sapphire Wind as Dmen Qeres might have—as his creation, his responsibility, his property. Teg forced herself not to grin. Uten Kekui might be different in many ways from Dmen Qeres, but the soul was definitely the same.

Peg looked around the group. "Grunwold? How about you?"

"I need to go home, see my parents. Tell them about what happened, about my bond with *Slicewind*. Need to find out what I can do to buy the ship from them. I know I'm not ready to settle down as a gentleman farmer who writes poetry to fill the lonely evenings, but maybe I can serve the family business in other ways."

He glanced sideways at Vereez. "Maybe I could come to the Library, bring supplies. Help out."

Vereez nodded and smiled automatically, but if Grunwold was hoping for encouragement that she saw him as other than a friend, he didn't get it.

"Xerak," Peg said, "I suppose you'll be helping your master at the Library."

"Some," Xerak agreed. "I think that it's likely I'll inherit Ba Djed when Master moves on, since it is already attuned to me, so I want to learn everything I can about the responsibilities of those who protect the roots of the world—and not just from Uten Kekui-va. If Cerseru Kham-va will accept me as a student, as well, I would be grateful."

Cerseru Kham smiled. "I think I could manage more than one student."

Xerak gave her a deep bow. "However, I've developed an itchy foot. Maybe I'll see if Grunwold can use an assistant with some wizardly skills aboard *Slicewind*."

"Yeah, you might be useful," Grunwold said, grinning broadly. "You're good for a lot of hot air, if nothing else."

"Kaj?" Peg prompted, almost gently.

Teg thought that, of all of them, Kaj was the most changed by their ordeal. When they'd met him, anger and defensiveness made it easy to overlook his talents as a caregiver. She bet Kaj still had a lot of anger, but now he knew where to direct it. Moreover, he knew that he wasn't a failure. Far from it. Although completely untrained, he'd done magic side by side with masters like Xerak and Uten Kekui.

Kaj had a place as one of the guardians of the roots of the world, too, if he was willing to accept the responsibilities that went with it. Kaj's reply made it clear that he intended to do so.

"I need to go to Sky Descry, and tell them that Qes Wen has a new trustee. However, this trustee isn't interested in making it easier for them to grant miracles. After that . . ." Kaj shook his head, a wide, sweeping gesture, like someone trying to shake off flies. "I'm also going to need teaching about a lot of things, but I don't want to get it from anyone in the Creator's Visage Isles. That place has been twisted by generations of people expecting miracles. When the expectation gets to the point that a little kid like Brunni is going to be sacrificed to that need—things must change."

Cerseru Kham made a soft whistling sound. "They're not going to like that."

Kaj shrugged. "I'm incredibly used to people not liking what I do. Now that I've been honest about what I will and will not do, I'd like to ask you and Uten Kekui-va if you would to teach me what I need to know as a trustee."

Uten Kekui said, "I owe you that and more. I would be pleased to help."

Cerseru Kham nodded. "It should prove interesting."

"But," Kaj said, "in addition to learning how to be a trustee, I need grounding in the basics of the magical arts. Xerak? You started as my teacher because we were all desperate, but would you continue? I really can't see myself at any university, magical or not. Not now, at least."

Xerak studied him. "Only if we get a few things settled first. You saved my life, and I'm grateful. I'll always be grateful. But if I'm teaching you, the fact that you saved my life is not going to be something you'll hold over me whenever I give you some boring exercise to do."

"Of course not!" Kaj looked genuinely shocked.

Xerak continued, his expression remaining very serious. "Because of your bond with Qes Wen, you're going to have the potential to tap—quite literally—the power to do miracles. Access to that level of raw mana is contrary to the basic skills a wizard needs to develop. I'd like to work out—if possible, in collaboration with Uten Kekui-va and Cerseru Kham-va—a way to block your ability to tap that power, except in a major emergency."

Kaj panted laughter. "You expect me to protest. No surprise, there. But you forget. I saw what associating with only one third of Ba Djed did to my mother. And even without the actual artifact in hand, I've felt Qes Wen's incredible intensity. The great artifacts aren't just tools, like a shovel or rake. They have agendas. I'm not interested in Qes Wen running me—I'd rather work out a partnership. Until I can do that, I think it can remain safe wherever my predecessor hid it."

"Then I think I can teach you," Xerak said. "If our teacher/student relationship doesn't work out, we'll find someone who will suit you better."

Kaj grinned, looking honestly happy for the first time since Teg had met him.

Teg thought about her conversation with Vereez about Kaj, what seemed such a very long time ago, soon after their arrival on Sky Descry. She'd told Vereez that Kaj needed sexual conquests because he needed to feel like he wasn't a loser. Was that still true? Would that part of him change?

Maybe. Maybe not. Certainly not all at once.

Along with Teg's breakfast, Peg had brought a large carafe of poffee on deck. Under the guise of filling her bowl, Teg snuck a glance at Vereez, dreading that she might see the young woman staring in wide-eyed adoration at Kaj. But Vereez's gaze was only approving, the same as she'd given Grunwold when he said he was going to find a way to claim *Slicewind* for his own.

She's over Kaj. That doesn't mean she's not going to fall for him all over again, but this time it won't be a fourteen-year-old's first crush. And Grunwold's not going to give up on her, either. And what about Xerak? Will he follow Uten Kekui's example and rule students off-limits or will he make a play for Kaj? One thing's for certain, rather than going their separate ways now that they're no longer holdbacks, the journey that began at Hettua Shrine has bound all four more closely together.

"So," Peg said, "our inquisitors have answered their questions— and we even took on a bonus mentee in Kaj. Our holdbacks are looking to the future. What does that mean for the three of us humans? Do we vanish into the mist, our tasks completed?"

She spoke casually, but a definite sadness leaked through nonetheless. After all, that was how the books always ended: neither the wise teachers nor the kids from another world got to stay in the imaginary realm that had become their heart's home.

Gandalf sailed into the west with the elves. The Pevensie kids got too old for Narnia. Merlin got locked in a tree. The Magic Knights left Rayearth, even though they had found love and friendship there. Mary Poppins drifted off on an umbrella or balloon. Alice woke up to find Wonderland was only a dream. Adventures ended.

Cerseru Kham asked, "Is that what you would like?"

Peg frowned. "Does what I'd like have anything to do with this?"

"Of course, it does. When Hettua Shrine chose you three from all the millions..."

"Billions," Meg muttered.

"... on your world, it chose three who would not be shattered by being taken from their homes and lives. It chose three who could come here without drowning in miserable longing for all they had left behind. The desire to go home again might be beneficial for young ones coming of age, but mentors are different. Mentors must be able to teach, to guide, to advise. They can't do that if their hearts and souls are somewhere else, if their only agenda is getting back to where they feel they 'belong.'"

Cerseru Kham glanced to where Thought and Memory were patrolling the *Slicewind*'s deck, hoping for treats or pats. "You even brought part of your world here, so your souls must be very powerful."

"You mean we can stay?" Meg asked. "Here?"

"Do we need to choose?" Peg added. "Can we come back and forth like we've been doing? Maybe my family doesn't need me as much as I'd like to think, but I need to keep in touch with them."

"There is the time difference," Teg mused. "A week here is a day there. That should make it easier to keep a foot in each world."

"I do not know why you should not be able to continue traveling back and forth," Cerseru Kham said. "Souls from this world cycle through yours. Our worlds are continuously connected."

"Covering for absences would take some managing," Peg said, "but I'm good at that. And there's still work for us to do. I've been thinking about Grace. We really shouldn't leave her stranded there on that mesa. Maybe Grunwold and I can figure out how to airlift her out. She'd probably love to settle near the Library, maybe down by the lake."

Teg laughed. "I might come along for that trip. Once my sabbatical is over, I'll be able to visit here less frequently, but I would like to do so. After all, I've discovered I'm a bit of a wizard. That's something I don't want to give up. But I've also learned a few things about holdbacks—including that I've been holding myself back. The place where I need to start making changes is back there."

Fleetingly, she thought of Heath Morton.

Maybe I should ask him out. A date doesn't mean I'm signing on for life, just signing on to Live.

Peg mused aloud, already working out the tactics, "If we're coming back and forth, we'll need to work out an enhancement on our bracelets, so we don't take a chance of ending up at the wrong place. It's certain to be complex, but with all these powerful wizards..."

"You would need an anchor," Xerak began.

"You can use me as an anchor," Meg interrupted. "I want to stay."

Silence, then Peg said cautiously, "You do?"

Meg's smile mingled sadness and a touch of a twinkle.

"I do, Peg. I know it's hard for you to envision, but I'm not involved in my children's lives. I haven't been for decades. We have become friendly strangers. My grandchildren are interesting little people I see a few times a year, if I'm lucky. And for most of those visits, I'm on the sidelines, watching some sports team or school play or graduation or other rite of passage."

She swept her hand in the direction of the four young mentees.

"I feel a much greater involvement with our inquisitors. I'd like to see what they'll do with their lives. Then there's the Library. It needs a proper librarian, not just a bunch of wizards. I quite like Sapphire Wind. I believe we could get the Library nicely in order. And, to be frank, there's the chance that I'll live much longer if I stay here. I'm in my midseventies. In our world, based on my family history, I can expect another ten years of life, maybe twenty. Here that will stretch sevenfold. I like that idea, quite a bit, actually. After all, I've promised Kuvekt-lial that I'll write up our travels for him. That will take time."

"When you put it that way," Peg said. "Yes. I can see it. Maybe I'll choose an active retirement here, too, but I'm not quite ready to retire."

Teg nodded. "Nor am I. Neither here nor there. After five decades and some, I think I'm finally discovering how much there can be both to life and to living."

SF/FANTASY

Lindskold, Jane
Aurora borealis bridge
: Over where. Book 2

05/11/22